Discovering
BALANCE

To Parkside Jr. Hi.
I hope you like it!

Discovering BALANCE

T.L. HOCH

A CHIP FULLERTON/ANNIE SMITH SPORTS NOVEL
BOOK TWO

TATE PUBLISHING
AND ENTERPRISES, LLC

Published by Tate Publishing & Enterprises, LLC
127 E. Trade Center Terrace | Mustang, Oklahoma 73064 USA
1.888.361.9473 | www.tatepublishing.com

Tate Publishing is committed to excellence in the publishing industry. The company reflects the philosophy established by the founders, based on Psalm 68:11,
"The Lord gave the word and great was the company of those who published it."

Book design copyright © 2014 by Tate Publishing, LLC. All rights reserved.
Cover design by Anne Gatillo
Interior design by Jomel Pepito

Published in the United States of America
ISBN: 978-1-62854-925-6
Fiction / Sports
13.11.13

Dedication

To Riley, Brody, and Ellie

Acknowledgements

Even though there is only one person sitting at the keyboard, it takes a dedicated group of people to produce a good story. Here is where I give thanks to:

My wife, Louann, for her support and constructive suggestions.

A heartfelt thank you also goes to my two daughters, Abby and Jessie, for the time and effort that they put in and for their insightful comments on how to improve the story.

My two other manuscript readers and critics, Tina Wilkinson and Kathie Temple. They both did a terrific job and their advice was greatly appreciated.

My brother, Gene, for his expertise on railroads and how they operate.

Dave Baisden, long-time coach and official, for his help with track and basketball questions that I could not answer.

Kathy Kelsey Holmes for her awesome sketch that appears on the back cover.

Thanks also go out to the people at Tate Publishing for taking a chance on me. I hope we have a long and fruitful relationship.

Contents

Preface

I've been told that middle books in a series are more difficult to write because there is no beginning and no end. Fortunately, for me, this was not the case. As many times as I went over the story, I never really tired of it. A series, in my opinion, is just one long story that is broken up into logical parts at a point where the reader wants to be done with it for a while. I'll admit that when I'm asked to talk about the first book, *Chasing Normal*, I had trouble placing the right events in the right book. I'm sure that this will become more difficult as the series progresses.

One of the surprising things to come out of writing this series is the actual ownership of the story and its characters. In the beginning, I was the only one that was privy to their thoughts and activities. Then the manuscript readers were let in on the action. Now anyone who has read the first book can claim to know the characters and their unique personalities. I guess what I'm really saying is, "It's not my story any more. It belongs to anyone who takes the time to read it." At this point it's up to the reader to take some of what I'm saying to heart or just chalk it up to another entertaining sports story. Either way, thanks for spending some time with Annie, Chip, Jenny, Luke, and the other members of the Reston crew.

I hope the people that are familiar with Texas high school softball will forgive me for taking liberties with the seasonal schedule and the state playoff format. Some deviation was necessary to bring the story to a logical conclusion.

Once again I want to convey to coaches and players that the techniques and strategies put forth in the book are just one guy's perspective on the game. I certainly don't want to give the impression that my approach to any of the sports mentioned is better than anyone else's. If a player or coach can use anything I have written, go for it. Feel free to let me know your thoughts on anything that I propose in the series. My e-mail address is: thoch58@gmail.com.

—Tom Hoch
August 22, 2013

Payback

Melinda "Chip" Fullerton was bent over with her glove resting lightly on the dirt in the ready position. From her location at short, she could see the batter's eyes. They looked confident. The batter was Cranston's cleanup hitter, and she already had two hits and had driven in two of her team's runs. The Reston Lady Eagles were up four to three, and the bases were now loaded. One more out and the Lady Eagles would go home with a victory. It wouldn't be a decisive win but a win over a much bigger school like Cranston would be huge. Chip looked over at her pitcher, wondering why it was taking her so long to deliver the ball. Tammi Olsen had been Chip's nemesis in every sport since fifth grade. Now she just stood there like a statue, looking in at her catcher.

"C'mon, Tammi," hollered Chip. "Fire it past her and let's go home."

Tammi glared at the little shortstop. As usual, she took Chip's comment as criticism and not as typical softball chatter. She looked back at the catcher and unleashed her fastball at the heart of the plate. The batter was on the ball as soon as it left Tammi's hand. She had been guessing fastball all the way. She snapped her bat around, catching the bottom third of the ball and lofted it softly toward left field. Chip turned with her left shoulder toward the outfield. Pop-ups were seldom a problem for her. She had great quickness and excellent footwork. The left fielder was playing deep, so the ball was all Chip's. The little shortstop sprinted toward left, and at the last possible moment, extended her glove. She felt the weight of the ball in the webbing and started to smile. Her smile was short-lived. The ball still had some spin on it, and it squirted out. She reached for it with her bare hand and got a piece of it, but it fell to the ground at her feet. Chip quickly picked it up and looked toward home. The girl who was on third was standing there with her arms in the air, signaling the runner behind her not to slide. With two outs in the inning, both of them had taken off as soon as the bat hit the ball. The game was over. Tammi threw up her hands and screamed something that Chip luckily couldn't make out. Chip slammed the ball into her glove and walked slowly toward the Reston dugout with her head down.

"Nice play," said Tammi sarcastically.

"Be quiet," scolded Tammi's twin, as she jogged in from first base and met Chip in front of the dugout. She draped her arm over her teammate's shoulders.

"Tough break, Chipper," consoled Jenny Olsen. "That sucker must have had a lot of juice on it. We'll get them next time."

B. A. Smith came running in from right field and added to Jenny's statement, "It'll hurt for a while, bud. I'm sure every one of us has been in the same position. We've got a lot of ball to play, so don't let it get to you."

"She's right," added their coach as he walked up. "A lot of shortstops wouldn't have even laid a hand on that one."

Chip, Jenny, and B. A. sat in the back of the bus on the way home and discussed the game. Chip was still dejected, and her friends' efforts to cheer her up were to no avail.

"I had it," moaned Chip. "What a stupid play! I know I'm better than that. I'm gonna get Luke to hit me a hundred pop-ups, so I won't mess up again. It's my fault we lost."

"My sister was out of line," said Jenny. "It must have slipped her mind that she gave up a hit and two walks to load the bases in that last inning. Have you ever made a mistake that cost your team a game, B. A.?"

"Yeah," responded B. A., remembering an incident that occurred during her first year of high school ball. "When I was a freshman, I caught a fly with runners on second and third. I tried to throw the first girl out at the plate. I threw it halfway up the backstop, and it hit one of the support poles. The ball bounced all the way back out to first base. The girl on second was the winning run. She just strolled across the plate."

"See," said Jenny, "it happens to the best of us."

"Are you making that up just to make me feel better?" asked Chip.

"No," said B. A., leaning back and putting her earbuds in. "It happened just the way I described it." B. A. failed to add that she had made up for her mistake by hitting a grand slam to win the game the next time the two teams faced each other.

Chip sat at the kitchen table, eating an apple and watching her mom make supper. It had been months since Chip had been allowed to use the stove, and she was anxious to try her luck at meal preparation as soon as her mom gave her the okay.

"Mom, has my banishment from cooking expired yet?" she asked in a hopeful voice. "I've seen the error, uh errors, of my ways and feel perfectly confident that I can cook up a tasty meal without blowing the place up. Besides, you've got insurance, so what's the big deal?"

"The safety of those who live here is the big deal," responded her mom as she stirred the spaghetti sauce. "Cooking is serious business. For safety's sake, food must be heated to a certain temperature for a certain length of time. If you're serious about preparing a meal, you have to know what you are doing. A good cook does more than just pour something out of a can and heat it up."

"Okay, you've convinced me," said Chip as she got up to throw her apple core away. She stepped on the garbage-can lid opener and tossed the apple's remains away. "Wait a minute here. Did I hear you right about not pouring something out of a can or in this case, a jar?"

Chip picked up the glass jar that the spaghetti sauce came from. "Busted."

"You got me," laughed Mrs. Fullerton. "I've been so busy with the hardware-store books. I just didn't have time to make something from scratch."

"I won't tell Dad about the fake sauce if you lift my cooking ban," said Chip.

"What, you're trying to negotiate a lesser sentence?"

"Yup. It's called *plea bargaining*. I learned that in government class. And I'm not admitting any guilt on my part for the first incident. The fire was purely circumstantial and beyond any rational person's control. Pretty slick, huh?"

"You do sound like you're learning something at school," said Mrs. Fullerton, considering the length of Chip's original six-month sentence. "All right, you can make chili for Saturday night if you want to. And it's not because of your threat to expose tonight's sauce. Your dad will know the minute he tastes it. But just to be safe, I will be in the other room with a fully-charged fire extinguisher."

"You're hilarious, Mom. Can I invite B. A. and Jenny over for a chili extravaganza?"

"Why don't you ask Luke and Rod over too? We might as well make it a full fledged chili fest."

"Do you think Jenny will mind if B. A. and I have our boyfriends over, and she doesn't have anybody to bring?" asked Chip.

"I like this new side of you," said her mom. "Consideration for other's feelings is a sign of a mature, compassionate person. Did you learn that from B. A. too?"

"Probably," answered Chip as she stood up and headed for her bedroom to text her invitations. "There's no way I learned it from my parents."

Chip was the quickest athlete in her school, but she wasn't quick enough to dodge the wet dishcloth that hit her in the back of the neck. Next to B. A., she had the strongest arm on the softball team. It was obvious where that trait came from. She reached behind her and caught the wet cloth as it slid down her back and lobbed it back to her grinning mom.

"Thanks, Mom. I will do you proud, and my chili will be the talk of the neighborhood."

"Let's just make sure the neighborhood is still standing after Saturday night. And to answer your question, no, I don't think Jenny will mind. She'll find someone when she's good and ready."

Jenny Olsen and B. A. Smith sat at the Fullerton dining-room table, waiting for their teammate to dish up the world's most fabulous chili as it was described to them. Next to B. A. Smith was her boyfriend, Rod Martin. Rod was an incredible physical specimen. He stood 6'7" and had a body that was the result of countless hours in the weight room. He was a little self-conscious about his appearance, so he usually wore a shirt that covered his arms. Rod was also Chip's cousin. Across from Rod sat Jenny Olsen. Jenny was a tall, slender girl with long brown hair. Several people had already told her that she should consider modeling as a career. In addition to her looks, she had a positive attitude that was reflected in her smile, and she was always smiling unlike her identical twin, Tammi. Tammi's attitude was the total opposite of Jenny's. She didn't realize that her poor attitude hampered her performance on the athletic field. It constantly weighted her down like she was dragging around a bag of heavy rocks. When it came to sports, Tammi was caught up in being the star of every team she played on. She obviously didn't care much for the new girl when B. A. showed up right before school started. B. A. surprised the community when she moved to town and played basketball at a level that they had not seen before. She was only 5'8" tall, but she played much bigger. B. A. and Chip averaged over fifty points a game between them for the last half of the season.

B. A. had dark blonde hair and sparkling green eyes that would often illicit a second look from someone who was seeing her for the first time. She was a positive influence on Chip and Jenny, and they would be the first to admit it. She was also the basketball teammate that Chip had been hoping for.

Luke Slowinski sat at one end of the table. He was Chip's boyfriend and the only non-athlete in the room. At six feet two and two hundred pounds, he looked like an athlete, but long ago he resigned himself to just writing about sports. The decision was a good one for all concerned.

Chip's mom and dad sat in the living room, waiting to be served. There wasn't enough room at the kitchen table for all of them, so they volunteered to eat in the other room. Luke carried in their bowls and set them on their TV trays. After looking over his shoulder to make sure Chip wasn't watching, he leaned over and whispered, "Tell her it's good even if it isn't. She's been talking about this for days."

"Kid," said Mr. Fullerton, "you've learned a lot about women in your short time here on earth. Around here, everything my wife cooks is absolutely fabulous."

Karen Fullerton snickered as she sniffed her bowl. "You've got that right. Cooks in this house accept compliments only. The first time you complain, you're the new cook. Hey, this doesn't smell half bad. You taste it first, John."

"Mine's awfully hot. I don't want to burn my mouth. Go taste yours, Luke, and give us a thumbs up if it's a go."

Luke shook his head and went back to join the others. Chip had set a huge bowl of corn chips in the middle of the table and was in the process of sprinkling some on her chili.

"In Texas," she explained to B. A., "we eat our chili with corn chips. How do they eat chili in Arkansas?"

"We usually eat it with a spoon," responded B.A. "These little chips don't hold much. It would take way too long to eat it."

"Ha!" said Jenny. "She's got you there, Chippy."

Chip's eyes went wide when she saw Luke crush up a bunch of chips before dropping them into the bottom of his empty bowl.

"No, you don't crush them. It ruins the flavor. They go on top, in their original shape."

"They do not," argued Luke. "They go on the bottom of the bowl, and the chili is poured over the top. That's the way the early settlers ate it. I like to stick with tradition. Why mess up a good thing? They knew what they were doing."

"What are they talking about in there?" asked Chip's dad. His wife had a better angle and could hear bits of the kitchen conversation.

"They seem to be arguing about how to eat chili," said his wife as she strained to follow what was being said.

"What's the big deal?" asked John. "You just spoon it up and eat it."

"Not if you're a natural-born Texan," said Karen. "We have a certain flair with some food like chili and, of course, barbecue."

"Hey," hollered John toward the kitchen, "Where's our chips?"

A fresh bag came flying out of the kitchen and almost hit Karen in the head.

"Kids," she said. "Makes you glad we only had one, doesn't it?"

"I heard that," hollered Chip from the kitchen.

"How's the team looking?" asked Luke as he spooned chili over his corn chips. "Has Pops got people in the right positions, or will parents and fans be second-guessing him for the rest of the season?"

"I think we all know our spots," said Jenny. "If my sister would just keep her mouth shut, things would go a lot smoother. She's already putting her two cents in on who should play where.

Pops knows what he's doing. She should just pitch and leave the coaching to him."

"I agree," said Chip. "But with so many players, I think he needs an assistant. A player has to hit infield grounders when Pops is working with the outfielders, which means the hitter doesn't get her turn fielding."

"Chip hit around .400 last year," said Jenny. "What did you hit back in Arkansas, B. A.?"

"I was pretty close to that," responded B. A.

"It would be cool to have two .400 hitters on the same team," continued Jenny as she took a corn chip out of the bowl and flicked it at Chip. "You two would be the talk of the softball scene just like you were in basketball. You're going to put Reston on the map with your sports heroics."

"Let's not get ahead of ourselves," said Luke. "Individual stats are nice, but the team is the main thing. Some players build their numbers by going three for four against a weak pitcher, and then they strike out against a strong hurler. I'm just saying there's a lot more to the game than individual stats."

"Well said, sports guru," agreed Chip, as she headed for the stove. "Who wants more of the most fantabulous chili they have ever eaten?"

Rod looked at the others and started clapping. The rest followed suit and then stood for emphasis. Chip was beaming. Her parents also clapped from the other room.

"I hope we haven't created a monster in there," said Mr. Fullerton to his wife.

"We're way past that, dear," came the response. "I was hoping to keep her out of the kitchen for a while longer, but I have to admit, her chili isn't bad. And the house is still standing."

They both laughed as they glanced over at the fire extinguisher standing against the wall by the kitchen door.

Rod and B.A. got into Rod's car for the drive home. They made small talk until they pulled into B. A.'s driveway.

"By the way," said Rod. "What did you hit last year?"

B. A. looked at him for a moment before she responded, "Around .500."

"How many home runs did you hit?" was his next question.

"Like Luke said, it's not about the individual stats. It's about the team. It might sound corny, but I really believe that."

"I know, Annie." He called her Annie when they were alone. "Just humor me, okay?"

Annie kissed him on the cheek and opened her door. She leaned back into the passenger side window and whispered, "Sixteen."

"Cool," hollered Rod as he started to back out the drive. "It sounds like softball will be just exciting as the basketball season was. I can't wait."

Rod and Luke sat in the front seat of Rod's car while Chip and B. A. sat in the back, talking about the upcoming game. The season was a few weeks old when the basketball girls showed up, so the team's makeup was about to change as their coach slowly moved them into the starting lineup. Chip had decided that she needed a new glove due to the fact that the webbing in her present one was falling apart. Her parents wouldn't let her drive to the big city alone, unless she was going to her dad's hardware store on the north side, so she recruited the other three to go along. It wasn't difficult because Rod and B. A. wanted to look at sports equipment too, and Luke was lured in by the promise of a free meal.

"Pull in to that barbecue place up ahead," said Chip, pointing. "They've got great roast-beef and chicken sandwiches. And like I promised, B. A. and I are buying."

"Since when did I get involved with the finances on this trip?" asked B. A. as they got out of the car.

"Look at the size of those guys," said Chip, nodding in the direction of the car. "They could clean this place out if they were hungry enough. You wouldn't want me to go bankrupt feeding those two, would you?"

"I was just kidding. I'll pay my share. We better get them two sandwiches each and some fries if we don't want to hear their stomachs growling all the way home."

The girls ordered six sandwiches, fries, and drinks all around. When they got outside the door, Chip grabbed B. A.'s arm and steered her against the side of the building.

"Are you ready for a flash of mental geniousness?" asked the little shortstop as she pulled a sandwich from her wind shirt pocket. She then took it out of the bag it was in and switched it with one of the sandwiches in the bag they had just purchased. The fresh sandwich went back into her shirt pocket. B. A. watched with a confused look on her face.

"I've been planning this for a while," explained Chip. "All you have to do is play along."

"I'd rather not be involved with one of your little plans. They seem to backfire more often than they succeed."

"C'mon, this is a perfect setup to get even with Luke for the voodoo-doll incident. You have to admit, he's got something coming for his rash behavior. I promise no one will get hurt, at least physically, although it might take him a while to get over the psychological aspects of this well-crafted plan."

Okay," agreed B. A., "but this better not make Luke mad at us. He's a schemer just like you, and this could get out of hand."

"Once we pull this off, he will be afraid to mess with either of us for a long time. Just follow my lead," said Chip as they walked back to the car. "This is going to be hilarious. You probably don't know this, but Luke is real sensitive about his food. It's like a fetish or something. He's always worried about somebody tampering with it or getting poisoned right from the food factory. I took a bite out of the sandwich that I switched and put on a little green food coloring for effect. And I added a few hairs to maximize the grossness factor. Just play along, all right?"

The girls got back in the car and Rod steered them toward Fort Worth. The bag sat between the girls in the backseat.

"Could you believe that guy, B. A.?" asked Chip. "Those teeth were disgusting. That dude must have had some kind of gum disease. And what kind of hair was that? It looked like something from a bad movie."

"They were pretty bad," added B. A. "He should have stayed in the back where the customers couldn't see him."

"It's weird you should say that. He went back to the kitchen area to get our order. Usually they just wait for it out front. Maybe he saw your Reston basketball T-shirt and messed with your sandwich."

"Stop yapping back there," said Luke. "Quit teasing us with the food. We can smell it up here ya know? How about passing some of that this way?"

"All right, jaws," said Chip. "We were just talking about that guy's nasty-looking teeth and hair back there. Those teeth were green and black like he had just finished off a bag of licorice. I don't think he would get many takers at an old-time kissing booth."

"Stop it," hollered Luke. "We're about to eat here. Pass up the goods, please."

Chip gave Luke and Rod a sandwich and their fries, and B. A. handed them their drinks.

"I got you two a chicken and a roast beef, knowing what huge stomachs you both have," said Chip as she and B. A. watched Luke unwrap his sandwich. When Luke saw the hairy bite out of his sandwich with the green food coloring for effect, he yelped and threw it up like it was a hot potato. It hit the car's roof and came back down in his lap. Chip looked at B. A. with wide eyes. It was obvious that she didn't expect such a dramatic reaction from her boyfriend. Now he was just sitting there, staring out the passenger window as if he was in shock.

"What are you doing?" asked Rod. "You're getting food all over my car."

"That creepy guy back there took a bite out of my sandwich," wailed Luke. "I don't think I'm hungry any more."

"I'm sorry, sweetie," said Chip in an innocent voice. "I must have given you mine by mistake. I took a bite back there to see if the sauce was too spicy. I was just testing it out. You know, like when someone else tested out my doll by stabbing her with a pin."

"What a memory!" exclaimed Luke. "Once you latch on to something you never forget it, do you? What are you, some kind of bulldog?"

"It's kinda hard not to forget something that almost kills your coach. The plan here was for you to be mildly disgusted. We didn't expect you to go ballistic and throw food all over the place. Here's your real sandwich, so be careful with it."

"Does this type of behavior run in the family?" asked Luke as he inspected his new sandwich.

"Nope, she's one of a kind," said Rod. "Hey, speaking of family, the Major's coming back soon."

"Where's he been anyway?" asked Luke.

"He's been overseas for about a year. We think he'll get to stay for quite a while this time. You'll like my dad, B. A. He's a very interesting guy."

"I'm looking forward to meeting him," said B. A. "If he's half of what you say about him, he must be pretty awesome."

Rod turned into the mall parking lot, and the group got out and headed for the sporting-goods store. Once inside, they went their separate ways. Rod went over to the weights, and the girls headed for the softball equipment to check out the gloves. Luke wandered for a bit and then took off for the bookstore. He was hoping to get some ideas for future articles on the Reston baseball and softball teams. A good reporter could never do too much research. A quote or short story about an old-time player showed the human-interest side of sports. Luke had successfully used this approach before. It didn't take him long to find a book on the bargain table about Christy Mathewson. Mattie was a pitcher for the New York Giants at the turn of the century, and he was considered by pretty much everyone to be the epitome of sportsmanship. After buying the book, Luke went out to the main mall area. He found a seat and immediately became engrossed in the pitcher's life story.

Chip and B. A. were sitting on a bench around the corner and out of sight from Luke. Chip was pounding her fist into her new glove and describing to B. A., who was looking at a flyer from the sporting goods store, all the amazing plays she was going to make with it. The two were engrossed in conversation and didn't notice the half a dozen rough-looking girls until they were standing right in front of them. Two of the girls had tats on their arms and one of them had one on her leg. It was obvious that these girls weren't looking for autographs.

"Well what do we have here?" asked one of the girls, noticing B. A.'s Reston basketball shirt. "Looks like a couple of Reston preppies. What are you little chickies doing so far from home?"

The rest of the group laughed and made a few nasty comments about small-town girls coming to the city without any *cover*.

"What's 'cover'?" asked Chip.

"You can't be that stupid," said the girl that initially addressed them. "Cover, sweetheart, is someone to back you up in case you run into trouble."

"We're not looking for any trouble, so I guess we don't need any cover," said Chip, trying to figure a way out of their situation.

"We're waiting for our boyfriends," said B. A. "They should be here any minute."

"And that's supposed to scare us?" asked the girl as she reached out and ripped Chip's glove out of her hands. "Two little Barbies like you probably have a couple of real studs for boyfriends. I'm sure your hot stuff at the country club, but you're on our turf now. This looks like a nice glove, and look, it fits my hand perfectly."

"Hey," hollered Chip. "Why don't you leave us alone? We're just sitting here, minding our own business."

B. A. stood up slowly and looked around for Rod or a security guard. She was about to say something when a pair of arms reached around her from behind and grabbed her forearms, pinning them to her stomach. Chip let out a squawk and looked over at her friend. Before B. A. could react, a threatening voice from behind them hollered, "Hey, what are you doing to my girl?" Rod was standing there smiling.

"Just keeping her from punching this chiquita's lights out," answered Victor loosening his grip on B. A. "Tigrita, how have you been?"

B. A. relaxed when she heard Victor's voice. She turned around and gave him a hug. "I've been good. Chip and I were just making some new friends."

"I don't think these girls are the friendly type," said Victor, looking directly at the group's spokesperson. "Why are you still here? Shouldn't you be out stealing cigarettes or something? Go somewhere else."

The leader turned and started to walk away with the rest of her crowd. She knew who Victor was and wanted no part of him or the people he used to run with. She didn't know that he had left that life behind and was now going to college.

"She's still got my glove," blurted Chip.

Victor said something in Spanish that didn't appear to be a compliment. The girl dropped the glove to the floor and kept walking without looking back. Chip ran over and scooped up her recent purchase. She clutched it to her chest like a favorite stuffed animal.

"Man, am I glad ya'll showed up," said B. A. "Things were getting pretty tense."

"They're more bark than bite," said Victor. "I've seen that little pack around. They think they're big-time rebels, but they have no idea what they're rebelling against. They're real tough when they have an advantage in numbers. We're you thinking about punching her, B. A.?"

"No," laughed B. A. "I didn't want to be sitting if Chip attacked them. I figured I'd have to pull her off when that girl took her glove. What did you say to her?"

"I mentioned some people that she definitely wouldn't want to be involved with. She got the message."

"It's good to have people," said Chip, still hugging her glove and looking past the two guys as Luke walked up. "Nice timing, Lukey-come-lately. Where have you been?"

"What's going on?" asked Luke.

"Nothing now," answered Chip. "Victor and Rod saved some strange girls from getting a severe beating."

"If you fight like you play basketball, there might be some truth in that." Victor laughed. He then turned to Rod and said, "Can I talk to you for a minute?"

The two of them went off to the side and had a short conversation. When they were done, Victor gave them a wave and headed in the opposite direction. The four of them headed for the parking lot and the fifteen-mile drive home.

"Just another day in the life of the action magnate," said Chip when they were all safely in the car.

"Who's this action magnate?" asked Rod as he steered the car out of the lot.

"B. A.," answered Chip. "Wherever she goes, there's bound to be something going on. That's why I hang around her so much. She's like a party all by herself."

"I thought you hung around her, hoping some of her athletic ability would rub off on you," said Rod.

"Yeah, that too," laughed Chip.

Pops

B. A. stood in right field and watched Tammi put the finishing touch on a six to three victory. The team was four and one since the basketball girls brought them up to full strength. The one loss was the game where Chip muffed the pop-up. She bounced back and went two for three the next game with a couple of spectacular plays in the field. B. A., on the other hand, was anything but spectacular. She was hitting .250 and hadn't made any plays that were considered all-star quality. That was fine with her. The team was winning, and even Tammi hadn't said much since the game they lost on Chip's error. Tammi was four and three overall, but in her mind, the losses were all due to poor play by her teammates. Carmen Lopez, the other starting pitcher was two and two.

B. A. stared intently at the batter as she made a smooth swing and lofted a fly down the right-field line. She was off and running as soon as the ball hit the bat. B. A. ran as if she didn't have a glove on her hand. Her arms were close to her body, and her gait was smooth and efficient. She got there with time to spare and waited for the ball just a few feet inside the foul line. She caught it at shoulder height, making the whole process look effortless. B. A. learned early in her softball career that good footwork was a big part of playing defense no matter what position you played. She only raised her glove when she was about to make the play. A couple of girls on the team ran with their gloves out when they were chasing a fly or a line drive. Coach Brown had coached them to stop it, but some habits were hard to break. Also, he still hadn't gained their confidence, so some of the girls were skeptical of his coaching abilities. There weren't too many schools around where the school janitor was the coach. Tammi had voiced her opinion on this fact more than once.

The players gathered in centerfield and waited for Pops to come out and give them their post-game talk. As usual, he went over the negative things first. He would then cover the things they did well, so they would end on a positive note. B. A. knew this was good coaching strategy. Sometimes a coach had to get on a player in practice or in a game, but that was just part of athletics. After the constructive criticism, an effective coach will find something positive to say about the player's or team's performance, letting them know that there were some aspects of their game that the coach approved of. And the positive part had to be legitimate because young people are real good at spotting phony compliments. The tough part of this strategy was when a coach had a player who would fold any time they heard something that was other than complimentary. These players had to be handled with great care.

B. A. remembered back in eighth grade when her coach hollered at one of the guards on the basketball team. He loudly told her to stop taking the ball down the left side of the floor. The opponents were using a trapping press, and they were herding her to that side of the floor. He wasn't shouting to be mean. The gym was loud, and it was hard to hear. Anyway, the girl he hollered at wouldn't look at him or talk to him for the rest of the season. This incident opened B. A's eyes, and from then on, she had a lot more respect for the challenges, obvious and not so obvious, that coaches had to face.

As the team walked off the field, Pops held back and spoke quietly to B. A. "Are you still coming?" he asked her.

"Sure, coach," she answered. "Can I just follow you? I have no idea where we're going."

"No problem. We'll get packed up and head north to Ponder. There's nothing tricky about the route. My niece is super excited. She read every article about your basketball exploits and has wanted to meet you for quite a while. I planned on having her come to a couple of games, but it's tough for my wife to coordinate with so many young ones around our place. Actually, everyone at the homestead is excited to meet you. My wife makes a mean barbecued chicken. We were hoping you would stay for supper."

"Sounds good to me," said B. A. with a big smile on her face. "Who's going to catch us?"

"Don't crack wise with me, little missy. I can catch anything you can dish up."

"I can see Slowinski's article now," said B. A., holding her hands up in front of her face like she was reading a paper. "Washed-up pitcher beans coach and sends him to the hospital. Tammi Olsen to coach team for the rest of the season."

Pops and B. A. were both laughing as they loaded the equipment bags into the coach's car. Tammi and Darby Quinn were watching from a distance.

"What do you think that's all about?" asked Darby.

"Just Smith trying to get in good with our so-called coach," answered Tammi. "Just like she did in basketball. Well, it won't work this time. She's not nearly as good in softball as she was in basketball. Maybe I'll set her straight at practice tomorrow. If I can get her away from Coach Brown."

"Maybe she's just off to a slow start," said Darby. "She sure looks like she knows what she's doing."

"Not you too," said the exasperated pitcher. "I think she's shown us all she's got in softball, and it ain't all that much. Let's go, I can't stand watching them yuk it up together."

Tammi would have been even more annoyed to see B. A. follow the coach's car out of the lot and on to the road, heading north to his place. A few months ago, B. A. had promised Pops that she would help his niece with her pitching technique. Even though Pops knew all about her past pitching exploits, he had not asked her to pitch for the high school team. He respected her decision not to pitch and figured she would bring it up when she was good and ready. And if she spent the season playing right field, well, that was her choice.

B. A. followed her coach up a small gravel lane into an area that was shaded by several tall mesquite trees. There were a total of four houses arranged in a diamond pattern. Four children ages six to ten came running up as the two vehicles pulled in. They stood staring as B. A. got out of her truck. Pops came back to her truck and introduced her to them and then told them to go play.

"Interesting arrangement," said B. A. as she followed Pops toward the biggest house.

"Yep," said Pops, stopping at the steps. "After I built this house, my sister liked it out here so much she talked me in to building a house for her and her husband. My two daughters and their husbands live in the other two houses. I'm fifteen years older than my youngest sister, so my grandchildren and nieces are close in age. I have about ten acres, so the kids have a lot of room to roam. We jokingly refer to it as the Brown Ponderosa. C'mon in. I want you to meet my wife. She's only been to one game because she's always watching the little ones that you saw outside. I'm sure Ellie is in there too."

They walked in the front door and were immediately hit by the appetizing aroma of barbecue sauce and chicken. The lady with the apron on turned around and smiled when they walked in to the kitchen. Pops introduced his wife, Gendra, and looked around for his niece.

"She was helping me with dinner," said Gendra. "But she ran outside to warm up as soon as she heard you pull in. You've got quite the reputation around here, young lady. Leroy has kept us all up-to-date on your basketball and softball exploits."

"I'm sure he's exaggerated somewhat," said B. A. "I hope I can live up to Ellie's expectations. I haven't pitched to a batter in a long time."

"Don't worry," said Pops. "You'll do fine. Let's get out there. If we stand here any longer, the smell will make us lose our focus. Don't burn that chicken, Gen. That's one thing I never have to exaggerate about."

B. A. couldn't believe her eyes when she and Pops walked out into the backyard. There was a baseball field complete with a screen backstop. Ellie was busy playing catch with a tall black man that was obviously her dad. When she saw her uncle and B. A., she ran over and stuck out her hand.

"Hi, I'm Ellie Winters," exclaimed the excited twelve-year-old. "Thanks a lot for coming. My uncle says you're the best girl athlete he's ever seen."

"I hope I can live up to his description of me," said B. A., shaking the young girl's hand. "Is this your dad? He looks like he's played some basketball."

Ellie's dad, Nate, smiled and extended his hand. "Started at TCU my last two years. I hear you've got an awesome hook shot."

"I need it to get it over the tall girls," responded B. A.

"I'd like to see it," said Nate. "We've got a hoop over behind our house and—"

"Let's save the basketball demonstrations until after dinner," interrupted Pops. "Right now we need to get on with the pitching lesson. You two head out there. I'll get my mask and bucket."

For the next thirty minutes, B. A. went over the basics of pitching with Ellie. She showed her how she held her pitches and how to use her lower body to help generate more power. Ellie was a quick study and improved immediately. B. A. also talked to Ellie about pitching strategy. She explained how she usually threw her change-up toward the inside part of the plate. That way, if the batter guessed right or recognized the pitch and was waiting for it, they were usually way ahead of it and hit it foul.

Pops sat on an upturned bucket and did the catching chores while Nate sat in a lawn chair off to the side. His job was to chase down the pitches that got by the catcher. Gendra opened the back door and told them dinner was ready. Pops said they needed five more minutes and walked out to the mound. B. A. knew what was coming. He wanted to see her throw a few at game speed. She agreed to pitch a few, and after a few warm-up throws, began to increase her speed. Her arm felt strong, so she decided to pick up the pace. Ellie just stood there and stared in awe. After five hard throws she looked at Ellie's dad.

"Mr. Winters," she hollered. "Would you stand in there like a batter and give me a strike zone?" B. A. winked at Ellie when her dad put on a helmet and stood in the right-hand batter's box with a bat in his hands.

"You can try to bunt it, but no swinging away," said Pops. "If you get lucky, you might drill one at my star player, and I can't risk that."

Nate shook his head that he understood and stepped into the box. He went in to an exaggerated crouch to try to simulate the height of a high-school player. The big guy watched several pitches go by before he tried to bunt one. He managed to foul off one ball. He was amazed at the rise balls that B. A. threw. In baseball, a good curve ball breaks away and drops sharply, but the ball doesn't rise. Even if he tried to hit it with a full swing, he didn't think he would have had much success.

Gendra opened the door and made a threatening motion to her husband with a spatula. That was their clue to hustle inside or risk the wrath of the cook.

"All right," he shouted.

He started to stand up when B. A. pleaded for just one more. Pops held up one finger to agree to one last pitch.

"Watch this," whispered B. A. to Ellie. She threw her hook right at Ellie's dad. When the ball was halfway there he jumped out of the box and let out a little yelp.

The ball broke back to the middle of the plate where Pops caught it and said loudly, "Strike." They all were still laughing as they trooped up the steps and tied into the best barbecued chicken B. A. had ever tasted.

After dinner, while Pops helped with the clean up, Ellie and B. A. went into the den to talk more about pitching. While B. A. answered questions, her attention was drawn to pictures of her coach on the wall. He was young and in a military uniform. Ellie saw B. A. looking and whispered to her, "Would you like to see something special?"

"Sure," said B. A. "But only if it's okay with your uncle. He's a great guy, and we really like him as our coach."

"I don't think he'll mind," said Ellie as she stood up and opened a desk drawer. "Check this out. The president put this on Uncle Leroy when he was at the White House."

B. A. walked over to the opened drawer and looked down at the object Ellie was referring to. She couldn't believe her eyes. The medal lay on a black-cloth background. There were thirteen little white stars on some blue material. Beneath the stars was the word *Valor*. Below that was the rest of the medal.

"Do you know what this is?" asked Ellie in a low voice.

"I do," answered B. A. "It's the Medal of Honor. I can't believe our coach has won the highest award that a soldier can earn. This is incredible!"

"Let's close this," said Ellie, looking over her shoulder. "Uncle Leroy doesn't like to talk about this very much. I just thought you would like to see it."

"Thanks for showing it to me," said B. A. as she walked back to her chair. "Ya'll should be very proud of your uncle."

"I'm proud of all my family," said Pops as he came in to the room, holding a softball bat.

"C'mon outside, B. A. There's something we need to cover."

Ellie and B. A. followed the coach outside. It was dark, but the outside house lights lit up the yard. He gave B. A. the bat and told her to take her stance. He then explained to her and Ellie that at contact a good hitter, especially a power hitter like B. A., should have their hips turned so they almost face the pitcher. B. A. took several swings, exaggerating her hip turn. She still felt a little awkward. Then Pops told her to turn her left toe out a little. As soon as she did that, it all fell in to place. Her lower body cleared itself, and she could feel the torque that was being created between her lower and upper body. It was a simple thing, but that's what often makes the difference in sports. B. A. had probably turned her foot out in the past, but with several months between softball seasons, she had, no doubt, forgot about it. She thanked Pops and told Ellie that she would have to shoot baskets with her dad some other time. As B. A. was getting into her truck, Pops said something about bringing the Fullerton girl next time so she could demonstrate three-point shots.

B. A.'s mind was very busy on the drive home. Now she knew why the custodian was coaching a varsity sport. He was obviously no ordinary janitor. She wondered if she was the only student at Reston High who knew that Leroy Brown was a highly decorated soldier. Leroy Brown, it just hit her. The song by Jim Croce, "Bad, Bad, Leroy Brown." She laughed at the irony. In deference to her coach, B. A. decided to keep her newfound information under her hat. She was good at keeping secrets about herself, so it should be no problem keeping Pops's secret. She also decided to stop calling her coach *Pops*. It would be more respectful to call him coach or Coach Brown. She made a mental note to pass that on to the rest of her teammates.

When Martha Smith came home from her job at the hospital, B. A. was waiting as usual with a cup of hot tea. She listened to the events of her mom's day and then told her about her visit to the Brown Ponderosa. She kept the medal information to herself as planned. Tomorrow was going to be a very exciting day. The Lady Eagles were playing Ferguson, and their star pitcher was none other than "Crazy Jane" Miller. B. A. couldn't wait to bat against her. She had a feeling that the toe-out stance would produce good results. It was about time she came out of her hitting slump. So far, her contribution to the offense was minimal. Tomorrow couldn't come soon enough.

Tammi spent most of the next school day telling anyone who would listen that the team's offense and defense wasn't doing their job. She and Darby had a big discussion at lunch on how B. A. should be moved down the batting order, or even better, on the bench. And why was the janitor coaching a sport? Wasn't it his job to clean the building? They even changed his schedule so he was off at three. Things were sure messed up with the Reston softball team. Maybe they should write an anonymous letter to the editor of the local paper and express their concerns. That would open a few eyes.

Chip was soft-tossing balls to B. A. on the other side of the centerfield fence when she saw a familiar figure jogging across the grass. When Miss Harbison got closer, they could see that she was wearing a Reston softball shirt and visor. Chip looked up at B.A. and smiled. Coach Harbison was their assistant basketball coach. Actually, she was the assistant, then the head coach, then the co-head coach. The ending to their basketball season was a little strange and quite memorable.

"Out of the way, Fullerton," said Miss Harbison. "I'll take over the tossing. Get a bat and start warming up. Smith, clear those hips. Don't hit the ball. Smash it."

"Yes, ma'am," responded B. A. as she took her stance. She met the last two solidly and drove them over the girls' heads that were fielding them. Those last two felt like old times.

"So what is this, Coach?" asked Chip as she swung two bats back and forth. "Are you the assistant softball coach now?"

"Yup," said coach Harbison. "The school board approved me as a volunteer coach last night. And unlike basketball, I actually played softball in high school."

"So you actually know something about softball, where in basketball you—"

"Watch it, Fullerton," said Coach Harbison smiling. "I pitched some in high school, and Pops will probably have me pitch some batting practice. I have no problem throwing inside."

All three of them laughed as B. A. grabbed her glove and headed out toward the group of fielders. She stopped after only taking a few steps and looked over her shoulder. "Hey, Coach, we're glad you're here. You were an awesome basketball coach."

"Hear that, Fullerton," said Coach Harbison as she knelt to toss a few to Chip. "At least she appreciates me."

"You know we love you, Coach H.," said Chip as she held her bat out waist high. "Toss them right here. I'm feeling a surge of power coursing through my powerful muscles."

"Still working on that vocabulary I see. That's good. A girl should be able to express herself in more than one syllable words."

"Speaking of expressing herself," said Chip as she smoothly hit line drives to all fields. "I wish B. A. would start expressing her softball self. I mean, I thought she'd be hitting better than this. Coach Brown bats her third, and everyone knows that's the spot where the best hitter should be. Some of the girls are griping about it."

"I wouldn't worry about it," said Coach Harbison. "You see how she moves. She's a natural athlete. She'll come out of it. It happens to all good hitters from time to time."

"I hope so," said Chip. "This would be the perfect game to start hitting. I'm sure Crazy Jane hasn't forgotten how B. A. humiliated her in basketball."

Jane Miller, the Ferguson pitcher, had not forgotten the treatment that B. A. had given her on the basketball floor. Chip lead off the game with a double down the right field line and then advanced to third on a ground out by Kris Ritter. B. A. stood in the box and watched the first pitch go by. She thought it was a little outside, but the umpire called it a strike. She dug in and waited for the next one. Miller cranked it up and plunked B. A. with a fastball in the left thigh. B. A. kept her head down and gritted her teeth as she trotted to first. Coach Harbison was waiting for her in the first-base coaching box and called time as soon as B. A. got there.

"How is it?" whispered coach Harbison as she looked over at Ferguson's grinning pitcher. "Do you think that was some sort of payback?"

"If it was," responded B. A. "It was a good place to get hit. On the bright side, I'm going to have a cool-looking bruise tomorrow."

The Ferguson first baseman gave B. A. a respectful look. She didn't know many girls that could take a fastball in the leg and then kid about it when they got to first base.

Tammi Olsen stepped in to the batter's box and hit the second pitch to short. The Ferguson shortstop gathered the grounder in, stepped on the bag, then threw Tammi out by two steps. B. A. was ten feet from second base when the shortstop reached the bag, so she veered out toward right field to get out of the way. She wasn't moving very fast on her sore leg, and she certainly wasn't going to slide on it. B. A. stood at second and waited for Chip to bring her glove out. Tammi came over and berated her for not sliding or at least standing in the baseline so the shortstop would have to throw around her.

B. A. decided not to inform Tammi that if you weren't going to slide on a double-play ball, you were expected to get out of the way. Standing in the way might cause a good umpire to call the batter out for interference, and it was considered a "bush league" play anyway. B. A. also didn't inform Tammie the Great that she had also seen a girl take a throw to the chin when she refused to give up the line of flight to the first-base bag. The shortstop that made the throw was looking down at the bag to make sure she didn't miss it and then fired it to first before she realized the base runner was just standing there in the way. The broken jaw that resulted served as a valuable lesson to the base runner and everyone else that saw the play. The bottom line was to play the game the way it is supposed to be played or accept the consequences.

One of the things that irked Tammi, and there was a long list of things that made her mad, was the fact that B. A. usually ignored her. Tammi had hollered at B. A. more than once in softball and basketball, and she usually just smiled at the taller girl and had no comment.

B. A. figured out early that Tammi was pretty much all for show with just a little something to back it up. She didn't see any reason to play Tammi's game. She remembered something Tank had said to her once. The big catcher from Jones Ferry told her, "If you haven't got much to say, say it loud. Maybe you can make up for your lack of insight with sheer volume." B. A. thought that Jenny's twin fit that description perfectly.

Jane Miller and her Ferguson teammates were sporting a one-run lead when B. A. came up for the second time in the third inning. Chip stood on first base and was hollering encouragement to the right fielder. Before B. A. stepped in, she ran some facts through her mind. Jane threw at her once and probably wouldn't do it again. A girl as cocky as the Ferguson hurler probably thought she had B. A. scared. What could she do to try to make B. A. look foolish? She didn't have a big curve or a *hook* as B. A. called it, so she would probably throw her change-up. If the Reston star took a big early swing expecting a fastball, it would draw a lot of laughs from the Ferguson bench and their fans.

B. A. stepped into the box and squeezed the bat tightly. She then exhaled and loosened her grip a little. She turned her left foot out and waggled the bat. Jane went into her windup and slapped her thigh with her glove as she released the ball. B. A. had guessed right. She almost didn't wait long enough as she led with her lower body and snapped the bat around. The ball was only fair by a couple of feet when it cleared the left field fence. An elementary school kid on a bicycle raced over, scooped up the ball, and took off with it. B. A. ran the bases quickly with her head down. That's the way Roger Maris, her idol, did it. It was her first home run in a Reston uniform. Jane just stood there and stared at her with contempt.

B. A.'s second home run came in the fifth inning with the bases empty. It was a shot over the scoreboard in center field. It was off a Jane Miller fastball, and it proved that the first one was no fluke. It helped a little, but due to some fielding mistakes and some wild pitches on Tammi's part, the score stood at six to three in favor of Ferguson. With two outs in the bottom of the seventh inning, B. A. came up for the last time. Chip was standing in the door of the dugout after popping up to make the second out. Kris Ritter then walked to fill the bases. B. A. stood just outside the batter's box and watched as the Ferguson coach went out to talk to his pitcher. Pops walked in from the third-base coaching box.

"What do you think?" asked the coach.

"I think your wife makes the best barbecued chicken in all of Texas," answered B. A.

The eavesdropping plate umpire chuckled as he bent over to sweep the plate off.

"That's a no-brainer," said Pops. "What's he telling her out there?"

"I think he's telling her not to walk me because then a hit would tie the game. With two outs, we will be running on contact. So he is probably advising her to pitch me outside. Close but nothing down the middle. They're hoping I will get impatient and might swing at a bad pitch."

"Good thinking," said Pops. "Be smart and try to make solid contact. We don't need a big knock here. Start on everything and react to the pitch. Hit it where it's pitched. Don't try to force it. Got it?"

"Got it," said B. A. as she watched the Ferguson coach cross the first base line on his way back to the dugout.

"Hey," screamed Chip from the dugout entrance. "Keep this one in the park. It's the last good ball we've got." This brought some laughter from the fans.

Miller stared daggers at Chip then in at B. A. She threw the first pitch a little outside. B. A. started on it then let it go. The second pitch was a little closer to the plate, so B. A. stepped in to it and made a smooth, compact stroke. It wasn't a big powerful cut, but she hit it right on the sweet spot of the bat. The ball flew down the first-base line and dropped neatly over the fence just inside the foul pole. It was the shortest route over the fence, but a home run nonetheless. The home fans went crazy high-fiving and hugging each other. Miller made a noise like she was going to be sick as she stormed off the mound. What more could this Reston girl do to her?

Chip sat at the kitchen table, watching her mom make supper. Her dad was in the other room, reading the paper and watching the news on television.

"Can you believe it?" asked Chip. "Three home runs in one game! We only had one home run all last year, and it was my inside-the-park job. B. A. hit three over the fence, one to each field. And the last one was a slammer. All that after Miller nailed her in the first inning. This girl is incredible!"

"How many hits did you have?" asked her dad as he came into the kitchen.

"I had two but popped it up in the last inning. I think I tried to do too much and wanted to be the big hero. But that's not my role on the team. I'm supposed to get on base so the big sticks behind me can clean things up. Lesson learned there. I'm starting to think that B. A. is as good in softball as she was in basketball. When are you two coming to a game?"

"So now you want us to come?" asked her dad.

"Well, yeah. If you haven't noticed, I'm a lot more mature and balanced now. I got over my fetish of having my parents at games."

"I think you mean phobia," said her mom.

Chip stood up and hugged her mom. "How did you get so smart? You must be where I get my mental abilities."

"Hey," said her dad. "One-half of the parental team is sitting right here. What did you get from me?"

"My in-depth knowledge of tools and their use," said Chip as she sidestepped her dad who made a grab at her. Chip headed to her room to do some deep thinking about a school project. "Don't forget to call me for supper," she hollered over her shoulder.

"I'm only going to call once," responded her mom.

"No, I mean call me like on the phone. I'll have my headphones on."

"Technology," said Mr. Fullerton. "How did we ever survive without it?"

◖◗

Chip lay on her bed with her eyes closed, listening to Carlos Santana play guitar. Once B. A. had introduced her to some of the older music, she was hooked. Chip pictured Santana standing in front of her, leisurely plucking his guitar strings. She wished she could play basketball and softball the way he played guitar. The really good athletes always seemed to be so smooth like they weren't putting out that much effort. She saw that in B.A.'s performance at times. How did she get so good? Scrutinizing B. A.'s abilities had to wait for another time. She needed to focus on a more immediate problem. Her sociology teacher had recently given the class an assignment. They had to do something nice for someone at least once a day for a week. She had no problem completing the assignment, but that was three weeks ago, and she was still thinking about the experience. The task had the effect on her that the teacher intended. It made her feel real good in ways that were hard to describe. What if she took it a step further? Not just doing a small thing for someone but a real big thing. Doing something for someone that might totally change their life would be an awesome accomplishment. She was deep in thought about helping her fellow man when her stomach started vibrating. She smiled and took off her headphones. Her mom was calling, indicating the food was ready. Her small part in making the world a better place would have to wait until after supper.

"So what's the prognosis?" asked her dad as they ate chicken fajitas. "Are ya'll going to be as good in softball as you were in basketball? Does B. A. have any more surprises up her sleeve other than the fact that she can hit the ball a mile in any direction?"

"Well," answered Chip, reaching for a second fajita. "I think she knows a lot about softball too. The coach and her are always talking—sometimes real low, so it's hard to hear what they're talking about. Oh yeah, Coach Harbison is back. She's our new volunteer assistant, and she actually knows something about this sport. I mean, she's more knowledgeable when it comes to softball."

A concerned look from Chip's mom made her add the last sentence.

"I'm sure Tammi will throw a wrench into the works sooner or later. How's that for injecting tools into the conversation, Dad?"

Mrs. Fullerton just snickered.

"It's too bad that Tammi went over to the dark side," continued Chip. "If she didn't have such a toady attitude we would be a much better team. She is our best pitcher as much as I hate to admit it. Did you know that there is a town in Arkansas called *Toad Suck?*"

"Can't say I've ever heard of it," said Mr. Fullerton. "Why can't you get along with her?"

"We've gone over this before, Dad. Mom will have to explain it to you in mature, adult terms. I'm all out of opinions and theories on why this girl is a psychotic lunatic bent on destroying everything in her path to superstardom."

"All right," said her mom. "Why don't you extend your school *niceness project* that you did a couple of weeks ago and try to become better friends with her? She is your teammate, and her sister has been your best friend for years."

"Mom, this girl lives in a fantasy world where she is the center of everything. If she had her way, we would all bow down to her every time she passed by. I refuse to sacrifice my dignity on her behalf. I promise to be civil, but that's where I draw the line. And I have several sane friends who will back me up on this. Can I be excused? I have some serious work to do."

Chip's parents watched her retreat to her room. Mr. Fullerton turned to his wife. "Our kid has the makings of a trial attorney. 'Sacrifice my dignity, psychotic lunatic, and went over to the dark side'. Where does she come up with this stuff?"

"I don't know," answered Chip's mom. "I just wish Tammi and her would come to some sort of agreement. High school is too short to waste time feuding with someone. Normally I would advise her to just stay away from the Olsen girl, but that's impossible when you play three sports with her."

"I'm sure she will figure it out. Didn't she just explain to us that she is becoming more balanced and mature? Do you think there really is a town called *Toad Suck*?"

"If she says there is, there probably is. Now that's a bit of information I can do without."

Mystery Thief

Chip, Jenny, and B. A. stood in the snack aisle of Mr. Kim's store, discussing which foods were healthier when they heard a loud voice exclaim something about a robbery. The three of them froze and stared wide-eyed at each other. Before the other two could stop her, Chip crouched down and moved up the aisle slowly toward the front of the store. Jenny and B. A. quietly followed their teammate, keeping as low as they could. They could hear Mr. Kim and someone else that sounded like a kid arguing. Chip was peering through the shelves, trying to get a better look. They heard Mr. Kim holler, and then it sounded like the would-be robber was running toward the door. When the figure—dressed in black with a mask—passed their aisle, Chip stuck out her foot and tripped him. Her two friends couldn't believe it, but they immediately sprang into action. Chip had a hold of the robber's legs when the other two pounced on him. Mr. Kim came around the corner and shouted for the girls to let him go. Reluctantly, the three released their grip, and the young boy scrambled to his feet and was out the door in an instant.

"We had him," exclaimed Chip, getting up from the floor. "Why did you tell us to let him go?"

"He might have had a weapon," explained Mr. Kim. "He said he had a knife, but I never saw it. Besides, he sounded like a desperate kid. He was more scared than anything. He was so nervous he could barely talk. I don't think he'll be back. No harm was done. Are you three all right?"

"We're fine," said B. A. "He didn't get anything, did he"?

"No. He panicked when I walked toward the end of the counter."

"You know judo, don't you, Mr. Kim?" asked Chip.

Mr. Kim smiled. "Tae kwon do, Korean-style karate. I haven't practiced it in a while. Maybe I should start up again."

"As long as no one got hurt, I guess that's the main thing," said Jenny, dusting off her shorts.

"You're right," said Mr. Kim. "I'm glad my wife wasn't minding the store. Thanks, girls. Your courage is appreciated."

Later that evening, the three girls sat in the front seat of Jenny's car and watched the sun sink below the horizon. Mr. Daggert's farm was their favorite spot for watching the sunset and for discussing important issues. Most of the time the discussions centered around sports or school. Jenny had backed up to the field gate, which gave them a perfect view of the western sky through the front windshield. The field across the road had a few trees off in the distance and about forty head of cattle milling around. All three were thinking about the attempted robbery. Finally, Chip broke their silence.

"Well," she asked, "did either of you get a look at the homemade tattoo on that guy's left hand?"

Without looking at Chip, Jenny and B. A. both said in unison, "JFR."

Just before they went to bed, Chip and Luke were on the phone, discussing the events at Mr. Kim's store. She was positive that the culprit was a student at Reston High School—probably a freshman because between Luke, Chip and Jenny, they pretty much knew all the students that were a year behind or ahead of them. The only class they weren't that familiar with was the freshmen class. That was one of the benefits of going to a small school. Everyone knew everyone else and quite often everyone else's business. In a small town, it was hard to keep secrets. Luke was the sports editor on the school paper, so he had access to some student records. He couldn't get into grades or personal information like health issues, but he knew how to bring up photos, addresses, and class schedules. The plan was to take the limited information that Chip had and create a list of possible suspects. Since they didn't know that many freshmen, they would have to check out everyone on their list for the tattoo. They decided to keep everything on the down low—observation only. Asking questions would raise suspicions. The guy was already crazy enough to attempt a robbery, so there would be no telling what he would do if he thought people were investigating him.

The self-proclaimed super sleuths had a stroke of good luck the next day at school. Chip volunteered to do a freshmen survey for her sociology class, and the only time they were all together was at lunch. The teacher provided a list with all the freshmen in the school. Jenny was the other volunteer, so between them, they had a chance to check out every freshman that was in school that day. When they came up empty, they surmised that the guy either wasn't in school that day or he had the tattoo covered. Six of the guys in the cafeteria had those little half gloves on that skateboarders sometimes wear. No one seemed even a little nervous when the girls came by with their clipboards, asking questions.

The two friends stood against the lunchroom wall and tabulated their results. "I had four guys with gloves on," said Chip. "And one of them was Luke's size, so we can rule him out."

"I had two skinny guys," added Jenny, "So they are both possibles. There's no way this is a no-brainer, and the guy just carved his own initials on his hand and then traced it with ink?"

"That's the first thing we checked on," responded Chip. "There is no freshman or sophomore with the initials JFR."

"I can't believe you or your partner in crime haven't figured this out yet. This kind of stuff is right up your alley."

"Don't worry, we'll find this guy. You've got to have patience. He could be absent today, or he's from another school. Luke and I have solved tougher cases than this."

Chip failed to mention that they were way off when they investigated B. A. Their Witness Protection Program theory fell apart as well as their undercover FBI theory.

"A big piece of this puzzle," continued Chip as the two of them walked back to class, "would fall into place if we could figure out why this guy wanted to rob the grocery store. Motivation is a key factor in any investigation."

"How about he needed money?" asked Jenny.

"That's too easy. Maybe he needed money, and maybe he didn't. What if it was a dare or a gang initiation thing? What if somebody told him they were going to beat him up if he didn't rob the store? Stick with me, weedhopper, and you will learn the ins and outs of sleuthing. In fact, I'm going to anoint you as assistant sleuth. It helps your confidence to have a title. Bow down so I can make it official."

Jenny bowed her head and Chip touched her clipboard to one shoulder then the other. She was about to say something clever when their sociology teacher opened the classroom door.

"I hope that's not some sort of satanic ritual you two are doing out here," said Mr. Cutler, smiling.

"You're lucky you didn't hear anything," said Chip in a voice that was barely above a whisper. "Members of the Raging Beagle Cult don't like eavesdroppers, and we deal harshly with them."

"Get in here, you two, and share your survey results with the rest of the class."

Chip and Jenny stood together on the far side of the center field fence, watching B. A. take her last batting practice cuts before they played Lakewood. "You see that smooth swing, Chippy?" asked Jenny. "If you copied it, you might be able to get the ball out of the infield once in a while."

"I'll have you know. I've got six doubles and two triples so far this season," responded Chip.

"What's this, do you have your stats memorized?" asked Jenny.

"No, it's just that my mind is like a computer. Once information goes in, it's stuck in there forever."

"Is that so? What did you get on your last statistics test?"

"I got a B- but that stuff wasn't important. I only process the important stuff."

B. A. totally whiffed on her last swing. It was tough to keep from laughing when her two best friends were distracting her. She looked over at them and saw a player in a Lakewood uniform standing behind them, smiling.

"Hey, Cheryl," said B. A., extending her hand. "It's been a while. How's your team doing?"

Cheryl Williams was Lakewood's best athlete. She averaged eighteen points a game in basketball and was her team's starting shortstop. The Reston girls were also impressed with Cheryl's sportsmanship. They often talked about how much better they would be if Cheryl went to Reston High and played with them.

"We're having a pretty good season," answered Williams as she shook hands with the three from Reston. "We've only lost two games."

"B. A.'s hit seven homers this year already," exclaimed Chip as she stepped in to take her swings.

"I've been reading about her," said Cheryl. "I think we'll walk her every time today. Hey, I hope you have been thinking about the Michigan camp. My uncle needs an answer in a couple of weeks. It's two weeks of softball and then two weeks of basketball. It should be an awesome time. We get to stay in the college dorm and everything."

B. A. and Chip looked at each other. Neither of them had brought the subject up since Cheryl asked them about it a few weeks ago. With all that was going on, it had just slipped their minds.

B. A. steered Cheryl off to the side and asked her a few questions about the camp. She also wanted to ask her a few questions about a guy that went to Lakewood. Jenny had been e-mailing this guy for a couple of weeks, and Chip and B. A. wanted to know more about him before things went any further. Chip was just being her snoopy self, but B. A. wanted to know more about a guy that might be dating one of her two best friends. She had heard a few rumors about Morrie Schreider but wanted some unbiased facts. She had planned on calling Cheryl, but when she saw that Lakewood was coming up on their schedule, she decided to wait and talk to her in person. The news wasn't good. Cheryl gave her honest impression of the guy—user and loser. He was out for a good time without considering the consequences of his actions. He was famous for throwing parties when his parents were away from home. In short, he was not the kind of guy that Jenny should be getting involved with.

The two friends parted when their coaches whistled at them. Pops and the Lakewood coach were both laid-back kind of guys. They had no problem when they saw their players fraternizing with the opponent before a game. The players from both teams hustled in to their respective dugouts.

As far as high school softball games go, the game with Lakewood was pretty tame. The score was three to two in favor of Reston. Tammi had walked in both runs. It was one of those outings where she either struck out the opponent or walked them. Williams was Lakewood's only offensive bright spot. She was two for three when she stepped in to the box for the last time. She had also scored both of Lakewood's runs. There was one out and a runner on third when Cheryl lofted a high fly down the right field foul line. B. A. sprinted over in plenty of time, but then she did something that immediately incensed Tammi. She just stood there on the foul line looking confused, acting like she couldn't locate the ball. When she made no attempt to catch it, Coach Brown smiled to himself. He was the type of coach that refused to holler out instructions to his team every time a situation came up. He did his work in practice and let his players mostly think for themselves once the game started.

The ball dropped foul. B. A. picked it up and lobbed it to Kris Ritter, the second baseman. It was nothing but a long strike. Tammi didn't see it that way. She screamed something at B. A., who ignored her while motioning to the center fielder that there was still just one out. It was obvious to anyone with a bit of softball sense that if B. A. had caught the ball, the girl on third probably would have tagged and scored. Even with B. A.'s incredible arm, the ball was hit too deep to risk it. Cheryl stood outside the batter's box and shook her fist at B. A. The right fielder waved her glove in response.

Cheryl lined the next pitch at Chip, who snagged it and almost doubled off the girl at third. The next batter popped up to end the game. Jenny, Chip, and B. A. all waved at Cheryl as they headed out to center field for their post-game talk. Pops broke down the mistakes and then complimented their good plays. As usual, the team stood and put their hands together. Before the coach said, "Eagles on three," he looked at B. A. and said, "Nice thinking on that fly. If you would have caught it, they would have tied the game."

B. A. nodded and smiled. Tammi just stood there, glaring at her, chomping on her gum.

Chip, Luke, and B. A. sat at their usual table at the Pizza Palace. They had several issues to discuss as they waited for their pizza. First was the kid with the JFR tattoo. So far, they had come up with no leads, which meant he probably wasn't a student at

Reston. This would make the whole investigation more difficult. Second was B. A.'s conversation with Cheryl Williams. If what Cheryl said was true, and they didn't doubt her, then this Morrie Schreider guy was not someone Jenny should be hanging around with. Chip was all for telling Jenny what Cheryl said.

"I don't think that would be a good idea," said B. A. "Let's not be too hasty. We're not even sure she wants to go out with him."

"She does," volunteered Chip. "She told me yesterday morning. He called and asked her to go out for pizza after Lakewood's baseball game on Saturday."

"You both should talk to her together," said Luke, looking over his shoulder for their order. When it came to pizza, he had an internal timer. He knew exactly how long it took to make and cook their usual order. Sure enough, their server came through the kitchen doors and headed for their table.

Chip spun the plate so Luke's side of the pie was in front of him. His half was loaded with every possible ingredient, while the girls' side was a more modest Canadian bacon and pineapple.

"Don't even think about stuffing one of those slices in your face," warned Chip. "You do it every time and end up burning your mouth."

"What are you, my mother?" asked Luke as he used his fork to separate a piece. "In the interest of decorum, I will wait the standard two minutes. Then I'm willing to risk it."

"Whatever," said Chip as she served B. A. then herself. "So what do we do, B. A.? Do we confront her?"

"This is going to sound weird," said B. A. "I feel like you two are drawing me into your web of subterfuge, but how about Rod and I go out for pizza at the same place they go to. That shouldn't be too hard to figure out. Then we can keep an eye on this guy to see what he's like."

"*Subterfuge*, I like that word," said Luke. "While you're at it, why don't you just introduce Rod to him? You know, like ya'll just ran into each other by accident."

"Yeah," added Chip. "Once this guy gets a look at Rod's ugly mug and hulk-like body he'll—"

B. A. gave Chip a discerning look. Chip forgot that she was talking about B. A.'s boyfriend.

"Hey, he's family," said a defensive Chip. "We talk like that about each other all the time."

B. A. laughed. "I know. You should hear what he says about you."

"Back to the subjects at hand, you two," said Luke as he lifted a slice of pizza and tested it for possible mouth burn.

Luke had just finished his half of the pie when Chip threw another iron into the fire. "There's another thing I wanted to bring up. It's probably nothing, but there's been a strange guy in the stands for our last three or four games, and it seems he's very interested in you, B. A. Do you think he's some kind of college scout?"

"The guy with the deep tan and sunglasses?" asked Luke. "I noticed him too. Up until a few games ago I've never seen him before. He doesn't just come to home games either."

"Wow," said Chip. "We've got mysteries all over the place. We better get to solving them. I like your idea about spying on Jenny and her date, B. A. Well, Pizza King, can you take me straight home, or do you need to stop for a couple of burgers?"

"I can't help it if I'm built like a SUV. I need fuel. You're just a little sports car that can run all day on a piece of lettuce. I need something more substantial."

"All right, all right. I was just kidding. By the way, B. A., what does my darling cousin say about me?"

"Oh no, I'm not going there. You two have been getting along fine lately, and that's the way it should stay. And we won't be spying on Jenny. We'll just be there for support."

The three friends paid the bill and headed out into the parking lot. Chip and Luke got in the *punkin*, as Luke's vehicle was affectionately known around town, and B. A. got into her truck. B. A. was about to pull on to the street when Luke started honking his horn. She waited for him to pull up alongside. Chip rolled down her window, and Luke hollered over at B. A.

"Hey, what if the initials on his hand aren't his? Maybe they could be his girlfriend's initials or a parent's. It might be the clue we're looking for."

B. A. waved and headed home. She was worried about how Jenny would react when she saw her and Rod at the same restaurant on Saturday. Hopefully, Jenny would understand that they were just looking out for her best interest. Luke's idea about the tattoo had some merit. And who was the strange guy in the sunglasses that kept showing up at their games? Chip was right. They had a lot of mysteries to solve.

Chip rode the next day to school with Jenny. She peppered the taller girl with questions about the baseball player from Lakewood. Jenny just smiled a lot and insisted that he was a real nice guy. She said she was excited about Saturday night and was a little surprised that her parents gave her permission to go. Lakewood was about fifteen miles from Reston. It was a little bigger than Reston but still considered a small town. If it were any closer to Fort Worth, she wouldn't have even asked. Chip, on the other hand, was worried that Jenny had fallen for the "but he's nice to me" kind of guy. The type of guy that could put on the believable act of being a decent person, when in reality, he was an entirely different animal. One surprising piece of information that Jenny didn't share with Chip was that her sister told her that she had heard that Morrie Schreider was not a very cool guy.

By the time Chip and Jenny arrived at school, Luke had already uncovered some vital information. He arrived early and had used the school's computer to do some sleuthing. When he passed Chip in the hall between second and third hour, he passed her a note. All it said was, "Jorge Fernando Reyes."

Chip, B. A., and Luke sat in the bleachers before practice that afternoon and discussed their newfound information. Luke had searched the archives of the local papers and came up with a death notice. Jorge Fernando Reyes was a freshman in Dallas that was killed two years ago in a car accident. His older brother was driving when he left the road and hit a tree. Jorge was the only fatality. The story was that Jorge had taken off his seat belt to get something in the backseat when his brother went into a curve too fast. He lost control of the car, went down an embankment, and hit the tree head on. His seat belt and airbag had saved the older brother.

"So," said Luke after relaying the results of his search, "there are three Reyeses in school, but only one of them is a freshman. Diego Reyes could very well be our guy."

"Do you think the tattoo is in memory of Jorge?" asked Chip. "Maybe he was a brother or a cousin or something."

"I think so," responded Luke. "Now all we have to do is track down Diego and get a look at his hand. He might be covering it up if he thinks ya'll saw it at the store. Here's an idea. Why don't all three of you start talking to him? You know, say hello to him in the halls. It could spook him into making some kind of move and tipping his hand."

"That's not bad," said Chip. "Most freshmen guys would get spooked if three gorgeous female athletes started talking to him. All right, if that's the best you've got, let's give it a try."

B. A. sat and listened to the two amateur detectives cook up a plan. She had to admit, they sounded like they knew what they were doing. They were certainly entertaining.

Jenny walked up as practice was about to start. It wasn't like her to cut it so close. It didn't take much for her two best friends to figure out that she was probably talking on the phone to Morrie, her upcoming date on Saturday.

After stretching and two laps around the field, Pops called them in and informed them that they would be doing some instructing today. Teaching the game was another way to sharpen their own skills. The plan was to go over to the middle school diamond to help the younger girls with their fundamentals. Coach Harbison would work with the outfielders and Pops would work with the infielders. The middle school diamond was only about a hundred yards away, so the Lady Eagles just jogged over.

B. A. and the rest of the varsity outfielders each took two of the younger girls and played catch with them. Then they started to toss shallow pop-ups to check on their technique. They weren't too bad with pop-ups, but when Coach Harbison started to hit medium flies, everything broke down. The little girls had problems judging the ball and a couple seemed to be afraid of it. They all ran around with their gloves out, which didn't help the matter. After two attempts each, B. A. asked the other varsity outfielders if she could try something with the middle schoolers. No one objected, so she called them in and told them to drop their gloves on the ground. They looked at her like she was crazy.

"Okay, let's go over here," instructed B. A. as she moved them away from the pile of gloves. "Our coach will hit a fly, and I will run under it, then I will step aside and let it drop. Then I want you to do it—one at a time, of course. I want you to get used to doing the footwork first. You need to run like an athlete with your arms pumping at your sides. The only time you stick your glove out is when you are preparing to catch the ball."

Coach Harbison lofted a lazy fly, and B. A. took off running. She got to the spot in plenty of time, camped under it, then she stepped aside and let the ball drop. The varsity outfielders ran alongside the younger girls and talked them through the drill as Coach Harbison hit flies to them. It didn't take long for them to get the hang of doing the footwork first before preparing to make the catch. It was a good idea for the older players to run with the younger girls because one girl got a little confused and just stood under the ball as it came down. Courtney Grimes, the left fielder, grabbed the girl and moved her out of the way at the last second. When it was time to put the gloves back on and actually catch the ball, the younger girls showed real improvement. They kept their arms in tight and sprinted to the spot where they thought the ball was going to land. By sprinting and getting there early, they had time to make adjustments in case the wind blew the ball of course or the ball was hit harder or softer than they had originally judged it.

B. A. also told them to catch the ball right above their left shoulder. No more putting their gloves in front of their faces. This really helped with a couple of them, who still appeared to be afraid of the ball. B. A. even missed one on purpose to demonstrate the safety aspect of this technique. If you misjudged the ball, you wouldn't pay for it by getting hit in the face. When B. A. missed the fly, the ball fell harmlessly to the ground behind her. The little girls all shook their heads, showing that they liked the idea of not putting their face at risk just trying to catch a fly. Pops hollered at his team to head back to their field. As the varsity jogged back, Courtney fell in beside B. A.

"How do you know all this stuff?" asked Courtney.

"I don't know," answered B. A. "I guess I just paid attention when I was little. I had a couple of older guy friends that showed me a lot. They were awesome players."

"Well, I wish I had learned what you just showed them at a younger age. I was afraid of the ball right up to last year. I took one on the chin when I was in seventh grade, and I was terrified it might happen again. That's when I decided to be an outfielder. Thanks a lot. I learned something today."

"You're welcome," said B. A.

Chip, Jenny, and B. A. jogged over to the track, hoping to get there in time to watch the last couple of events. They had promised Lu to come and support her when she ran the 1600 meters. Lu was one of the best milers around. It was her specialty, and she had not been beaten yet in the six dual meets that she had run in this year. There would be more runners today as this was a triangular meet with two other schools. When the girls walked up on the far side of the track, it looked like the 1600 was about to start. Jenny explained to her teammates that the 1600, or mile run, was one of the most exciting events in track and field. It combined aerobic and anaerobic skills. The first part was aerobic, where you used oxygen from outside your body to help provide energy. The last part, the sprint to the finish line, was anaerobic. That meant there isn't enough time for the respiratory system to take in enough oxygen, so energy is produced with the help of the oxygen that is already in the body. There was a lot of strategy involved, depending on the runner's style and the style of her competitors. The gun went off, and when Lu ran by her basketball teammates, she was in third place behind two taller girls.

"C'mon, Lu," screamed Chip. "Get those stumpy legs moving. You're behind already."

B. A. and Jenny gave Chip their usual look of dismay.

"I can't believe you said that," said Jenny. She then went on to explain that Lu would draft behind the leaders, letting them break the wind. It would take less effort if you weren't in the lead fighting the wind. Breaking the wind was the wrong term to use in front of Chip.

"Ha!" exclaimed Chip. "If they're breaking wind out there, I'd want to be in front of the pack not behind."

"Funny," said Jenny. "Let's do something cool when she comes by again. What should we do, B. A.?"

B. A. thought for a second. "Okay, how about you and I act like we're rowing a boat? Chip can be the caller and instead of row, she says Lu, Lu, Lu."

"That's goofy," said Chip. "But it'll have to do until I can think up something really clever."

When Lu passed them on her second lap, they went into their rowing routine. She cracked a smile, but that was it. The next time around, they acted like they were doing the backstroke. That was Jenny's idea. Chip's contribution was to do the Macarena dance when Lu went by for the last time. The fans on the far side were howling at the girls' antics. Lu was still in third place with half a lap to go.

"Watch this," said Jenny. "This girl's got an awesome finishing kick."

As soon as she passed the comedy trio, Lu went to the outside and picked up speed. If the pace of the race was to her liking, this is where she usually made her move. When she came around the final curve, she was in a dead sprint. Her competitors didn't have the chops to stay with her, and she won by twenty-five yards going away. After crossing the finish line, Lu pointed at them and gave them thumbs up with a big smile.

"Let's walk over and see if the superstar runner wants to go out for supper with us," said B. A.

"We can ask," said Chip, "but I think she's only allowed to eat stuff like bean sprouts and tofu. I've got to admit, those miniature legs can really move when she gets going."

Once again, Chip was a little off the mark. Lu said she would meet them at the Pizza Palace in thirty minutes.

The dinner conversation covered a myriad of subjects. Chip got strange looks from Jenny and B. A. when it appeared she was getting a little too nosey. Lu didn't seem to mind as she answered everything Chip could throw at her. Chip and Jenny didn't know very much about Lu's background because she moved to town with her parents two years ago when she was a freshman. She explained that she was adopted when she was only a few months old. Her little brother and sister were also adopted. Running was her passion, but she started to appreciate the game of basketball when she decided to become somewhat of a defensive specialist. B. A. asked her what made her such a good runner.

"I think I'm a natural runner," answered Lu. "I usually eat sensible and drink a lot of water. The one thing I do different from most of the other girls is I overtrain. When we did the learning unit in psychology, Mrs. Crandall wrote several techniques for better learning on the board. You remember, Chip, stuff like *paraphrase*, *tie it to something you already know*, and the big one, *overlearn*. Don't just do the minimum, go farther than what was assigned. Well, I do that with running. The other day at practice, the middle and long distance runners were supposed to run three miles. I ran the three miles, then I ran three more when I got home."

"Hey, we do that sometimes after basketball practice," observed Chip. "We'll have to come by so we can all run together. That is, if you can keep up, Lu."

"I think I can keep up with those short little legs of yours."

"What? My legs are longer than yours. Stand up, Lu. Jenny, compare our legs and tell us whose are longer."

"Sit down," ordered Jenny. "People are looking at us." Some of the other patrons were watching and smiling. Chip didn't seem to notice as this was a common occurrence for her.

"I really appreciate ya'll coming by and rooting for the track team today," said Lu. "We don't draw very many fans like the softball and baseball teams do. If you want to see a tough race, come by next Tuesday. Tracie Morgan from Staunton hasn't lost a race this year either. Our times are pretty close, so it's going to be a real battle."

"We'll be there to cheer you on," said B. A. "I need to head home for an exciting night of studying. Jenny, I'll give Chip a ride if you can take Lu home."

"Fine by me. We'll talk about how awesome the basketball team is going to be next year. See you at school tomorrow."

B. A. pulled into Chip's driveway and turned off the engine. "I hope this whole surveillance thing on Saturday night doesn't backfire on us," said B. A. "Rod and I will be at the Lakewood pizza place before Jenny and this Morrie dude show up. I think it will look better that way. How about if I ask Cheryl to meet us there? Then we can talk about the summer sports camp. She'll be a nice cover if Jenny asks what we're doing there. Pretty good, huh?"

"You're learning, rookie, but you're not in our league yet. Your plan does have merit though. If Luke or I were involved, she would immediately sense something was up. I say go with it. If there are any problems with this guy, Rod can just beat him up in the parking lot."

"No one is going to get beat up," said B. A. "I just want to make sure Jenny is safe. Hopefully this guy will say something to reveal his true character before she gets too serious about him."

"I've got one more thing to throw in to the mix," said Chip. "As if we don't have enough going on with the attempted robbery and Jenny's bad dating decisions. Who do you think our new fan is? You know, the guy that's been showing up at most of our games and staring at you. Do you think he could be a college scout?"

"Yeah, he could be a college scout, but I doubt it. He just doesn't have that look about him. He's probably just a guy that likes to watch cute girls like you and Jenny play softball. I wouldn't worry about him."

Lu Battles Back

B. A., Cheryl, and Rod sat at the Lakewood local pizza place, munching on breadsticks and waiting for Jenny and her date to show up. Cheryl explained in detail about how the camp was run. It was at Western Michigan University in Kalamazoo, Michigan. Her uncle was a local high school coach and had been running the camp for several years. The first two weeks were softball and the last two were basketball. Cheryl seemed pretty excited, and in the end, she sold B. A. on the idea. Her mom had given her permission a couple of weeks earlier. She said she would be busy taking a nursing class when she wasn't working, so the timing was perfect. Cheryl let out with a loud "yes" when B. A. said she was in, and she thought Chip would come too. Rod tapped the table to get their attention and nodded in the direction of the door. Jenny and her date were just arriving.

B. A. was glad to see that there was a whole group of guys and girls. This would be a good way for her friend to get to know this guy a little better without being alone with him. Jenny gave them a strange look as her group pushed a couple of tables together. A few minutes later, Jenny walked over to their table.

"Hi, Cheryl. What are you two doing here?"

"We're talking about the summer sports camp in Michigan," said B. A. "How did the game go?"

"They lost by one run," said Jenny. "Sorry for being kinda rude. I thought you might be spying on me. Anyway, they recognized you, B. A., and I said I would introduce you. Could you come over for a couple of minutes?"

"Sure," said B. A. "We were just about to leave anyway."

Rod went over to pay the bill while B. A. and Cheryl went over to talk to the Lakewood group. When Rod came over and put his hands on B. A.'s shoulders the crowd went silent. Rod was used to this sort of reception. It was hard to hide a six-foot-seven muscular body. After exchanging a few more pleasantries, the three of them said their good-byes.

Outside the door, Cheryl asked, "Were you really spying on your friend?"

"Heck, yeah," said B. A. "After what you told me about this guy, wouldn't you? The main thing was to give Morrie a look at the big guy here. I hope this is a one-time thing with Jenny. Some guys are awfully good at hiding their true selves when they see something they want. Present company *excepted* of course."

"I know what you mean," added Rod. "I've seen guys do it, and it's pretty low."

"Hopefully she will come to her senses and that will be the end of it," said Cheryl. "It sure is nice to have such good friends that worry about you. Anyway, I'm glad you can go to Michigan. It's going to be a lot of fun. Please let me know if Chip is a definite." Cheryl started to walk away and then turned around, "I almost forgot. The next time I hit a potential game-winning fly, catch the darn thing."

"No problem," said B. A. "I'll think about it if you'll do something for Chip and me."

"What's that?" asked Cheryl.

"Move to Reston."

"That's not a bad idea. I'll pass it by my parents."

B. A. and Rod both laughed and gave her a good-bye wave. The ride home was a quiet one. Both of them had a lot to think

about. Rod had final exams coming up and B. A.'s mind was full of
Jenny's situation, robberies, and strange guys lurking around the
ball diamond. When they got to Rod's place, they went through
a short workout in his garage weight room. Their lifting routines
were very efficient. They went about their business and seemed
to know exactly when the other needed a spot. B. A. wondered
as she watched her boyfriend do some light curls if his dad knew
Coach Brown. Rod's dad was in the Special Forces, so chances
were he would know about a Medal of Honor winner that lived
close by.

Chip sat at her desk, looking over the schedule for the rest of the
season. There were twelve regular season games to go. They were
winning most of their games, but she would be the first to admit
that the softball season didn't have the spark that the basketball
season had. Something seemed to be missing. B. A. had finally
come out of her slump, and in a big way. She had nine home runs
and a ton of RBIs. It seemed like every time Chip got on base, B.
A. would come through with a hit. The last game was a thing of
beauty. Reston was only down by a run. Chip was on third, and
Kris Ritter was standing on second. B. A. came up and hit the
second pitch to the gap in left center. Chip wondered why the
coach didn't tell her pitcher to walk B. A. Maybe it was because
she had never seen the Reston star hit before. Still, she should
have known how dangerous Reston's leading RBI producer could
be in the clutch. She was getting plenty of write-ups in the local
papers. There's no way the opposing coach was afraid of the next
batter, Tammi the Great. Tammi was hitting something like .280.
She had a triple and a few doubles, but she wasn't half the hitter
that B. A. was.

Chip headed in to the living room where her parents were
doing their usual thing. The television was on low and both of
them were reading. *What a boring life these two lead*! She decided to

liven things up a little. She limped up to them and said in a raspy voice, "Mom, Dad, how can you tell if a snake bite is poisonous?"

"Don't fall for it," whispered her mom without looking up from her magazine.

"What?" screamed Chip's dad as he leapt from his chair and wrestled his only daughter to the floor. "Quick, Karen, get the big knife from the kitchen. I saw an episode on snakebites last week on *Animal Planet*. We'll have to cut it open and suck the poison out."

Chip's mom ran to the kitchen and came back with a steak knife. "This was all I could find. Hold her still, and I'll make the incision."

"Are you crazy?" hollered Chip as she struggled to get free. "I was just kidding."

"You don't kid about these things, dear," said her mom laying the knife down and pulling up Chip's right pant leg. "You're already getting delirious. Now where did that nasty thing bite you?"

Chip's dad held tight as her mom inspected her leg. She struggled and squawked but couldn't break free. The little shortstop looked over her shoulder and saw Luke looking through the kitchen door window.

"Luke, get in here and help me," screamed Chip. "My parents are losing it."

Luke let himself in and surveyed the situation. Chip's dad was holding her upper body down, and her mom had her legs pinned to the floor. Now she was trying to pull her daughter's other pant leg up. It was all Luke could do to not break out laughing.

"Forget helping," said Chip still struggling. "Call Officer Rubio and tell him to bring his tazer."

"Help us, Luke," said Karen. "I think she's going in to snakebite shock. We might have to amputate."

"It might be the only way to save her," offered Luke.

"No, no," screamed Chip. "Luke, do something. Get these thugs off of me."

"I know what we need," said Karen, sitting back and looking at her husband. "Ice cream."

"Yeah, that might do the trick," said her dad. "Keep her quiet, Luke. We're going to make an emergency ice cream run."

Chip's parents got up off of her and casually headed for the door. After a few steps, her mom turned around and snatched the knife off the floor. She tossed it on the kitchen counter as she walked by. A few seconds later, Luke and Chip could hear the car leaving the driveway. The two teens looked at each other and started laughing. Luke offered his girlfriend a hand and helped her up.

"It's a wonder that I turned out the way I did with parents like that," said Chip, brushing herself off. "Why didn't you push them off of me?"

"I don't like to get involved in family problems," answered Luke. "Domestic squabbles can be tricky."

"Well, because of your amazing lack of courage while your girl was getting mauled, you are treating tonight. C'mon, let's get out of here before those two insanos get back. Let me ask you this. If we were outside and two bears were attacking me, would you jump in and help?"

"What kind of bears?" asked Luke as they headed out the back door.

"Black bears, not grizzlies."

"Adults or cubs?"

"Teenage bears."

"Let me think about it. When it comes to bears, you can't be too hasty. Did you do something to aggravate them?"

"Never mind, superhero. It's obvious that a girl needs to be able to take care of herself. It's a rough world out there. Maybe I need to start carrying pepper spray or something."

"You know," said Luke, getting serious. "That's not a bad idea. You never know what some real crazy person might do. Does your dad carry it at his store?"

"Yeah, he does. I'll get some if you think I might need it. And maybe some for the other girls too."

"Good thinking," said Luke as he opened the car door for his girlfriend.

The following Tuesday was a big day for the softball team and the girls' track team. Chip and the rest of her teammates were playing at home against the top-rated team in the area. Kennedy High had only lost one game all year and had one of the top pitchers around. Carrie Booth was fast and had a wide assortment of pitches. The rumor was that the University of Texas was interested in her. B. A. and Chip were both excited to bat against her. The rest of the Lady Eagles were extremely apprehensive and were already intimidated even before Carrie threw her first pitch. The odds of the home team scoring a lot of runs was slim, so Tammi needed to be on her game if the Reston squad had any chance of winning. Whatever the outcome, the three friends wanted the game to get over in a timely fashion so they could get over to the track. Lu was racing her big rival in the mile, and they wanted to support the new member of their inner circle.

Carrie Booth was everything the press had been saying about her and more. When the public address system broke down, it appeared that the playing of the national anthem was not going to happen. When Coach Brown went over to explain this to the Kennedy coach, he turned to his team in the dugout and said something to them. Four girls, including their pitcher, came out to the first base sideline and sang a very impressive version of "The Star Spangled Banner." The visitors received a huge round of applause for their efforts.

"So Carrie Booth can sing and pitch," muttered Chip. "What else does she do? Sell popcorn?"

"Don't worry, Chipper," said Jenny. "If she strikes you out every time, maybe she'll sing you a little blues number to make you feel better."

"What?" wailed Chip. "That's how you encourage your teammate just before she goes up against the best pitcher she's ever seen?"

Little did Chip know but the best pitcher she would ever see was standing right next to her in the dugout.

"Hey, Chip," said B. A. as she winked at Jenny. "I just talked to Coach, and he wants you to crowd the plate on Booth. Get in there real tight, and take one for the team if you have to. It's all about commitment, babe."

"You can't be serious," said Chip only half believing what B. A. was saying. Jenny was usually the one pulling stunts on her. "This girl is fast. If I get plunked, it's gonna hurt real bad."

"A week from now you'll be laughing about it," said Jenny with a straight face. "If you're out of the hospital by then." That last statement caused Jenny and B. A. to break out laughing.

"Stop it!" hollered Chip as she grabbed her glove and ran out to her position at short.

Coach Brown looked questionably at Chip and then at B. A. and Jenny. They just shrugged their shoulders and headed out onto the field. A little pregame humor to loosen up your teammates was not always a bad thing. This proved to be true when Chip led off the bottom of the inning with a single to right. She stood on first and glared at B. A., who was now in the on deck circle. B. A. just smiled back at her. The visiting pitcher settled down and lived up to her reputation by striking out Kris and B. A. Courtney, now batting clean-up, popped up to end the inning. The Lady Eagles went hitless for the next five innings.

B. A. did her best to give the home fans something to cheer about. Reston was losing four to zero with Booth leading off the fifth inning. The Kennedy first-base coach was a large lady with an even larger voice. Apparently, she thought her job was to coach the players and entertain the fans at the same time. She was constantly hollering at her hitters. Most of her routine was just old baseball clichés that she adapted to the game of softball. Jenny and B. A. thought she was hilarious while Chip just stared at her in disbelief. B. A. watched the first base coach from her position in right and decided to try an old baseball trick if the opportunity presented itself. Sure enough, Booth was the next batter, and she hit a solid grounder between Jenny and Kris. B. A. came in fast on the rolling ball and knelt down on one knee to field it. With the ball safely in her glove, she stood quickly and started to run toward the outfield fence.

"Dig it out, Boothie, dig, dig," screamed the coach as she windmilled her left arm. "Go two. She missed it."

The pitcher followed her coach's instructions, and with her head down, she rounded the bag and headed for second. B. A. took three quick steps toward the right field fence as if she were chasing a ball that got by her. She then quickly planted her right foot and threw a strike to Chip, who was standing on second base. Booth was only halfway to second when she looked up and saw Chip on the bag, holding the ball in her bare hand so the runner could see it. She hit the brakes and tried to retreat to first, but Chip easily chased her down and tagged her on the rear.

The first base coach was furious. The Reston right fielder had just fooled her with a play that probably went back to the beginning of organized ball. B. A. avoided her stare by looking over at Rachel in center and signaling one out. Rachel motioned for B. A. to look toward first, but the right fielder refused. She wasn't looking for trouble, so she tried to downplay what just happened. B. A. looked in just before Tammi threw to the next batter. She almost laughed when she saw Jenny in her crouch with her right hand behind her giving B. A. a thumb up. When the inning was over, B. A. made sure to give first base a wide berth as she jogged toward her dugout on the third base side of the field. You don't celebrate one play no matter how spectacular when your team was down four to nothing.

"Sweet," said Chip as B. A. stepped into the dugout. "I love it when you do something to amaze and amuse us at the same time. I wouldn't look over there, but their assistant coach is having a serious conversation with that Booth girl. Now go out and make us proud. "

"Yeah," said Tammi. "Instead of hot-dogging it, why don't you do something that will get us some runs?"

"You always want more, don't you?" asked B. A. smiling. One thing that annoyed Tammi was the fact that she couldn't rile B. A. no matter how hard she tried.

B. A. grabbed her helmet and bat and headed for the on deck area. For some unexplained reason, it seems to be the case in baseball and softball that when a player makes a great play in the field, they invariably come in to lead off their half of the inning. This time was no exception. B. A. had popped up and struck out against Booth, but she had learned something in those two at bats. Booth liked to get ahead of you so she could deal from a position of strength. That way she could use more than her fastball on ensuing pitches. She had great speed, but overpowering the batter was just one of her strategies. The Reston slugger figured that Booth would throw her first pitch down the middle with everything she had. Once she was ahead in the count, she could toy with her a while. It would be a nice payback for the girl that just made her look foolish on the base paths.

The batter looked down at her third-base coach. Coach Brown was busy tying his shoe. B. A. was on her own. She dug her back foot in the dirt, looking for good traction. Booth was calmly waiting for her to get settled. The pitcher's wind up was smooth and the ball came thundering out of her hand. B. A. timed the fastball perfectly, and with a stroke as smooth as the pitcher's delivery, she lined the ball over the left fielder's head. The ball was still rising when it passed over the girl in left. She turned and only took one step. There was no reason to go any further as the ball landed several feet on the other side of the fence.

The crowd was stunned for a few seconds, then they broke into a loud cheer. Chip was up off the bench in a flash. The timing was perfect for her little plan. She got Coach Brown's attention and signaled for him to act like he was tying his shoe again. A few days earlier, Chip talked to the team when B. A. was out of earshot. On B. A.'s next home run, they were to act like they were focused on something else and didn't see the ball clear the fence. Chip grabbed a bat and had her teammates gather around. Tammi, now batting sixth, just sat at the end of the bench and didn't move. She usually didn't congratulate B. A. when she hit a homer anyway. When B. A. crossed the plate, Courtney, the next batter, was busy talking to a fan on the other side of the fence. When she got to the dugout, the rest of the team was gathered around Chip, who appeared to be showing them something about her bat. B. A. stepped in and put her helmet on its peg. Chip turned around and gave her a smile.

"Back already? Don't feel bad, Barbara Ann. That girl is one awesome pitcher. You'll get her next time."

B. A. sat down on the bench and surprised everyone in the dugout by putting her head in her hands. Her shoulders started to shake like she was sobbing. Chip looked over at her teammates, as they just stood there expressionless. It was all Coach Brown could do from his vantage point in the third-base coaching box to keep from busting out, laughing. Chip felt really bad about her little act. She immediately blamed Luke because he was the one that gave her the idea. She sat down next to B. A. and tried to console her. Her teammate mumbled something that she couldn't quite hear, so she leaned in close.

"You are so easy," whispered B. A. through her hands.

"What? Are you kidding me?" Chip looked over at her teammates, and they were all laughing.

"Looks like something backfired on you, Chip," said Rachel. "You better come up with something a little more elaborate next time."

"Hey, B. A.," said Jenny. "That Kennedy first-base coach was still staring at you while you ran the bases. I don't think she likes you very much."

"What do you expect," said Chip. "B. A. makes a fool of her, then she takes her star pitcher deep. You don't have anything else up your sleeve do you, B. A.?"

"What the heck," said B. A. "We're losing four to one, and we've only got three more outs to go. If Darby will go along, we could make this interesting."

The girls watched Tammi go down, swinging for the third out. B. A. and Jenny went over to Darby as she was putting on her chest protector. They talked for a minute, and Darby nodded her head in the affirmative. Coach Brown walked back from a conversation with the umpire and stood outside the dugout with an inquisitive look. The rest of the team was out on the field, including the four subs that he had just put in. He made a grand gesture for the three of them to take the field.

"No worries, Coach," said Jenny as she passed by. "You're gonna love this."

The plan was simple. The problem was, they had never practiced it before, so it was risky. When Coach Brown saw it develop, he mentally kicked himself for not thinking of it.

The first Kennedy batter grounded out to Sandy Johnson, who was now playing second. The second batter was a notorious slapper and, true to form, she punched one to Carissa Bender, who had just come in to play third. The batter easily beat out Carissa's throw. With a fast girl on first, the plan was on. Jenny put her right hand behind her and wiggled her fingers. Darby called for an outside pitch on the next batter. She caught Tammi's delivery and rifled the ball to Jenny at first, hoping to surprise the runner who had stepped off the bag. The ball flew over Jenny's outstretched glove down the right field line. Jenny jumped and grunted for effect. That was enough for the first-base coach, who sent the runner sprinting for second. Ten feet short of the bag, she saw Chip standing there with the ball in her hand. She just stopped and let the shortstop tag her. The Kennedy coach had been fooled twice in the same game.

B. A. had started to walk toward the right field line when Tammi looked in for her sign. The right fielder didn't want to draw any attention to herself, so she just sort of drifted over. When the pitcher went into her windup, B. A. picked up the pace and ran to and then down the foul line toward first. The Kennedy coach didn't see B. A., who was positioned about twenty feet behind Jenny when the ball flew over the first baseman's head. B. A. caught Darby's throw and pegged another strike to Chip. The normally boisterous first-base coach looked down at the dirt and kicked it. This was the second time the right fielder had decoyed her. The Kennedy head coach was in the third-base coaching box with his hands covering his face. It was obvious that he was laughing. He appreciated a well-enacted plan even if it was against his own team.

The three friends walked over to the track after losing four to one to Kennedy. They knew that if they were going to get better, they had to put up a couple more runs against pitchers like Carrie Booth. That or Tammi would have to throw equally as well, and that didn't seem likely.

"Okay," said Chip. "Who gave away my little plan? Was it Luke?"

"It was pretty easy to figure out something was up when our coach wouldn't even acknowledge me as I came by third," said B. A.

"Just tell her the truth, B. A.," said Jenny. "Luke might have let it slip that you were planning something. He didn't say exactly what it was going to be, but we were supposed to be ready."

"I knew it. He's trying to get even for the chicken sandwich thing. That guy has some serious problems. He's lucky that I'm so good-natured. A normal girl would have dumped him a long time ago."

"A normal girl?" asked Jenny. "I'd say you two were a perfect match. You're always up to something. I think that's why you are attracted to each other. It makes things exciting."

"Speaking of exciting," said B. A. as they walked up to the far side of the track. "Our timing is perfect. Lu is about to start. Let's not do anything weird to break her concentration, okay? She's going to need everything she's got to beat this Morgan girl."

"Why did you look at me when you said let's not do anything weird?" asked Chip. "I'll have you know that I'm a sane, well-balanced person."

"You just keep telling yourself that," said Jenny. "That attitude and a good psychiatrist will keep you out of the asylum."

"Here we go," said B. A., looking at the runners lined up for their race.

There were five girls lined up for the 1600-meter run. Two of the girls were from Staunton and the other three were Reston competitors. Lu's main competition was almost a foot taller than her. Because of this, Lu, with her shorter stride, was at a disadvantage before the race even started. Everything went smooth for the first twenty yards or so. Then disaster struck. Lu had just fallen in behind Morgan when the other Staunton runner stepped on her heel. Lu and the girl that stepped on her, both went down. Her hands kept her face from plowing into the track.

"Hey, foul," hollered Chip. "She can't do that. Restart, restart."

"She's getting up," observed Jenny. "She doesn't look so good."

Lu pulled her shoe back on and stood up on the track, inspecting her leg. Blood was running from a gash just below her knee. She started to jog to see if she should continue. The girl that tripped her was already off and running. Morgan was quite a ways up the track. Lu picked up her pace and began to run.

She had a very determined look on her face when she passed her three friends.

"Do the math, Lu," screamed Jenny. "Do the math."

"What the heck are you talking about?" asked Chip.

"I'm telling her that she doesn't have to make up the distance between her and Morgan right away. It's a long race. She needs to figure out how much to make up every lap. That's her only chance of winning."

"Do you think Lu has winning on her mind?" asked B. A. as she watched Lu go around the far curve.

"Absolutely," answered Jenny. "Did you think you could hit one out off of Booth today?"

"Yeah, I did, if I got the right pitch," said B. A.

"There you go. Like you have told us a hundred times, 'you've got to believe you can do it before it actually happens'. Here comes Lu. Let's show her some support."

Jenny started clapping in a slow cadence. The other two joined in and added a chant, "Lu, Lu, Lu." Halfway through the third lap, Lu had cut the distance down to twelve yards. Her gait was smooth, and her focus was on Morgan's shoulders. The blood that was dripping down her leg had finally stopped. When she went down, she felt a mixture of shock and anger. This was a race that would test her abilities, and she had been looking forward to it for weeks. Quality teams and individuals don't practice to beat poor or mediocre competition. They practice to beat the best. That's their measuring stick. Smoking a team that is outmanned doesn't prove much. Lu had a lap and a half to go to prove she had the mental toughness to compete at a high level. When Morgan crossed the finish line for the gun lap, Lu was only five yards behind. Morgan was running smooth with a lot of confidence. She knew something had happened behind her and felt that all she had to do was finish strong and the win was hers. The cheers from her school's fans and her teammates didn't sound like she had the race in the bag. She didn't realize Lu had been gaining ground on her for the last three laps.

When Lu heard the cheers for the last lap, she felt a surge of adrenaline. She fought back the urge to kick it in and pass Morgan right there. Logic and experience told her to wait and start her kick on the last curve. If Morgan went out earlier than that, Lu would have to answer her, or the race would be over. Her legs felt good, but her wind was being tested. When she passed her friends on the far side, they were still chanting. *What great friends those three are*, she thought. *They're so good at basketball and softball. I have to make a good showing here to prove myself to them.* With half a lap to go, a strange transformation overcame Lu. She was now right behind the leader. Her focus was razor sharp. All she was aware of were her arms, legs, and lungs. She could feel her heart pounding, trying to push the blood to the parts that needed it the most. Lu was in a place that she had never been in before. She had run literally hundreds of miles, but she had never felt like this. It was as if she were running in a dream, and running was all that mattered. The only thing on her mind was to run light and loose. The only sound she heard was her breathing and two sets of shoes hitting the ground—hers and Tracie Morgan's. She was totally oblivious to the cheers from the fans.

When the two leaders hit the home stretch, they were in a dead sprint. Morgan figured out that she would have to give it her all if she was going to beat the girl that had been dogging her. She thought it was the short girl from Reston but wasn't sure. Ten yards from the finish, Morgan made a huge mistake. The girl sprinting next to her was much shorter, but that was usually the case. There weren't many 6'1" female milers in this area. The Staunton star looked over to see who was giving her everything she could handle. She assumed it was Lu but wanted to make sure. She only turned her head for a second, but that was her undoing. That little glitch in her stride enabled Lu to gain a slight advantage, and she stayed a quarter step ahead as they crossed the finish line.

Fifteen yards past the line, Lu was still running hard. It finally dawned on her that the race was over, and she slowed down. Her arms were too tired to raise them above her head. She looked over at her friends, and they were jumping up and down, hugging each other. That was the last thing she remembered as she sunk slowly to the ground.

"Girl down," shouted Chip pointing across the track.

Lu was on her hands and knees when her coach and the athletic trainer got to her. They assisted her up and walked her slowly back to the bullpen area. The Reston fans were making up for their lack of numbers with sheer volume. Lu smiled and waved back at them. Somebody shoved a sports drink in her hand, and she took a couple sips. As Lu stood there, gathering strength she looked over at her opponent, who was standing next to her coach and an adult fan. The coach and the man appeared to be arguing. Lu's coach went over to see what the commotion was. When he came back, he explained what was going on.

"The guy is Morgan's dad. He is telling the Staunton coach that he should file a protest for excessive coaching."

"What?" was all Lu could say.

"It has to do with your softball friends across the track," said her coach. "He is claiming that they were giving you advice on how to run the race. Fans are allowed to do that, so I don't know what his problem is."

Lu and her coach looked over and saw Morgan, her coach, and her dad heading their way. The dad had a smug look on his face. Before he could say anything, Tracie held her hand out to Lu and smiled. Lu took it and smiled back.

"You just ran the most incredible race I have ever seen," said the Staunton runner. "And I barely got to see any of it, 'cause you were behind me for most of it. What happened back there at the beginning?"

"Someone stepped on my heel, and I went down," said Lu, looking at her leg with all the dried blood on it.

"It was me," said the other Staunton miler as she walked up. "Sorry, Lu. I was trying to stay right behind you and cut it too close."

Lu stuck out her hand to the other girl. "No problem. I figured it was an accident."

The dad's smile had disappeared, and he started to say something, but his daughter raised her hand to shush him. She turned to Lu and smiled. "The bottom line here, Dad, is that this girl just ran an awesome race and caught me in the stretch. That's the first time that's happened this year. You better train hard, Lu. Next time, I'll be ready for you."

"I think I'll run home from here," said Lu as the Staunton people walked away. Morgan, her teammate, and her coach just laughed. Morgan's dad was not happy, but he didn't say another word. It would take awhile for him to recognize that his daughter had the mentality of a true competitor. The way he just acted, it was obvious that she got it from her mother.

To Catch a Thief

Four of the best female athletes in the area sat in Jenny Olsen's car and discussed their current situation. Lu was now a full-fledged member of the group. It was her first time at Mr. Daggert's farm, and she was excited to go along. They watched the sun set and talked about the robbery and their ongoing efforts to unmask the thief. Lu couldn't believe that the three of them had actually tackled a would-be robber. She wasn't much help when it came to the JFR tattoo. They also talked about the strange guy that had been coming to their games. One thing they didn't talk about was Jenny's relationship with Morrie Schreider from Lakewood.

"I guess this is as good a time as any," said Chip as she reached into her pocket and brought out three little boxes. She gave one to each of her friends. "My dad sells these at his store. He wants to give one to each of you. A girl needs more protection out there than just her wits and superb physical condition. There are a lot of creepos running around loose, and babes like us should be prepared for anything."

The three of them opened their boxes to discover a bottle of pepper spray inside. Chip was surprised when Jenny didn't have a witty comeback.

"Read the instructions so you know what you're dealing with," continued Chip. "I thought about trying this stuff out on Luke, but he's the one that came up with the idea, so that would be sort of ungrateful. Hey, maybe we could douse the big guy to test it out. If the stuff in those bottles can bring down a big goof like... uh, never mind. I'm told it's powerful stuff, so be careful with it. Just treat it like it's a gun. Do ya'll know the four basic gun safety rules?"

The three of them were speechless. Chip was actually sounding like a responsible person with something important to say. They shook their heads to indicate that they didn't know the four rules.

"Okay. One is always assume the weapon is loaded. Two is never point it at anyone unless you intend on using it. Three is be aware of your target and what's behind it. And four is...wait a minute, oh yeah. Never put your finger on the trigger unless you intend to fire the weapon. Not bad, huh?"

"What you're saying makes sense," said Lu. "How do you know all that stuff about guns?"

"My dad sells them at his store. The guy that usually works in that department is a real expert. He's going to take my dad and me to a firing range sometime and show us the basics. Texas girls should know as much about weapons as the guys do. We'll be taking over some day anyway. The men have messed things up pretty bad, so when the women get their chance they should be ready to move."

"How soon do you think the women of America will move on the guys in power?" asked Jenny feigning seriousness.

"Could be any day now," answered Chip in a no-nonsense tone. "Look how bad things are in this country. Politicians selling their votes and big city bankers that are so greedy they would sell their own mammas for a profit."

"Wow," said Jenny. "You must be paying attention in Mr. Torrison's current issues class. You sound just like him."

"He might be a little out there, but a lot of the stuff he says makes sense," said Chip.

"Time to go," said Jenny as she fired up the car. "We've got a game tomorrow, and Lu has a big meet. What do you say, Lu?

Do you want to hang around with us, or is Chip a little too weird for your taste?"

"Ya'll are pretty weird," said Lu. "Actually, that's why I like you. I don't think I'll have a problem fitting in with this group. I think I've got Jenny's and Chip's roles figured out, but what is B. A.'s function?"

"Action magnate," said Jenny and Chip at the same time. All four were laughing until Jenny started singing, "I am woman hear me roar," from the Helen Reddy song. The other three quieted down and stared at her. Then they all started singing.

When Jenny dropped Lu off at her house, Chip leaned out the window and hollered, "You better roar tomorrow, woman. We won't be there to cheer you on."

Lu waved at them and turned to go into the house. She didn't have any homework, so she planned on going to bed early. She needed a lot of sleep if she was going to run a personal best tomorrow. As it turned out, her personal best the next day was good enough for a new school record.

Later that evening Chip sat in her dad's chair and looked over at her mom. The Texas Ranger game was on the television, but the sound was muted. Mrs. Fullerton was reading as usual. Chip was glad to see her reading an adventure novel. She looked a little closer and saw that the author was the guy that Luke read all the time—the one who didn't know much about judo.

"Mom, do you think I'm a well-balanced individual?" asked Chip.

"What are you talking about?" replied her mom as she closed her book. She was used to strange questions from her daughter, but this one caught her off guard. "You have terrific balance. I haven't seen you fall in years. Although when you were little, you used to fall a lot. You would take the bread out of the drawer and throw it on the floor. Then you would lose your balance and down you would go, right on the bread. The guy's at the store made fun of your dad's sandwiches because the bread was always in different shapes."

"Cute, Mom. What I meant was do I put too much emphasis on sports? The sociology teacher had us draw circles the other day to help us put our lives into perspective. You know, stuff like school, family, relationships, church, sports, and hobbies. My sports circle was huge. My family circle was just as big, but the rest of them were pretty small."

"How big was Luke's circle?"

"That depends on the day. He's on probation right now for telling Jenny about a scam I pulled on B. A. Right now he's just a speck on the page. You can see it, but you have to look close."

"Well," continued Mrs. Fullerton, "I think your love of sports is a healthy thing. It keeps you out of trouble, and you learn a lot from it. If you weren't involved in sports, you might not have such great friends like Jenny, B. A., and now Lu. Plus your boyfriend would probably dump you for a more gifted athlete."

"Not a problem there. B. A. is already taken. What I mean is, I don't do anything for the community. I've been thinking about making some sort of contribution. I don't have a lot of money to give because my parents are somewhat poor, so I was thinking that my time would be the next best thing. But I don't know what to do. I went to the food pantry, and they said they didn't need any help."

"How about starting with something smaller? Maybe just help out an individual from time to time rather than a large group?"

"That's a great idea," exclaimed Chip. "Rather than save the whole town, I'll look for individual acts of kindness. I think I'll start with my own family by not asking dad for a raise. Technically, working on Saturday like I do, I should be getting overtime."

"I wouldn't mention that to your dad with us being so poor and all. Be careful how you approach this new project. Sometimes good intentions aren't enough. The person you are trying to help might take it the wrong way."

"That's great advice. You're so smart. Why don't you run for public office? I could be your campaign manager. It's time for women to make their move while the guys are messing around with stuff that's not that important. We could move right in and take over. I'm going to put that on my list. Number one: Help out locals; number two: Get even with Luke; and number three: Take over the world. I should be able to get it all done in about a month or so."

"That's the spirit," said her mom as she opened her book again. "Don't go too fast. People will need to get used to such a high-spirited female giving them orders."

"They better get on board real quick. I won't have the time or patience for slackers."

With that Chip jumped up and headed to her room to study. She sat down at her computer and read an e-mail from Luke. After reading his short message she clicked on the attachment.

Lady Eagle Softball Team Rapidly Improving

By Luke Slowinski

The Reston softball team has finally come together and is currently firing on all cylinders. Earlier in the season, their run production was lacking, but a change in the batting order and the emergence of B. A. Smith as the top run producer in the area has made a world of difference. Smith has sixteen home runs and forty runs batted in. Chip Fullerton and Kris Ritter are doing a great job of getting on base in front of the Reston slugger. Between them, they have crossed the plate thirty-six times. Jenny Olsen appears to be comfortable with her move to the fourth spot. She now has sixteen RBIs, while the fifth batter,

Courtney Grimes, has thirteen. Softball at this level is definitely a pitcher's game, so every run is crucial.

Tammi Olsen is doing a commendable job on the mound. She is currently seven and four and can hold her own with most of the pitchers in the area. Carmen Lopez has also shown improvement. She is four and three as the number two pitcher. In addition to Smith's bat, the other bright spot on the team is the defense. Fullerton, Smith, Ritter, and Jenny Olsen are all candidates for the all-area defensive team. Smith showed her arm in a recent game with Kennedy, gunning down two runners at second base. The ball got there so far ahead of the runners that neither one of them even attempted to slide. The girls have eight regular season games to go. The next home game is on Tuesday with Grand Prairie. The visitors have one of the top pitchers in the area, so it should be a good game.

Switching gears, no pun intended, is something Xiu Lu has recently perfected. Lu goes all out on the final curve and sometimes before it. She recently defeated Tracie Morgan from Staunton in a terrific race. After falling, Lu recovered to take the 1600 meters in a race that featured two undefeated milers. Her time of 5:24 is getting close to what it would take to be a state qualifier. Lu's gutsy performance was incredibly inspiring. Hopefully, her performance will inspire more fans to come out to see her and her track-and-field teammates for the rest of the season. All our Reston athletic teams appreciate the support of their fans.

Chip sat back and thought about the article. It actually wasn't too bad. She knew from past experience that B. A. didn't like people to make a big deal about her accomplishments. That type of thinking had rubbed off on her and Jenny. It's too bad that "Tammi The Great" didn't have the same attitude. She thought about the rest of the starters on the team. Kris Ritter was solid at second and had a good attitude. Courtney Grimes in left was much better than she was last year and was starting to contribute offensively. Maria Baltierra was barely holding down her spot at third. She had made several costly errors this season, but there really wasn't anyone Coach Brown could put in for her in a tight game. He had given Sandy Johnson and Carissa Bender opportunities at the hot corner, but neither of them had proven they were as good as Maria. The only other infielder was Katie Renfro, and she was a true space cadet. Half of the time, she didn't even know how many outs there were. Rachel Moon was okay in center. She hustled and was a team player. It obviously helped to have B. A. next to her in right. Darby Quinn was just fair behind the plate and a loyal Tammi subject. She had shown signs of wavering but always went back to her idol. Chip was the backup catcher. She had better hands than Darby and a much stronger arm. She had only caught a couple of innings this year but could step in at a moment's notice.

B. A. never ceased to amaze Chip. She was worried about a letdown after the basketball season, but after a short slump, the new girl came on like a true superstar. How could one girl be so good in two sports? She was glad B. A. didn't play shortstop. If she did, she might be out of a job. She had played short since she was nine years old. It's not that she couldn't play anywhere else; she just liked being in the middle of the action all the time. She didn't know it, but she was about to find out that B. A. did play another position, and it wasn't shortstop.

The next afternoon proved to be an exciting one on the Reston softball diamond. The Grand Prairie leadoff batter slapped one to Maria at third and beat out her throw. On the next pitch, she stole second. Tammi got the second batter to pop up to Kris at second. Chip looked over at the speedster on second and decided to decoy her if she got the chance. Sure enough, the next batter hit a hard grounder to Chip on the second pitch. The little shortstop fielded it cleanly and came up throwing to first. She never even looked at the runner on second, who was a few steps off the bag, waiting to dash for third. Chip faked the throw and held on to the ball. The girl on second bit on Chip's fake and started for third. The look on her face was priceless when Chip tagged her out as she ran by. All of the fielders, except Tammi and Darby, held their gloves above their heads and beat their fists into them. Jenny came up with this little maneuver early in the season. She called it the *defensive salute*. Any time a member of the defense made a great play, they would salute her this way. They would even do it for Tammi or Darby, but those two would reciprocate only if anyone but Chip or B. A. made the play.

Chip ended the inning with another brilliant defensive play. She gobbled up a hard grounder to her left, stepped on second, and threw the batter out by a half a step at first. Tammi was doing an acceptable job against the Grand Prairie pitcher. The offense needed to generate some runs or she would rack up another loss. Chip stepped up to the plate in the bottom of the sixth with the visitors up three to one. She hit the second pitch into the right center gap and legged out a double. Kris came up and ripped a hard single that just got over the shortstop's head. Chip had to hold her ground to make sure the ball wasn't caught. Pops gave her the stop sign at third. Tammi, in her usual arrogant manner, loudly complained about not sending Chip home. Chip could have probably beaten the throw to the plate, but what Tammi didn't understand was the fact that Chip's run wasn't all that important. Kris was the tying run now, and B. A. was coming up to bat. It wouldn't make sense to take meaningless chances in front of your best hitter. B. A. looked toward the third-base coaching box as she stepped in. Surprisingly, her coach wasn't even looking at her. He was staring in to the dugout at Tammi who was still chirping away at Darby. It looked as if the coach was going to call time out, but then he turned to B. A. and acted like he was swinging a bat. It was obvious that he wasn't happy with Tammi, and maybe he had had enough of her antics. B. A. tipped the bill of her helmet and dug in.

The Grand Prairie pitcher relied mostly on her fastball and threw it about eighty percent of the time. She was also a leg slapper, which was extremely annoying. B. A. figured that some goofy coach years ago told his pitcher to slap her leg after she released the ball to distract the batter. This didn't make much sense because anyone that has ever pitched before knows that the first thing you need to do after releasing the ball is to come to a fielder's stance. A hard shot up the middle can get back to the pitcher in a hurry, and she needs to have her glove in the ready position and not slapping it against her leg.

The girls discussed this little move one evening while watching the sunset. Chip volunteered that if your strategy was to distract the batter, why not have the second baseman jump up and down and make faces as the pitch was delivered? Jenny added that the catcher could bark like a dog. That would definitely be distracting. They all decided that the coach that came up with the slapping idea was probably the same one that told his players to hit themselves in the back with the bat when they took a practice swing. Slapping your leg and hitting yourself with the bat just didn't make any sense to them.

B. A. stepped aggressively into the first pitch and hit it on the sweet spot of the bat. The ball cleared the center field fence by twenty feet. When she rounded third, she could see the distressed look on Pops' face. Even though they were now in the lead, she could tell that he was not happy. Win or lose when coaching teenagers, there was always something going on. Pops surprised everyone when he sent Carmen out to pitch the last inning. From her position in right, B. A. could see both coaches talking to Tammi at the end of the bench. Carmen sealed the victory by getting the first two hitters to ground out to Chip. B. A. made a running catch in right for the last out. As the team headed out to center field for their post game talk, Jenny gave the signal, and they all threw their gloves at Chip. Chip squawked and tried to get out of the way. This was another one of Jenny's ideas. The glove throwing was now the tribute to anyone who had an outstanding day in the field. When Tammi and the rest of the players on the bench came out to join them, she had a serious look on her face. That lasted until she got in to the car with Darby. Then she let her battery mate know what she thought of the Reston coaching staff.

"I'm getting pretty sick of all the favoritism around here," complained Tammi to her battery mate. "Coach Brown told me this is my last warning. I guess he doesn't realize that your number one pitcher is the most important player on the team. Without me, we would have to score ten runs a game to get a win."

"I don't know," volunteered Darby. "When my dad played high school football, he said the coaches played favorites all the time, and it was the right thing to do. The guys that worked hard and didn't complain got the benefit of the doubt over the slackers and the whiners."

"Look, I know B. A. is a good player. I'm not blind or stupid. But can't you see what a phony she is? Her whole act of not wanting attention is just a way to get more attention. And she's got half the girls on the team following her lead, including my sister. The coaches are always falling all over her like she's some kind of celebrity. Am I the only person that can see through her little act? She makes me want to puke."

"Can't you tone it down a little?" asked Darby. "We're a pretty good team, and it would be cool to win some games in the state playoffs."

"No way," said Tammi. "I'm a leader not a follower. Trust me; this whole thing is going to blow up in her face. And we're going to be there when it does."

Another situation presented itself when the girls left the field. There were two reporters from the city, standing there talking to

Coach Harbison. Chip spotted them first and grabbed B. A. by the arm.

"Code blue, babe," observed Chip. "Those dudes have to be reporters. It's obvious they're here to talk to the Reston slugger. What are we going to do?"

"Fullerton, Smith," hollered Coach Harbison as she waved at them. "Come over here will you?"

B. A. stopped in her tracks and thought for a moment. "Bend over and grab your stomach," she whispered to Chip.

Chip bent over and grabbed B. A.'s arm. She threw in a few moans for effect. Courtney just smiled, but Kris and Jenny had to turn away to keep from laughing.

"Hey, Coach," said B. A. as she faked helping Chip off the field and toward her truck. "This little one has a bad stomachache. I better get her home to her momma. See you tomorrow."

The two of them hustled into B. A.'s truck and headed for Chip's house.

"Those two reporters didn't look very happy," said Chip, looking through the back window. "Do you think they bought the stomachache routine? It looks like they're still talking to Coach H. She'll give them some good copy. They don't need our goofy comments anyway. Copy, that's what an interview is called you know. Luke told me that."

"I didn't know that," said B. A. "You don't feel bad about not answering their questions, do you? It sounded like they wanted to talk to you as much as me."

"Naw, I've adopted your philosophy on the whole press thing. We're just kids playing for fun. Who cares what our opinion is on stuff? How about this:

'Reporter—Fullerton how did you feel when you slid into second base on that awesome hit to left center?

Me—Gee, I think I felt like I got some dirt down my uniform pants. Oh yeah, save the whales.

Reporter—Did you think you could win this one?

Me—No, our coach talked about how much we were going to lose by during our pregame discussion. It turned out he was dead wrong. When our super slugger crushed two over the fence and when her sidekick made some awesome plays at short, we somehow pulled it out. It was a softball miracle, totally unexplainable.'"

"So, you're my sidekick now?" asked B. A.

"Sure. It's like you're Spiderwoman, and I'm your sidekick, Web Girl."

"Let's keep those nicknames to ourselves. You did touch on one of my pet peeves though. That part about getting dirt down your pants."

"That's a pet peeve—dirt in your pants?"

"No," explained B. A. "When major league players slide into a bag, they get up and call time out right away, and the umps usually give it to them. If I were umpiring, I'd ask why they wanted to stop the game. The real answer would be, "So I can parade around for a while and maybe get the camera on me some more." It's pretty silly if you think about it. I mean, they're playing ball. You're supposed to get dirty playing ball. You slide into a bag. If you're safe, you stand up on the bag and brush yourself off. If you're out, you run off the field and brush yourself off in the dugout. What's the big deal? Please stop the game. I've got some dirt on me. Bunch of sissies."

"Wow!" exclaimed Chip. "You're starting to sound like me. Cool, we're sort of turning into each other. I mean, little bits of us. I've got something to add to your peeve. How about when the batter gets a hit and when the ball is thrown back in, the infielder catches it and usually calls time out. Why are they asking for the game to be stopped? Are they afraid that they're going to throw the ball over the pitcher's head and the runner will take another base? Hey, if you can't throw the ball to the pitcher from second or short, the runner should get another base. If your arm is that bad, just run the ball back to the pitcher and hand it to him or her. I hope you've noticed that I never call time out in that situation."

"I have noticed and neither does Kris. Good for you two. You should go over and talk to the boys' team. I haven't watched them play very much, but their infielders do it all the time."

"I watched a whole game with Luke last weekend. They do some strange things out there, but I suppose they think we do some strange things too. One thing I wish would change in softball is the bases need to be farther apart. I think they're too close together."

"I agree," said B. A. "Moving the pitching rubber back a few years ago was a start. It would make it tougher for the slappers and bunters to get on because with more distance between the bases, the fielders would have more time to throw them out. Don't get me wrong. I think there is a place for slappers and bunters in the game, but a real fast girl should have to do more than just beat the ball into the ground to get a hit."

"Yeah, I'd rather smoke one out to the fence. What's it feel like when you hit one out of the park?"

"It feels great. The best feeling is when you hit one to the opposite field. You swing late and don't hit it as efficiently compared to a ball that you pull. But you hit it on the sweet spot, and it just explodes off the bat."

"Is that what happened when you hit your third one off of Miller from Ferguson?"

"Yeah. Coach said to shorten my swing and try to hit it solid. It was a cheapie that's for sure."

"I'd settle for just one cheapie. I need a hurricane wind behind me to get one over the fence."

"You do what you can do. I wouldn't want to come in and play shortstop even for one out."

"Hey, maybe we should all switch positions for a game. Playing the outfield doesn't look all that difficult."

"I don't know if coach would do that," said B. A. "It might look like we're making fun of the other team. You know, playing different positions because they aren't very good."

"You always think of that stuff, don't you? Maybe just for one inning then. He'll let us do that. Speaking of coach, I think he's had it with Tammi. She's had two lectures this week, and it doesn't seem to have any effect. Why is she so weird?"

"All I know is we've got bigger problems than her. Jenny and Diego are on the top of our list of wrongs that need to be righted. There I go, talking like you again. I'm getting stranger by the day. It's like I'm slowly sinking into some kind of bizarro world, where you live."

"I think you meant you're getting cooler by the day. I know I'm secretly your idol. It's okay, you can admit it."

"I've got him," exclaimed Luke the next day as he sat down next to Chip and her three friends at lunch. "Diego Reyes is our guy. He was getting something out of the vending machine this morning, and his JFR tattoo was easy to spot. He must have had gloves on when you did your survey."

"So what's our next move?" asked Jenny.

"I don't know," said Luke. "This part could be tricky. Without positive identification like facial recognition, it would be tough to prove anything. You all saw the tattoo but the situation was very intense. A lawyer would grill you in court and maybe get you to stumble under cross-examination. Like maybe only one of you saw some letters on his hand, and talking about it later, you all believed you saw it. Or maybe one of you thought you saw an *R*, and maybe in the past, you saw Diego's tat and you subconsciously put two and two together, and your mind created a memory that didn't really happen."

Lu looked over at B. A. and asked, "Does he always talk like this?"

"Only when he's hot on a case," said B. A.

"One more thing," added Luke. "I think I have it figured out why Mr. Kim told you to let Diego go. He and his family aren't

US citizens yet. I think he didn't want to do anything that would draw attention to them. Knowing Mr. Kim, he's probably filed all his paperwork, but it takes a while for that stuff to go through the proper channels. I'm pretty sure you even have to pass a test on the constitution."

"You're a citizen, aren't you, Lu?" asked Chip in her usual straightforward manner.

"Yes. The rules are different for adoptions. I will tell you that I took government class real serious in the eighth grade. Not being born here, I wanted to feel like I deserved to live in such a great country. The sad thing was a lot of the kids in our class said it was a waste of time and did really poor. They seem to take everything for granted. Their attitude was like they were entitled to everything just because they were lucky enough to be born here. Sorry. It's sort of a pet peeve of mine."

"I'll bet your list of peeves is shorter than Chip's," said Jenny. "Hers is several pages long, and it's in a small font."

"That's right," responded Chip. "Hey, I got a *B* in eighth grade government. Go on, Lu, ask me a government question."

"Okay, here's an easy one. The main topics of first amendment spell R-a-p-p-s What do the letters stand for? Ya'll can help her out if she gets stuck."

"I know freedom of religion is the first one," said Chip. "And one of the *P*s is freedom of the press."

"I think the other one is freedom of petition," said Luke. "People are allowed to let the government know when they're not happy about something. You know, sometimes they don't want to wait for new elections to roll around so they petition for a recall election. I think that's how Arnold Schwarzenegger got elected as the California governor the first time."

"Assembly," said B. A. "It's okay to get together to discuss or protest things. The police can't break up crowds if they're not breaking the law or if they're not doing something dangerous."

"You got four of them," said Lu. "What's the last one?"

They looked at each other, but no one volunteered an answer.

"Is it against the law for me to stand up in the cafeteria and say I think the governor or president is doing a terrible job?" asked Lu.

Luke hit his forehead with the palm of his hand. "Freedom of speech. We should have gotten that one right away. It's the easiest of the bunch. But I will add, you can say a lot of things but not just anything. Like I can't stand up and holler, 'He's got a gun', if he really doesn't have one. You know, just to see what people would do. If everybody started to run, someone could get hurt. So there are limits, which is a good thing. It's not a *free country* but we do have a lot of freedoms."

The bell rang and the group stood to go to their next class.

"Good job, guys," said Lu. "I guess you can keep your citizenship cards for a while longer."

"Wait a minute," said B. A. with a look of surprise. "Victor's last name is Reyes. You remember, Rod's friend, the guy at the mall that grabbed me from behind."

"What are you saying?" asked Luke. "Do you think they're related? Victor seems like a pretty cool guy."

"He might be worth talking to," said B. A. "Let's think about it for a while. We don't want to jump to any conclusions without thinking them through first. Right, Chip?"

Chip was deep in thought about jumping to conclusions, and she jumped when B. A. addressed her.

"Uh, right. Only an inexperienced rookie would do something like that."

Lu smiled to herself. These guys were fun to hang around with. She imagined what most of the other students were talking about during lunch. It was a safe bet that they weren't discussing government or trying to solve crimes.

"We're going to have a short practice today," said Coach Brown as the team gathered around him that afternoon. "I want to go over a few situations with runners on base, then we're heading over to the middle school diamond again." He saw the questioning looks on some of their faces, so the coach explained it one more time. "By working with them, we get two things accomplished. One, we do our part to keep the Reston program strong. The little girls love it when ya'll pay attention to them. Often, they will listen to an older player more than they will their coach. Two, you always learn something when you teach someone else."

After going through the situations with runners on base, Pops had the catchers go behind the plate where Coach Harbison was waiting for Darby, Chip, and Sandy. The drill was an easy one. A pitcher would throw one pitch, and the catcher that caught it would come up, throwing to second. The infielders took turns handling the throws at second. B. A. and the other outfielders were told to go over and stand at first and wait. It didn't take long for the infielders to get the hang of the drill. As soon as a throw went to second, a new pitcher and catcher stepped in. After four throws each, Pops called for a halt. He ran over to the fence where he had a sliding mat all rolled up. He lay the mat down in front of second and explained that they would continue with live runners.

Earlier in the season, they had practiced sliding on the outfield grass. They did this to avoid the damage that a dirt infield does to a runner's legs. It got exciting when Chip followed B. A. at a sprint and hollered for her to slide right. Chip then slid on the left side, and they both slapped a hand on the bag at the same time. They told their coaches that they wanted to try it one more time with a third runner. This time Jenny slid right, B. A. slid left, and Chip went between them head first. Pops jumped in and shouted, "Safe, safe, out!"

He pointed at Chip when he cried, "Out."

Chip jumped up and started screaming, "What do you mean *out*? I was way ahead of the ball. My grandmother could have made a better call. You better have a day job, cause umpiring ain't your thing."

Pops just stood there with his hands on his hips, then he gave Chip the old heave-ho. "You're out of here, Fullerton!"

Everybody broke up at Chip's and the coach's antics. Pops knew how to have a good time with the team and tried to make things fun. As the team headed back to the dugout, Tammi whispered to Darby. "He does have a day job. He's the janitor." Her comment drew a quiet snicker from her catcher.

After laying down the mat, Pops explained that he wanted the runners to practice sliding on the outfield side of the bag first. The second time around, they were to slide on the infield side. He went on to say that a runner sliding on the infield side would quite often get in the way of a low throw on a close play. The drill went off without a hitch. There was a lot of action, and everybody was involved. The big surprise was that Chip threw out every runner but one.

The team jogged over to the middle school diamond where the younger girls were taking batting practice. They stopped when the varsity showed up. Coach Brown had put Chip in charge of the infield instruction. She had been thinking about something special to teach the younger girls when they got together again. The last time they had a teaching session, they worked on keeping their gloves down and bringing the ball up into their body. The body worked as sort of a backstop if the ball wasn't fielded clean. Today, Chip wanted to work on throwing. The last time there was only one girl that attempted a crowhop when she threw to first. She decided to exaggerate the move so they would all get the feel of taking a short hop on their right foot before they delivered the ball to first. This move kept the player on balance and brought her into an efficient throwing position. It also didn't take much time, which was important for an infielder.

After explaining what she wanted, she signaled for the coach to hit one to her. She scooped up the grounder and then hopped ten times on her right foot before throwing to first. This maneuver brought laughs from the infielders and even some of the outfielders that were watching. When the first middle school girl tried, it she fell down. Each varsity infielder had two of the younger ones to work with, so they hopped alongside them, voicing encouragement. It took a while to get them all to do ten hops. Once they could do ten, Chip reduced the number to five, then to three, and finally to one. A half hour later, all the younger girls could do a decent crowhop before throwing the ball to first. When Pops called a halt to the exercise, the varsity players held their gloves above their heads and pounded their fists into them, acknowledging the younger girls' efforts. This put huge smiles on the faces of the middle schoolers.

When the varsity got back to their own diamond, Coach Brown asked for a report from the outfielders and the pitchers and catchers. B. A. told him they worked on going deep and catching flies while moving toward the base they were going to throw to. She said they had all the girls doing it but two. The rest of the outfielders shook their heads in agreement. When the coach asked Tammi and Carmen how the pitching went, Tammi answered before Carmen could speak up. She said the pitchers weren't very good so they just worked on how to hold the ball. Coach Brown pressed her by asking if that's all they did. Tammi responded by saying that the girls were so bad it was impossible to teach them anything else. When she said this, the two coaches looked at each other. Tammi just shrugged and asked if practice was over. She didn't realize it, but the hole she was digging was getting deeper by the moment. She also didn't realize that both her coaches had been bending over backwards to accommodate her.

After supper, Jenny picked up her two teammates, and they headed out to their favorite spot to watch the sunset. They stopped by Lu's house to pick her up, but Lu's mother said she went out for a run. "That girl is definitely an overachiever," said Chip.

Jenny backed up to the field gate, and the three of them got out and sat on the front of the car. B. A. and Jenny sat over the headlights and Chip sat on the hood. She was the lightest of the three, and the hood supported her with no problem. Chip and B. A. were unusually quiet during the ride out. They had decided to tell Jenny what they thought of the guy from Lakewood. They also needed to come up with a plan for Diego. It was obvious that Mr. Kim wanted them to drop the issue, but they felt they had to do something to let Diego know that they knew he was the guy in the store that day.

Chip stated her opinion first, "I say we corner him in the hall at school and get him to confess."

"What good will that do?" asked Jenny. "He'll probably just deny it. On the other hand, if he does confess, what do we do next? Mr. Kim wants us to drop the whole thing. I don't think we should do anything crazy here."

"We need to do something," said Chip. "If we don't, he might try another robbery and then he might end up in jail, or somebody might get hurt. We would feel pretty bad if we did nothing, and this guy turned to a life of crime. Some day we'll see him on a most wanted list, and we'll feel bad, knowing we could have prevented the whole thing."

"I've got an idea," said B. A. "I talked to Rod, and he said that Victor is actually Diego's uncle. Victor's mom and dad are divorced, so he's like the male head of the family. He helps out a lot with his little brother and sister and with the rest of the extended family. Maybe he will know what to do with Diego.

He could have a talk with Diego to figure out why he did such a stupid thing."

"That's not a bad idea," said Chip. "If we let the family handle it, Mr. Kim won't even know about it. And if Diego doesn't listen to his uncle, he can give him a good pounding."

"What is it with you and beating people up?" asked Jenny. "I don't recall you ever being in a real fight. I'll bet you have never even hit someone."

"No, I haven't, but sometimes that's the only way to get through to people. Have you ever been in a fight, B. A.? I mean a real fight not a girly pull each other's hair thing."

"No, but I did punch a guy once."

"Really?" asked Chip. "What happened?"

"He went down, and my hand swelled up for a couple of days. I don't know how, but my mom found out. She didn't say anything about it until we moved here. Tank and Riley, my two best guy friends, were there so all I can figure is one of them told their mom, and then she passed it on. The guy really deserved it. I saw him slap this other girl, and it made me mad. I had plenty of 'cover' like the girl at the mall said, so I went for it."

"Wow, you're a real brawler," said Chip.

"Not hardly."

"Okay, change of plans," said Chip. "We catch this guy outside of school and B. A. punches his lights out. Then we tell him to straighten up, or she is coming back for more. What do you think?"

"Nobody's getting punched," said Jenny. "I say we go to Victor and let the family handle it. That relieves us of our responsibility. What do you think?"

"That's the smart thing to do," answered B. A.

Chip agreed but still wanted to keep the punching strategy as plan B. It was decided that B. A. and Rod would go talk to Victor about his nephew. Hopefully, he would appreciate the fact that Mr. Kim didn't want to go to the authorities. Maybe a stern talk from his uncle would keep the kid from doing something that would get him into real trouble. The three friends sat silently for a while, watching the sun drop lower in the western sky. Chip pointed to their left down the gravel road at a speck that appeared to be coming toward them. They watched for a couple of minutes, then they figured out it was a person running. They broke out in big smiles as they recognized Lu. Chip looked at B. A. hoping for some assistance with their next topic for discussion. This one would be more difficult than confronting a would-be thief. B. A. motioned for Chip to bring up the subject of Jenny's new guy friend, Morrie Schreider.

"Uh, Jenny," said Chip, taking the lead. "We want to talk about something else."

"I know, it's my crazy sister," responded Jenny. "I don't know what to do with her. She won't listen to reason when it comes to sports. She thinks everyone is plotting against her. I told her if she keeps up her comments and snotty attitude, the coach might kick her off the team. She said he'll never do that because then we won't have a decent pitcher to finish out the season. I'll talk to her again. I know she's causing problems for everyone except her faithful follower, Darby."

"We hope you make some progress there," said Chip. "We're playing really well right now, and we need everyone to be on the same page. It's better if we all pull together. What B. A. and I want to talk about is your new boyfriend. We've heard some bad stuff about him, and we think you should know about it."

Jenny didn't respond right away. She looked up the gravel road at Lu who was only about a hundred yards away. Her gait was smooth and appeared to be effortless. She slowed down to a walk for the last twenty-five yards. When she got to where her friends were sitting, she wasn't even breathing hard. Lu could tell something serious was going on when the three of them gave her a little wave.

"What's up?" asked Lu looking from face-to-face. "Uh-oh, you must have told her."

Jenny looked at B. A. with a scowl. "So you were spying on me the other day? I knew it. What, you don't think I can take care of myself? That was a rotten thing to do."

"We were just concerned about your safety," said B. A. "We've heard stuff about Morrie that you need to hear."

"Like what?" asked Jenny with her eyes tearing up.

"Like he's a real user," said Chip, getting right to the point. "He goes through girlfriends faster than B. A. hits home runs. He's a huge partier, and we don't think he's right for you. Is that it, guys?"

"Our information is pretty solid," said B. A. in agreement. Lu was shaking her head too. "How much do you really know about this guy, Jenny?"

"I suppose you got your info from Cheryl Williams," said Jenny in an accusing tone. "Maybe she wants him for a boyfriend. He is a big time athlete at Lakewood. He's got looks, status, and he's been real nice to me."

"That might be the problem," said Chip as she tried to reason with her best friend. "He might be real nice to you for a reason other than he is a real nice guy. Let me ask you this. Have you heard anyone else say he's a great guy? I mean someone that has nothing at stake here? That would go a long way to *unprove* our information."

Jenny was now in tears. She didn't know what to think. Her friends looked at each other not knowing what to say. Chip put her arm around Jenny's shoulder. "We're your best friends, Jen. We just want you to be safe. That's what good friends are for. We're not saying this guy is an axe murderer or anything. Will you at least agree to keep an open mind about things?"

Tears rolled down Jenny's cheeks as she slid off the car and headed for the driver's side. She was hoping that her friends' information was coming from a potential rival and not based on fact. Morrie was always considerate and thoughtful around her. He even opened the car door for her. B. A. came around and held her hand out for the keys. She said something about not letting a teary-eyed girl get behind the wheel. Jenny gave them up and went over to the passenger side.

Chip looked at Lu as they got into the backseat. "Speaking of friend responsibility, what are you doing running on a country road all by yourself? It could be dangerous, ya know. Did you bring anything for protection?"

Lu reached into her pocket and brought out the pepper spray that Chip had given all of them.

"A lot of good that will do against bears or rattlesnakes," said Chip.

"She'll just out run them," said B. A. from the front seat.

"Bears can run up to fifty miles an hour," responded Chip. "She's fast but not that fast."

"I usually don't run in isolated places, but I figured ya'll were out here. From now on, little mom, I'll stick to the crowded streets. And by the way, *unprove* isn't a real word."

"It is if you know how to use it right," said Chip.

Jenny would have normally snickered at this exchange, but she was busy looking out the window. Not much was funny to her right now.

It was somewhere around midnight, and Jenny was still wide awake. Normally, she fell asleep as soon as her head hit the pillow. She could hear Tammi snoring softly in her bed on the other side of the room. Why would her friends say those things about Morrie? She had never seen him act anything but the perfect gentleman. Was it an act? Was Cheryl trying to get even with him for something? She didn't seem like the type of person who would do something like that. This whole thing was very confusing. She knew she wasn't the type of girl that was always desperate for a boyfriend. There were a lot of girls like that at school. They weren't happy unless they were walking the halls, holding on to some guy. It was like some sort of status symbol with them.

She turned on her side and adjusted her pillow. *Just because my friends are pretty smart*, she thought, *that doesn't mean they know everything about everything. I'll keep my guard up, but I'm still going to see Morrie. If he's putting on an act for my benefit, he sure is good at it. I can take care of myself. I'm not a little kid anymore.*

Busted

B. A. and Rod sat on his porch swing that evening after a short lifting session and an even shorter pitching session. She threw about twenty pitches, and everything was working fine, so they took a break. They discussed how they should approach Victor with the news about his nephew. Victor was renting a place with some other guys in Denton while he went to the University of North Texas. Rod said he was going up there this weekend to attend Victor's twenty-first birthday party. He would lay everything on the line then. Rod knew that Victor had been a gang member for a few years until he figured out there was no future in it. His early years were pretty rough, but he was a survivor, and he was now seriously thinking about going in to law enforcement.

"If we left it up to Chip," said B. A. as she sat cross-legged, facing her boyfriend, "she would confront Victor and demand that he beat the stuffing out of Diego. She's been into violence lately. She wanted you to punch Jen's new boyfriend out at the Lakewood restaurant."

"She's always been like that," said Rod. "When she was younger she got into a lot of scraps with her little friends. She's definitely a type-A personality. She can be annoying at times, but she's got a good heart. Luke and her are usually up to something. You were the focus of intense scrutiny when you first showed up. It drove her and her detective buddy crazy, trying to figure out your background. At first, they thought you were in the Witness Protection Program, then you were an FBI agent, and finally, you were an older lady with fake records, so you could relive your high school years. You do realize that when you moved here, it was the answer to her prayers? My mom tells me her new thing is to start helping out the less fortunate. Don't tell her I told you any of this. She's usually antagonistic toward me enough as it is."

"I've always wondered about that," said B. A. "Why does she act like that toward you?"

"You won't believe it. I think it's because I'm so tall, and she's not. I think she actually believes that I stole the height in the family and didn't leave any for her."

"Haven't you been like a big brother to her?" asked B. A.

"Yeah, I can't tell you how many times I've bailed her out of tough situations. Once, in the eighth grade, some weirdo was hassling her and Luke. He was a sophomore, so he was a couple of years older than they were. Apparently he didn't know that we were related."

"What happened?"

"I picked him up and held him against a locker in front of his friends and explained what would happen to him if he didn't leave them alone. He got the message. It was a good thing too. I think she was plotting some evil scheme to get even with him. Even back then, she was a planner. Sometimes it just gets her into more trouble. Most of the time, she wasn't even aware that I got involved."

"Well, it's nice to have someone looking out for you. She really thought I was in the Witness Protection Program?"

"Yup. When those two ran into difficulty, digging up information on you, they came up with that theory. When they latch on to something, they go all out, looking for answers. My mom gets a big kick out of her and Luke."

"Jenny does too. She can get Chip riled up quicker than anyone. She and Jen are the best girl friends I've ever had. How about we throw a few more?"

"Okay," said Rod, slowly getting up and offering her his hand. "So you really aren't interested in pitching at all this season?"

"I don't know," answered B. A. "The team's been winning, and we're all getting along so well except for you know who. I figure, why mess up a good thing? There was a big city reporter lurking around after our last game, but Chip and I gave him the slip. Luke sort of ran interference, and while he was distracting him we slipped away. I don't care if they write about us, but why do they have to have a quote about the game? When most athletes are interviewed, they say just about what you thought they would say. Uh, it was a good pitch, and I nailed it. Did I think it was going over the fence? Uh, no, I thought it was only going to be a single. The wind must have got hold of it."

Rod and B. A. were still laughing when they got to their special pitching spot between Rod's and the neighbor's garage. B. A. threw a couple of easy tosses then she ramped it up to game speed. When she threw hard, she could throw as fast as the top college pitchers. She signaled for one more and threw a smoker that cracked into Rod's glove. The proximity of the two garages amplified the sound and gave off a little echo. Rod's eyes went wide after B. A.'s last pitch. It wasn't because she threw it so fast, he was used to that. It also wasn't because it hurt his hand. He had a bandana stuffed into his glove to deaden the impact. He looked surprised because his pint-sized cousin had come around the corner as B. A. threw her last pitch.

"What's this!" exclaimed Chip as she stood there, puffing. It was obvious that she was out of breath. "I ran to your house, and you're not home, so I head over here thinking we could run by Jen's and Lu's. And now I catch you pitching to sugarlips here. So you're a pitcher? Don't answer, I saw the last one. I'm your best friend. Why haven't you mentioned this?"

"Let's go out front, best friend," said B. A. "We can sit down and have a little talk."

The two girls went around to the front of the house. Rod conveniently disappeared into the garage. He didn't need to hear any more of Chip's tirade. As far as he was concerned, he had done nothing wrong. He knew that Chip was capable of twisting everything around and blaming him, so it was best that he kept out of sight. He did chuckle to himself that he, at two hundred fifty pounds, was trying to avoid a little person like her.

"Okay," said B. A., once she and Chip got settled on the front porch swing. "Here's the whole deal. Back in Arkansas, I was hassled by people for my basketball and softball abilities. We've been through this before. I just didn't want to go through all that nonsense again. I decided not to tell anyone about my pitching skills until I saw how the season would develop. And you've got to admit, it's going great. We've won nine out of our last ten games, and you are by far the best shortstop I've ever seen. You make plays on balls that other girls wouldn't even touch. And Jenny, she's hitting like .350 or close to it, and she's getting better every game. Except for her sister, we're having a lot of fun playing together. Our coaches are awesome, and we get along so well. So you do see my side of it, right?"

B. A. was surprised that Chip sat there and listened quietly without interrupting. It was obvious that she was trying to take it all in. What wasn't obvious were the thoughts running through Chip's head of Reston winning the state championship with B. A. on the mound and Chip making a spectacular play to save the game.

"Okay," said Chip after few moments. "I understand, sort of, what you're saying. And I will admit that you're quite the schemer. That's a compliment coming from me by the way. But why would you keep this a secret from your best friend? Why does the big guy get to hear information like that and I don't?"

"You and Jenny are my best girl friends, and Rod's my best guy friend. You can't tell me that you don't talk about stuff with Luke that you haven't mentioned to me. Stuff like, oh I don't know, like the Witness Protection Program."

"You know about that?" asked Chip. "Well, what did you expect us to think? You come in here with a boatload of secrets. It's just not normal. Okay, we're even on that score. I forgive you. The big question is, are you going to tell the coach you are a pitcher and take the starting job from Tammi? Man, this is going to be so sweet. You are better than her, right? I mean, I only saw one pitch."

"Let's just keep going like we were," answered B. A. "We've got enough reporters snooping around. If things get tough, I'll make the decision. It's not really that big of a deal."

"All right, but don't wait too long. It's time Tammi was put in her place. I don't think I can hold my tongue much longer. I know the coaches are fed up with her. On the bad side, if Tammi were humiliated, how would Jenny take it? I mean, she's not real happy with us right now. I wish there were some way we could blame it on Luke or Rod."

"No more schemes for a while," said B. A., stepping off the porch and stretching. "Let's run over to Jenny's to see if she wants to join us. We need to get her talking again anyway."

Two days later, B. A. showed up a few minutes before practice and asked to speak to her coaches in private. Chip was all smiles anticipating what was happening between her new best friend and the coaches. Tammi was going down in a ball of flames. This could be one of the best days of her life. This was stuff that dreams were made of. This was...

Chip saw the dejected look on B. A.'s and the coaches' faces when they were through talking. It didn't look like B. A. had torpedoed the *evil one.*

"Gather around everyone," hollered Coach Brown. He waited until everyone was quiet then informed them that their starting right fielder was ineligible. The eligibility sheet would come out the next day, but B. A. wanted to give her coaches a heads up. She just looked down at the ground too embarrassed to face her teammates. After failing her last algebra test, her teacher asked her to stay after for a few minutes. Mrs. Lawton offered to tutor her right after school. B. A. said she would think about it and get back with her. She knew why she didn't do so well on her last test, and if Chip found out, she would probably never hear the end of it. The night before the test, she lifted weights with Rod in his garage and then they sat on the porch for a long time—longer than she should have. They talked and sat real close to each other on the swing. It was such a nice evening, and B. A. didn't want it to end. She arrived home just before her mother got home from work, and after a short talk with her, she went straight to bed. B. A. never even opened her algebra book to study for the next day's test.

"Well," Tammi whispered to Darby as soon as they were out of earshot. "It looks like Little Miss Perfect has finally slipped up. I hope some of these girls will now see what this chick is really like. She's nothing but a show-off and a *grandstander*."

"I don't know," said Darby. "She's leading the team in RBIs and has something like twenty homers. She also has the best arm that I've ever seen on a high school player."

"Not you too," said Tammi in an exasperated tone. "So she's hit a lot of homers. Most of them were off of lousy pitchers and when the game wasn't on the line."

"Are you sure?" asked Darby. It was rare for her to question her idol, but it appeared that she was having trouble with her facts. "I'll admit she hasn't done much the last few games, but that's because the other coaches know about her now. They intentionally walk her a whole lot more than at the beginning of the season. And I wouldn't call Booth a lousy pitcher. B. A. ripped her good. I heard it was the first homer hit off that girl in her whole high school career."

"Come on," said Tammi. "So she closes her eyes and gets a hold of one. What did she do the other two times, a strike out and a pop-up. Don't tell me you're falling under her little I'm-better-than-everyone-else spell like most of the girls on the team."

"You really don't like her, do you? Why do you hate her so much?"

"Like I told you the other day," said Tammi, pointing her finger at her catcher. "I think she's a phony. She puts on big act about not wanting a lot of attention. She's pretty devious. She gets a couple of the girls, my sister included, on her side, then she goes to work. You have to admit our coaches think she's a little darling. Have you ever heard them get on her the way they get on everyone else when we make a mistake? Never!"

Darby had always been a Tammi supporter. Mainly because in middle school, Tammi was the top athlete and the other students looked up to her. But now, a lot of girls had caught up and passed her in athletic ability. Even her sister, Jenny, was now twice the athlete that Tammi was. Was that the source of Tammi's anger? Was it because Jenny looked up to B. A. now instead of Tammi? It was something to think about.

It didn't take Chip long to get to the bottom of the failed test. She was sitting at the kitchen, ranting to her mother who was listening halfheartedly. When her daughter was in this mode it didn't do any good to offer another side to the story. It was best to let Chip blow off a little steam until the rational side kicked in.

"Mom, B. A. will be out for a whole week because of this algebra thing. It couldn't have come at a worse time. We've got two games coming up against tough teams. We really need her. And I know why she failed that test. She spent the whole evening with you know who, lifting weights and probably swapping, uh, doing the kissy face thing. The bottom line is, she didn't study at all. How could she do this to us?"

"She'll get herself straightened out," said Mrs. Fullerton. "B. A. is pretty capable as you have pointed out on numerous occasions."

"I know," continued Chip. "But now I'm in possession of some new information that will totally shape our destiny, and B. A. is ruining everything."

"Calm down. All winter and spring all you could do was praise this girl, now she's the source of all your problems? And what's this new information?"

"Sorry. I lost my head for a minute. I still love her and respect her, but doggone it, we're just starting to play like a really good team. Oh yeah, I can't tell you about my new discovery until I talk it over with Luke. I haven't told him yet. He is going to flip out. Plus I get a check mark for finding out something that he should have come up with. Maybe I should get two checks."

Chip Steps Up

The Reston softball team took the field minus their starting right fielder and RBI leader. B. A. had offered to do the books for the two games she would be missing. She went in and talked to her algebra teacher and got some extra help. If tomorrow's quiz was anything like the practice problems she had finished the night before, she should have no problem bringing her grade back up to passing. She was embarrassed, but she knew she had to take the necessary steps to solve her problem, and she had done it. Tammi snickered at her when she took the scorebook, but B. A. ignored her. She had learned to do that way back during the basketball season. It was pointless to trade barbs or anything else with a girl like Tammi. She obviously had her mind made up about B. A., and there was no changing it. B. A. had seen girls like Jenny's twin before, and she refused to be bothered by her lack of class and general nastiness.

Chip Fullerton fielded grounders thrown by Jenny and rifled them back to her at first base. B. A. and Chip had a little talk before the game. She told Chip to stay focused and not to let any of the extra-curricular activities affect her performance. She also told her that really good players could shut out everything that wasn't part of the game. Chip decided to totally throw herself into the task at hand and worry about B. A.'s and Jenny's problems later.

The first batter for Colfax, a small private school from the Fort Worth area, hit a hard grounder to Chip's right. She took two quick steps, backhanded the ball, and threw a bullet to Jenny. The speedy runner was surprised to see the ball beat her to the base by three full steps. The Colfax first-base coach was impressed but not as impressed as she was going to be when the third inning rolled around. The game was still scoreless in the top of the third. The Colfax leadoff batter had started off the inning by hitting a hard single to right. The next hitter cracked a line drive to Chip's right. The little shortstop dove and was totally airborne when she caught the liner. She hit the dirt and rolled to a seated position. Looking back toward first, she saw that the runner was halfway to second and was scrambling to get her momentum turned around, so she could get back to the first base bag. Chip threw from a seated position and doubled the runner off. The play drew a huge ovation from the home crowd and from most of the visitors. The first-base coach hollered at Chip, and when she looked over, the coached tipped her cap to her.

Back in the dugout, B. A. marked the play in the scorebook. She wondered if the first-base coach would talk to the runner later. She had just made one of the dumbest moves in softball or baseball for that matter. Often, when a runner on first saw a ball ripped to left, they would take off running with their head down as fast as they could. They don't even wait to see if the ball gets through. Coach Brown went over this earlier during one of their practices. B. A. liked the way he presented it to the team. He used the Socratic method. The coach asked them logical questions that would hopefully guide them to an understanding of the problem. That's the way Socrates used to lead discussions when the talked about philosophy or politics with the people of Athens.

"If you're on first and the hitter gets a hit to left field, what is your goal?" asked Coach Brown.

"To get to second," several of them responded.

"Right. So if your goal is to get to second, how fast do you have to run, assuming you took two slide steps off the bag when the ball was hit?"

"You could probably jog there," answered Chip. "I mean, once the ball clears the infield, it has to bounce or roll out to the left fielder. She will probably field it cautiously on one knee because she can't afford to let it get past her. Then she will make an easy throw back into the infield, assuming the runner on first is stopping at second. It's pretty much impossible to go to third on a hit to left that the left fielder fields cleanly in front of her. A ball down the line or in the alley is a different story though."

"Exactly," said Pops. "So why wouldn't you wait to see if the ball gets by the infielders before you take off in a mad dash toward second? Good base runners are thinking all the time, and sprinting toward second in this situation is something a nonthinker does. Don't just go through the motions. Learn something while you play the game. Hey, someday you could be teaching it to your kids."

The Reston shortstop capped off her stellar play in the field by making a smart base running decision in the bottom of the seventh. With Reston losing two to one, Chip stepped up and led off the home team's last chance with a single up the middle. She stole second on the first pitch to Kris Ritter. Kris hit a routine grounder to short on the next pitch, and Chip bolted for third, passing behind the fielder. It was a smart move, and Chip would have made it easily except the shortstop misplayed the ball, and it got by her. Chip was right behind the Colfax shortstop when the ball went through her legs, hitting Chip in the foot. The ball caromed off her foot and headed out to short left field where it crossed the foul line and came to a stop. The third baseman started to walk toward the ball, assuming the ball was dead, and the runner would be called out. Chip never broke stride as she rounded third and headed for home. The Colfax catcher was standing with her mask in hand, jabbering at the home plate umpire and pointing to her foot, showing the ump where the ball hit Chip. Kris slowed down for a second, but when she saw Chip running hard, she picked up the pace and ended up at third because no one was covering the bag.

Through all of this, Pops didn't say a word. He just waved his runners on and then gave Kris the stop sign at third. He saw the opposing coach call time out and head on to the field, so he walked slowly toward the plate to hear the conversation. The umpires stood and smiled at the Colfax coach for about ten seconds. At that point, the plate umpire told him to be quiet or he would be ejected. The ump then calmly explained that the rule was if a batted ball passed an infielder—other than the pitcher—and hit a runner, the runner was not out if she didn't show any intention of letting the ball hit her. Pops knew the rule and so did Chip. The bottom line was, Chip did not interfere with the ball before the shortstop had a chance to make a play on it, and she certainly didn't let the ball hit her on purpose.

The visiting coach was still fuming when Courtney hit a fly deep enough to right that enabled Kris to tag at third and score the winning run. At the post-game meeting in centerfield, Coach Brown complimented the base runners on knowing the rules. When asked why he didn't holler at his runners, he said he didn't want to alarm the fielders. If he would have shouted at his runners to keep running, the third baseman might have hustled out to get the ball, which would probably have kept Kris at second. It was the visitor's fault that neither they nor their coach knew about the rule. Everyone but Tammi and Darby clapped Chip and Kris on the back.

"What about Courtney?" asked Chip. "She had the winning RBI." Courtney came in for a round of shoving and good-natured slapping too. B. A. was right in there with the rest of them congratulating her teammates. She was so happy for the players involved in the last couple of plays that she didn't worry about being a bystander to all of the action. She felt good that the glory was spread around to some different players for once. It made them feel like a real team and not just a bunch of individuals playing together. This is what she had hoped for when she moved with her mom to Reston. The funny thing was her ineligibility helped her to see the situation a little more clearly.

Jenny said good-bye to her teammates and headed for her car. Chip asked her if she wanted to go to the Pizza Palace to celebrate their victory, but the tall first baseman said she had some things to do. This didn't set well with Chip. She went over to B. A. and expressed her concerns.

"She doesn't want anything to do with us because we told her the truth about her new boyfriend. Why won't she listen to her best friends, who are only looking out for her?"

"I don't know," answered B. A. "She does seem to be a little hardheaded when it comes to this guy."

"Let's go get Lu," said Chip. "We need to have a meeting. Somebody needs to do something about this jerk before it gets too serious."

The three friends pulled up to their favorite spot on the edge of Mr. Daggert's field. The sun turned the whole western sky to an orange red as it neared its final resting spot for the day. Chip had called Lu on the phone, and then B. A. and her went in to Chip's kitchen to make supper. Ten minutes later, they came out with a big bag filled with chicken salad sandwiches, carrot sticks, chips, and apples. The three of them sat in the back of B. A.'s truck, eating sandwiches and discussing their strategy. Chip, in her normal fashion, wanted to confront Jenny's boyfriend right in front of Jenny. The other two said that was a bad idea. Morrie would deny everything, and they would lose Jenny as a friend maybe—forever.

Mr. Daggert pulled up on his tractor to say hello, and the girls invited him over for a sandwich. He stood next to the truck, munching on a sandwich and made polite conversation with the high-school girls. He talked a little but mostly listened. The three of them didn't talk about the usual things that teen girls talk about. He knew because he had two nieces about the same age. Their looks, likes and dislikes, and boys were quite often the main topics of their conversations. That's why he liked these girls so much. They were interesting and very unpredictable. Chip proved that a moment later when she looked over at him and asked, "Mr. D., what would you do if a friend of yours was dating a low down dirtbag but didn't believe you when you told her about him?"

"Well, that's a tough one," said the farmer. "She doesn't believe you, huh? And you're sure this guy is that bad? How about you put him in a situation where his true colors have to come out? You know, force his hand so to speak."

The three of them looked at each other for a few seconds. "That's a great idea," said Chip. "If Jenny won't believe us, she'll just have to see what this guy is really like for herself. Mr. D., you're a genius. Now, how do we do it?"

"Easier said than done," said Mr. Daggert as he headed back to his tractor. "You'll have to figure that one out for yourself. Thanks for the sandwich, girls. Tell your mom, she makes a great chicken salad."

"Her salads are good, but my chili is better," hollered Chip.

"That was a good idea," said B. A. "But how do we set it up. Morrie hardly ever comes to Reston. She usually goes over to his place to watch one of his games or to hang out."

"We better do something soon," added Lu. "I heard some stuff about a group of Lakewood guys that's not very nice."

"Like what?" asked Chip.

"It's not all of them, but some of them have this big contest about how many girls they can date and, you know, *score* with."

"What? Are you kidding me?" screamed Chip as B. A. just sat there with a concerned look on her face. "This is awful. What a bunch of jerks! Jenny's too smart to get involved in something like that, isn't she?"

Chip's two friends sat quietly and thought about the situation that Jenny might have gotten herself into. Chip repeated herself after getting no answer to her previous question. "I said, Jenny's too smart to get involved in something that low class and stupid, right?"

"Let's hope so," said B. A. finally. "Yeah, she'll see right through this guy after she spends a little more time with him. We've got to believe that."

The two softball stars and the track star got back into B. A.'s truck and said very little on the way home. Chip was thinking about Rod and Victor punching Morrie's lights out. Lu was wishing that her information wasn't accurate and maybe blown way out of proportion. B. A. was worried about their friendship with Jenny but mostly about Jenny's safety.

Later that evening, Chip sat at her desk and did her homework. She wanted to do some planning with B. A., but she figured the right fielder was studying her algebra. She sent Luke a quick e-mail, asking for his opinion on the Jenny matter. Chip was working diligently on a paper for her English class when a message appeared on her screen that she had mail. She clicked on the icon and saw Luke's latest article.

Reston Softballers Exhibit Throwback Traits

By Luke Slowinski

With B. A. Smith on the sidelines this week because of eligibility problems, the Reston Lady Eagle softball team is finding ways to plug the huge hole left by Smith's absence.

The latest game with Colfax provided several opportunities to show what the rest of the team is capable of.

Juanita Esperanza did a nice job replacing Smith in right. She fielded two balls cleanly and went one for three at the plate. Courtney Grimes did what the number three batter in the lineup is supposed to do—bring runners home. Her sac fly in the bottom of the seventh sealed the victory for Reston. Tammi Olsen did a good job on the mound keeping Reston in the game. Chip Fullerton was outstanding at the shortstop position, making several plays that drew applause from the home fans as well as the visitors. Her quick thinking on the base paths set up the situation for Courtney's final RBI. Kris Ritter's grounder went through the Colfax shortstop's legs and hit Fullerton, who was running from second to third.

When asked about it later, Chip said she knew the ball was still live after it hit her because the shortstop had a chance to field it. She was surprised when the ball hit her in the foot but had the presence of mind to keep running. The opposing coach was a little confused about the rule, but the umps set him straight. An interesting note here is that B. A. Smith, who was keeping the official book, had no idea how to mark the play down. Normally, you should be able to look at a scorebook and figure out what happened on any given play during the game. A fielding error by the shortstop might let a runner score from second, but how did the batter, Kris Ritter, end up at third? Smith asked the home plate ump how it should be recorded after the game was over. He smiled and told her to make a note somewhere on the page explaining what happened.

Smith's approach, along with several other members of the Reston squad, remind me of one of the all time greats in the game of baseball, Christy Mathewson. Mattie is considered by most baseball experts as baseball's first superstar and was one of the original five players to be inducted into the hall of fame. He pitched for the New York Giants at the turn of the century. Christy played hard, and he played fair. It was something our Reston girls' teams are known for. He played a huge role in the Chicago Cubs's World Series Championship in 1908—the last time the Cubs won it all. Mathewson wasn't scheduled to pitch for New York, so he was coaching first in a play-off game that would decide who would go to the series. With two outs in the ninth inning, the New York batter singled to right and the runner on third scored. Game over? You would think so, but the runner on first never went to second. He jogged about halfway, and when the fans started to pour on to the field, he turned and ran for the dugout. The Cubs came up with the ball and stepped on second for a force out, which means the run should not have counted. They protested the game and the commissioner called for a hearing. When Mathewson was called to testify at the hearing, he told the truth. His guy never made it to second, so another game was scheduled. The Cubs won this one and then went on to win the championship.

I get the feeling, after watching our girls compete in basketball and now softball, that the majority of them would do just like Mathewson did. Compete fairly and with integrity. Is there any other way to do it?

Chip thought the article was pretty good. She liked the historical aspect of Luke's writing. She didn't know that the Cubs got in to the 1908 World Series on a technicality. Luke was shaping up into a pretty good sportswriter. Tammi would, no doubt, not be happy with her limited exposure. *Hey*, she thought. *Do something a little more spectacular out there, and you will get noticed more if that's what you're in to. B. A. and Jenny and me and some of the other girls, we just want to play and play well. The rest of that stuff is just small potatoes.*

She sent Luke an e-mail, congratulating him on a fine article. She suggested they go out for ice cream to celebrate. Luke messaged back that he would meet her there in fifteen minutes. He had to get rid of the girl that was currently over at his house.

Chip made a mental note to get even with him for that comment. She walked into the living room to see the usual sight—her mom and dad in their respective chairs, reading.

"Hey, you two bookworms," she said. "I'm going out for ice cream with my future Pulitzer-Prize-winning boyfriend. Do ya'll want me to bring something back for you? Oh yeah, how are you supposed to hold a knife if you get into a knife fight? There's a couple of people stalking me, and I might have to take matters into my own hands soon."

Neither of her parents put down their books. "Nothing for me, thanks," said her father. "Your mother might want a banana split or something."

"If I had a banana split, I might do the pants split. No thanks, dear."

Chip was surprised at the calm demeanor in her parents' answers. They must be trying to psyche her out. She would have to come up with something more shocking next time.

"Oh yeah," said her dad as she reached for the doorknob. "The best strategy in a knife fight is to bring a gun. A big one."

"No problemo," said Chip. "I never hit the streets of Reston unless I'm packing heat. See you later."

"I'd be careful with your suggestions," said Mrs. Fullerton. "That little one is quite unpredictable, if you haven't noticed."

"I've noticed," said Mr. Fullerton. "What's up with her and Jenny? There's some kind of trouble between them."

"Her little group is not happy with Jenny's new boyfriend. They were hoping she would find some nice boy to spend some time with, but apparently he's not that nice, and Jenny didn't believe them when they told her."

"Teenagers. Do you think it's tougher today than when we were that age?"

"Maybe," said Mrs. Fullerton. "They've got a totally different set of problems to solve in addition to the ones we had to deal with. So yeah, I think it's tougher for them. They'll get through it. Melinda inherited her mental toughness from me."

"Is that so? What did she get from me then?"

"Like she said, her knowledge of tools and their uses."

"Funny," said Mr. Fullerton going back to his book.

The next game was an easy one for the Reston softballers. Carmen pitched a good game, and with some solid defensive play behind her, she allowed only two runs. Chip, Courtney, and Kris provided enough offense for the Lady Eagles to score five runs. After the game, Tammi heard B. A. tell the coaches that she would be eligible for the next game. She made a comment to Darby that they should all be grateful that the team would be saved when the superstar returned. Darby had no comment to her battery mate's opinion. She had been thinking a lot about Tammi and her ugly attitude. Darby was impressed with the slugger's behavior during the last two games. She didn't complain or mope around, and she volunteered to do the scorebook. B. A. also cheered for her teammates on offense and defense. If she was a phony, like Tammi said, she sure did a good job of hiding it.

When the team met after the game in short center field, a heavy set man wearing Bermuda shorts, a golf shirt, and a ball cap stood patiently just out of earshot. As the team stood with their hands in the middle, Coach Brown looked over at Chip and B. A. and told them to stay after practice. The two stars saw an interview coming, and it looked like there was no way to avoid it.

"Don't bother with the stomachache routine," warned Pops as they walked slowly over to the waiting reporter. "That was a good one by the way, but you can only use it once. This man is from the *Dallas Morning News*, and he is a well-respected journalist. Fullerton, keep your answers short and be polite."

"What about B. A.?" asked Chip. "Does she have to be polite too?"

"She's not the one I'm worried about," said Pops as he approached the sportswriter with his hand out. After introductions, Coach Brown took his leave and went to check on the equipment.

"How did you think that went?" asked Chip, after their interview with the Dallas sportswriter.

"I thought it went fine," answered B. A. "He was real nice and not pushy at all."

"It was a good idea to invite him into the dugout, where there was some shade," observed Chip. "That guy was sweating pretty bad. I was hoping we wouldn't have to do CPR on him if he went down. Did you know that you're not supposed to do the mouth-to-mouth thing anymore? The experts say it's a waste of time?"

B. A. gave Chip the usual, "where did you come up with that" look. "I did know about the CPR change. My mom told me. That guy sure did his homework before he drove all the way over here. Did you know that you were on a pace to set a new school record for runs scored?"

"I never even thought about it," said Chip. "And what about you? He said you already broke the area home run and RBI record. You're really tearing it up. If this were baseball, the professional scouts would be all over you. Would you like to play professionally someday?"

"I don't know. It would probably seem more like a job than a sport you play for fun. Have you ever thought about playing in college?"

"Heck, yeah. It would be awesome. A huge stadium with thousands of people watching would be very cool."

"It's obvious you haven't seen many college softball games," said B. A. "Their fields look similar to the ones we play on. And I don't think they draw many more fans than we do. I have noticed lately that our crowds are getting bigger. I think it's due to your spectacular play at short and all around perkiness."

"Remember, I'm just Web Girl. You are the real Spiderwoman."

"Whatever," said B. A. as she opened the door to her truck. "Hey, on Sunday, Rod and I are going to talk to Victor. It's his birthday, and he's throwing a party, so we're going up for a while."

"Great, but break it to him in a nice way. You don't want to ruin his birthday."

"Don't worry, little mom. We'll be nice. And if he doesn't take it too well, Rod will beat the stuffings out of him. How's that?"

"Now you're talking my language," said Chip as they pulled into her driveway.

Problems Solved

Saturday started out as a beautiful day in northern Texas. After breakfast, Chip headed in to Fort Worth to help at her dad's store. When she was younger, she would ride in with him, and her mom would come in and get her if she had an activity to attend. Now she drove herself in and worked until two o'clock. She enjoyed working at her dad's hardware store. She got along great with the other employees, and it was nice to spend some time with her dad while he was doing something he loved so much. Both of them considered it quality time spent together. Chip was going to miss these Saturdays when she was in Michigan for a month. Even though he didn't say anything about it, she knew her dad felt the same way. Chip also helped to cover for vacations in the summer. Luke volunteered to fill in for her until she got back.

B. A. was still working a couple of hours on Saturday mornings at Mr. Kim's grocery store. Lu was going to take her spot while she was gone. B. A. was still helping out, even though Mrs. Kim had fully recovered from her illness. B. A. had called Jenny to see if she wanted to work for her, but she didn't answer her phone. Jenny wasn't talking much to any of her three friends lately. B. A.'s mom advised them not to press Jenny too hard. Earlier in the week, B. A. had invited the three of them over for lasagna, but Jenny said she couldn't make it. Chip was impressed with B. A.'s lasagna. She said it was world class and ranked right up there with her chili. Lu had a big race the following Monday, so she was grateful for the carb-intensive meal. She amazed the others by putting away enough for two people.

B. A. said good-bye to her mother and ran out the door when she heard Rod honking. It was only a half hour to Denton, which meant they would arrive at Victor's about an hour after the party had started. B. A. kidded Rod about being fashionably late.

"Actually, I had to go pick up his present," explained Rod as he handed a bag to B. A. "There's a lady that does custom embroidery and screen printing over in Lakewood, so I had her design this shirt for him."

B. A. took the shirt out and held it up. The saying on the front said, To the Victor Goes the Spoils. There were all sorts of guy toys underneath the saying—cars, motorcycles, and an ATV. There was also and an assortment of pretty girls.

"Cute," was all B. A. said.

"Trust me," said Rod. "He'll love it."

"It must be a guy thing," said B. A. "Do all guys look at girls as toys?"

"No, that's not what it means. It's just supposed to be a funny shirt with a play on words."

"I was just kidding," said B. A. "Girls wear a lot of goofy shirts too. You know, like the ones that say, You Can't Handle My Game or Come On Back If You Want Another Lesson. Most of the time, they can't back up the saying on their shirt, but I don't think that ever occurred to them. It's as if by just wearing the shirt, they turned into a great athlete. It seems to me that the sports scene and even the music scene is all about trying to impress the other guy. Why can't people just go out and do what they do without worrying about their image all the time? I remember a saying that my dad told me one time. He said, "If you're good, you don't need to talk about yourself; other people will talk about you." That wasn't exactly how he said it, but you get the idea."

"That's a good saying. You seem a little hostile today. Did my cousin get you all riled up or something?"

"No, I'm just worried about Jenny. She's got another date with her new boyfriend, the sleazebag."

"Do you think there's anything to what Cheryl said about this group of guys from Lakewood? I'm not saying that Cheryl is making it up or even exaggerating. It just sounds like something from a book or a movie."

"Cheryl doesn't seem like the type of person that would make up something like that," said B. A. "Jenny hardly ever talks to the three of us any more. I don't know why she is taking it so hard."

"Matters of the heart are hard to explain sometimes especially when young people are involved," said Rod.

"Aren't you the philosophical, mature one." B. A. laughed.

"Speaking of mature," said Rod. "You know there will be alcohol at this party? A lot of people there will be over twenty-one."

"I know. It's okay for a high-school student to be at a party, where adults are drinking beer. You're not going to drink, are you?"

"Naw, it's against the law. Besides, I had a few beers at a party once when I was a college freshman, and it wasn't that big of a deal. It's weird, when you're young, you want to be older, and when you're older, you want to be younger. Go figure."

"Here's another saying from my dad. I don't know where he got it, but I always liked it. It goes something like this: "You've got to be what you is, 'cause if you is what you ain't, you ain't what you is." It sounds silly, but if you think about it, it makes a lot of sense. If people would stop acting and just be themselves, the world would be a better place. It's hard enough to be yourself without trying to convince people that you're cooler, smarter, more talented, or whatever. Sooner or later, people will figure you out. Then where will you be?"

"Now who is being philosophical?" asked Rod. "I do like that one though. Tell you what, I don't think Victor will let anyone under twenty-one drink at his place, but if there are underage drinkers, we'll leave. You especially don't need to be at a place where minors are drinking. If the cops showed up, it wouldn't do for the top female athlete in the whole area to be there. Even if you are innocent, some people will look down on you. It's the old guilt by association thing. You know how that goes."

"I knew there was a reason I liked you," said B. A. in a wispy voice. "In addition to your great looks and awesome body."

"Yeah, yeah," said Rod as he looked for a place to park along the busy street. "Hey, if Diego is here, how do you want to handle it?"

"Let's just tell Victor straight out," said B. A. as she got out on her side. "He's pretty cool. He can handle it any way he wants to. Once we tell him, we are done with this whole robbery mess."

The party was going full bore when Rod and B. A. walked in. The backyard was a small fenced-in area, and it was packed with people. Music was blaring, and the grill was full of burgers and brats. Victor saw the two from Reston and hurried over to greet them.

"Dudes," said Victor hugging both of them. "Thanks for coming. We've got food and drink all over the place. No beer for you, Tigrita. You're still a baby."

"Thanks, old man," said B. A. laughing. "Check out the present Rod got you."

Victor took the bag that Rod held out. He held up the shirt and laughed. "Very cool." He whipped off his shirt and put the new one on. B. A. checked out Victor's body before he put his gift on. He was skinny but still muscular with a lot of definition. *Nice,* she thought. *But not as impressive as the guy standing next to me.* Victor went off to show his shirt around.

"I saw you checking him out," Rod said quietly as he took her hand. "Do you wish I looked more like that? You know, somewhat malnourished."

B. A. had never heard Rod say anything along those lines before. She thought it was cute. He didn't sound jealous. It was more like he was fishing for a compliment.

"He was okay," she said. "But I'm into the big muscular types."

"So you would date the Incredible Hulk if he was available?"

"You know it. We'd have to do something about the green color though. It would make me nauseous and draw too much attention."

"Speaking of drawing attention," whispered Rod. "People are looking at us already. Victor did tell me that a bunch of his family and friends want to meet you. He talks you up all the time. Let's get something to eat. That grill is looking too full, and I don't want any of that food to burn."

"Now you sound like Luke. I'll get us drinks if you'll round us up some eats."

Rod and B. A. sat in lawn chairs and talked to the people around them. A lady in her mid forties said she was Victor's aunt, and she had a favor to ask. She asked quietly and in a very serious tone, so Rod responded in kind by leaning forward and stating if it was possible he would attempt the favor. Then the lady waved at a couple of junior-high girls that were watching them across the yard. They came scampering over with a pen and paper in hand. Rod's face lit up when he figured out what the girls wanted—an autograph.

"Mister, could you get your cousin, Chip Fullerton, to sign this piece of paper?" asked one of the girls. "She's the best shortstop and the best point guard we've ever seen. She can send it to the address on the back of the paper. Thanks." With that, the two of them ran back across the yard.

Rod was speechless. He had signed a few autographs when he was in high school and a lot more when he started for UNT as a tight end. He looked over at B. A., and she was trying hard to keep from laughing, but that didn't last long. A few heads turned when they heard the sound of her laughter above the loud music.

"Chip is going to have a heyday with this," said B. A. still chuckling. "Rod Foster, former high school and college football star, will now be officially known as Chip Fullerton's cousin."

"Man, talk about being put in your place," said Rod. "They even called me mister. That's embarrassing."

Victor walked up with a chair and sat it down between his two guests. "What's so funny over here?" he asked.

"Your relatives are hitting Rod up for Chip's autograph," said B. A. "His new claim to fame is his family connection to one of the best athletes around. He's going to have to get used to it because she's petty awesome."

"Both of you are awesome," said Victor. "And once people find out who you are, B. A., you'll have a few autographs to sign yourself."

"Hey, amigo," said Rod turning serious. "Is this a good time to talk about something important? If it's not, let us know, and we'll talk later."

"No, it's cool. We're sitting here face-to-face. There's no better time. What's up?"

Rod relayed most of the attempted robbery story, and B. A. filled in the blanks. Victor sat very still and listened to every word. When Rod was done, Victor stared at the ground for a while B. A. put her arm around Victor's shoulders. After a few minutes, he said he would be right back. He rose and went into the house with a purposeful look on his face. When he came back out, Diego was right behind him. Rod and B. A. looked at each other. They didn't know Diego was even there, but the would-be robber knew they were in the backyard. He saw them through the window as they walked up the drive and was conveniently staying out of sight inside the house. Victor walked the high-school freshman up to them and stood there for a moment, gauging Diego's reaction.

"These two are good friends of mine, and I don't think they would come here on my birthday and make up a story about an attempted robbery," he said in a low, serious tone. "Now, I want to hear what you have to say about being in Mr. Kim's store with a mask on, claiming you had a weapon."

Diego was shaking and didn't say anything for a while. He stared at B. A. then at Rod. He finally looked up at Victor and admitted, "It's true. I was tired of there being no food in the house. I didn't want my little sister to cry anymore. I'm sorry. I really am. It was really stupid."

"I am not pretending to be your father," said Victor quietly. "In the future, if you have problems that you need help solving, you come to me, okay?"

"What are you going to do?" asked Diego.

"Monday, after school, we're going to see the store owner," said Victor. "I don't know what he's going to say, but whatever it is, you're going to say 'Yes, sir.' If he wants to press charges, then you will cooperate. Got it?"

Diego solemnly shook his head in the affirmative. Victor told his nephew to go back into the house. When he was out of earshot, B. A. told Victor that Mr. Kim was a great guy and didn't want to take the incident any further. Victor seemed somewhat relieved but reiterated the fact that they would cooperate no matter what Mr. Kim wanted to do. He then surprised both of them by thanking them for bringing the matter to his attention.

Rod and B. A. were unusually quiet on the way home. They knew they did the right thing by telling Victor about his nephew's activities, but they didn't have to like it. B. A. broke a long silence by commenting on something that happened in sociology class recently.

"We had this intense discussion about *no snitching*. A few in the class thought that you should never tell on anyone no matter what they did. Mr. Cutler shot that thinking down by saying if that were true, the only way a robber or a murderer would be caught was if the police actually saw him do the crime. If people wouldn't speak up when they saw others breaking the law, very few crimes would ever be solved. There would be no eyewitnesses in court unless they were policemen because that's their job. Then he went on to say that if the people of this country wouldn't help, our nation of laws would be reduced to a nation of warlords and gangs. That no-snitching philosophy is one of the dumbest things I've ever heard. I'm not saying you should run around, looking for people that are jaywalking or spitting on the sidewalk. I'm just saying we need to look out for each other."

"Did most of the students get it?" asked Rod.

"Most but not all. Mr. Cutler showed a short video after the discussion. Some entertainer guy that I've never even heard of said he wouldn't tell the cops even if a serial killer lived next door to him. He told the interviewer that he would move somewhere else."

"Really? That's pretty gutless. Why not make an anonymous phone call to alert the cops?"

"If I was doing the interview, I would have asked him this: So while you're out, looking for a new house so you can move away, the serial killer goes to your house and kills your family. Now do you think you should have said something?"

"Well said. You sound like a future lawyer or maybe even a politician."

"You can scratch that politician talk," said B. A. "I wouldn't want to go through what those guys go through to get elected. It's embarrassing."

B. A.'s phone rang. She looked at it and saw that Cheryl Williams was calling. "Hey, Cheryl, what's up?" B. A. mostly listened with a couple of "what's" and "no ways" thrown in. Her last statement got Rod's attention. "Well, I've got the snake killer right here with me. We'll think of something."

"What the heck was that all about?" asked Rod as B. A. hung up and gave him a scared look.

"Cheryl heard through the grapevine that Morrie was going to make a serious move on Jenny tonight. This is awful. We need to do something."

"What was the bit about a snake killer?"

"Cheryl said that Morrie and his bunch are real snakes. I told her that I was with you. We can't just hope for the best on this one. Will you help us once we come up with a plan?"

B. A. saw Rod's forearm muscles tense up as he gripped the steering wheel. They looked like ropes that ran from his elbows to his hands. She thought that it wouldn't take much for him to rip the steering wheel right out of the dashboard.

"Sure, I'll help. Do you think we should tell Chip and Luke?"

"Yeah, you've got to admit, they're pretty good at planning things."

"You mean scheming things, don't you?" asked Rod as he eased up on the steering wheel.

"Yeah, that too."

B. A. called Chip, who was on her way home from her dad's store. She got Chip's attention right away when she said it was a code blue situation. Chip said she would call Luke, and they could meet in half an hour.

"What's this code blue stuff?" asked Rod as he looked over at B. A.

"It's how Chip and Luke talk to each other," answered B. A. "I'm surprised you haven't heard them before. Blue is total disaster, red is trouble, and yellow is just an everyday alert."

"I've heard that stuff before but really didn't pay any attention to it," said Rod. "Don't tell her I said this, but those two were made for each other. She's usually peeved at him for something, but I've never seen them have a serious fight or anything like that."

"Their weirdness sort of complements each other. There's never a dull moment with those two. What do you think Chip will want to do?"

"Knowing her, I'd say she opts for the frontal approach with both guns blazing."

"Well," said B. A., laying a hand on Rod's bicep. "If we go in with both guns blazing, we're going in with some pretty big guns."

Rod looked over at her and smiled. "You know what they say, if you're gonna bring a gun to a gunfight, bring a big one."

The four of them sat on Rod's porch and discussed possible strategies. In the end, they decided to cruise over to Lakewood and check out the make-out spots that the local teens used. If they spotted Morrie's car, they could just watch from a distance. Luke reminded them that if they were going to play the part, they would have to look legit to anyone that would happen to walk or drive by. Chip said she had no problem with that as long as it was for a friend. Luke looked a little dejected, so she grabbed his face and gave him a big kiss. When she pulled away, he was all smiles.

"Will that hold you for a while, or should I ask these two to leave?" asked Chip.

"I don't know," said Luke as if he was trying to decide. "How about one more with feeling?"

Chip obliged with her cousin and B. A. looking on. This was a side of her that they had not seen before. It was obvious that beneath her feisty exterior, there lurked an affectionate, caring side.

"All right, you two," said Rod. "Break it up. We need to stay focused here. Let's not forget our mission."

"I'd listen to him," added B. A. "He's our snake killer."

"Ha," said Chip. "I happen to know that he doesn't like snakes. He's afraid of them."

"Not the kind that walk on two legs," said Rod as he headed for the car.

"Can we stop and get a burger or something?" asked Luke as he got in front beside Rod.

"Sweetie," said Chip from the backseat. "If this works out right, I'll cook you a gourmet meal. Two cheeseburgers and a small pizza."

"Deal," said Luke. "And you better not be teasing."

Jenny and Morrie came out of the movie theatre with different opinions on how good the movie was. She didn't like all the violence, but he seemed to enjoy it. He even laughed at one of the gory scenes. This reminded Jenny of a paper that one of her classmates had written and then read to the class. The main point of the paper was that gory movies were so stupid that they were actually funny. She thought she had a good idea of what funny was, and she didn't see slasher movies as comedy. They were just gross.

After the guy in her class finished, the teacher named half a dozen movies that he thought were quality pictures. By a show of hands, only a couple in the class had seen the ones he mentioned. Then he asked how many had seen the latest installment of a low-budget horror flick. Every hand but Jenny's and two others went up. She couldn't figure out why her peers went for shallow special effects compared with something that made you feel or think. Oh well, she had no problem being in the minority on that topic. One comforting fact was that her sister felt the same way about movies and music. Now if she could only get her to change her philosophy on athletics and sportsmanship. She looked at Morrie and realized he was saying something to her.

"I'm sorry," she said sheepishly. "I was sort of zoning out there. What did you say?"

"I said, let's go out to a spot where a lot of high-school people hang out. I want them to see me with a gorgeous babe. It will be good for my rep."

"I thought you already had a good rep," said Jenny.

"It never helps to improve it," replied Morrie. "You're only as good as your latest accomplishment. Know what I mean?"

Jenny looked at him and shook her head to show that she wasn't following him.

"It's like this," continued Morrie. "If you're a singer and haven't had a hit for a while, people tend to forget about you. It's the same with actors or athletes. Have a down movie or bad season and people are looking for somebody else to worship."

"So it's all about hero worship?" asked Jenny, trying to figure what he was getting at. This was a side of him that he had not shown before, and she was somewhat confused.

"Worship might be too strong of a word," said Morrie as he made a left down a country road just outside of town. "I prefer adulation. Now there's a thousand-dollar word."

"And if people think you're really special, even if you might not be as special as they think, that's all that matters? Where are we going anyway? I thought it was some sort of restaurant where the local kids hung out."

"It's all about image, Jen. You know that. If you're not stylin' all the time, your numbers will drop drastically. And to answer your question, it's sort of like an outdoor hangout. You know, a place to relax and have a few refreshments."

"I'm not too crazy about this. I'm not a drinker, and besides, I told my parents I'd be home before ten."

"Geez, lighten up a little," said Morrie as they turned off the road and crested a small hill. Before them was an open area about forty yards across. Trees and high grass, along with the hill behind them made the place almost invisible from the road. In the twilight, Jenny could see a couple of areas where small fires had burned at one time. Morrie backed in to a spot next to a big oak tree. There were two other cars parked across the way. Jenny couldn't see anybody in them as the light was fading fast. Morrie looked over at her with a sinister grin on his face. "I think it's time you and I got to know each other a little better. I've got a little something in the trunk to enhance the mood. I'll be right back."

What have I gotten myself into? thought Jenny. *It looks like my friends were right. They were being honest with me, and I got mad at them. How stupid am I? Now they're going to think that I'm just a naïve small-town girl.*

Jenny heard a noise and looked down on the seat. Morrie's phone was lying there, and it appeared that he had just received a text message. She picked up the phone and looked over her shoulder. Whatever was in the trunk, it was obvious that he was having trouble finding it in the dark. She hit *view now* on his phone and read the message.

> m, have u dun the deed yet time is runing out remember shes worth 30 pts

Jenny stared at the phone. It only took a few seconds to figure out that she was part of some kind of sick game. Her eyes started to leak. She took a deep breath and got her composure back. *No, I'm not going to handle it this way. What would B. A. do in a situation like this? She'd be smart and explore all her options. Then she would take action.* She jumped when her phone rang. It was Chip. She told Chip they were parked somewhere just outside of Lakewood, but she didn't know exactly where. Holding back a sob, she admitted she might be in trouble. The trunk slammed, and she jumped again. Her last words were she needed help. As she was closing her phone, Chip said something she couldn't quite understand—something about snake killers and Spiderwoman. Didn't she hear that her best friend needed help? She thought about locking the doors, but Morrie took the keys with him to open the trunk.

"All right," said Morrie as he got back in with a small bottle and two plastic cups. "I had trouble finding the cups. I usually drink it straight, but with you being a classy lady and all, I figured we'd sip it from cups with our little fingers raised. Plus I figured you would want to mix yours with some soda." With that, he reached behind him and grabbed a can of Coke that was lying on the backseat floor. "This is going to be a special night for you, young lady. Actually, it's going to be a special night for both of us."

"When you say special, do you mean like a night where you score thirty points?" asked Jenny in her best sarcastic voice.

"So you know about that, do you?" asked Morrie as he poured himself half a glass of rum. He poured Jenny the same amount and gave it to her. "Mix in some of the Coke. It'll go down easier. Go ahead, it ain't half bad."

"I think I want to go," said Jenny in a firm voice. "People told me about the real you, and I didn't want to believe them. Obviously they were right, and I was wrong. So start the car and take me back to my car. I'm out of here."

"Nice speech," said Morrie as he took a big gulp of liquor. "Listen, little miss prissy. This is gonna happen tonight whether you like it or not."

"I forgot. It's all about your rep, right?"

"Damn straight. Morrie gets what Morrie wants."

"Well, Morrie," said Jenny with more conviction than she ever thought she could muster. "I'm not one of your low self-esteem followers, looking to move up the social ladder. I now see you for what you are, and frankly, I'm not impressed. You think you are a great athlete and can take what you want. I have played on two teams this year with two female athletes that are both better than you are. Tonight, Morrie the Magnificent, or whatever your little followers call you, is not going to get what he wants. So start this car and take me back to my car."

Morrie threw back the rest of his drink and looked at Jenny with a sickening smile. "It ain't gonna happen, babe. You got in my car willingly, and I've been fighting you off all night. Did I mention that my dad is a lawyer? I can't tell you how many girls have come on to me to improve their social standing. I'm just another example of females trying to manipulate men with their bodies. You might as well relax and enjoy it."

Morrie's sick grin was barely discernable as Jenny slowly slipped her hand into the lower pocket of her cargo shorts.

"Rod," said B. A. "Put your foot down on that gas pedal. I'm calling Cheryl to see where Morrie and Jenny might be."

"You better listen, cuz," said Chip. "Spiderwoman is on the case. I got a feeling that this is going to get ugly. You ready to go into battle, Luke?"

"Relax back there," said Luke. "Let's not let our emotions get the best of us. When Jenny turns this guy down, he'll accept defeat and look for other conquests. I'm not saying that's right, but our mission is to rescue our friend not save the world. Right?"

"I'm not agreeing with that," exclaimed Chip. "Dirtbags shouldn't get off the hook that easy. This guy needs a good thumping. You are going to pound him, aren't you, Rod?"

"Let's just see how this plays out," answered Rod in a calm voice. "Hopefully everyone stays cool and nobody gets hurt."

"I can see that B. A. and I are going to have to take the lead on this," said Chip smacking her fist into her open hand. "You two can stand behind us if it gets too rough."

"Okay," said B. A. closing her phone. "Cheryl says they're probably at the local party place just north of town. I told her where we're at, and she said we're real close. Turn right on Longhorn Road and then left on to a grassy lane a mile and a half later. If we see a barn that has fallen down, we went too far. Morrie drives a red Ford Taurus. She said she's coming out with her dad. This is getting serious."

Spiderwoman, the snake killer, and their two sidekicks turned on to Longhorn Road and found the grassy lane with no problem. Rod turned his headlights off, but left his running lights on. The moon was out, and it was a clear night, so that helped a little. They parked in the middle of the clearing and scoped out the area.

"There's a car to our right," observed Chip. "But I can't tell what color it is."

"There's another one straight ahead," said B. A., pointing.

"And one to our left," said Rod. "With our luck, they'll all be red. I guess it's time to do some recon, up close and personal. You girls stay here. Luke and I will start checking cars."

"No way," said Chip. "We're coming too."

Rod was now standing outside with his door still open. He leaned over the seat and pointed an oversized finger at his little cousin. "Stay! Who knows what people will do when two strangers approach them at night. This is Texas. They might have firearms."

Chip looked over at B. A. for support. B. A. put her hand on Chip's arm and shook her head to show that she agreed with her boyfriend. This was not a game. Rod and Luke took only a few steps toward the car on their left when the driver's door opened on the car to their right, and someone came out holding his face and gasping for air. B. A. leaned over the front seat and turned on the headlights. The car's lights weren't shining directly at the Taurus, but they lit up the clearing enough to see what was going on. Both of the girls jumped out of the car and ran over to the passenger side where Jenny was standing with a confident look on her face. In her right hand was a little can of pepper spray.

"Jenny," hollered Chip. "Are you all right?"

"I'm fine," said a relieved Jenny. She didn't really have a plan after the pepper spray. She did think about leaving her date out here and driving back to her car, but Morrie's lawyer comment made her think. His dad could probably twist things around and make it look like Jenny stole his son's car. "Are ya'll checking up on me again?"

Both of her friends shook their heads in the affirmative. Jenny hugged them both while thanking them profusely.

Rod walked over and picked up Morrie like he weighed about twenty pounds. "Whoa, tough guy. Are you all right? You don't look so good."

"I was okay until this witch sprayed me with something," wailed Morrie. "My dad's going to hear about this. I'm pressing charges."

Rod slapped Morrie hard across the face twice. "You're delusional, dude. Have you been drinking?"

Two car doors slammed on the far side of the clearing, and two very large guys approached the group. The one in the lead appeared to be about six feet three, weighing around 230 pounds. The guy behind was just a little smaller, but well over 200 pounds. Rod was still holding Morrie up as he was still recovering from the face slaps. His biceps looked like two baseballs resting on top of his arms.

"What's going on here, Morrie?" asked the guy in the lead. Morrie's face lit up in a smile, thinking reinforcements had just showed up.

"The little guy here has had a rough night," said Rod without looking at the two new additions to the group. "He made an offer that our friend was not supposed to refuse. But she refused anyway and glamour boy wouldn't take no for an answer."

"You know," said the big guy, looking strangely at Rod, "I could make a few calls and get half the Lakewood football team out here in short order. But I'm guessing you could make a few calls and get half the UNT football team over here. Am I right, Foster?"

Rod dropped Morrie on the ground, and he started to crawl back to his car while sneezing and rubbing his eyes. Rod turned and looked at the guy's face for the first time. He looked somewhat familiar. "Do I know you?"

"Probably not, but I know you. I was a freshman when Reston played us, and you kicked our butts. You were awesome, man. You went ten yards with three of our guys hanging on to you before you drug them across the goal line. I'm Josh Traynor and this is Jimmy Davis." The three of them shook hands and Rod introduced the rest of his group.

"So our prima donna here is still trying to score points," observed Josh. "I thought that was just a rumor going around. What did you do to him, Jenny?"

"She pepper sprayed the scum," said Chip.

"Ha, good for you, girl," said Josh. "It looks like he got what he deserved. Just because his dad's a lawyer and on the school board, this little toad thinks he runs the school. Now what?"

Luke went over to Morrie and helped him up. Morrie pushed Luke away and took a swing that grazed the side of Luke's head. Luke retaliated with a hard right that sent Morrie back to the grass. The rest of the group was in shock. Luke gave them a sheepish look as he walked back over to the group.

"Don't worry about it," said Rod as he gave Luke a fist bump. The other two guys followed suit. "He's a jerk. He got what he deserved."

Rod looked over at the two newcomers. "What did ya'll see here tonight?"

"If anybody asks," said Josh, "we saw a drunken Morrie having a problem with this girl and then Luke here, with your help, reacted when the prima donna here attempted to start a fight. Isn't that what we saw, Jimmy?"

"That's what I saw," said Jimmy as he and Josh turned to leave. "It was nice meeting ya'll."

Morrie pulled himself up by the car-door handle and stood there, swearing at the five of them. He was saying something about getting even, lawsuits, and the integrity of the Reston female population. The Reston contingent turned to walk away when another set of headlights came over the little hill that shielded the area from the road. The car stopped, and Cheryl Williams got out of the passenger side. An older man stepped out from behind the wheel.

"What's going on here, men?" asked the driver. He was obviously Cheryl's dad.

Rod turned to the older gentleman. "A small difference of opinion, sir. This idiot tried to make unwanted advances to our friend here. The problem has been solved, and no one got hurt much."

Mr. Williams went over to check on Morrie. Cheryl came over and hugged the Reston girls. When she was satisfied that Jenny was okay, she told them not to worry about anything. Her father was a lawyer. When they laughed at that statement, she gave them a funny look.

"Morrie said his dad was a lawyer too," explained B. A.

Cheryl snickered. "We call his type an *ambulance chaser*. I know attorneys don't like to hear that term, but in his case, it's true. Jenny, I'm so glad you are okay. Didn't these guys warn you about Morrie and his little club or whatever they call themselves?"

"They did," said Jenny. "But I was too stupid to believe them. I want to apologize to all of you. I should have listened. You are my best friends."

"C'mon, best friend," said Chip. "We'll take you back to your car. We'll ride back to Reston with you so you so you don't get into any more trouble along the way."

Mr. Williams put Morrie in the backseat of his car. He decided to take Morrie home and deliver him to his parents. He was in no condition to drive home anyway. He and Cheryl said their good-byes, and they headed in separate directions.

"Hey," said Mr. Williams once they were back on the road. "Were those the two girls that you are going to Michigan with?"

"Yup," answered Cheryl, looking at Morrie in the backseat. "They're nice girls too. I guess you found that out, huh Morrie?"

"Why didn't you introduce me?" asked her dad. "Those are two of the finest female athletes around."

"Hello, athletic daughter sitting right next to you."

"I know, sweetheart," said Mr. Williams. "You know, I think those girls would make great teammates."

"Yeah," said Cheryl. "Now all we have to do is get them to move to Lakewood."

"That's not what I was thinking," said her dad.

"You keep thinking, dad," laughed Cheryl. "That's why you make the big money. Let's get Senor Stud home. I'll clean up the backseat tomorrow."

"Who was the big guy with the huge arms that did all the talking?"

"That was Rod Foster, B. A.'s boyfriend. He is one muscular dude."

"He looks like a good guy to have around in a confrontation."

"I don't know anyone that would want to mess with him. How about you, Morrie?"

Morrie didn't respond. He just sat there feeling his fat lip.

Rod drove back to Reston with Luke in the front seat. The three girls followed in Jenny's car. The guys discussed Morrie and his sleazebag buddies. It was obvious that they had no respect for the opposite sex. Luke wondered out loud if some of the music they listened to had anything to do with it.

"A lot of songs guys sing today talk about how attractive girls with low morals are," said Luke. "And to be honest, a lot of female singers do the same thing. It's as if they don't know the difference between slutty and sexy. I mentioned that in a class discussion one day, and I got hooted for it. They said I was still living in the forties or fifties. If appreciating class and good manners makes me look like I'm not with it, then I don't think I want to be part of the self-proclaimed "cool" crowd. Is that why you like B. A.? I would say she's pretty classy."

"Yeah, that's one of the reasons," said Rod. "She's her own person, that's for sure. She doesn't complain much, but she does have a list of pet peeves. Some of them are pretty funny."

"Like what?" asked Luke.

"Oh no, I'm not telling you anything personal like that. That little spitfire would get it out of you in no time. I will say she still has a secret that you haven't figured out yet."

"What, like she's an awesome pitcher?"

"You know about that?" asked Rod in a surprised voice.

"Yeah, Chip told me. She's got a vault, but the door isn't locked all the time. She said B. A. will pitch when the time is right. Knowing her, she thinks B. A. will step up when the state championship is on the line and save the game. She fantasizes about that sort of stuff all the time. That would be some story though. I'd love to write that one up."

B. A. followed Rod and Luke in Jenny's car. She convinced Jenny that she shouldn't be driving because of her emotional state. Jenny surrendered the keys without an argument.

"Did ya'll see Luke drop that scum with one punch?" asked Chip.

"Does he get a superhero name too?" asked B. A.

"Naw, one lucky punch does not make a superhero," answered Chip. "I am proud of him though. I thought the big guy went too easy on him. Whatever, Morrie got what he deserved. I wanted a shot at him too. What do you think the guys at his school would have said when they found out that a girl punched him out?"

"I don't think that little fist of yours is capable of punching anybody out," said B. A.

Jenny snickered.

"It looks like she's back," said Chip, leaning forward and patting Jenny on the back.

"I can't tell you how stupid I feel," said Jenny. "I don't know why I ever doubted you. When you want something so bad, I guess your thinking can really get messed up. You won't believe it, but my sister even cautioned me about Morrie. If it's okay with you two, I don't think I'll tell anyone about what happened tonight. He didn't get very far. He refused when I asked him to take me back to my car. Then when he started to slide over on the seat, I just let him have it. You should have seen the look on his face. That pepper spray really works. I was holding my breath, but I had to get out of there fast or I would have been choking like him. Thanks again for getting it for me, Chip. I don't know what I would have done without it."

"No problem," said Chip. "So I'd say it was a good day, sort of. I mean we solved two problems. B. A. says Victor is going to handle Diego, and we got our friend back nondamaged and in good shape. So how about we focus on softball? From now on, except for the obvious, it's going to be smooth sailing right to the state championship."

Jenny looked over at B. A. and mouthed *nondamaged*. B. A. raised her eyebrows and shook her head from side to side, signifying that Jen should let it go. They both knew what Chip meant.

Big Shirley to the Rescue

Big Shirley Fosse was feeling pretty good about herself. She hadn't been in detention for a month, and her grades weren't too bad; she was only failing two subjects. History was all about a bunch of dead guys and math was just a waste of time. When were you ever going to use that stuff anyway? To her way of thinking, school was stupid except for the foods class she was taking. Now that was something a girl could use. Maybe she would open her own restaurant someday. In her mind, she would be a great boss. She was good at ordering people around, so why not get paid for it?

Chip stood at her shortstop position and watched Tammi throw her warm-up pitches for the top of the seventh inning. With Reston leading six to three, Chip, B. A., and Jenny were all having a great game. Jenny was back to her old self, and if anything, her ordeal with Morrie strengthened her friendship with Chip and B. A. They were worried about the side effects, but Jenny seemed to be coping nicely. All three of them had two hits and had played flawlessly in the field. B. A. came back in typical form by blasting the second pitch to her over the left-field fence. The whole team couldn't help but notice the increase in crowd size and the amount of sports reporters that were now showing up for their games. Coaches Brown and Harbison told B. A. and Chip to be nice and answer their questions. So far, against their will, they had been cooperating.

Tammi walked the first girl to start the seventh. The second batter popped one up along the first baseline, and it looked like a simple play for Jenny. Darby, the catcher, even hollered for Jenny to take it. Tammi didn't see it that way. There were a lot of people and reporters there to impress. She came over at the last second, calling loudly for the ball. Before Jenny could get out of the way, Tammi crashed into her, taking both of them to the ground. The ball fell to the dirt in foul territory. Coach Harbison slammed her clipboard on her knee. She had had enough of Tammi's shenanigans. Whether it was basketball or softball, that girl was a huge pain in the backside. She looked over at Coach Brown, and he was staring intently at his pitcher. It was obvious that he wasn't happy either. He finally called time and went out to settle his team down. Tammi was indignant and wouldn't listen to her coach or her teammates. She said the ball was hers, and Jenny should have backed off. As Coach Brown turned to go back to the dugout, he did a strange thing. He turned and stared at his right fielder for about five seconds. The people around the diamond didn't catch the significance of the look, but Chip knew what it was all about. B. A. didn't see the stare as she was looking and talking to Rachel over in center. Her coach muttered to himself all the way back to the dugout.

The visitors ended up scoring two runs in the top of the seventh, but it wasn't enough. Tammi and the team racked up a six to five win. They had now won twelve out of their last thirteen games.

Their only loss in that stretch was to Kennedy and Carrie Booth. They would have their chance to get revenge on Kennedy because the next game was at their place in two days. The rematch was on the girls' minds when they met for lunch on Wednesday. Chip laid it on the line.

"If we don't score more runs, we're toast. That Booth girl is tough. She throws hard, and she's deceptive. Do you think you can hit another one off of her, B. A.?"

"I wouldn't count on that. She's the best and smartest pitcher we've faced all year."

"Keep an eye on their assistant coach," added Jenny. "After what B. A. did to her last game, she might have something up her sleeve."

"What can a first-base coach do to her?" asked Lu. "Trip her on her way to second?"

The group was still laughing when Luke came over and sat down. He looked extremely stressed about something.

"What's going on?" asked Chip.

"I think I might have done something that I'm going to regret," admitted Luke.

"That punch you threw the other night might have been the first step to a whole new you," observed Chip. "What did you do now?"

Luke explained what had just happened in history class. "Mrs. Gunderson has been real mean to our class lately. I'm not exaggerating here either. As classes go, we're not too bad. They're a few goof-offs in there, but basically we pay attention to her dry lectures, and we do the worksheets that she loves to hand out. She can turn an interesting subject into a dull one in a matter of minutes. You know how much I like history, so it must be pretty bad for me to complain."

"Give us the short version," said Chip. "Lunch is about over."

"Okay, so she hands out this true-false quiz, fifteen questions on the Civil War, and announces that the best grade will probably be no better than a *C*. The she tries to be funny and says why bother taking the quiz if we all just agree to a *D-*. That way, she won't have to grade them. A couple of the guys said they were all for that. You know, thinking she was serious. I'm getting one of the only *A*s in there, so I'm a little insulted. I look the quiz over and decide to pull something out of B. A.'s playbook. I went for the totally unexpected."

Now he had the group's full attention. Chip impatiently motioned for him to go on.

"The first question was, 'The battle of Bull Run and the Battle of Manassas were fought on the same day.' If you remember, a lot of the time, the south named the battles after the closest town, and the north named them after a physical feature like a creek, a river, or a hill. So they were actually the same battle. The two sides just called it by a different name. So the answer is true, but I mark it false."

"Why would you do that?" asked a skeptical Chip.

"Stick with me. This gets better. The second question was, 'Stonewall Jackson was not at the Battle of Gettysburg because he was back fighting in Virginia.' That is false, because Stonewall was already dead by the time that battle was fought. I marked it true."

"All right," said Chip. "This makes no sense at all. I don't know anyone that makes mistakes on purpose. You better come up with something to impress us in the next two minutes, or we're going to forget this whole thing."

"Get ready to be impressed. I missed them all on purpose."

"I get it," said Lu. "You were telling her that if you get them all wrong, you must know the right answers."

"And," added B. A., "if you messed up and got one of them right or in this case wrong, you showed that you would be willing to settle for a score of one out of fifteen."

"Cool," said Lu. "You are quite the gambler. Did you get them all wrong?"

"When she had all the quizzes, Mrs. G. asks, 'Who thinks they got a hundred?' She had this sick little smile on her face, so I raised my hand. Now she starts to give us the answers, and she grades my paper as she's doing this. She says I missed the first one so there's no way I could get a hundred. Then she makes a big red check mark on my quiz like she's making fun of me. Here's where I made my mistake. I kinda rubbed her face in it. I said something like, 'I wouldn't bet on that.' She gave me a weird, 'you're just a stupid kid look' and continued. You should have seen the look on her face when she got about halfway through. She stopped making the check marks at about number ten. Her face went red, and she stared daggers at me."

"The old stink-eye," said Jenny.

"Yup. At that point, she said she would see me after school. If she wouldn't have made such a big deal out of it, I wouldn't have either. I got my hundred. They were just all wrong instead of all right."

"That's gutsy," said Chip. "You're turning into a real tiger in more ways than one. I like it. Do you think she'll give you a zero just for spite?"

"I don't know," said a dejected Luke. "I guess I'll find out right after school."

The action didn't wait for the last bell of the day. It started much earlier.

Reston High School had eight classes per day. Fifth hour was the lunch period. There were about four hundred students in the building, so there were three lunch periods. About one third of the students ate before fifth hour, one third ate after fifth hour, and the remaining third went to lunch halfway through fifth hour. The split class was the longest class of the day and the toughest for student and teacher alike. Halfway through the split class, everyone had to stop what they were doing and break for lunch. After lunch, it always took a while for the students to get settled down. Some settled down too quick. They were the ones that had to fight falling asleep. Some of them didn't put up much of an effort.

Shirley Fosse walked slowly down the hall with her passbook in hand. Unbeknownst to the teachers and the administration, she had two passbooks. The second book came courtesy of a freshman that left it in the gym on the very first day of school. Shirley carefully erased the freshman's name and entered hers. She took great pains to make the books look alike. Now she had twice as many hall passes to use, and she took full advantage of this fact. Shirley ate during first lunch, but felt the need to socialize during second lunch also, so she filled out her book and went up to the teacher. Normally a teacher wouldn't let a student out of class right after they had spent a half hour in the lunchroom, but this was Shirley. The class ran smoother when she wasn't in there, which meant the teacher was only too happy to sign her book. She would have liked to add, "Take your time coming back," but decided to just enjoy Shirley's absence along with the rest of the students in her fifth hour class.

Shirley made a right into the girls' restroom and was disappointed to see no one in there. Usually a couple of her buds would be in there, planning some sort of mischief. The main topics ranged from the usual drama to where they could get cigarettes or beer. Shirley looked under the stall doors and saw two pairs of legs in stall number three. Interesting. The feet were facing each other and the occupants were whispering back and forth. A drug deal? She went over to the sink and washed her hands. The whispering stopped. Now she was intrigued. What the heck was going on? She decided to pretend to leave. Maybe the people, she assumed they were girls, would start talking again. She walked to the door, opened it, then let it close by itself. Now she was standing silently just inside the door. The occupants in the number three stall started up again.

"I'm telling you it's true," said one of the girls. Shirley couldn't make out the owner of the voice. "Some dude paid Charlotte Murphy two hundred dollars to start a fight with B. A. Smith. It's supposed to happen between sixth and seventh hour."

"I ain't believing it," said the second girl. "Why would they do that?"

"The story is there are some guys betting on high-school games, even softball. They bet on all sorts of stuff. Not just who will win but by how much. I think it's called the spread. Also there's extra money if a team gets shut out or if they win by the ten-run rule. It's all pretty complicated. Anyway, the story is there's a lot of money on Kennedy shutting us out tomorrow. That Booth girl is a real good pitcher. The guys betting on Kennedy probably have to give odds. Don't ask me what that means. All I know is, if Smith gets suspended for fighting, there's a good chance we won't even score, and the betters will make some extra cash. We only scored one against them last time, and that was on Smith's homer. Pretty slick strategy, don't you think?"

"It all sounds pretty stupid to me," said girl number two. "What's the penalty for betting on high-school sports?"

"I don't know, and I don't need to know 'cause I ain't betting. What I am gonna do is hang around the biology room right after sixth hour. That's where Charlotte is supposed to take Smith down."

"Charlotte better be careful, or she's going to get a two hundred dollar beat down. She will get some cash and a couple of days off of school though. That's a pretty sweet deal. I'll bet she's got somebody lined up to pull them apart right after the action starts. Smith will walk right through her. I gotta admit, I didn't think Charlotte was that smart."

"She ain't that smart," said girl number one. "Do you think these guys would pick a smart person to do the job? The only one dumber in this school is Shirley Fosse."

Both girls laughed at that last statement.

"Let's get back to class," said girl number one. "I'm going to get in trouble for being gone so long as it is. Remember, biology room, right after sixth hour."

Shirley slipped out the door before the two talkers came out of the stall and walked a few quick steps to the drinking fountain. She wanted to see who the two girls were. Maybe she could put a name to the voice that called her dumb. If she couldn't decide who said it, she'd just have to kick both their butts. The girls came out and headed in the other direction. They were both freshmen. No wonder she didn't recognize their voices. She didn't think she'd have any trouble picking them out of a crowd in the future. She saw just enough of their faces, and she wasn't likely to forget what they looked like.

Shirley had some thinking to do. B. A. was not one of her favorite people, but she did respect her. Smith didn't make a big deal over the arm wrestling thing last fall. In fact, Smith usually said hi to her when they passed in the hall. Not when it was crowded, but when there were only a few people in the hallway. She was an awesome athlete, and her boyfriend was really hot. Shirley walked back into class and went to her seat. The teacher didn't say a word about her being gone for fifteen minutes. She smiled to herself. Sometimes it was good to be Big Shirley.

B. A. stayed to talk to her algebra teacher for about a minute after her sixth-hour class. She had brought her grade up to a *C*, and she was feeling good about it. She headed down the hall and saw Jenny coming from the opposite direction. When she slowed down to talk to her, a girl she didn't know bumped into her real hard.

"Hey," hollered Charlotte. "Watch where you're going, klutz. You think you own the hallway or something, superstar?"

"No, sorry," said B. A. Jenny caught up and stood a few feet away. She gave Charlotte a strange look, trying to figure out what was going on. The hall traffic stopped as soon as Charlotte hollered at B. A.

"She thinks she owns the hall," shouted Charlotte even louder. Surprisingly, there weren't any teachers in the area yet.

"I don't like being pushed. Maybe I'll slap you around a bit. Someone should teach you some hall etiquette."

"C'mon, B. A.," said Jenny. "This girl's nuts."

"Punch her, Charlotte," said one of her friends. "She's not so tough."

"Are you going to talk or fight?" asked one of the boys in front.

Shirley hustled out the door as soon as the bell rang. The teacher was about to say something about lining up at the door before class was over but decided to let that go too. The big girl could move pretty fast when she wanted to. She figured she had about one minute to get over to the other hallway. It was a good thing that B. A. had stayed to talk to her math teacher. Otherwise, the timing would have been off. As it was, Shirley pushed her way through the crowd just as the boy in front asked his question.

Shirley assessed the situation and decided to take action. "I've been looking for you, Charlotte," said Shirley in a loud voice. "You've been bad-mouthing me all over the place." With that, Shirley picked up a confused Charlotte Murphy and slammed her up against the locker. The breath went out of the stunned antagonist as Shirley held her off the ground. The crowd didn't know what to think. Finally, the boy in front that wanted to see Charlotte and B. A. fight let out with a loud, "Yeah! That's what I'm talking about."

Mr. Fox saw the crowd and hustled over to it. There were several students between him and Shirley when he saw the big girl pick up the smaller one and slam her against the locker. "All right," he shouted. "Get to class people. Shirley, be nice and put her down."

"Anything you say, Mr. Fox," said Shirley as she let Charlotte slide down the locker. "She's a little too puny to hit. She might break. She's got an awfully big mouth though." With that last statement, Shirley looked over at B. A. and Jenny and winked.

B. A. couldn't believe it. She remembered winking at Shirley when she slammed the big girl's hand to the table in their arm-wrestling contest. Now Shirley was winking at her. What was going on? Before she turned with Jenny and headed to class, she returned the wink. Shirley laughed, while Charlotte just stood there, still shaking with a scared look on her face.

"What the heck was that all about?" asked Jenny as she and B. A. hurried to their next class.

"I don't know," answered B. A. "But somehow I get the feeling that Shirley just did me a favor. Who was that Charlotte girl? I don't even know her."

"Just a sophomore tough girl wannabe," said Jenny as they turned into their English 3 class. "I'm beginning to think there's something to this action magnate thing. I was just playing along with Chip before, but now I'm a believer. Wait 'til Chip hears about this."

"Word travels fast around here," said B. A. "I'm sure she already knows about it."

Sure enough, when Jenny and B. A. filed out of their seventh-hour class Chip was already standing there.

"Now what are you up to Spid—"

"Don't call me Spiderwoman," interrupted B. A. "You're starting to give me a complex. To answer all the questions running through your little imaginative mind, some weird girl tried to start a fight with me. Then Shirley Fosse stepped in and slammed her against the locker. Mr. Fox took them both to the office. End of story."

"Tell her about the wink," added Jenny.

"Oh yeah, and Shirley winked at me. I have no idea why. There, you have it."

"I already knew all of that except for the wink," said Chip. "I'll pass the wink part on to Luke to see if he wants to do an investigation. Do me a favor. Don't start any trouble for the next two periods. We can't afford to lose you for any more games. You get at least a two-day suspension for fighting you know."

It dawned on B. A. as she sat in Spanish class why Charlotte tried to pick a fight with her. Someone was trying to get her suspended. Maybe it was Morrie. No, it had to be someone else. It sure was tough to lay low in this environment. She looked over at Jenny and the tall girl made a face at her. B. A. rolled her eyes back at her. The phone rang, and the Spanish teacher answered it, then she motioned for B. A. to come up to the desk.

Mr. Woodley, the assistant principal, told B. A. to sit down when she entered his office. It was her first time in there. There were pictures of his wife and children on the wall along with some of him playing college baseball. She didn't know that he played for TCU. He was about to say something when Coach Brown walked in and sat down.

"All right, B. A." said the A. P. "What happened between you, Charlotte, and Shirley? I want to hear your side."

"I'm not sure what that was all about," said B. A. "This Charlotte girl said I pushed her in the hall and started hollering at me. I don't even know her. Then some other students tried to get us to fight. Before anything happened, Shirley showed up and slammed her against the locker."

"You didn't say anything to her to set her off?" asked the A. P.

"No, I think I just said sorry when she accused me of running into her."

"That's pretty much the story I heard," said Mr. Woodley, looking over at Coach Brown. "I've got one more question for you. Do you think you can hit another homer off Booth tomorrow? An old college buddy of mine teaches at Kennedy, and we've got a friendly little bet on it."

"I'll do my best," said B. A. "Am I in any trouble?"

"No, you're fine. Just go out and hit that homer tomorrow. Oh yeah, and win too."

"See you at practice, Coach," said B. A. as she walked out the door.

When B. A. had left, Mr. Woodley looked over at Coach Brown. "I probably shouldn't have made that comment about betting with my buddy. Murphy cracked immediately when I threatened to get the police involved. She told me that someone offered her two hundred bucks to start a fight with Smith. Someone sure wanted her to miss the Kennedy game. I don't know about you, but to me that sounds like there's money on the game. What's next, betting on quiz bowl?"

"We've got our hands full enough dealing with these kids," added Coach Brown. "Now the adults are getting involved and messing things up even more."

"Believe me, I've had enough adults in this office, trying to mess things up for their kids," said the A.P. "We need more like Smith and her group around here. It sure would make things go smoother."

"I hear you," said Coach Brown as he got up to leave. "But if everything ran real smooth, you and I wouldn't make the big money, now would we?"

"True that, Coach. Go get them tomorrow. You're going to need a little something extra to beat Kennedy with Booth pitching."

"I was thinking the same thing myself," responded Coach Brown as he walked out.

⚾

Mr. Woodley looked over at Shirley Fosse as she sat outside his office, waiting for a parent to come and pick her up. Shirley had the strangest grin on her face, and she seemed to be humming quietly to herself. She sensed that he was looking at her and turned toward him. Her little grin broke into a big smile, and then she gave him the thumbs-up gesture. As he returned the gesture, he figured out what had just happened. Shirley had just put a whole knew twist on *taking one for the team*. He shook his head and chuckled. Shirley went back to her humming.

B. A. was on her way back to class when she passed by the open door to the biology room. She could see Chip and a lab partner, working on something. She got Chip's attention and shook her head like she was in big trouble. Then she waved like she was leaving. When Chip hollered, "What?" she quickly moved on down the hall. B. A. didn't hear the biology teacher chastise Chip for not staying focused and for scaring her lab partner and most everyone else in the room. She had better start taking the labs seriously, or she'd be sitting the next one out in the office.

Introductions

Chip, B. A. and Jenny were sitting in the back of the bus on the way to the Kennedy game. They were excited for the upcoming game and for Lu. She was running in the conference championship this afternoon. Lu had just broken her own school record again and appeared to be in the best shape of her career. She had recently beaten Tracie Morgan by three seconds in their highly touted rematch. Everything was in place for her run at the state title.

"So Diego has to work at Kim's store for a month without pay, is that it?" asked Chip.

"Yep, that's the deal," answered B. A. "Rod said Diego and Victor went over to the store, and Diego fessed up to everything. He also said Mr. Kim was real calm about the whole thing."

"He's getting off too easy," said Chip.

"How about twenty lashes too?" asked Jenny.

"That's barbaric," said Chip. "I think he should have to wear a T-shirt that says he's a thief. He should have to wear it for a month."

"Some people don't have it as good as we do," continued Jenny. "He was just trying to do something for his family. It was the wrong thing to do, but he's just a kid like us. Kids make mistakes you know. Trust me, I know all about making big mistakes."

Jenny's comment about some people having it better than others started Chip thinking about her personal project. She decided that to achieve better balance in her life, she should help someone else out. Hanging around with Luke all these years had taught her to be a keen observer. Lately she had been watching a little freshman girl, Stacy Wellington. She had noticed that Stacy wore only two different sets of clothes to school, and sometimes they weren't all that clean. Were those Stacy's favorite clothes, or was that all she had to wear? She decided to do some investigating, but she had to do it without arousing anyone's suspicion. She wasn't even going to bring Luke in on this one, at least for a while.

Jenny brought both of her friends back to the task at hand when she said, "We really need to win this game. We've beaten some good teams, but a victory over Kennedy would make us one of the best teams in the whole area. People are talking about us especially since we had so much success in basketball. They'd really be talking if we beat Kennedy. I think they've only lost two games all season and to bigger schools too."

"I can do without all the talk about us," said B. A. as she closed her eyes for a little nap.

"That didn't come out right," said Jenny. "We've been playing so well. Courtney is starting to hit, and Kris is playing an awesome second base. If our shortstop would shape up, we would be incredible."

"Hey," said Chip. "Who was all-area player of the week last week?"

"Just kidding, short stuff," said Jenny, laughing. "But B. A. has won that honor twice."

"Home runs are just like dunking a basketball," retorted Chip. "It's easy if you know how to do it. Sometimes B. A.'s uniform never even gets dirty. She just hits it over the fence and trots around the bases. Big deal. She's making a mockery of the game."

"It's easier to get your uniform clean that way," said B. A., opening one eye. "I toss it in the washing machine after each game, and I'm good to go. I'll bet your mommy washes yours, doesn't she?"

"Most of the time," admitted Chip. "I messed up a load a few months ago and was told to stay away from the machine for a while. Before you ask, I doubled up on the soap, thinking it would help get the clothes extra clean. It got all over the laundry-room floor. It was a mess, and mom was not happy."

"Cute," said Jenny. "Listen, I know the real weak spot on the team is my sister. It sounds funny saying your pitcher is your biggest problem in fast pitch softball especially when you are winning most of your games. But if she would stop worrying about what makes her look good or bad, we could be awesome. Don't you feel us coming together the way we did in basketball?"

"Come together, right now, over me," sang B. A. in a whispery voice.

"I'm trying to be serious here, and she's singing Beatles's songs," said Jenny.

"Leave her alone," said Chip. "She's got a big game ahead of her."

The first two-and-a-half innings of the Kennedy game were noneventful. Chip and Jenny had seeing-eye singles, but that was it. B. A. struck out in her only appearance at the plate. The bottom of the third was a different story. Tammi walked the first batter on four pitches. A wild pitch sent the runner to second. The pitcher made a gesture at her catcher, indicating she thought Darby should have caught the ball. Tammi didn't realize she was picking on the only teammate that supported her. The next batter bunted, and Maria, at third base, didn't field it cleanly, so she held on to it, not wanting to risk a bad throw on a girl that was obviously going to be safe. The tall pitcher was now fuming. The opposing coach, sensing a meltdown, gave the take sign to his batter. Sure enough, Tammi walked the third batter on four pitches to load the bases. She was out there, making gestures and exhibiting just plain poor sportsmanship. Coach Brown had finally had enough. He told Carmen to go behind the dugout and warm up in case they needed her. Then he called time out.

"Are you going to pull her?" asked Coach Harbison.

"Yes, and I've got something else in mind," said Coach Brown as he got up and headed out on to the field. Leroy Brown walked out of the dugout and straight past his pitcher. He was headed toward right field. He motioned for his shortstop to join him. The rest of the team didn't know what to make of this unconventional move. The umpires gave each other a questioning look. When her coach stepped on the outfield grass, B. A. dropped down and pretended to tie her shoe. She was still down on one knee when his feet came into her field of vision. A smaller pair of softball shoes showed up a second later.

Tammi asked the umpire if she could toss a few to her catcher. She figured B. A. was either hurt or in trouble with the coach. She had no idea what was really going down in right field.

"Hello," said Coach Brown, extending his hand. "I'm retired Gunnery Sergeant, Leroy Brown, and I'm a Congressional Medal of Honor winner. And you are?"

B. A. stood up slowly. Her coach had a very serious look on his face. She got the impression that this was going to be a one-time thing. He was asking her to pitch. If she turned him down, he wouldn't bother her about it again. Chip looked at her coach then to B. A. She was totally confused. The base umpire started to walk out toward them.

B. A. looked Leroy straight in the eye and asked him in a serious voice, "You got it on you?"

Coach Brown grinned. This girl sure had some brass. "Would it make a difference?" he asked.

"No," said B. A. "I've seen it before."

"I know," said Coach Brown. "Do you have any secrets you'd like to divulge?"

"Well?" asked the base umpire as he caught up with them.

With a sigh of resignation, B. A. extended her hand. "I'm Annie Smith, a transfer student from Jones Ferry, Arkansas. I play right field, and I pitch a little."

Coach Brown's hand closed firmly around hers. "Would you consider pitching a little now? Your team needs you."

"Please do," said the umpire sarcastically. "It's getting dark out here."

B. A. looked at Chip's pleading eyes. She nodded to her coach and then inclined her head toward Chip. He got the message. Coach Brown turned and told the ump that he had two substitutions and a couple of position changes. As they walked back toward the infield and a whole bunch of confused players and fans, the coach told Chip to put the spare catching gear on. It would probably be a good idea not to have Tammi's friend catch the new pitcher. Chip whooped and ran toward the dugout.

"What's going on?" asked Jenny as they passed her on the way to the mound.

The coach went over to her before he went to the home plate ump with his changes. He put his hand on her shoulder. "I'm sorry, Jenny. I'm going to pull your sister. I...this whole team has had enough of her antics."

"I know," said Jenny with tears in her eyes. "You're right, Coach. Do what you think is best."

The coach waved Darby out to the circle and told her and Tammi he was subbing for them. Then he went to the plate umpire and made his changes. Annie played catch with Maria, the third baseman, while they waited for Chip to get her gear on. As soon as she was ready, Chip called for time and ran out to her pitcher.

"You've already got the longest time-out on record," hollered the ump. "Let's get going. You get seven pitches and that's it."

"You have been promoted to the title of action queen," said Chip. "This is going to be awesome. Okay, one for fast, two wiggled for change, and three for a rise ball. What else do you have?"

"Four wiggle for a hook and fist for a drop ball. One more thing, and this is gonna seem weird. I throw the first three pitches overhand. It's like a tradition that I used to do with my dad. Don't let the fans bother you. They will make some comments when they see it."

"No worries," said Chip. "How do you think Tammi's going to take this?"

"Not well, but we've got a game to win right now. We'll worry about that later. She brought all this on herself. One more thing, would you call me Annie?"

"I'm not even going to ask about that. I heard sugarlips call you that once. I figured it was a pet name."

"Nope, it's just my name."

"Ladies," said the ump as he approached the pitcher's circle. "If you're not too busy. I'd like to get started. I don't want to have to turn the lights on."

"Yes, sir," said Chip with a salute. She ran back to the plate and got ready for Annie's first delivery.

Annie looked over at the dugout and saw Tammi and Darby sitting next to each other in quiet conversation. She felt bad for Tammi. With all her bluster and hubris, she was still just a high school girl trying to get through all the trials and tribulations that most teens go through. Her misguided approach was definitely annoying. Annie wondered what started it all. Was it a defining moment, or did she gradually become the person she is today little by little? It would be interesting to see or hear her take on Annie's pitching debut. Annie looked toward her catcher who was settled in and waiting for her teammate's first Texas pitch. Annie Smith, transfer student from Arkansas, did not disappoint her. Annie threw her warm-up pitches then looked around the infield at her teammates. *This is going to be much better than it was back in Arkansas*, she thought. *I've got some quality friends here, and my teammates support each other especially when somebody messes up. Our coaches are the best too. Dad, I wish you were here.*

Your little girl isn't so little any more. Thanks again for all the things you taught me. She wiped the tears from her eyes and looked in at her catcher. The umpire was pointing at her to get on with it. She went to work and proceeded to strike out the next three batters. She used mostly fastballs and riseballs, but she sent a message to Booth. After two fastball strikes, she threw her hook and got the other team's star to back away from the pitch. It curved nicely back across the plate for a called strike three. The home plate umpire said, "Wow," after that pitch. Carrie Booth walked away and didn't say a thing.

Annie held Kennedy at bay for the rest of the game. Neither team had scored yet when Chip lead off the bottom of the seventh with a bunt single. Kris sacrificed her to second with another bunt. Annie promptly hit Booth's first pitch between the pitcher and second baseman. Chip took two slide steps and paused to make sure the ball got through the infield. She raced around third, expecting a play at the plate, but the throw never came.

"We beat Kennedy," hollered Chip, as the team walked up to their bus. "Can you believe it? I thought those reporters would never stop asking questions. I was glad when Coach told them we had to leave."

Jenny, Annie, and Chip stopped halfway up the aisle. Tammi and Darby were already in their customary seats at the back of the bus. Annie plopped down in the nearest seat, and Jenny and Chip sat across from her. Jenny had a concerned look on her face. She wondered if she should go back and sit with her sister. Tammi had to be hurting. She pretty much lived for her role as one of Reston's star athletes. Playing a supporting role was not going to suit her. Jenny looked over at Annie. "So we're supposed to call you Annie now?"

"Yeah, it's what people have always called me," said Annie. "Well, until I moved here. The B. A. experiment is over. I hope the FBI doesn't have a problem with it."

"What's that about the FBI?" asked Chip as she fiddled with her iPod.

"Nothing," said Annie. The transfer student then did something that she was becoming famous for. She looked Jenny in the eye and motioned with her eyes to go to the back of the bus and sit with her sister. With a sigh, Jenny got up and headed back. "Sisters are forever," whispered Annie as she put her earbuds in.

Later that evening, Chip walked into the living room with Luke in tow. They had been in her room, discussing the game and Annie's emergence as a top pitcher in the area, maybe the whole state. She made Luke promise that he wouldn't make a big deal about it in the school newspaper. He agreed only if they could go out for a late snack. Surprisingly, Chip agreed to the deal. Even to the part where she was buying.

"Watch this," said Chip over her shoulder. "And get ready to run."

As usual, her parents were quietly reading.

"Mom, Dad, what are some of the early signs of a pregnancy? It's, uh, for a survey in my health class."

Luke froze in his tracks. Both parents looked past their daughter and gave him the super stink eye. He moved his hands back and forth in denial and shook his head from side to side. They could tell that he was taken by surprise as much as they were. When her dad started to get up, Chip broke for the door. "Run, Luke, he's got a shotgun."

The two teens ran to Luke's car and sped out the driveway. "Don't ever do that again," said Luke, breathing hard as if he had just raced Lu in the mile.

"They knew I was joking," said Chip as she messed with the radio. "I had to come up with something to get even for pretending they were going to cut my leg open."

"Is that what life is about with you, getting even with people?"

"You make it sound so sinister when you put it that way. But yeah, I like to keep the books balanced so to speak. Speaking of balance, I need to talk to you about something. I'll mention it to my parents too as soon as they cool down. Luckily, they don't hold grudges."

"Where did you get that little trait then?" asked Luke.

"I don't know," said Chip as she contemplated the question. "Just developed it all on my own, I guess. Listen I've been thinking about giving a bunch of my old clothes and some other things to a girl at school. She doesn't appear to have much, and I'm sure she could use them. We're about the same size. Think it's a good idea?"

"Maybe. Give me a kiss first."

"What? Why?"

"I'm giving you a reward for being so thoughtful."

Chip pulled her seat belt out at the shoulder so she could lean over and kiss him. "There, I think you were rewarded as much as I was."

"You know it," said Luke with a smug look. "Now, what were we talking about?"

"We were talking about me giving some things to a freshman girl."

"Oh yeah. I think it's a good idea, but maybe you should do it through a third party. That way you would remain anonymous, and she wouldn't be embarrassed if you saw her at school, and she thought you were looking at your old clothes. Did I go back on your list for tricking you out of a kiss?"

"Actually I tricked *you* out of the kiss. And you are on my list for events that are much more gravitational than something as silly as that."

What a night! thought Luke. *Annie is a star pitcher, I'm getting a free pizza, and I tricked the mistress of subterfuge into giving me a kiss. This has been a good evening in the life of future sports reporter for the* New York Daily News, *Luke Slowinski. Heh, heh, heh.*

"What are you chuckling about?" asked Chip.

"I'm just thinking what your parents are going to say when you get home. I think you finally got a legitimate rise out of them. I'd be careful if I were you. They still have strong gravitational grounding power."

"I'll just lay low for a few days. It will blow over. I'll do something really nice that they don't expect from me. I should be doing more of that kinda stuff anyway. Speaking of doing something nice, can you get us some little Reston softballs like the basketballs we distributed at the hospital? I'm working on a little field trip for the four of us. Do you think the school has something that Lu can hand out?"

"I think I can get the little softballs," said Luke as he turned into the Pizza Palace parking lot. "Mrs. Jackson has a whole closet full of that kind of stuff. I've never seen any track items in there. Maybe we could have the shop class make up some little batons. We could put Lu's school record time for the 1600 on them. That would be sorta cool."

"Excellent," said Chip. "I'll leave that little chore up to you. We need them by next week though. The nursing-home lady is supposed to call me back tomorrow. She seemed pretty excited about having us visit."

"Good for you. The high school students need to do more of that community service stuff. It would definitely improve our reputation. I'm sure you've noticed that our rep isn't the best with the older generation."

"Yeah," agreed Chip. "We talked about that in class the other day. A lot of teens are nepotistic. You know, really in to themselves."

"I think you mean narcissistic—extremely self-centered. And to be honest, I agree. Do you remember in our freshman world history class on the first day? Mr. Canfield said that we're special but not nearly as special as our parents think we are or as special as we think we are."

"Well, one little miss special was put in her place at today's game. I feel really bad for Jen. Tammi is her sister even though she is a pain most of the time."

"You know what?" asked Luke as he turned off the car and looked over at his girlfriend. "I feel bad for Tammi. It might sound corny, but she pretty much lives for sports as much as ya'll do. I don't think she's going to take this very well. Do you think she'll quit the team now that she isn't the number one pitcher?"

"I'm glad to hear you say that about Tammi," said Chip in a serious tone. "I feel bad for her too. I've spent years hoping she would fall on her face, but now that it's happened, it's not what I expected. Rooting against people especially your own teammate is poor sportsmanship. How's that for maturity and balance? And to answer your question, I have no idea what she'll do next."

"Hopefully, Jenny can talk her out of quitting," said Luke. "I hope your checkbook is as balanced as you are because this stimulating conversation has increased my appetite from snack to major feast."

The two of them got out and walked across the parking lot hand in hand. Chip was thinking about Jenny, her multiple projects, getting even with Rod for something that presently escaped her mind, what her parents would do when she got home, and tomorrow's biology quiz. Luke was thinking about a sports article that focused on self-centeredness and today's teens.

Mr. and Mrs. Fullerton were both waiting up for their only daughter when she walked in. Her little comment didn't just blow over.

"Melinda," said Karen Fullerton, once the three of them were seated around the kitchen table. "Your father and I are somewhat worried about your little comment when you and Luke were leaving earlier."

"Mom, Dad, you don't have to worry about Luke and me," explained Chip. "You did a great job raising me and you filled my head with good stuff. I was just kidding about the pregnancy thing to add some excitement to your otherwise dreary lives. Y'all practically live in those chairs out in the living room. When I go to the Michigan camp, why don't you two take a vacation, or at least throw a wild party? It will be good for you. Luke and I have enough excitement in our lives. We're not going to mess things up in a moment of craziness."

"Just the same," said her dad. "We still worry about you. There seems to be a lot of 'moments of craziness' going on with today's teenagers."

"Dad, you shouldn't lump my friends and me in with a bunch of narcolistic teens. I get good grades and I respect my elders. I don't spend much time talking about nothing on the phone or texting nonsense. And, you have to admit, I even know how to speak like I'm learning something in school. Most of the other kids put themselves first in a conversation, even though the teachers are on them all the time about the way they talk. Thanks to you, Dad, I can even make change for customers at the store. That alone should prove to you about how well-balanced I am. I appreciate your concern, but there's nothing to worry about. Your kid turned out just fine. Great job, you two."

Mr. and Mrs. Fullerton watched as their only daughter walked out of the kitchen heading for her room.

"I had this whole lecture prepared," said John, "then she took over the conversation. Maybe she's right. We did do a great job raising her."

"Just the same," said Karen, "when she gets back from her trip, let's tell her we joined a cult. We could tell her that we did it on her suggestion to spice up our 'dreary little lives'."

"So that's where she gets her off-the-wall ideas. Join a cult if you want. I'm going to finish the chapter I'm on in my book, and then I'm going to bed. By the way, what does narcolistic mean?"

"It means self-centered. You'd know that if you were paying attention."

Annie had an uneventful evening. After a quick supper at home, she went to Rod's, and they did a short workout in his garage. Afterward, they sat on the porch and talked about the day's events and what the rest of the team's reaction would be. When Annie told Rod what Coach Brown had said in the outfield, Rod told her he knew about the medal. When she gave him a surprised look, he reminded her that his dad was in the Special Forces, and that he'd been out to the coach's place with him more than once. Coach Brown had even shown them the medal. Annie was impressed at her boyfriend's ability to keep secrets—hers and her coach's.

Jenny's evening, on the other hand, was anything but uneventful. She sat up with her sister until midnight. They talked about a lot of things. There were also some tears, from both of them. Tammi finally opened up and explained what started her on the path to her attention-seeking behavior. It all started with a compliment. She asked Jenny if she remembered the trip that the whole family took to some friends of their parents over in Dallas. Jenny said she couldn't forget it. She didn't feel well, and they ended up coming home early. Tammi went outside to play some driveway basketball with the neighbor kids. The twins were sixth-graders and were by far the tallest in their class.

"When dad hollered that we were leaving," explained Tammi, "the girls and two boys that I was playing with told me that I was the best kid basketball player they had ever seen. They said if I went to their school I would be a big star. I remembered that I scored a lot, but they were short bank shots that I could get off because I was taller than them. That's all I could think about on the way home. I was going to be a big star, and everybody would look up to me. I even had a dream about it that night. Pretty stupid, huh?"

"No, I don't think it was that stupid," consoled Jenny. "We were little girls. There's nothing wrong with dreaming. You just expected too much from yourself. There's only one best player on a team, and only one best player in the state. It's okay if you're not the best."

"And when I found out that I wasn't the best, I didn't handle it very well. I can't believe you didn't tell me off. Why didn't you try to set me straight?"

"You're my sister," explained Jenny. "And would you have listened or would you have been mad at me?"

"Mad," said Tammi starting to sob again. "I've been a stupid jerk. Do you think the rest of the girls hate me? And I guess the important thing is, will they forgive me and let me try to make it up to them?"

"I wouldn't say they hate you," said Jenny as she put her arm around Tammi. "That attitude of yours has been tough to deal with. You might find this hard to believe, but the first person to forgive you will be Annie. And she's the one you've been the hardest on. Once you get to know her, you will find out how incredible she is."

"Annie?"

"Yeah, that's what we're supposed to call B. A. now. It's the name she's always gone by until she moved here."

"That doesn't make sense. Why would she want to go by her initials just because she moved to a new school?"

"It made sense to her," explained Jenny. "Haven't you noticed how she shuns all the attention people try to give her, especially the sportswriters? She just wants to be a regular kid. Obviously that's not possible for her because she's such a tremendous athlete. She's the reason Chip and I have gotten so much better. You might as well throw in the rest of the basketball team and the softball team while you're at it."

"Everybody but me and Darby. What a little follower that girl is! Whoops, I shouldn't complain about her. She was only following my rotten lead. And I have noticed her attitude toward me has changed lately. Am I the only one that couldn't see what an idiot I was?"

"Hey, sis, you can only see the world from one perspective— your own two eyes. That is, if that's all you want to see. Our psychology teacher called that confirmation bias. You have your mind made up, and you go around looking for only the things that reinforce your opinions."

"Okay," said Tammi with some conviction in her voice. "Enough sobbing. The big question is what do I do now? I'm serious. What do you think I should do?"

"First, I'd meet Chip and Annie in the parking lot before school starts tomorrow."

Chip sat in her first-hour class, thinking about what had just happened in the parking lot. It was like she was living in bizzaro world as Luke liked to say. Tammi had actually come up to her and Annie with a look of something like humility on her face. She said she had been a jerk and asked them if they could forgive her. Chip looked at Annie for guidance, since she had born the brunt of Tammi's abuse. Annie looked from Tammi, to her twin, and then back at Tammi. Jenny's look convinced her that Tammi was remorseful, and she was being sincere. Annie remembered something Tank had said to her back in Jones Ferry, "Life's too short to stay mad at people." She smiled and stuck out her hand. Tammi smiled back and took Annie's hand, following it with a big hug. Chip was in total shock. She stuck out her hand and also received a big hug. Both of the twins had tears in their eyes.

"Ms. Fullerton," said the teacher. "Can you leave your world for a short while and come into our world? That's the second time I've asked you a simple question, and it appears that you have zoned out on us."

"To be honest, sir," answered Chip, "my world is a whole lot more exciting than what's going on here. I do, however, appreciate your efforts to make this class as interesting as possible. I will soon be writing a letter to the school board commending the—"

"All right, all right. Don't get overly dramatic on us. I suppose your world is more exciting than this class. However, since you need this class to graduate, how about making a little more effort to stay with us? Deal?"

"Deal," said Chip, sitting up straight in her seat and folding her hands on her desk.

The teacher shook his head in dismay and went back to his lecture. Chip got some strange looks from her classmates, but it was nothing that she hadn't seen before.

Scott and Gina

Scott Milligan sat at his desk, staring at Jenny Olsen. Not only was she the most beautiful girl he had ever seen, but she appeared to have a wonderful personality to go along with it. He couldn't believe that she didn't have a regular boyfriend. He knew a lot of pretty girls, and most of them behaved like their looks were everything. They flaunted themselves at every opportunity. Jenny wasn't like that at all. He knew; he had been watching her from the moment he walked into the class a month earlier. Scott's dad had recently taken a new position at a Fort Worth hospital, and he gave Scott the option of staying with friends so he could finish out the school year at his old school or moving immediately to the house he had purchased in Reston. Scott was still trying to decide when an inside pitch broke a small bone in his left hand. On the way home from the hospital, since his junior year in baseball was over, he told his dad it was time to move on and make some new friends.

Scott was somewhat of a rarity himself. At 6'3" and 180 pounds, he was the consummate three-sport athlete. Along with his athletic prowess, his natural good looks made him a very popular young man in his hometown of Fenton, Texas. Scott was lean and muscular with short black hair and smiling brown eyes. He lost a great deal of that popularity when he made a decision to right an incident that he felt was unacceptable. He had called a press conference at the end of last fall's football season and asked that his name be stricken from the state record books. He found out that the opposing coach had told his defensive backs to let Scott's receivers add on yards after making a catch. In the fourth quarter, Scott's team was down forty-five to twenty-one, so the winner of the contest had already been decided. However, he was on track to set a new state record in single season, passing yards for his class. The two coaches were old friends, so what was the harm in helping one of the other guy's players out? A week after he had broken the record by five yards, the junior quarterback became aware of the rumors that were floating around. The opposing team's defensive secondary had leaked what their coach had asked them to do. They were supposed to play their regular pass coverage, but if a pass was completed, they were expected to let the receiver get some extra yards after the completion.

After studying the game film for hours, it was pretty apparent that the defense was letting the receivers rack up extra yards after the catch. One linebacker tried to "bulldog" Scott's tight end and was carried for about ten yards before being brought to the ground. If a linebacker on his team had tackled like that, he would be watching the game from the sidelines. Milligan decided to go to his coach and ask for the truth. His coach told him not to worry about it. It didn't affect the outcome of the game, so it was no big deal. He should be proud of his accomplishment. So what if he got a little help.

Scott didn't see it that way. In his mind, records were not supposed to be manufactured; they should happen in the course of normal play. Getting help from an opponent was just wrong. When he told his coach what he was going to do, his coach wasn't very happy. He did tell his quarterback to do what he had to do. His job was safe at the school because of his winning record. If his whiney little quarterback didn't like the way things were done, then maybe he should go somewhere else to play.

His dad gave him the news in January. He was thinking about taking a new position in Fort Worth. The hospital had an opening for an orthopedic surgeon that specialized in sports-related injuries. Scott's dad, Dr. Milligan, was considered one of the best in his field in all of Texas. Scott had no problem moving to a new school for his senior year. His coach and football teammates were still giving him the cold shoulder after his press conference. They took their football very serious in Texas, and like most high schools, if you did anything to cast doubt on the program, you were not to be trusted. A few close friends and some community members stood behind his decision, but they were in the minority. He could've gotten through it. His physical toughness was matched by his mental toughness. Athletics and his dad, had taught him how to be both. Moving away from Fenton was just fine with him.

When Dr. Milligan asked Scott where they should look for a new home, his son had already researched the place where he wanted to live and go to school—a little town called Reston. Surprisingly enough, it wasn't because of the boys' sports programs at Reston. He wanted to meet three people that went to Reston High School—B. A. Smith, Chip Fullerton, and the guy that wrote the insightful sports articles, Luke Slowinski. He had read all the positive reports about the Reston girls, and he was looking forward to meeting them. Discovering Jenny was a bonus.

When he showed up at his new school, Scott made it a point to introduce himself to the football, basketball, and baseball coaches. The small cast on his left hand would be there for another two months, but his dad was confident that there wouldn't be any lasting effects. The three coaches seemed genuinely happy that Scott would be part of their teams next year. He appeared to be a solid kid, and he had the body and carriage of a top athlete. After a month in his new school, he had not even talked to any of the three people that he wanted to meet.

He had a class with each one of them, but he didn't sit close enough to start up a conversation. New kids usually sat in the back of the room where there was an empty chair. He did hold the classroom door for Jenny once, and she smiled and said, "Thank you, Scott." At least she had remembered his name when the teacher had introduced him to the class a few weeks earlier. Now he needed a reason to actually meet and talk to her. He wanted it to look natural and not like he was trying too hard. He ate during a different lunch period, so that wasn't an option. His big break came one day after school when he was cruising through town. He saw the three girls he knew and an Oriental girl out for a run. It was time for him to start running again anyway.

As usual, Gina was arguing with her mother. She considered her mom to be an imbecile. She had no idea what it was like being a teenager today, and she had no right bossing her around. In her mind, Gina was a top athlete in basketball and softball, and she was not getting the respect she deserved at home or in school. At five feet ten, Gina did have some athletic ability. The problem was, she was in a Dallas school with about seven hundred students in each class. This meant there was a lot of competition for starting spots and playing time on all the sports teams. Gina was pretty good, but the old saying about "buying somebody for what they are worth and then selling them for what they think they are worth", fit her to a T. Gina had two main problems—her attitude and her mouth.

Her disagreements with her mom were almost daily now. The way she dressed, whom she hung out with and her grades were all heated topics. Gina's mom was a divorced socialite that didn't have to worry about working for a living. She didn't think her monthly alimony payments were high enough, but she did receive enough to keep her and her daughter living in style. Her daughter was the source of enough problems without money entering the equation. Community activities took up most of her time and, of course, the obligatory parties that went along with them. She hadn't made it to one of her daughter's sporting events all year. Social commitments took up a lot of time if you fancied yourself as a pillar of the community. Gina was acutely aware of her mother's priorities but convinced herself that it was no big deal. Their last argument was the clincher.

"I hate this place," screamed Gina. "I want to go live with dad. At least he will appreciate me."

"You can't be serious," responded her mom, slurring her words. It was late and she had been partying with the *in* crowd for several hours.

"I am serious. Any place is better than here."

"Well, darling," said her mom with a touch of arrogance. "Why don't we call your dad tomorrow, and if he agrees, you can go live with him."

"Just like that?" asked Gina somewhat dismayed. "After you fought so hard in court to keep me?"

"I only want what's best for you, sweetie," said her mom, faking sincerity.

"I hardly believe that, Mom. With me out of the way, you can do whatever you please. Not that you don't do that already. All right, let's do it. We'll make the call."

Gina's mom went to mix herself another drink. She was smiling all the way to the kitchen. *Let the little brat be Henry's problem for a while.* Her big worry was keeping the alimony payments the same. She knew how bad he wanted their daughter to live with him after the divorce, so that should be a nice little bargaining chip. This way, they both would get what they want. Besides, wasn't she doing good things for the Dallas community? Her latest project of acquiring shoes or coat or mittens or whatever for the poor, was a very worthwhile project.

The call was made the next day, and the lawyers were put to work. Gina found out that she wouldn't be going to Fenton to live. She was going to a little town north of Fort Worth called Reston. She couldn't believe it, but she had heard of Reston before. Anyway, Scott—her twin brother—and her dad would be waiting for her to move in. *Scott*, she thought. *God's gift to the sports world. In a little hick town like Reston, I'll be making some headlines myself. I'll probably be the first decent female athlete they've ever seen.*

Four high school girls running through the streets of Reston was a regular sight to the inhabitants of the small town. Most of the residents waved to them and the girls waved back. They slowed down a little so they could discuss the game they had just played.

"So tell me again what happened in the fifth inning," said Lu.

"It was no big deal," said Chip. "It was just one of those things."

"I'll tell you," offered Jenny. "Here's how it went down."

The game against West High was supposed to be a rout. West didn't have a very strong record, so Coach Brown started Carmen. Annie said she would come in if there were any problems. The score was seven to four in Reston's favor when Chip led off the bottom of the fifth. She was acting kind of funny when she was in the batter's box. This didn't draw any attention from her teammates or coaches as they had grown to expect strange things from her. She singled up the middle on the first pitch. From the third-base coach's box, Coach Brown immediately gave her the steal sign, but Chip didn't move from the bag when the pitcher threw her first pitch to Kris.

"Are you paying attention?" asked Coach Harbison, standing a few feet away in the first base coach's box.

"Sorry, Coach, I must have missed it."

Kris grounded the next pitch to first, and the first baseman decided to take the out at first instead of going after the lead runner. Chip probably could have been thrown out at second as her run to the bag was a little unorthodox to say the least. It was a half scamper with a few skips thrown in. Coach Brown gave her a funny look as if to ask if everything was all right. Everything was not all right. Before Annie could step in, Chip called time. She went straight for her teammate, signaling for her coach to stay where he was. The umpire appeared a little miffed. This had better be serious. Coaches, not players, usually called time to confer with the batter. Chip jogged up to Annie and whispered in her ear.

"Look, I've got to go to the bathroom real bad. So don't mess around here. Hit the first pitch somewhere, preferably over the fence, and get me in, okay?"

Annie couldn't believe it. She just smiled and shook her head. Chip went back to the bag, and the umpire restarted the game. Coach Brown looked across the infield at his assistant with a "what's going on?" gesture. She gave him the same gesture in return. Meanwhile, Chip was all but dancing on the bag at second. Annie stepped in and then called time and stepped back out. She acted like something was in her eye. The plate umpire did a good job of showing restraint. When Annie stepped back in, she did all she could to keep from laughing out loud.

"C'mon, blondie, quit stalling," hollered Chip from second. "Slap that thing somewhere."

Annie responded by hitting the first pitch high and deep to left field. Chip took off as soon as the ball hit the bat. She ran right by Coach Brown at third with her head down. He said something about waiting because there was only one out. At this point, she didn't care. The left fielder was playing Annie deep, so it didn't take much for her to get back to the fence. She stood there, gauging the flight of the ball. At the last possible moment, she reached over the short fence and snagged the high fly. Chip was opening the door to the port-o-potty when she was doubled off at second.

A lot of coaches would have been upset at Chip's antics and decision making, but Coach Brown wasn't one of them. He walked back to the dugout with a serious look on his face, then he sat down and started chuckling. The chuckling quickly turned into an uncontrolled laugh that brought tears to his eyes. The rest of the team joined in. They were used to Chip's somewhat strange behavior, but this was something that they had not seen before. Leave it to her to find a totally different way to amuse them. Tammi and Darby laughed right along with their teammates. The opposing coach shook his head in disbelief as he took his position in the third-base coach's box. Coach Brown finally recovered enough to put Sandy Johnson in at short and Juanita Esperanza in right field. Annie went from right to pitch. The game ended with the same score, seven to four.

"Why didn't you call for a sub?" asked Lu.

"I told you. I didn't think I had to go that bad until I got to first. Then it hit me. It would have been too embarrassing to ask Coach for a sub so I could go to the bathroom."

"Good thinking," said Jenny. "As it turned out, no one was paying any attention to you as you ran the bases oblivious as to what was going on. And then straight to the port-o-potty."

"It wouldn't have been a problem if Annie would have hit it over the fence like I told her to," responded Chip.

"She did hit it over the fence," said Jenny, laughing. "Except their left fielder caught it."

"They told me she didn't even have to jump," said Chip, looking at the Reston slugger. "Where were you when I needed you?"

"Sorry," said Annie. "Next time I'll be more selective on the pitches. It was a little high, and I didn't get all of it."

"Don't turn around," said Lu. "Some guy is coming up behind us."

Scott didn't have a plan when he caught up to the four runners. He figured he'd just wing it. All he wanted to do was meet them outside of school and give them some information about an addition to their softball team. A couple of days ago his dad had told him that his twin sister was coming to live with them. He had always considered his sister a spoiled brat. She was annoying and extremely opinionated. Her mediocre athletic ability had gone to her head. He knew that he was inadvertently part of the problem. People expected her to be athletically inclined because she was his sister. She had used this fact to convince herself that she was not only an awesome athlete, but she was also an expert on almost every subject under the sun.

The girls were running in a two-by-two formation with Lu and Jenny in front. Scott picked up the pace and pulled up on the outside next to Jenny. He was amazed at how fast they were moving. They weren't running hard, but they weren't jogging either. He decided to play it very low key.

"Hi, ladies. Do you mind if I run with you for a few minutes?"

"Only if you can keep up," answered Chip. "We don't wait for stragglers."

"I'll do my best. I'm Scott Milligan. I moved here about a month ago with my dad."

"I think we've all got a class with you, Scott," said Jenny. "I'm Jenny, and this is Annie, Chip, and Lu. What did you do to your hand?"

Scott still had a small cast on his left hand. He had to keep it on for three more weeks.

"I got hit by a baseball that I didn't think was going to hit me. You know, sometimes you know when you're going to get hit, and other times it's a complete surprise. Well, this time it was a big surprise. It broke a small bone in my hand."

"I bet that sucker hurt," observed Chip.

"Oh, it hurt all right. My dad said when I was little and got hurt I would to run around in circles and yip like a puppy. I didn't think that would be very dignified in front of hundreds of people, so I just stood there, holding it. It was tough to hold the tears back."

"Have you ever cried in front of a bunch of people, B. A., uh, Annie?" asked Chip.

"Yeah. We were at a fair, and my ice cream fell right out of my cone. My dad picked it up and slapped it back in there and told me to go ahead and finish it. My mom gave him a disgusted look and threw it in the trash. My sister stood there and laughed at me. It worked out in the end. I got a new cone and chose a better flavor."

"How old were you?" asked Lu.

"I think I was five."

"That sounds about right," said Jenny. "You usually don't remember things before you are four, unless it's something really traumatic."

"Well, I remember something when I was about four," said Chip. "I was crying because Rod did something mean to me in public. We were all out to dinner or something."

"No way," said Jenny in disbelief.

"Way," countered Chip. "I had my mom write it down so I wouldn't forget it."

"I'm not believing that for one minute," said Jenny.

"All right, I made that up about her writing it down. But he did do something to me, and I cried right in front of a whole bunch of people." *And I don't recall getting even with him for that little stunt,* thought Chip. *That little piece of information is going in the memory bank to be dealt with later.*

Scott couldn't believe the conversation that passed back and forth between these girls. They went on as if he wasn't even there. And they actually talked about interesting stuff. They certainly were different from the girls he was used to.

"What about you, Scott?" asked Lu. "You ever cry in front of a bunch of people? It doesn't count if you were under eight years old."

"I remember my tenth birthday when I was in fifth grade. I wanted this Al Kaline ball glove. There was this company that put out a list of names they could put on a glove, and Kaline was one of them. He played back in the sixties, and he was my dad's favorite player."

"I've heard of him," said Chip. "He played for the Yankees."

"Close," said Scott. "He played for the Detroit Tigers. He was awesome and a great guy too. Anyhow, when I opened my present and saw Cal Ripken's name on my glove, I burst into tears. It should have been embarrassing, but I didn't care. I wanted that Kaline glove."

Wow, thought Jenny. *This guy seems pretty nice. He's not trying to impress us with how smart or how brave or how tough he is. No, he's probably another Morrie in disguise. How did he just happen to be running the same route that we were running?*

"Anyway," said Scott. "I want to tell you about a new addition to your softball team. My sister will be at school tomorrow, and she's got permission from your coach to practice with you. Obviously she can't play, transferring in at this time, but she will be at practice. And I guess I'm not just telling you; I'm warning you. Gina has been living with our mom for the past couple of years since our parents divorced. She's loud and obnoxious, and she can be a real handful."

"Coach Brown gave us a heads up on her yesterday," said Annie. "Don't worry, Chip's a real handful, and we keep her under control most of the time."

Jenny and Lu snickered at Annie's assessment of Chip.

"There are a few big differences between Chip and Gina. One is, Chip's got a boatload of talent. And number two is, Chip doesn't pretend to be an expert on everything. I've watched your team play several games, and you are awesome. I mean it. You do stuff that not many other teams can do. Although I was a little confused about the all-out sprint to the port-o-potty play."

Everyone but Chip laughed at that comment.

"It was obvious that the batter in question missed her signal on that play," said Chip in defense of her actions.

"What signal was that?" asked Annie.

"The plan was for you to hit a home run, so I could go to the bathroom. If you would have done that, everything would have been fine."

"You know what I like about the way ya'll act at games?" asked Scott not expecting an answer. "When your coach takes you out, you cheer for your replacements and don't mope around because someone came in for you. I think that's pretty cool."

"Annie taught us that," said Jenny. "We play to have fun and to work together toward a common goal."

Scott could tell that Jenny was being sincere. He could tell that the other three agreed though they didn't say anything about her comment. It didn't take him long to figure out that this group of girls was definitely different than the ones he was used to dealing with. The group slowed down to a walk when they hit a blue mark on the sidewalk. Lu had several routes around town marked off. Today, they ran the three-mile route.

"There's one more reason I wanted to talk to you," said Scott as his breathing returned to normal. Jenny and Chip gave him a suspicious look. Here it comes. "Chip, would you introduce me to your boyfriend?"

"What for?" asked Chip in a loud voice that made an elderly couple across the street stop and look over at them.

"I hope this doesn't sound corny, but I want to meet the guy that writes the amazing sports articles for the school newspaper. The Dallas papers have printed a few of them. He seems to really know his stuff for a high-school kid. I really liked the one that he wrote after you lost the tournament game to Dunbar. And I think it's cool the way he throws in the historical info. Anyway, with school getting out soon, I need to make some guy friends, or it's going to be a lonely summer. I'll meet the football players when practice starts, but I can't do any of the summer camps because of my hand. I will go and watch, but it's not the same as participating."

"Tell you what," said Chip. "We'll be at the Pizza Palace in about an hour. Luke and Rod will be with us. They're huge eaters, so we'll probably have to order an extra pie. Why don't you join us?"

"Thanks, I'll see you there," said Scott as he jogged toward home.

"Why did you make that crack about the guys being huge eaters?" asked Annie.

"I was hinting that he should bring some cash for his share," said Chip. "We don't know this guy. He could be a first-class pizza moocher."

"Well, he seemed pretty nice," said Lu.

"Yeah," added Jenny. "Maybe a little too nice."

Supper at the Palace was typical for the Reston group. The talk ranged from sports to politics to history. Scott enjoyed every minute of it. There was no discussion about other people—who they liked or disliked or who said something about someone else. His dad told him about a famous quote when he was back in the seventh grade: "Bright people talk about ideas, mediocre people talk about things, and small people talk about other people." That was one of his favorite sayings. Tonight, he mostly played the role of listener. He didn't want to get off on the wrong foot with his classmates and hopefully, future friends. It didn't take him long to come to the conclusion that Chip was a real character and that Jenny could get a rise out of her with very little effort.

"So, Chip," said Jenny as she dipped a breadstick into some sauce, "Do we need to come up with a new signal for a bathroom break? How about you form a *J* with your fingers?"

"What's the *J* for?" asked Annie.

"It means she has to go to the john," explained Jenny.

"Ya'll think you're funny, don't you?" said Chip. "I was almost in crisis mode out there. If blondie here would have messed around at the plate any more than she did, we would have had a major disaster on our hands."

"What's a crisis mode?" asked Scott.

Jenny started to explain when she was cut off by Chip.

"You don't need to know all about that," said Chip. "All you need to know is who to hang out with here in Reston."

"Yeah, and you're off to a good start," laughed Luke. "Because we know who those people are, and tomorrow we'll point them out to you."

"I thought y'all were the right people," said a confused Scott.

"Oh no," continued Luke. "We're just the people who know the right people. It's a very complicated system. Don't worry, there's a lot of math involved, but you'll catch on."

"Don't listen to him," said Chip. "He's just trying to be funny, and that's not his job. His job is to write interesting articles so he can get a high-paying job at a New York City newspaper. And just to clarify things, Jenny's job is to be a beautiful but down in the dirt athlete. Rod's job is to scare away anyone we think is undesirable. And my job, which is the toughest by far, is to keep everyone focused on our goals."

Chip's comment about Rod brought her a nasty look from Annie.

"And entertained," said Jenny. "You forgot that."

"That's purely a sidebar from my main objective."

Scott was looking at Chip as she explained everyone's purpose, but her last statement confused him. When he looked to the others for help, they all shook their heads from side-to-side, signifying for him not to pursue her logic or use of the English language.

"Thanks for clearing that up, but what is Annie's job, to hit home runs and pitch no-hitters?"

"No," said Chip. "That's a sidebar too. Her job is simple— action magnate. You will find out that wherever she goes, strange, unexplainable things will happen. She has strong gravitational pull. It's like a cosmic gift. Very few have it, not even one in a million. And now that she's come out of the closet, I expect things to get even more hectic."

"Stop it," said Annie. "He seems like a nice guy. Don't scare him with that talk. And I wished you had phrased that last comment a little differently. Our new guy here might not understand what you're talking about."

"It's true," said Jenny. "Before Annie got here, we just walked around in circles, mumbling to ourselves and drooling all over the place. She has shown us the light so to speak."

"Enough," said Annie, getting up. "You've got this, right, Scott?" asked Annie pointing toward the empty pizza pans and breadstick baskets.

"Uh, sure," said Scott a little confused.

"She's kidding," said Chip as she and the rest of them dug into their pockets. "We all chip in. You better walk out to your car with me in case you have any more questions. I am a plethora of information."

"Hey, did any of you get a hold of Lu?" asked Jenny. "I called and sent her a text but didn't get an answer."

"I tried too," said Annie taking hold of Rod's arm. "I didn't have any luck either. I did notice that she was struggling during our run today. Usually she just glides along, but when we were done, she took a long time to get her breathing back to normal. Maybe she's catching a cold or something."

Chip was walking ahead of the group, holding on to Scott's arm. She was talking a mile a minute, and he was trying to follow her. The last thing she said before he got into his car was something about what a great person Jenny was, but that was something Scott already knew. The problem was how was he going to get her to talk to him one-on-one? She didn't pay much attention to him while they were eating pizza. He smiled as he started his car and left the lot. He was used to being the center of attention due to his athletic accomplishments. It was refreshing to be just one of the gang, if that's what he was in this new town. He didn't know it, but his situation was similar to another transfer student that showed up in Reston several months earlier.

Later that evening, Chip called her two best friends. "We've got trouble," she said in a somber voice. "I talked to Lu's mom, and she said Lu is sick. They think she's got mono. I don't understand how someone so healthy and in such good shape can get sick so fast. Those mono germs must be nasty little dudes." She also called Luke to give him the news and to ask his opinion on the new guy. They both decided that a background check was in order. That was one of Luke's roles that Chip failed to divulge at dinner. Like any good sleuth, one did not show their entire hand to others.

It was confirmed by lunch the next day that Lu had mono. Her run toward the state finals was over. They couldn't believe that Lu, of all people, could get sick like that without any warning. One day she was fine and the next day she was seriously ill. Luke informed them that anyone could catch a virus. It did help though to be in good physical condition. It put you in a better position to fight it and get over the complications sooner. He remembered reading an article about a guy that was on his bicycle when he was hit by a pickup truck. The article said because he was in such great shape, he survived the accident. Someone who wasn't in as good of physical condition might have died from something that traumatic.

Chip and Luke left the lunchroom together as they headed for their next class. She told him she had a bag of clothes that she wanted him to give to the counselor. Then the counselor would pass them on to the freshman girl that was in need of them. It was a slick plan that she considered foolproof. Chip's community service circle would now be twice the size that it was when she first drew it in sociology class. And after they visited the nursing home next Saturday, it would be almost as big as her sports circle. She was on her way to becoming a truly balanced person.

Practice after school that day was definitely memorable. Gina Milligan was introduced to the squad as they were warming up. Scott's description of his sister was spot on. She was definitely a handful and then some. After Coach Brown introduced her, he asked her what position she played. She looked at the team and said wherever he needed her. She was there to help the team out next year of course. The girls thought that was a pretty cocky answer for a girl standing in front of a team that was nineteen and eight with a win over the top-rated team in the area. The coach went on to explain it was their last day with the middle schoolers. The fresh/soph team had been working with them on hitting, so the varsity was going to do some base running with them at the end of practice.

Carmen, Tammi, and Annie took turns throwing batting practice pitches to the rest of the squad. Annie went third and started to walk off after the last batter.

"Wait a minute," shouted Coach Brown. "You've got one more." Coach Harbison was back behind first base where Annie couldn't see her. She was stretching and swinging two bats. She walked down the line, grabbed a helmet, and stepped into the box. Annie turned and signaled for all the fielders to come in several steps. She wound up and threw the ball about twelve feet in the air. Coach Harbison relaxed and watched the ball come down and land about three inches beyond the tip of the plate—a perfect strike in slow pitch. Annie looked in at Darby and said, "Call it."

"Strike one," hollered Darby as she stood and threw the ball back to her pitcher.

"No way," objected Coach H. "Coach Brown, a little help here."

"Illegal pitch," he warned. "No more of that, Smith, or you'll be on double-secret, suspendable probation."

Annie threw her fastball on the second pitch, and the batter made a beautiful well-balanced athletic swing about two seconds after the ball hit the catcher's glove.

"The bat's too big," hollered Chip. "Get her a smaller bat."

"No, no," added Courtney from short left field. "Her right shoulder's too high. Get that shoulder down, Coach."

"That's not it," said Kris from second. "She's not holding the bat right. Separate your hands a little like Cobb used to."

"Open up," shouted Rachel from center field. "Get those hips in there, Coach."

Coach H. ignored the ribbing and got ready for the next pitch. Annie threw her hook and was surprised that her coach did not back away. Coach H. took the pitch mainly because she just froze when she saw it coming right at her. Darby called it a ball even though it looked pretty good. The rise ball came next, and Coach H. missed it by a foot.

"Open your eyes, Coach," hollered Rachel from center. "You can't hit it with your eyes closed. That's how Fullerton hits."

Annie looked in at her coach and saw the serious intent in her eyes. She knew that Coach H. had played some college softball, so at one time she was probably a decent hitter. Annie mouthed, "Change-up, so wait for it." Only the batter and the catcher saw the pitcher's tip. Annie wound up and threw a smooth change at about half the speed of her fastball. The batter waited a little too long but made a nice level swing and managed to hit a grounder toward Kris at second. The second baseman casually bent over but not far enough, and the ball went right between her legs. Juanita fielded the ball leisurely in right field and lobbed it into Chip, who was covering the bag at second.

Everyone was surprised when their coach rounded first and came barreling into second. Chip saw this and purposely made an awkward stab at the ball deflecting it with her glove toward Kris. The outfielders screamed for Coach H. to take third. Kris picked up the ball and waited for a few counts then threw the ball about six feet wide of third as Coach H. was sliding in. The ball hit the fence in front of Reston's dugout. The runner jumped up and headed for home. Maria was laughing so hard, she had trouble picking up the errant throw. She surprised everyone by flipping the ball back to Coach Brown, who was standing in the third-base coaching box. He caught it and proceeded to throw it over Darby's head into the backstop. Coach Harbison slid into home and jumped up, raising her hands above her head. Everyone cheered except for Gina.

Dang, Gina thought. *It looks like I probably could play any position I want here. Smart move, Milligan. Next season can't come soon enough.*

"All right, you fumbly-fingered female defenders," shouted Coach Brown. "Two laps for letting an older, uh, just past her teens woman make a fool out of you. Then jog over to the middle-school diamond."

Chip started a chant when they were halfway around the field on their first lap.

"I know a coach named Harbison. She embarrassed us all by hittin' a home run."

Jenny picked it up from there. "For an older lady, she was pretty fast. Maybe the team should get her an oxygen mask."

"What are they singing out there?" asked Coach Harbison as she looked for something to cover the strawberry she earned, sliding into home.

"I think they're singing about you and your four-bagger," replied Coach Brown. "Also it sounded like they thought you needed an oxygen mask."

"You better be careful with your little lyrics out there," hollered Coach Harbison. "Unless you want to run a few more."

"Better you than me," laughed Coach Brown.

The lesson today was tagging at third on a fly ball to the outfield. The middle-school coach teamed up with the varsity coaches to get everyone in the right position. Coach Harbison stood there with a bandage on her leg, explaining the varsity strategy. When the ball was hit, they were to go down into a sprinter's starting position with one foot on the bag and wait for the coach to tell them to go. There were two reasons for this: (1) The runner would not get excited and leave early, because the coach was watching for her; (2) It was easier to decoy and draw a throw from the left fielder. The coach would holler "go" and the runner would sprint for home. But if the coach put his hands on his knees, the play was off. When he hollered "go," the runner was then supposed to take three hard steps toward home and stop. Coach Harbison explained that if the left fielder threw home, a runner on first would be able to take second. And if the throw was wild, the runner on third might be able to score without a play on her. Another bonus that came from the coach telling the runner to go was the third baseman would be listening and would tell her left fielder to go home with the ball.

The varsity outfielders were supposed to throw first with varsity runners on the bag. Then the younger girls would move in and get their chance. Darby and Chip took turns taking the throws at home. Courtney, Rachel, Carmen, Juanita, Tammie, and Annie were standing in left with the middle school outfielders standing off to the side. The infielders were the runners. They took turns tagging from third and going if the call wasn't a decoy. The varsity outfielders went over the catch and throw technique that they had covered earlier in the season. All was going well until Sandy Johnson slipped on her way home and was thrown out by ten feet.

"Hey, Coach," hollered Gina. "Can I run? Somebody needs to show these squirts how it's done."

"Sure," said Coach Brown. He looked to the outfield and made a little switching motion with his index fingers. Tammi was next in line to throw, and she got the message immediately. She turned and told Annie to switch with her. Annie went to the head of the line and assumed the fielding position for outfielders. Coach Brown hit a lazy fly right at her. Annie gauged the ball and took a few steps back then she moved forward to make the catch. She was in a perfect position to throw home.

Gina went down into the sprinter's position with her right foot on the bag. Coach Harbison shouted, "Go" when the ball hit Annie's glove and Gina took off. The Reston varsity was impressed with Gina's speed but not nearly as impressed as Gina was with her own running ability. This was her first chance to make a big impression on these small-town girls, and she intended to make it a memorable one. There was only one problem with her thinking. She had no idea of the caliber of arm that was attempting to gun her down from left field.

Darby was all set to take Annie's throw, and it was right on the money. She caught the ball about two feet in front of the plate on the infield side. It should have been an easy tag—step to the left and kneel, covering the ball with her right hand in the catcher's mitt. The runner should slide right into it. Gina caught the flash of the ball and heard it hit the catcher's mitt. Instead of sliding, she tried to knock the ball out of Darby's mitt with her hands and consequently bowling her over at the same time. Darby and her teammates couldn't believe it. Both of the girls went down in a heap, but the catcher held on. Coach Brown dropped his bat and went to his catcher. His assistant came running in from third and checked out the new girl. It only took a few seconds to have both of them sitting up.

"Was I out?" asked Gina.

"By a mile," said Coach Brown as he helped Darby up. "What were you thinking, girl? You don't ever run into your teammates like that."

"I was just showing everyone what hard-nosed softball is all about," explained Gina. "If you want to win, you have to do whatever it takes. It's even on the softball T-shirts we used to wear at Sterling High in Dallas."

"At Reston High, we focus on hard work, fundamentals, and execution," said Coach Brown as he held back what he really wanted to say to the new girl after pulling a stunt like that. "And we take pride in playing smart and fair. Why don't you sit in the dugout, out of the way, for the rest of this drill. We play ball a little different here, and you need to make the decision to do it our way, or you won't be playing at all."

Gina went to the dugout, mumbling. There was no way that throw came from the outfield. That Smith girl probably held on to the one she caught and someone a lot closer to the plate must have thrown a different ball. What a rotten trick to pull on a new girl that's just trying to make them better. Bunch of hicks.

Chip, Annie, and Jenny sat in the back of Annie's truck at Mr. Daggert's farm and discussed the events of today's practice.

"That new girl is a nutcase," said Chip. "I can't believe it, Jen. Your sister finally comes to her senses, and now, she's been replaced by a girl from another planet."

"That was quite a stunt she pulled on Darby," said Jenny. "It's lucky no one got hurt. Our coaches weren't very happy. If that's the way the big-city girls play, I don't think I'd like it very much. Collisions at the plate do happen in softball and baseball, but you don't do it to a teammate in practice."

"All big city teams don't play that way," added Annie. "Most of them are just fine. Sometimes it's the girls, and sometimes it's their coaches. Whatever, we don't need that kind of attitude around here."

"Check this out," said Chip as she reached back into her book bag and pulled out a folded piece of paper. Jenny took it and opened it up. She stifled a laugh and handed it to Annie.

"Okay," said Annie, looking at Chip's drawing. "What is it?"

"It's Lu trying to outrun the mono virus," explained Chip. "It's a card I made for her to cheer her up. I figured we'd all write something clever on it."

"But she didn't outrun the virus," said Jenny. "It caught her and ate her up. And your virus looks like the blob that attacked Cleveland. What are you trying to do, make her feel bad? She's depressed enough as it is. Let's make a cheerful card and have everybody sign it."

"I was just trying to help," said Chip.

"Your heart is in the right place," consoled Annie, "Even if your weird drawing isn't. Now tell us about the nursing home visit that you want us to go on."

"Okay," explained Chip as she stuffed her card back into her bag. "We handle it the same way we did at the hospital. Mrs. Jenkins, the manager, told me on the phone yesterday that most of the residents want to see us. When we get there, the nurse in charge will tell us which people we are supposed to stay away from. I guess some of them are violent and might attack us if we get too close."

Jenny looked over at Annie after Chip's last statement. "You better be kidding about that. I don't want to have to use my pepper spray twice in one month."

"Yes, I was kidding. We go around and talk to the residents and tell them about our team. We've got little softballs to give them if they want one. The shop class made some little batons for Lu to give out, but I guess we'll have to save them for another day. It should be fun."

The car was silent for about thirty seconds after the girls came out of the nursing home. Each one was thinking about the people they met inside. Jenny finally broke the silence.

"This one man told me he wasn't sure about talking to a high school student. He thought I would be saying things like, "Oh my God," and "That is so, like, fabulous." He said his granddaughter talks like that, and it is very annoying."

"They did seem a little afraid of us at first," said Annie as she pulled her truck out of the parking lot. "But it didn't take long for most of them to relax. One lady asked if she could call me Beth because that was her granddaughter's name. When I told her that was fine, she lit up in a big smile. Chip, you did good. I'd say you are well on your way to becoming a balanced person."

"Thanks, ladies. I wasn't certain that this was a good idea, but it seemed to work out okay. What do you think about going back to the hospital?"

"That's not a bad idea," said Annie. "The kids there are all different now. How about we do it right after you and I come back from Michigan?"

The other two nodded their heads in approval. Chip was thinking about all the things she had to do before their summer trip. Her dad, trying to be funny, said he could cover her Saturdays at the store with just about any warm body off the street. She was very professional at his store, and she knew her dad enjoyed having her come in on Saturdays and during the week when school was out for summer vacation. She knew a lot about tools even though she didn't actually use them. Surprisingly, her expertise with tools was called upon a few days later at school.

Mr. Fouts, the shop teacher, had several tools laid out on one of the shop tables. "As I told you last week, we are going to have our tool-identification-and-use quiz tomorrow. I have about thirty different tools here, and you need to know every one of them."

"Every one?" asked a guy in the front. "That's a lot of tools. How about you ask us just half of them, and we get to pick which ones? There's a few of them there that I've never even seen before."

This brought a few laughs from the rest of the class.

Mr. Fouts looked out the small window in his door and saw Chip sauntering down the hall. "Tell you what," he offered. "I'll quiz the next student coming down the hall on these tools. If he or...what the heck, I'll ask the next girl that I see in the hallway, and if she doesn't know most of these tools, I'll give you all *A*s, and you don't have to take the quiz. Deal?"

His students weren't sure if he was kidding or not. One of the guys in front didn't wait for him to rescind his offer. "Deal," he said.

Mr. Fouts walked over to the door and opened it. "Miss Fullerton, would you come in here for a moment?"

Chip was a little leery, thinking she was in some sort of trouble. She walked tentatively into the shop class. There were about twenty boys and one girl standing there grinning at her. Because of her nature and past exploits, she figured she was being set up for something. Mr. Fouts was a regular customer at the store, so she knew him even though she had never taken a class from him.

"Would you be so kind as to identify these tools as I point to them?" asked the shop teacher. Chip looked the table full of tools over and hesitated. A few of the guys started high-fiving each other. A*s for everyone!* The boys misread Chip's hesitation. She didn't respond right away because she spied one tool that she couldn't identify. The rest were a piece of cake. She calmly identified each tool as Mr. Fouts pointed them out with a yardstick. He picked up the pace toward the end and finally hit the one that Chip didn't know. Without breaking stride, she confidently called it a *Stradle*. The teacher didn't even flinch on that one. He decided to add an extra credit question to the quiz. Five extra credit points if they knew which tool she missed.

"Thanks, Chip" said Mr. Fouts with a satisfied smile on his face. Chip bowed and headed back to her class.

When Chip got back to her class, her teacher accosted her. When she was asked why she took fifteen minutes to go to the restroom, she simply told the teacher that she had to stop to take a quiz for the shop teacher. The teacher decided not to press her for more information. But like most experienced teachers, she would make a call to verify Chip's story. She was surprised when Mr. Fouts confirmed Chip's story, and had she been in his class, she would have received an *A* for her efforts.

The Real World

Chip sat at the kitchen table, watching her mom make supper. She was drawing a new set of circles to illustrate the degree of her *balanceness*. At least, that's how she described it.

"Here it is mom," she said holding up the paper with several circles on it. "As you can see, my community service circle is much bigger than it was the last time I drew them."

Mrs. Fullerton came over to look at her daughter's drawing. The circles she drew were more proportionate than the first one Chip had shown her. Luke's circle was even big enough to have a small hole in the middle.

"I see Luke is back in your good graces," remarked Chip's mom pointing to his circle.

"Yeah, he gave me some good advice on my clothes giveaway deal."

"Good for him. It looks like you are making some real progress there. Keep up the good work. So how's the softball team doing? Your father and I should be able to make your next game. Is Annie going to pitch?"

"I think so. You won't believe what happened yesterday. This new girl, Gina, ran Darby over at the plate. She's a real piece of work from a big-city school. We sure get some crazies for such a little town. It's like the psycho train passes right through Reston. As soon as Tammi sees the light and starts acting human again, we get someone that's even worse. Boy, were the coaches mad. Coach Brown told her she couldn't do any more drills with us."

"That's not good. Hey, it might not be any of my business, but don't you think you're a little too hard on your boyfriend?"

"He can take it. Besides, if the women are going to take over, we need practice in giving orders and stuff like that. And the men need more practice in following orders. So in a way, it's good for both of us. It's like a win-win situation."

"I don't think Luke sees it that way. You better be careful, or that little redheaded freshman might steal him away from you. If I remember right, she's a real flirt."

"I'm not worrying about her too much. He rarely sees her. She's covering the baseball and track teams, so Luke can focus on softball. I think he likes to follow us anyway because we're a lot more interesting than the boys are. Speaking of boys, there's this new kid that I think would be perfect for Jenny. He's tall, and he seems nice. He's an athlete too although he won't be doing anything for a while because he's got a broken hand. Did you know that in the future they'll probably just unscrew your hand when you break it and screw another one back on? They'll probably do that with feet too. Will you call me when supper is ready? I have some stuff to do."

After seventeen years, Chip's mom was still amazed at the stuff her daughter came up with—"balanceness" and people unscrewing their hands and feet and replacing them with new ones. She definitely traveled to the beat of a different drum. Maybe she should start writing some of this stuff down. She might want to write a book about her someday.

Chip finished her homework, and her mother still hadn't called her for dinner. She figured that her dad must have been running late. They liked to eat their evening meal together as often as they could. Her dad said it was an American tradition that was starting to fade away. At dinner, her parents always asked her what she was up to and how school and sports were going. She appreciated the fact that her parents took a genuine interest in her activities—that is, the ones she could tell them about. They didn't need to know about her and Luke's sleuthing adventures. It was best to keep things like that just between the two of them. It's not that they were doing anything illegal or unethical, but there were some things that parents wouldn't understand. When her phone rang, she was expecting a call from her mom telling her that dinner was ready, but when she looked at the display, she saw that it was Luke on the other end.

"Hey," said Luke in a serious tone. "Are you eating dinner?"

"Not yet," said Chip. "We're waiting for my dad. What's up?"

"I'm on my way over. I'll be there in a few minutes."

Chip was a little surprised at her boyfriend's tone. He usually didn't invite himself to dinner. He must be on to something serious if he had to talk to her in person. She went out to the kitchen to talk to her mom until Luke showed up. Karen Fullerton was reading a cookbook when her daughter came back into the room.

"Mom, you shouldn't be reading cookbooks, you should be writing them. Everyone knows that you're the best cook in town. I'm surprised that dad isn't porkier than he already is."

"I'd keep that porky talk to yourself if I were you," responded Karen closing the book. "Your dad is just fine, thank you."

"Sorry. Can Luke stay for dinner? He's on his way."

"Sure, I always make enough. If we don't eat it all, your dad takes it the next day for his lunch."

Luke showed up at the back door, and they waved him in. He wasn't wearing his usual cheerful smile. Sitting down across from Chip, he motioned for her to give him her hands. She looked questioningly at her mom and put her hands in his.

"Okay," said Luke. "Remember, I'm just the messenger here. You know the clothes that you gave me to give to the counselor?" Chip shook her head. "Well, I stayed after school today to do some work in the publications room. On my way out the door, one of the janitors asked me to throw away some trash in one of the parking lot Dumpsters. I opened the Dumpster cover and threw the trash bag in. As I was closing it, I saw the clothes you donated, lying amongst the garbage. I'm sorry, Chip. I don't know how they got there."

Chip looked at her mom with tear-filled eyes.

"I'm sorry, honey," said her mom. "Sometimes things don't go the way you planned them."

"But why would she throw them away?" asked Chip going from being shocked to being angry. "It was an anonymous donation. There were some real nice clothes in that bag." Chip got up and went into the living room. She sat down in her dad's recliner with her arms folded across her chest. Luke and her mom followed. "Something stinks here. This doesn't make sense. Maybe the counselor threw them away."

"No," said Luke, looking at Mrs. Fullerton. "I actually saw Stacy, the girl who was supposed to get them, walk out with them. The publications room is right next to the counselor's office. She was paged to go there right after last period today. I couldn't see her face because she was walking away from me, but if body language means anything, she seemed very happy to get the clothes. I don't know what happened after that, but I don't think she was the one that went to the Dumpster and threw them in. It's a mystery."

"Well," said Chip, looking at Luke. "This is one mystery we are going to solve."

"I'd be careful on this one," said Karen as she stood up. "It might be a good idea to let something this strange go. In the real world, people's feelings get hurt or people get angry, and the results can be disastrous. I just heard your dad's car pull in. Why don't you two wash up for supper?"

Theories were thrown back and forth across the dinner table. John Fullerton sensed his daughter's disappointment, so there were no wisecracks. She was trying to do something nice for someone, and it had apparently backfired. He felt bad for her just as the others at the table did.

"So the clothes weren't salvageable?" asked Chip's dad.

"I don't think so," said Luke. "There was kitchen garbage all over them."

Chip stopped with her fork halfway to her mouth. "I'm going to get those clothes back." She looked at Luke. "We're going right after dinner. We'll need plastic gloves, a garbage bag, and a couple of flashlights." Her parents noticed that she didn't ask Luke, she told him.

"Melinda," said her mom quietly. "Don't you think you should ask Luke if he wants to participate in your salvage adventure? It sounds like a nasty chore. And don't bring those clothes into the house if they're all yucky. Wash them outside with the hose first."

"Good idea," said Chip, pushing back from the table. "C'mon, Luke, let's get our equipment together and go for an exciting Dumpster dive."

Her mom made a noise that said she should try again.

"I mean, Lukie, would you like to help me with a little project? There will be a free meal as a reward if we're successful."

Luke looked at Chip's parents. "How can I refuse an offer like that? We've got a bunch of heavy-duty rubber gloves at home. Let's stop by my house and pick them up. But first, you have to agree. If those clothes are too nasty, we leave them there. And I get to decide on that issue."

"Whatever, let's go. Once we get those clothes back, we're going to get to the bottom of this."

Chip and Luke stood outside one of the school's Dumpsters shining their flashlights into it. Chip was all for jumping right in, but he cautioned her that there might be rats hanging around. When they were positive that there were no critters in the

Dumpster, he went into a semisquat, and she stepped on his leg for a boost. She hopped in and threw her hands above her head as if she just stuck the landing in an Olympic gymnastics event. "Score, please."

"Stop messing around and check out those clothes," said Luke. "If they're too nasty, just leave them in there. This is creepy enough as it is. If the cops come by—"

Before Luke could finish his sentenced, the Reston squad car pulled into the lot. Officer Rubio got out and walked over to the teens with his hand hovering above his gun. "Watch it, Slowinski. There's a big varmint in that Dumpster. Stand back and give me a clean shot at her."

"Funny, Officer," said Chip, bending over and inspecting items. "Hey, could you give us some more light."

Officer Rubio went back to his unit and brought back a very powerful lantern. He shined it into the Dumpster. "Can I ask what you're doing in the school's trash bin? The citizen that called the station was worried that you were stealing valuable items."

"Retrieving my property," said Chip as she calmly put items of wet-stained clothing in the garbage bag that Luke was holding out for her. When she was done, she walked to the edge of the Dumpster and stood there. "Do you want to see a really cool Dumpster dismount, or do you want to help me down?"

Luke took off his gloves and grabbed her around the waist. He easily lifted her to the ground.

"Okay, you two," said Rubio. "Let's get away from this smelly thing so I can ask you a few questions." The two teens went over and stood by his squad car. Chip explained about the clothes and about Luke spying them in the trash earlier in the day. Rubio leaned back against the trunk of his car and mulled over the information she gave him. "What was the name of the girl who received the clothes from the counselor?"

"Stacy Wellington," said Chip. "It was supposed to be an anonymous gift so she wouldn't be embarrassed to wear them to school. I thought she could use some different clothes because she wears the same stuff every day. I guess we'll wash them and give them to Goodwill or somebody like that."

"This is the real world, Chip," said Officer Rubio. "Things are a lot more complicated than they should be. People do some of the craziest things. Your heart was in the right place though. I wish more teens behaved as you two do. It would make my job a lot easier. It would also be more interesting. Ya'll are always up to something. I would put those clothes in the trunk if I were you. They smell awful."

The two teens thanked him for his help and pulled out of the lot. Luke got half a block when Rubio, following behind, turned his overhead lights on. Luke moved to the curb and waited for the officer. As the town cop walked up, a carload of teens went by in the other direction. One guy leaned out the back window and hollered. "Slowinski, you lawbreaker. Throw him in the clink, Rubio. He's carrying drugs. Full cavity search."

"You've got some strange friends," said Officer Rubio, leaning in the window. "Listen, this is probably a long shot, but there might be something to it. Stacy's brother is somewhat of a hothead. We've had a few run-ins with him in the past. One thing I know is he is fiercely protective of his family. He's only twenty, but he's the father figure in the household. I'm thinking he is behind your clothes being dumped. It's just a theory. One other thing, I wouldn't pursue this any more. You two have a reputation for sticking your noses into other people's business, and this is something you should just let go. What I'm saying is, don't mess with Karl Wellington. He's bad news, anyway you look at it."

"Thanks, Officer," said Luke as Rubio retreated back to his car.

"This is the real world," said Chip mimicking Officer Rubio. "He's the second person to tell me that tonight. It's like they think I live in a fantasy world and don't know what's going on. Do you think I live in a fantasy world?"

"Uh, no, I don't think that. You are headstrong and stubborn most of the time. But that's not all bad—most of the time. You are a woman of conviction. That's the opposite of wishy-washy in case you didn't know. So what's your plan?"

"I know what conviction is," said Chip as she contemplated her next move. "I'm going to hose these nasty things off in the backyard, then they're going into the wash machine, probably twice. After that, I have to think about it. I've never heard of Karl Wellington, have you?"

"I think he's been out of the area for a few years, like away in some sort of juvenile facility. Rubio's advice was good. Let's let this one drop, okay?"

"I'll think about it," said Chip not willing to give up that easily.

Victor Reyes sat at his aunt's kitchen table with a stack of papers in front of him. He had volunteered to help her with her bills, and what he saw was very depressing. There just wasn't enough money. This is one of the reasons he was going to college. People with few skills, like his mom's sister, had very few options in the work world and were destined to have money problems their whole lives. Victor's mom told him stories about her sister when she was in high school. Everything seemed to be a big joke to her. She didn't try in school and was mostly worried about her appearance and what boys she'd like to go out with. The net result was another single young woman with children and no appreciable skills to help support her family. Thank goodness his mom wasn't anything like her sister.

Victor sat back and took a sip of his soda. It was going to take a miracle for his aunt and her three kids to stay in this house. The house wasn't worth much, but maybe she could sell it and move in with his mother. He decided to mention it to his mom when he went over there for dinner later. Victor looked at the stack of bills and decided to arrange them into three different piles—must pay, pay some of it, and it ain't gonna happen.

Diego came in the back door and saw his Uncle Victor sitting at the table. His timing was excellent. He walked over and without saying anything, slapped two hundred dollars down on the table. When Victor looked up, Diego broke out in a huge grin.

"What's this?" asked Victor.

"My contribution to the household finances," said Diego as he headed for the refrigerator. "Are those mom's bills? Wow, there's a ton of them."

"Hold it," said Victor, looking at the money in front of him. "Where did you get this?"

"You won't believe it," said Diego with his head in the fridge. He found a soda and sat down at the table. "I'm working for Mr. Kim, right? What a great guy! I was going to work at his store for as long as he wanted me to. And, just like we agreed, for nothing. Well, I'd been working three days a week for about a month. He did give me a couple of sacks of groceries, and he didn't have to do that. I did everything he asked, and I always tried to do something extra just like you told me. I could tell he was impressed. I even ran the register the last week I was there."

"The last week? So you're done working there?"

"Hold on. Where was I? Oh yeah. So Mr. K. tells me to deliver some sandwiches to the guys at the lumberyard. He's got this little sandwich business going Wednesday through Saturday. His wife usually delivers them, but she must have been busy. He told me she delivered thirty sandwiches one day. They're five bucks each, so that's a hundred and fifty dollars. I figure half of that is what the sandwiches cost them to make, so they made seventy-five bucks on the deal. That's decent for a couple of hours of work."

"So you're thinking like a businessman now. That's good. I'm glad to see that you are learning something. But that still doesn't explain where this two hundred came from."

"I'm getting there. So I ride my bike over to the lumberyard and ask for Mike. They sent me around back where this Mike guy, and two other guys were loading up some lumber. Mike pays me, gives me a two-dollar tip, and I start to head back. Then Mike hollers at me. 'Hey, kid' he said. 'Do you know why you're here?' I said, 'Yes, sir, I'm delivering sandwiches.' Then he told me I'm really there so he can get a look at me, you know, to see if I was the kind of guy that could handle real physical work. He said Mr. Kim spoke highly of me, so he offered me a job right there. Ten bucks an hour, three weekdays and Saturdays. Here's the clincher. I told him I would have to check with Mr. Kim first because I worked for him. I didn't mention that I was working for nothing to make up for my stupid behavior. Mike said that was the answer he was looking for. If I had said anything else, he would have withdrawn the offer right there. I guess he was testing me to see if I had any loyalty to my boss. Like if I was willing to jump to the lumberyard for more money, then I was probably the type of guy that would leave the yard for the first place that gave me a better offer."

"Now do you believe all the stuff I've been telling you about honor and duty and doing the right thing?" asked Victor.

"Yeah, you were right all along. Anyway, Mr. Kim told me to go work for Mike. And when he shook my hand, there was a hundred dollar bill in it. I told him thanks, but refused the money. What I learned working at his store was worth much more than that. Anyway, the two hundred is most of my first paycheck from the lumberyard. I should be able to help the family out now. From now on, I'm going to give half my pay to mom. Do you think that's about right?"

"That sounds fine," said Victor, standing and shaking his nephew's hand. "I'm proud of you, Diego. You dug yourself out of the hole you were in. Do a good job at the lumberyard. Who knows, you might end up owning it someday."

"I can't believe that we've got only two regular season games to go," said Jenny as the three of them played catch before the Wilson game. "And I can't believe that my sister is the starting pitcher today."

"I guess our coaches believe that she and Darby are sincere about their change of attitude," said Annie. "These last two weeks have been a lot more fun, except for—"

"Except for our new addition," added Chip before Annie could finish her sentence. "What's with that girl? How can she be so weird and have such a nice brother?"

"Just another challenge for us to overcome," said Jenny. "We sure seem to have more than our fair share of them." The three teammates had no way of knowing that the next challenge was less than an hour away.

It was the top of the fifth, and Tammi was cruising along nicely with a six to two lead. Chip made a dazzling play at short that resulted in a double play, or the score would have been much closer. Tammi led the team with their defensive salute. That gesture brought smiles from players and coaches alike. Those smiles turned to looks of shock when Maria hit a pop-up over in front of Reston's dugout. The Wilson third baseman came over cautiously, but she had plenty of room to make the play. As she was about to close her glove around the ball, Gina jumped off the bench, grabbed the dugout fence, and screamed at her. The unexpected move stunned the third baseman, and she flinched, failing to make the catch. The Reston players, coaches, and fans all froze. Coach Harbison was the first to recover. She went immediately to Gina, who was standing there with a smug little smile on her face. That smile disappeared fast when Coach H. told her she was no longer welcome in the Reston dugout. Gina had no idea of the gravity of her act.

"What was the problem? The girl dropped the ball, didn't she?" Gina reasoned. She looked at her future teammates as she headed for the bleachers, and they shook their heads showing disapproval.

Between innings, Coach Brown went over to the Wilson coach and apologized profusely. He explained that Gina was a recent transfer student and not really part of the team. And at this rate, it was questionable whether she would be part of the team next year. The visiting coach was very understanding about it. He told Leroy that he was aware of his team's reputation and wouldn't hold the act of one irresponsible girl against the Reston squad. Then the visiting coach said something you normally wouldn't hear from an opponent. He said he and his girls really wanted to see Smith pitch. They had heard so much about her and were expecting to see a true superstar in action. Coach Brown shook his hand and said maybe that could be arranged. Walking back to the dugout, Coach B. was smiling to himself. These girls were always involved in something. But then again, that's what made them such a challenge. And so far, the season was turning out to be a memorable one.

At the end of the home team's bleachers, another set of eyes was watching the whole incident evolve from Gina's yell to Coach Brown's reaction. Coach Devers, the boys' head basketball coach, decided then and there to make a phone call that he had been thinking about. Later that evening, he made his call to the Reston athletic director.

Reston had several subs playing in the field by the sixth inning. Tournament time was coming, but both the Reston coaches believed in playing everyone as much as possible. When they came in to bat at the bottom of the sixth, Coach B. went over to Tammi and told her he was going to let Annie pitch the seventh. He didn't explain that he was trying to atone for the behavior of a girl that wasn't even officially on the team yet. Tammi said what he hoped she would say, "No problem." The girls were finally coming together as a real team. Coach B. decided if they never won another game, he would be satisfied with the way things had turned out. He was confident that his assistant felt the same way.

Annie went out and finished the game in style—striking out the other side. When the teams shook hands after the game, the Wilson coach talked to Annie, Chip, and Jenny for longer than the normal "Good game, ladies." When Coach B. asked what that was all about, they told him the other coach was congratulating them on their basketball and softball seasons. He also told them they were a credit to their sport and to keep it up.

"Can you believe what the visiting coach said to us?" asked Chip as she and Annie sat in the back of Annie's truck, watching the sunset.

"Don't let it go to your head, Chipper," said Annie, munching on a piece of fried chicken. "There are a lot of great players in this state alone. Think of how many there are across the whole country."

"You really know how to deflate a girl's balloon, don't you? I'm not saying we're the greatest players to ever play the game. I'm just soaking up a little of the adulation that's coming our way."

"Adulation?" asked Annie. "Where did you come up with that word?"

"I'm trying to improve my vocabulary so Luke and I can have more meaningful conversations. He's pretty smart, ya know? I mean, for a guy. Where's Jenny? She should be here by now. It's not our fault if she has to eat cold chicken. By the way, I talked to Lu on the phone, and she says it's okay for us to visit her now."

The girls turned their heads when they heard Mr. Daggert's tractor rumbling down the dirt road. They always brought enough food for him when they showed up to watch the sun set. When the tractor got closer, they could make out the inside of the cab. Both of their mouths opened at the same time. Mr. Daggert wasn't alone in there. Jenny was with him, and it looked like she was driving!

"No way," hollered Chip as she stood on the tailgate and waved both arms at them. The tractor pulled up and came to a stop. Jenny and Mr. Daggert climbed down and walked up to the truck. Knowing how much Chip wanted to drive Mr. D.'s tractor, both of them had trouble keeping a straight face.

"Got any chicken left?" asked Jenny. "We're cattle people, but we'll settle for something smaller if we're hungry enough."

"I'm not believing this," exclaimed Chip. "How did you *fingale* your way into driving that beautiful piece of machinery?"

"Fingale?" asked Jenny as she handed the box of chicken to her fellow rancher.

"She's working on her vocab," volunteered Annie. "I think she means finagle."

"Whatever," said Chip. "When do I get to drive, Mr. D.?"

"Right after I finish this piece of chicken. We'll drive it up to the barn, and your friends can pick you up there. I'll help you with the controls on account of your—"

He was going to say short legs, but Jenny finished the sentence for him. "Abnormally short legs."

"As long as I get to drive it," said Chip, ignoring another zinger from Jenny. "Get your phones out girls. This is going to be a Kodak moment. C'mon, tractor buddy," said Chip, heading for the huge piece of farm machinery. "We're burning daylight."

"Sometimes," observed Annie, "Chip's world and the real world do come together."

"She's an original," said Jenny as they watched the tractor roll down the gravel road. "She does have a big heart though. Do you know about her quest for balance?"

"Yeah. I've seen the circles that she draws. I don't think she'll be satisfied until they are in perfect proportion."

"We should all be so lucky," said Jenny as she got into Annie's truck. "Chip's world isn't so bad."

A few days earlier, Mr. Ozello stood at his back door, watching the neighbor girl. "What's the Fullerton girl doing now?" asked his wife from the other room.

"I think their washing machine is broken," responded Mr. O. "She's got clothes laid out all over the lawn, and she's washing them with the hose. She'll get chiggers in them sure as shooting. That little girl is always up to something. Remember when she was younger and she put sandwiches all over her backyard and ours? She thought the squirrels weren't getting enough to eat. For days we had dozens of wild animals out back, looking for free food. And how about the time we caught her throwing rocks at our fake owl on the garage roof. She thought we put a real one up there to keep the squirrels from coming into our yard."

"Close the door and stop spying," said Mrs. O. "The neighbors will think you're a Peeping Tom. Maybe I should call Karen to see if she wants to use our machine until they get theirs fixed. Yup, that's just what I'm going to do. Close that door, old man, and come back and help me solve these Wheel of Fortune puzzles."

Tying up Loose Ends

Annie sat at the kitchen table, eating supper with her mom. Martha marveled at her daughter's ability to make new friends. Her athletic ability in two sports was definitely an asset, but even without it, she doubted that Annie would have had any problems in the friend department. Her friends were not what you would call dull either. In the past few weeks, Jenny pepper sprayed a guy and Chip, well if she knew everything Chip was up to she would probably have trouble sleeping at night. Chip told her two best friends about the Dumpster incident, but they were instructed to keep it in the vault.

"So what's Chip up to lately?" asked Martha as she cleared the dinner dishes from the table. "Anything exciting?"

"Uh, nothing real exciting unless you count driving Mr. Daggert's huge tractor. She's been bugging him about it for a long time, and he finally relented. You should have seen her face when Jenny pulled up in that thing. I know those two set it up just to get a rise out of her. Jenny has this incredible talent for that. Sometimes all it takes is a few words and bam, that little girl goes into overdrive. Oh yeah, the coaches banned the new girl from the dugout. She's not even on the team yet, and she's causing problems. I heard she plays basketball, so next season will be interesting, that's for sure."

"That's too bad. She should feel fortunate to be playing with such a nice group of talented girls like you and your teammates. You always wonder why people behave the way they do. Were they just born that way, or did they develop their ability to be mean or nice along the way?"

"We talked about that in psychology class last semester. We came to the conclusion that it was a combination of nature and nurture. You know, what you're given at birth and what you acquire from the people around you. And we decided that it wasn't a fifty-fifty proposition. Sometimes nature has more influence, and sometimes it's nurture. Our teacher had us write two paragraphs on what we would be like if we were raised somewhere different than where we are now. What would we be like if we were raised in the inner city or in a fishing village in Alaska? It was a pretty cool assignment. One of Chip's paragraphs was about growing up in southern California. She was a surf bum and a star beach volleyball player. She's got quite the imagination, but I know you have already figured that out. Like Jenny said, she's got a good heart. Right now she's...I can't tell you about that, but it's nothing bad. Spending a month with her in Michigan will be exciting."

"I'm sure you will have lots of stories to tell me when you get back. Do you have everything lined up, or do we need to go over it again?"

"I think we're good to go. Cheryl and her dad have arranged for everything. We ride the train to Michigan and her uncle picks us up. Sounds foolproof to me."

"I'd feel better if Rod were to accompany you."

"He's doing some sort of internship for school, Mom. It's important, and he can't reschedule."

"How much trouble could you get into if you don't leave the train? You're sure you don't have to get off anywhere until you get to Michigan?"

"Nope, there are restrooms on the train and everything. And I heard the food is really good."

"All right, but it's a mom's duty to worry. You know how much I worried about your sister when she went away to college?"

"Yeah, and when she didn't call you every night, you called her. I bet she took a lot of ribbing from her dorm buddies for that. 'Margie, is that your mommy on the phone again?' Do you mind if I go over to Lu's tonight? Her mom says it's okay to visit her now."

"Sure, as long as you've got all your homework done," said Martha as she headed for the living room. "I'm going to veg out in front of the TV. Oh, one more thing. You know how you have been encouraging me to socialize a little more? Well, there's a new doctor at the hospital that has hinted about going out to dinner. I'm thinking about taking him up on it. It will be like putting my big toe in the pool to test the water."

"That's great," exclaimed Annie. "When is this going to happen?"

"Probably the next time he brings it up. I don't know much about him at all, but he seems real nice. And he's not all that bad looking either, if you know what I mean."

"Go for it, Mom," said Annie as she headed out the back door.

The three softball players sat with Lu at her kitchen table and filled her in on everything that was happening at school and with the Reston sports teams.

"You don't look sick," observed Chip. "Are you sure you're not faking it to get out of school?"

"No," said Lu. "I wouldn't wish this on anybody. Ever since I caught this thing, I've been super tired."

"You were in such great shape," said Annie. "That should help."

"Yeah, the doc says my recovery should be faster than someone that's older and doesn't take care of themselves. I'll be okay. I'm going back to school tomorrow. I can stay as long as I don't get too tired. If I do, I can come home."

"Let me get this straight," said Chip. "You can leave school anytime you want? I'd say this is a gift, not an illness. Cough on me a few times. Wait, you better not. We've got the tournament coming up then our trip to Michigan."

"Ignore her," said Jenny. "What will you do once you've recovered? I mean with your track career."

"Go back to running," answered Lu. "It'll be tough, but if it was easy, anyone could do it. It's all about the journey, ladies. The journey is more important than the destination. I can't wait to lace up my running shoes again. I will even enjoy the pain of getting into shape. Pretty cool, huh?"

"You're the coolest, Lu," said Jenny. "C'mon guys, let's leave so she can get some rest. You better be ready to run when they get back from sports camp. We'll even slow down so you can keep up."

"Thanks, I appreciate that. You girls are great friends. Good luck in the state tournament. And thanks for the cool card that you made."

"You should have seen the rough draft," said Jenny. "It would have given you nightmares."

"What a great attitude, that little girl has," said Chip as the three of them crowded into Annie's truck. "She actually seemed positive about the bad break she got. Mono is also called the *kissing disease*. Did you know that? Did any of you ask her how she got sick in the first place? Do you think she was making out with some sick, leper dude?"

"Stop that," said Jenny. "Where do you come up with this stuff?"

"Just making an observation, tall girl. In the real world, that sort of stuff happens."

"So you're an expert on the real world now?" asked Annie.

"I am an enlightened individual on the subject," said Chip. "And let me tell you, the real world is a dangerous, vicious place.

We need to be on our toes all the time. That's because men have been in charge for so long, and they've messed it all up."

"Not this again," moaned Jenny.

"Tell me this, smarty," said Chip. "If women would have been in charge, do you think we would have had as many wars as we've had?"

"Maybe and maybe not," said Jenny. "The fighting might have been different though."

"Yeah," added Annie. "It would be a huge hair-pulling contest."

"I'm being serious," said Chip in her own defense. "When the call comes, the women of the world better be ready to take action. Are you with me or not?"

"We're with you, Chip," said Jenny. "We're with you all the way, win or tie."

Annie stood in the on-deck area, waiting for her first at bat in the game against Crane. It was their second to the last game and the team was playing well. They were scoring a lot of runs and giving up very few. All the reporters standing around bothered her. Apparently, her home run total was setting some kind of record. She knew she was somewhere in the low twenties, but she honestly didn't pay much attention to it. Individual accomplishments should be looked at after the season was over. Kris popped up for the second out, and Annie stepped in. Several cameras were held in the ready position.

"Focus, Karly," hollered the opposing coach to her pitcher. "This hitter is way overrated. She's a fence swinger."

It was obvious that the Crane pitcher wasn't going to give her anything good to hit. On the third pitch, Annie reached out and lined a single to right. Standing on first base, she looked over at Coach Brown, and he gave her the steal sign. She touched her helmet, acknowledging that she got the signal. She didn't even draw a throw as she slid into second. Crane's scouting report said that Smith rarely stole bases. With two outs, Annie was off and running when Courtney hit a line drive to right. She jogged across the plate as Crane's right fielder had trouble coming up with the ball cleanly.

"Way to pick up the pace out there," said Chip as Annie came back into the dugout. "What's that give you for steals this year, uh, about two?"

"Two more than your home run total," said Rachel.

"The game's not over yet," said Chip. "If our pitcher doesn't do something spectacular for those cameras, I'm going to have to step up."

"How about this, Chip," volunteered Rachel. "You hit one of your weak, sissified singles, then you do cartwheels all the way to first. That will get you in the papers for sure."

"Yeah," added Darby. "The funny papers."

Coach Brown turned his head when he heard his team laughing in the dugout. *Goofballs,* he thought to himself. *I hope they keep this attitude when tournament play starts. It's good to stay loose but not too loose.*

Annie was standing in the on-deck circle in the bottom of the third inning. Kris was up, and on the first pitch, Coach Brown signaled for Chip to steal second. Coach Brown was a little concerned with what happened next. There was no play on Chip as Darby was standing on third, but she slid in headfirst anyway. He immediately called time out and walked briskly out to second. When he got there, he held out his hands for Chip and motioned for Chip to put her hands in his. She figured this was bad news because this is what Luke would do when he had something serious to tell her. Coach Brown acted like he was looking at her hands for an injury.

"Look, Chip," whispered her coach. "You need to forget about the cameras and the reporters. I can't have you getting hurt on a play that should have never happened. So settle down and play your normal spectacular game, okay? Just your normal game."

"Sure, Coach, I'm on it," responded Chip.

"All right, take a breath and let's get on with it," said Leroy, letting go of her hands. The ump was right behind him, trying to move the game along. "Her hands are okay, ump. Just scratched up a little."

As Coach Brown went back to his third-base coaching box, he looked at Annie and rolled his eyes. She laughed and shrugged her shoulders. Jenny was standing in the dugout entrance, looking at Chip with a "what are you doing out there" look on her face. Chip waved and smiled back at her. Kris walked and Annie came up with the bases loaded. The Crane coach started in with what might again be considered harassing language directed toward Annie. The Reston slugger decided she'd heard enough of her nonsense and timed the next pitch perfectly. The left fielder, who was playing deep already, didn't even turn around to see it land on the other side of the fence. *So much for being overrated*, thought the left fielder. *Nice job, Coach. I hope they don't interview you after the game. You've embarrassed us enough already.*

The game finished with Reston winning seven to zero behind Annie's two-hit pitching. When the team met out in center field after the game, both Reston coaches warned them about talking to the press. "Don't try to be cute or funny. Just answer their questions politely."

Chip appeared to have calmed down, but they both looked in her direction to impress their point. "I'm cool," she said. "Don't worry, I just lost my head for a moment."

Surprisingly, the reporters wanted to talk to almost everyone on the team. Tammi was very gracious with her praise for Chip, Annie, and the rest of her teammates. Jenny was beaming. Now she had a sister and a teammate.

Gina watched the whole game from the bleachers. She didn't even want to come to the game, but she decided she needed to find Reston's weak spot. It might be her key to getting a starting position next season. She finally admitted to herself that these girls weren't too bad for country bumpkins. What happened next was something she had never seen before at a high-school softball game. When the reporters were done with their interviews, a middle-school girl from Crane went up to Annie and asked her to sign the ball she hit over the fence. The Reston star signed it with a smile and talked softball to the girl for a while. Soon, there were several people around Annie, Chip, and Jenny asking for autographs. Gina couldn't believe it. She was as good as these girls, and no one had ever asked her for an autograph. Obviously she was lacking something, but she had no idea what it was.

The Reston crew sat at the Pizza Palace that evening and discussed recent events. Lu was back, and Scott was now a regular. He had approached Chip, asking for advice on what it would take for Jenny to go out with him. This was unfamiliar territory for him as he rarely had a problem getting dates back in Fenton. Chip gave him a thoughtful answer without mentioning Jenny's experience with Morrie. She told him to be patient and not to try too hard. Jenny would let him know if she was interested. If not, there was a redheaded freshman she would be glad to introduce him to. If she did that, she wouldn't have to worry about Clarice, Luke's assistant, chasing after him all the time.

"Everyone, listen up," said Chip, banging on her glass with a fork. "Here's our status report. The attempted robbery has been laid to rest with an outcome better than we expected. Thanks to Annie and Rod for bringing that to Victor's attention. Jenny's, uh, adventure with Morrie is over. Thanks to all who were involved with that one. Tammy and Darby are now real teammates, and hopefully, soon to be good friends. Great job, Jen and Annie. And I'd like to announce that the clothing issue has been solved also."

"What?" asked Luke. "What did you do? Our lives aren't in jeopardy, are they?"

Scott whispered to Jenny, who was sitting next to him, "He's kidding about that, right?"

"Not necessarily," answered Jenny. "These two are quite well-known by officers of the law throughout the whole area."

"We don't know all of them," added Chip.

"The school year's not over yet," said Rod. "Give them time."

"What about the clothing?" persisted Luke.

"I decided to take direct action on that one," said Chip. "I saw Stacy walking home from school yesterday, so I pulled over and asked her if she wanted a ride. When she got in the car, I asked her point blank about the clothes and how they got into the Dumpster. She started to cry a little but finally told me that her brother took them from her and threw them away. He said their family didn't accept charity from anybody."

"So Rubio was right," observed Luke. "What happened next?"

"After I explained that I retrieved them and cleaned them up, I talked her into taking a shirt and a pair of jeans. If he asked, she was going to tell her brother that they came from the lost and found at school. Since the year is almost over, students are allowed to take anything that hasn't been claimed. And since no one gave them to her, it's not a charity issue. That way, she will be able to wear something different from time to time, and he won't question it. The lost and found thing is actually true, so we weren't lying about that. Most of the stuff in there is pretty grungy though. Pretty slick, huh?"

"So does this mean your circles will stay the same?" asked Annie.

"What are circles?" asked Scott somewhat confused.

"That would take too long to explain," answered Annie. "And you probably wouldn't believe it anyway."

"Status on big Shirley," said Chip as if she were an executive running a staff meeting.

"That issue has been brought to fruition," said Annie. Then she whispered to Scott, "She likes us to use big words. We're supposed to be working on our vocabularies."

Scott sat there, trying to take it all in.

"When she came back from suspension," continued Annie, "I cornered her in the hallway and thanked her for what she did. She acted like it was no big deal, but I still told her I knew why she did it and was grateful. She said don't let that get around because she had a rep to protect. Oh yeah, and I owed her a big soda. I think she's got a soft heart somewhere under all that swagger."

"Okay," continued Chip. "We've got one regular season game to go and then the state tournament. Then we get a short break, and Annie and I are off to Michigan. Jenny, Lu, and Luke, you're going to have to hold down the fort until we get back."

"Aye, aye, captainette," said Luke, saluting. "By the way, I've got some info that even you aren't aware of." This last statement got everybody's attention. Luke leaned forward for dramatic effect and, in a quiet voice, he said, "Your new basketball coach is going to be none other than..." He added a drum roll on the table that brought scornful looks from the basketball players. "Coach Bob Devers."

"No way," said Chip. "Why would the boys coach come over to coach the girls? You must have heard it wrong."

"Nope. He's going to have a basketball meeting in a few days to fill everybody in. You know, announce that he's the new coach and what the summer program is going to be like."

"But we'll be gone for the summer program," said Chip. "It's always in June so they can redo the gym floors in July. Not a problem. We'll tell Coach Devers, if he's really the new coach, about our *dew-lama*. He'll understand."

Scott made a strange face until Jenny set him straight. "That's Chipspeak for dilemma," she whispered. He looked at her with a thoughtful expression then shook his head indicating that he understood.

"One more thing," added Jenny. "What about the strange guy that kept coming to our early season games? You remember, he was dark and always wore sunglasses. Luke, did you find out anything about him? We thought he might be a college scout, since he seemed to be focused on B., uh, Annie."

"No luck on that," said Luke. "I just didn't have enough to go on. I even tried talking to him once, but he didn't have much to say."

"Why do ya'll sometimes have trouble saying Annie's name?" whispered Scott to Jenny.

"She didn't always go by Annie," answered Jenny. "That's a long story too."

"She went by another name?" asked Scott. "What is she some kind of spy?"

"Ha, that's what our two famous detectives thought," answered Jenny. "Sometimes they get out of control with their crazy theories. Their sanity has been questioned more than once by the residents of Reston." Then she added, "Lu, we're glad you're back. It's too bad about your quest for the state title. I guess there's always next year."

"I can't believe I missed out on so much action," said Lu. "I wish I would have been there to see the short one here drive that tractor. Did Mr. D. really put blocks on your feet?"

"We've been over this before, squirt," said Chip. "I'm taller than you, and you know it."

"I don't think so," challenged Lu shaking her head from side to side. Jenny wasn't the only one that could get a rise out of Chip.

"Okay," said Chip, looking around. "There's two nice-looking old people over there, *scarfing* down some pie. How about we go over there and stand side by side. Then they, two totally unbiased strangers, can judge who's taller."

"Don't fall for it, Lu," said Jenny. "Those nice people are Chip's next-door neighbors."

"You would cheat a sick girl?" asked Lu as if she had just been insulted.

"Spoil sport," said Chip to Jenny.

"Aren't you forgetting something?" asked Luke pointing to his feet.

"Whoops," said Chip. "You better explain that one, master of the scam."

"Okay," said Luke. "This was mostly Chip's idea, but I had a small hand or foot in it. Ya'll, except for Scott, know my assistant, Clarice. She's been after me to dump Chip and start dating her. And although I have given it some consideration—"

Chip interrupted him with a snorting noise.

"Anyway, since she's been such a busybody lately and likes to spread rumors, we decided to start one. We made something up and told only Clarice. We figured we would wait for a week to see if the word got around. It actually only took a couple of days for it to get back to us."

"What was the rumor?" asked Jenny. "I haven't heard anything out of the ordinary."

"Me either," added Annie.

"Well," said Luke, taking a big breath. This is where he lost it. He started laughing and banged on the table with his fist. His friends had never seen him like this before. It must have been a very creative rumor. Tears started to flow down his cheeks.

"Come on, laughing boy," said Chip. "It isn't that big of a deal. We told that little redheaded blabbermouth that—" Now Chip was laughing. She looked at Luke who had his hands in front of his face. Several of the patrons at the surrounding tables were looking at him.

"Finish it," said Jenny. "This place closes at ten."

"Okay, here it is," said Chip, composing herself. "Luke told me that in his modern history class they are studying movie stars from the fifties and sixties. And he happened to mention that Marilyn Monroe was believed to have six toes. We decided to tell Clarice that someone at school had six toes, and then we waited to see if she would spread the word. After only a few days, it was all over the place. I'm surprised you didn't hear about it."

The people at the table looked at each other and made gestures that showed they hadn't heard anything.

"You probably didn't hear anything because you know this person quite well," said Chip. "Keep in mind this was a harmless experiment to show little miss chatty Clarice that she should keep her mouth shut."

"We know this person quite well," repeated Jenny. "Who is it?"

Now Luke and Chip were laughing so hard they couldn't even speak. In unison, they both pointed at Annie.

"What?" hollered Annie. "You told her I had six toes?"

Now the whole restaurant was looking at them. The owner was explaining to some out-of-towners that this was pretty much the norm for this group. Then he told them who the girls were. One lady at the table jumped up and went out to her car. She brought back a softball and went over to the table. She apologized for interrupting and then asked for the three softball players to sign it. She said she was originally from Fort Worth but now lived in Austin. She had been reading about the Reston players in the newspapers that her brother sent to her. The three girls were very polite and answered all of her questions. Scott couldn't believe it. With all his athletic accomplishments, he had never signed a single autograph in his life, and these girls were signing things for people all the time. And they seemed to be used to it.

When the lady left, Annie leaned across the table and spoke in a low voice, "I can't believe you did that. I'm going to start my own list now, and guess who is going to be at the top?"

"Sweety, I wouldn't start something unless it was well thought out," explained Chip. "All we have to do is paint our toenails in the school colors and then wear sandals the next day. People will see your toes and will figure out that it was just a rumor, and that you're not a toe freak. Then we'll bust that little assistant sports writer. I can't wait to see her face when we tell her it was all made up, and she was the only one we told it to. You were a perfect subject for the rumor because you always wear running shoes to school. Those little toes of yours are always out of sight. Let's call the rest of the team tonight and tell them to do their toes. It will be like a school spirit thing."

"I'll go along just so people won't think I'm weird and have extra things on my body," said Annie.

"I think you are all weird," said Scott. "That's probably why I like hanging out with you."

"You want to hear weird," said Jenny. "During basketball season, Chip made this little doll that—"

"He doesn't want to hear all that historical stuff," interrupted Chip.

"How about the pliers incident?" asked Rod looking at his cousin.

"There was no pliers incident," said Chip. "You're making something up just to be part of the conversation."

"Let's hear it," said Annie.

"Okay," said Rod, holding his hands up for effect. "When little Melinda was in the third grade, she went into the kitchen where my mother and her mother were sitting at the kitchen table. When the little squirt tried to sneak something past them, her mom told her to stop and show what she was hiding behind her back. She had taken a pair of pliers out of the drawer. She said, and you won't believe this, that Luke had a red nose, and she was going to squeeze it with the pliers and make it pop. That way he would be all better."

"I never did anything like that," said Chip in her defense. "What a stupid story!"

"Luke," said Rod, asking him for verification.

"I remember that day," said Luke. "Chip's mom was watching me because my mom had to go into the city. It was my first zit or what was going to soon become a zit. My nose was all red and really sore. Chip said she could fix it for me. It was weird because when she came back into the room, she said to forget about it. So that's what happened. You got caught trying to sneak pliers past your mom. I can't believe it. You were going to squeeze my nose with those things. I could have been disfigured for life."

"Don't make such a big deal about it," said Chip. "Anyway, it might have left a really cool scar. You would have been the most popular kid in the third grade, thanks to me."

"Only because I would have looked like the scary brother in *The Goonies*. You were one dangerous little girl."

"I still am," warned Chip. "And don't you forget it."

"Enough," said Jenny, standing up. "We could fill the whole evening with the strange stuff that this little character has done. She's lucky she's not in juvenile hall for some of the things she's been involved with."

Now Scott wasn't sure what to believe. As they got up to leave, Annie spread her hand at the table and asked, "You're buying tonight, aren't you, Scott?"

"He can afford it," said Luke, digging into his pockets for some cash. The rest of them did the same. "His dad's a doctor."

"Not all doctors are rich," said Scott. "Uh, Jenny, can I walk you to your car?"

"Sure," said Jenny, trying to sound indifferent. "We're all going that way."

Behind Jenny's back, Chip gave Scott a thumb's up.

Chip walked by the table where the older couple was sitting. "Hi, Mr. and Mrs. Ozello. How was the pizza?"

"It was good, Melinda," said Mrs. Ozello. "You tell your mom she can use our washing machine any time she wants."

"Uh, okay, I'll be sure to tell her that."

"What was that all about?" asked Luke as the two of them walked away.

"I don't know," answered Chip. "You know how older folks are these days. Who knows what they're thinking."

"That Melinda sure is a nice girl," said Mrs. Ozello.

"She's always up to something," said her husband. "You know how young folks are today. Who knows what they're thinking."

Jenny was bummed and she had no reason to be. She was hitting over .350, fielding her position like a champ, and the team was doing great. They had high hopes for the state tournament. The basketball and softball seasons had surpassed her wildest dreams. And her sister was acting like a normal person. Down deep, she knew what the problem was. One, Chip and Annie were going away for a whole month. Two, she knew that the new guy, Scott, liked her, but she couldn't bring herself to talk to him alone. He had called her a couple of times, and both times she made up an excuse why she couldn't talk for more than a couple of minutes. She wondered how he got her cell number. That little busybody Fullerton probably gave it to him. One thing was certain; it was going to be a dull month with her two best friends away in a far-off state.

Annie lay in her bed, thinking about all the things that had happened to her and her friends lately. High school sports were sure a lot of fun if you put them in perspective. She didn't know what she would be doing if she wasn't playing ball. Maybe she would be a music geek. She sat up and grabbed her bass guitar that was next to her bed. She cued up Black Sabbath's "Ironman" on her mp3 player and played along. She hadn't been practicing all that much lately. Every time she picked up the instrument, it reminded her too much of her dad.

Chip was busy in her room, deciding on what she should take on their trip. She also needed to make up a list of things for Luke to do while she was away. Her dad had agreed to let Luke take her spot at the hardware store. Once school was out, she usually worked two days a week and Saturdays. Her dad needed her more because of summer-vacation coverage. She was sitting at her desk when her mom hollered at her.

"What are you doing in there, sweetie?" asked Karen.

"I'm looking up on the Internet on how to make homemade fireworks, Mom. Do we have any gunpowder in the garage or stuff I can make fuses out of?"

Karen was used to this kind of behavior, so she didn't even flinch. "I think we're all out, dear. I'll have your dad bring some home from the store tomorrow. Oh, by the way, we decided to get you a pet. He should be in your room somewhere. Maybe he's hiding under the bed. Good night and sweet dreams. Hahaha."

"I'm not falling for that," said the little shortstop quietly so her mom couldn't hear. "What kind of mom would say that to her own kid? And what was that goofy witch laugh? She is going back on my list. I'll have a lot of time on the train ride to Michigan to plan some get-even strategies. Right after we win the state title and Jenny, Annie and I are named coMVPs." She quickly looked under the bed and in the closet before jumping into bed. Just to be safe, she left the desk light on.

Tournament Time

School was almost out, and the softball team was rolling. They were getting huge coverage by the Dallas and Fort Worth newspapers, as well as the local radio stations. The Reston Lady Eagles had won their first four tournament games without being seriously challenged. Coach Brown did a good job distributing the pitching duties between Annie, Tammi, and Carmen. One big surprise was Jenny's play. She was hitting .500 for the four tournament games and had even bounced one off the left field fence. Another couple inches, and it would have gone out. She took a lot of ribbing after that hit. On their way to the bus, after being interviewed for the umpteenth time, Annie received a call on her cell. She had a serious look on her face when she motioned for Chip to hold up. The rest of the team kept walking toward the bus. Annie slammed her phone shut and whispered to Chip. Jenny was watching from the bus door, thinking that her two teammates were planning something. It paid to be suspicious of these two at all times. Letting your guard down was not the thing to do especially when Chip or Luke were involved.

Once the team was on the bus and settled in, Chip started to do a mock interview of Jenny. "Is it true, Ms. Olsen, that you have a new romantic interest, and that your recent surge of awesome play is an attempt to impress him?"

"No," answered Jenny. "And stop with the questions. They're annoying. Why don't you bother one of the other girls?"

"That's obviously a sore point with you," continued Chip holding the small end of her bat as if it was a microphone. "Let's talk about performance enhancing drugs. You are familiar with them, aren't you? Those little spaghetti arms of yours have grown quite a bit in the past few weeks. Didn't you recently hit an awesome shot over the left fielder's head? Care to comment on that?"

"Annie," wailed Jenny, "help me out here. Get this little bulldog away from me. Who does she think she is, Luke Slowinski?"

"She can't be stopped when she's hot on a story," said Annie. "It's best to just answer her questions. And I wouldn't tick her off. She's a bad go-getter if she feels she's been wronged. She has a list from here to Reston of people she wants to get even with."

"That's true," admitted Chip. "Do you think your trip to the Michigan camp will improve your basketball and softball skills?"

"Duh, fake reporter. I'm not going to Michigan. Hopefully I will get a job and make a little money while you two are playing up there in the snow. Do you even know where Michigan is?"

"I'll ask the questions here. And I will repeat myself because you seem to be a little slow today. Do you think you will be a better player after the camp with Cheryl's uncle?"

Jenny looked over at Annie who was smiling and shaking her head in the affirmative. Slowly, her face showed that she understood what Chip was getting at. She was asking her if she wanted to go to the camp with them to coach some younger girls.

"Are you serious?" asked Jen. "I mean you're not just messin' with me here? If you are that would be really mean." Jenny looked at both of them, and they were still shaking their heads and smiling. After a group hug, Annie explained how Cheryl had just called her and told her that her friend from Lakewood couldn't make it and would she ask Jenny. Annie didn't mention that she had tried very hard to get Cheryl's uncle to ask Jenny to come along too. But he said the dorm rooms were set up for only four to a room, and he didn't want to ask too many favors from the university since they were already very accommodating. As soon as Annie was done explaining how the invite came about, Jenny was on her phone to her mom. Her mom knew that Jenny was secretly disappointed that she wasn't asked, and it didn't take much persuasion for her to say she would probably be able to convince her husband that it would be best for all concerned that Jenny be allowed to go. She told her daughter to invite her two friends over for dinner that evening so they could answer any questions that they might have.

"Look, Mrs. Olsen," said Chip. "The train trip will be safe. There's like five train employees in each car and—"

"My dad is a dispatcher for the BNSF Railroad, Chip," said Jenny. "Mom knows that's not true."

"Okay, I was exaggerating a little on that," said Chip without losing a beat. "But we will have weapons, so there shouldn't be any—"

"Let me handle this, Chip," said Annie. "Mrs. Olsen, once we get on the train, we won't get off until we get to where we are going. Plus the train employees will know that we are minors traveling without parental supervision. They will help to keep an eye on us. Cheryl's uncle will pick us up at the train station and will take us to Western Michigan University. We will be staying in the university dorms close to the athletic center and the softball fields. There will be adult supervision in the dorms. Cheryl and her uncle have everything all planned out. There will also be other student coaches there. I think they will be from Lansing."

"You know I was kidding about the weapons, right Mrs. O?" asked Chip. "I get carried away sometimes especially when it looks like a plan is coming together."

"Chip," said Jenny's mom. "I've known you all your life. As my husband says, you're a live wire. We just want to be sure that you will all be in a safe environment. It's a crazy world out there."

"Tell me about it," said Chip.

The back door slammed and Mr. Olsen walked into the room. Jenny jumped up and gave him a hug. "That's a, 'I want something, dad' hug," said Mr. Olsen. "What is it this time, and how much is it going to cost me?"

As the meal wound down, the Olsen parents finally gave Jenny permission to go. Tammi was genuinely happy for her twin, and Jenny's younger sister, Cassie, was in awe that her big sister would be coaching alongside Chip and Annie. She made Jenny promise to e-mail her every day, telling her what they worked on and what they were doing after practice ended.

The next day at school was a routine one until right after last hour. At lunch the girls told Lu about Jenny's invite to camp, and she was ecstatic. She told the three of them that she wanted daily updates of everything that went on.

Chip and Jenny walked into the cafeteria right after school, where there appeared to be some sort of confrontation. Mr. Fox, the boys' counselor was standing with his back to the wall intently watching the action unfold. He was ready to step in if the situation called for it. When the two softball players got to where they could see what was going on, they were surprised to see that Scott was in the middle of everything. A junior girl named Trish was the other main character in the drama that was being acted out.

"What's going on?" asked Chip as she looked up at the taller girl. "You can see up there, can't you?"

Jenny shushed her. She wanted to hear the conversation between Scott and Trish, Reston's infamous high-school socialite.

Trish Sterling was known as the Reston debutante. From third grade on, her mom always dressed Trish to perfection, right down to the scarves that she wore even when it was ninety plus degrees out. Rumor was, she put Trish on birth control pills in the eighth grade, because according to her, Trish was so beautiful that the boys just wouldn't be able to stay away from her. Trish relished the attention and played her role to the hilt. For her, it was all about image. If they had allowed her to bring her little housedog to school, she would have carried him from class to class. Trish was used to getting what she wanted, one way or another. And recently, she had decided that Scott would be a worthy conquest. It didn't take long for the transfer student from Tyler to figure out this girl's game, and he wanted no part of it. She was a manipulator that used her dad's money and her mom's narrow-mindedness to get what she was after.

"Hello, new boy," said Trish as she sat down next to Scott at one of the cafeteria tables. He didn't need to look up from his book to see who it was; her perfume preceded her by several seconds. There were about fifty students in the cafeteria doing an assortment of activities while they waited for their busses or after school activities. A few were actually doing their homework or studying for their upcoming final exams. "I'm sure you've been dying to talk to me, so here's your chance. If I had to wait for you to get up the courage to come to me, school would be out. Me and some of my friends are going out to a special place for a little get-together tonight. Why don't you come by about eight and pick me up? We'll go together. There will be plenty of refreshments and who knows what else."

"Thanks, uh, Trish, but I've already got plans," said Scott looking over at a couple of grinning girls that were taking the whole thing in. They were part of Trish's entourage, and they usually followed her wherever she went.

"I guess you are a little confused," said Trish, refusing to believe that he had said no to an evening with her. "But that's okay since you're new and all. I'm asking you out, stupid."

"And I'm saying thanks, but no thanks," said Scott without trying to make a big deal about it.

"Are you blind?" asked Trish in a voice that betrayed her usual confident manner. "Look at me. Do you see what you're passing up? I promise it will be a very good time."

"No, thanks. I'm sure there are plenty of guys here that would want to go. My guess is that you can probably just pick one."

Trish looked around and saw that the crowd around them had grown in numbers. "So what are you saying?" she asked in a very loud voice. All the activity and conversation in the cafeteria stopped when she raised her voice. She looked around and saw that she had quite an audience. "You're telling me you don't like girls? Is that it? I mean, I heard rumors, but I just didn't want to believe it."

"Go bother someone else," said Scott, standing up and gathering his stuff. "I'm out of here." He turned to move but was blocked by a group of students that had gathered to see the show.

"I don't want to use the *G* word," continued Trish even louder, "because it's against school rules. But if the shoe fits, if you know what I mean. I can't believe it—a good-looking guy like you. Is that why you moved here from another town? To get away from your past?" Trish was not used to being rejected, and she was not handling it well. She was not going to come out of this on the losing end.

Chip and Jenny had walked in to the area at the moment Trish started to ramp up her voice. Chip grabbed Jenny by the arm and pulled her along. They got behind Mr. Fox, who was starting to move through the crowd. It was time to break this little scene up. When Chip figured out what was going on, she grabbed the counselor's arm and quietly asked him to wait a second. The counselor knew this was a little out of the ordinary, but when he saw it was two of Reston's prize athletes, who were also two of the school's top students, he told her she had better know what she was doing.

Chip turned to her friend. "Get in there and save the day. You know what to do."

Jenny looked at her with questioning eyes. Then she figured out what Chip was talking about and nodded her head to show that she understood. She turned and worked her way to where Scott and Trish were standing. If Chip were tall enough, she would have seen her teammate walk up to Scott and give him a big kiss right in front of everybody.

"Sorry I'm late, Scott," said Jenny, taking his hand. "Are you ready? Let's go." With that, she took a stunned Scott by the hand and turned to leave. "Nice blouse, Trish," said Jenny loud enough so the surrounding crowd could hear. "I bet that cost a lot of money." Jenny's comment drew several laughs from the crowd. A few even clapped. They recognized an awesome put-down when they heard one. Trish just stood there with a few of her camp followers as the crowd dispersed. They were speechless.

Mr. Fox looked over at Chip and discreetly put a closed fist out to her. With equal discreetness, she bumped it with her own. *Kids, they were a constant source of amazement and amusement at the same time.* He decided to let that little PDA go. In this case, it was completely warranted.

"Thanks, tall stranger," said Scott as they rejoined Chip.

"No problem," said Jenny as they walked out the front door together. "It looked like you could use a little help back there."

"Trish is like a python," said Chip. "Once they get their tentacles in to you, they don't let go."

Jenny and Scott both laughed at this comment. Neither of them bothered to inform Chip that pythons didn't have tentacles. Jenny and Scott were still holding hands when they got to her car in the parking lot. Tammi was sitting in the front seat, waiting for her sister. Scott finally let her go and thanked her again for her assistance. As Scott and Chip started to walk away, Scott turned and asked Jenny if he could call her. The first baseman looked into Chip's pleading eyes and said it would be okay but not too late.

Chip and Scott continued on through the parking lot where Annie was waiting for Chip in her truck. Chip saw Luke exit the school, so she grabbed Scott's hand. Walking hand in hand they passed Luke who was concentrating on a piece of paper in his hand. "Hey, Luke," said Chip, trying to get his attention.

Luke looked up for a couple of seconds finally recognizing them. "Hey, babe, I ended up getting an *A* on the history quiz. But she made me promise to never pull a stunt like that again. Actually, I think she was impressed with my creativity. You better hurry or you'll be late for practice. Hey, Scott." With that he returned to his paper.

"Ya'll are absolutely crazy," said Scott as they got to Annie's truck. "Did you know that, Annie?"

"It only took me a couple of days after I got here to figure that out," said Annie.

Scott spun Chip around so they faced each other and gave her a big hug. "I'm sure you had something to do with that back in the cafeteria. Thanks, I appreciate it."

"No problem, but now you're in our debt," said Chip in a serious tone. "And we do want something from you, don't we, Annie?"

Scott looked at Annie for some sort of explanation. She shrugged her shoulders, signifying that she had no idea what Chip was getting at.

"We want you to be extra nice to Jen. Show her you're a real gentleman. She's our good friend, and she deserves it."

"Of course," said Scott. "She's awesome, and trust me, that's the only way I know how to treat someone like her."

"Be careful with that *trust* word," said Chip. "Let's just say that word has caused her problems in the past."

"I'll be careful," said Scott as he turned to leave. When it dawned on him what had just happened, he had trouble keeping his mouth shut. He wanted to holler out loud that the girl he had been dreaming about had said he could call her. Oh yeah, and she had kissed him too. He knew that a sympathy kiss didn't really count, but maybe there would be some real ones in the future.

He wondered what Chip was alluding to when she mentioned Jenny's past. No matter, it was a good day. Now he had to decide what he was going to talk to Jenny about when he called her later that evening. He got to his car and his sister, as usual, was mad because he was late. Her snarky little comments directed toward him, and a host of others, couldn't wipe the smile off his face.

"Did you see that jerky boyfriend of mine?" asked Chip. "I walked right by him holding another guy's hand, and he didn't say a word about it."

"Does that move him up the list?" asked Annie laughing.

"No, he's usually at the top of his own special category. I'm thinking I need to plan something even more elaborate than the last time."

"No food, okay? That was pretty disgusting."

"I'll think about it. You won't believe what just happened in the cafeteria. Jenny blew "Trish the Dish" away. We'll have to be careful around her little clique for a while. Some people like to get even, you know?"

"Really? I don't think I know anyone like that around here."

"Whatever, let's talk softball. I'll bet there will be ten thousand people there tomorrow."

There wasn't ten thousand at the next day's game, but it was the largest crowd that anyone could remember for a small school Texas softball game. And no one left the game disappointed.

Annie toed the rubber and looked in at the Clarkston hitter. The Running Rebels from Clarkston were a perennial softball power in north Texas. Their pitcher didn't have as many pitches as Annie, but she threw hard and had good control. So far, each pitcher had given up only one hit. The Reston rooters were a little surprised when, in the first inning with two outs and no one on base, the Clarkston pitcher walked Annie on four pitches. It was obvious that they had Reston scouted, and their coach wasn't going to give the Reston slugger an opportunity to change the game with one swing if he could help it.

The game went in to the top of the sixth with no score. It had the makings of a marathon. The winner of this game would be the first team to scratch out a run. Clarkston appeared to be that team when their first batter bunted toward third, and Maria couldn't make a play on it. Annie struck the next batter out as she tried to bunt her teammate to second. The next batter successfully bunted moving the runner along. With a runner on second and two outs, the Clarkston coach tried something to shake up the game—he had his runner steal third. The batter faked a bunt, which drew Maria in from third. Chip was hedging a little toward the bag, and when the batter took the pitch she got to third in plenty of time to take the throw. It helped to have a shortstop that paid attention, and it also helped to have one as quick as Chip.

Chip's heads-up play made no difference as Darby's throw sailed over the shortstop's head into left field. The Clarkston coach made a smart decision. He looked toward left and held up his runner. Courtney was on the move when she saw the runner head for third. She fielded the overthrow cleanly and was standing with the ball about twenty feet past the bag at third. With a good throw, she would have easily thrown out the runner at home. Annie got the next batter to hit a weak grounder back to her for the third out.

"We dodged a bullet there," said Chip. "C'mon, ladies, let's win this thing right here. I'm getting hungry."

Chip led off the inning with Reston's second hit of the game. Kris came up and laid down a beautiful bunt to the third baseman. Her throw was low to first, and it was bobbled by the first baseman. As Annie approached the plate, the Clarkston coach called time. Before he headed onto the field, his assistant reminded him that she had seen Annie hit one about seventy-five feet over the fence earlier in the year when she was scouting Reston.

The Clarkston coach walked up to his pitcher. "I'm thinking about walking her."

"If we put the go-ahead run on third, they could score with a passed ball or even a tough grounder to the infield," said his pitcher.

"Let me pitch to her, coach. She doesn't look that tough. I've handled her so far."

"Rachel, this girl doesn't just hit softballs; she crushes them. She is probably the toughest hitter you will ever face in high school. I don't know. Do you think you can get her?"

"I know I can. Just give me the chance," pleaded Rachel.

"All right," he said, patting his pitcher on the shoulder. "Work the corners. Nothing down the middle. Go get her."

Annie looked down at Coach Brown in the third-base coaching box. She questioningly flashed the bunt signal to him. He grinned and shook his head. She had only bunted once this year and had popped it up. She wasn't the type of batter that was called on to bunt very often. He gave her the swing-away sign. Annie looked down along the right field fence and saw Rod and a couple of college friends standing there. She took a deep breath and tried to calm herself. Keep it smooth. Don't get overly excited and start swinging like a crazy woman, trying to impress your boyfriend and his buddies. The Reston slugger drew on her experience and stepped in focused and ready.

The game announcer introduced the Reston pitcher over the P.A. "Now batting for Reston, number fifteen, pitcher, Annie Smith."

Chip was standing on second, watching her teammate as she stepped into the batter's box. She did her own quiet introduction. "Now batting for New York, number nine, right fielder, Roy Hobbs." Hearing this, the Clarkston shortstop gave her an odd look. Apparently, she had never seen Robert Redford in *The*

Natural. Chip looked to the sky to see if any storm clouds were forming. No luck there; the sky was completely clear.

Annie leisurely swung her bat back and forth and looked at the pitcher. So far, she had walked and had flown out to right. All she was looking for was something she could drive. With Chip's speed, a single would probably send her home. The crowd was as loud as she had ever heard. But they sounded like one big blur to her. No one voice was distinctive. Chip was saying something at second, but it was impossible to hear her. Kris and Coach Harbison were also hollering. Annie relaxed her grip just a little. The first pitch was a little outside, and the ump called it a ball. The next one was a rise ball that started chest high and went even higher. *This is it,* thought Annie. *If she's going to pitch to me, she will try to get this one over. Quick bat, quick bat.*

The Clarkston pitcher threw a fastball that was supposed to hit the outside third of the plate. It came out of her hand and sped toward the catcher. It was about six inches to the right of where she intended it to go. It was a small mistake on her part but enough of a mistake for a hitter like Annie to cash in on. Annie stepped forward, snapping the bat through the hitting zone. Her technique was flawless. She made solid contact, sending the ball toward left field. It was still on its upward arc when it passed over the outfield fence. The Reston crowd went crazy.

"Yup," said the Clarkston assistant coach. "That's pretty much what I saw earlier this season. That girl is one dynamite hitter."

Annie came out in the top of the seventh and struck out the side to secure Reston's win.

"This is getting crazy," said an excited Chip as she sat in the back of Annie's truck. The sun had just set, and the four girls were sitting on the sides with their feet in the bed. They could hear Mr. Daggert's cattle in the background. "School's about out and if, uh when, we win the next game, we head downstate to the big time. How many great softball players do you think will be there, Jen?"

"Probably one less than you think," responded the first baseman, looking up the gravel road. Annie and Lu got the sly remark, and they both snickered. It went right over Chip's head. "Where are those guys with the food?"

The guys promised to treat the four of them if they won the game against Clarkston. They were supposedly on their way with a carload of chicken, salads, and pizza.

"Why don't you entertain us with your latest dream, Chippy?" asked Jenny. "Ya'll are going to love this."

"They're just dreams, Jen," said Chip. "They're not real."

"Humor us."

"Okay," said Chip. "A couple of days ago, I had this dream where sharks came out of the water and started walking around. I probably was subconsciously thinking about them because there have been a lot of shark sightings in the news lately. Anyway, they walked on their tail fins and were wearing really nice business suits, and they had bibs on that said, "Thank you for inviting us to dinner." I was standing at a podium, making a speech. I think I was like the president of the United States or somebody even more important like the governor of Texas. One really big shark started to come after me, so I pulled a softball bat and some balls out from behind the podium and started hitting balls at him. I hit him right on the nose, and he turned and ran away. There was one about three hundred feet away, and the crowd was chanting and pointing for me to get that one too. I threw the ball up and hit it in his direction. I nailed him, and he starting yipping like a little dog. It all came to an end when I turned around, and there were three big ones right behind me."

"What did you do then?" asked Lu. "Were you an hors d'oeuvre?"

"I did what every dream hero does when the situation gets impossible—just wake up. Did you know that if you die in a dream, you will probably die in real life too?"

"That's not true," said Lu. "I've died several times in my dreams, and I'm still here. I've been shot by a gun and a bow, and I've fallen off a cliff."

"What happened when you fell off the cliff?" asked Annie.

"I bounced about twenty feet in the air. The next time I hit, people gathered around and someone said I was dead. So there, your theory is just an old wives' tale."

"Wow," said Chip. "You are one violent little girl. There's some crazy stuff going through your head."

"Coming from you, I'll take that as a compliment," said Lu. "I see headlights. I hope it's the food."

Rod, Luke, and Scott pulled up in Luke's orange Topaz aka the punkin. He considered it a term of endearment and not a put-down, which was the original intention of the term's creator. The guys got out with enough food to feed the whole softball team.

"Why don't you two munchkins sit on the tailgate so there's room for the normal-sized people up there in the back?" asked Rod.

"Good idea," said Chip. "Annie, why don't you and Lu sit on the tailgate?"

"Don't start up with those two," warned Jenny. "Once and for all, you two are the same size. You're both high schoolers that look like fifth graders that's all."

"I'll sit on the tailgate with Lu," said Annie. "I don't want you two to start wrestling over matters of height."

"Speaking of height, have ya'll noticed anything about me lately?" asked Jenny.

"Like what?" asked Chip.

"My dad measured my sister and me the other day, and I am now officially six feet tall. And the strange thing is, I grew, and Tammi didn't."

"What did she say about that?" asked Luke as he shoveled half a slice of pizza in his mouth.

"It didn't seem to bother her," said Jenny. "I really think she has come to her senses."

"Good for her," said Annie. "Scott, how is your sister taking the ban from the dugout?"

"She hasn't said much lately," answered Scott. "Knowing her, she is up to something. She's a schemer, but thank goodness she's not in your league."

"Not many are," replied Chip with a sense of pride. "Schemes have to be thought out in great detail. You can't just slap something together at the last minute. It has to be a well-crafted plan. Ya'll probably don't understand what I'm talking about, right, Luke?"

"You mean like the fake toe you were going to glue to your foot on the day the team painted your toenails and wore sandals?" asked Luke.

"What?" said Annie. "I thought that was supposed to be a sting on Clarice?"

"It was," explained Luke. "Then the queen of stings decided she would make a fake toe in art class and glue it to her foot. The only problem was she didn't have time to make it look real and keep it from falling off, so she dropped the idea."

"That was confidential information, blabbermouth," said Chip.

Scott laughed and inwardly complimented himself on his choice of Reston for a new home. What could be better than sitting in a truck on a country road next to an awesome girl like Jenny? The thing that happened next startled everyone in the truck. Out of nowhere, a set of red lights came on followed by a quick burst of a police siren. Officer Rubio had driven quietly up on the group with his lights off. The group was so engrossed in their conversation that they didn't notice him. Rubio got out and approached the group slowly with his hand slightly above his sidearm.

"What do we have here?" he asked. "Teenagers partying on a country road? I should run ya'll in."

Scott was the only one of the group that looked worried. He wasn't sure what was going on, but it didn't look good.

"What's the charge?" asked Chip in a defiant voice.

"I don't know," said Rubio, relaxing his posture and his tone. "I'll think of something. However, I might forget everything if I wasn't so darn hungry and thirsty."

Chip slid the little cooler toward Officer Rubio. "There's one root beer left, but it's a diet. Pizza and chicken for the law, guys." Luke handed him a chicken bucket and slid what was left of the pizza over.

"Slide over, munchkin," said Rubio to Lu. This choice of words caused the whole group to break into hilarious laughter even Lu. Officer Rubio didn't know he was such a funny guy. Maybe he should have been a stand-up comedian. It would certainly be a lot more exciting than being a peace officer in a quiet little town like Reston.

"Officer," said Chip, looking over at Jenny. "Can I drive your squad car sometime right through town with sirens and lights blazing?"

"I suppose you'll want to fire the shotgun out the window too?" asked Rubio. "I'll think about it."

Chip looked over at Jenny with a look of triumph on her face.

The next day, Coach Bob Devers called for a meeting during study hall for the girls that wanted to play basketball the next year. He had to do some lobbying to get switched over to his new coaching position. His main selling point to the school board and the administration was that these girls had a real chance to go somewhere, and it would be risky to put them into the hands of an inexperienced coach. A small school like Reston usually attracted first-year teachers. You came to Reston if you were just starting out in education, or if this area was your home. Veteran teachers and coaches normally didn't move to a smaller district because they usually couldn't afford to pay as well. He also knew the girls' strengths and weaknesses and, most of all, their little idiosyncrasies. That last fact might have been the clincher. The school board had the athletic director's blessing, so they agreed to let his assistant coach the boys for one season while Coach Devers was running the girls' team. The entire community had high hopes for the Reston girl's basketball team in the coming season.

Being banned from the dugout put the damper on Gina's current softball situation, but she was in rare form during the basketball meeting. She was the first to respond when Coach D. asked for questions.

"Hey, Mr. Devers, what type of offense are we going to run?" asked the cocky junior. Then before he could answer, she added, "Remember you've got some new talent and that might change the whole picture." She gave Addie Gordon, a sophomore player, a big smile after this comment. Addie and Gina had hit it off right away, which probably wasn't a good thing. Addie seemed to find her share of trouble in and out of sports.

"I have a real good idea of what we're going to do," responded Coach D. When he opened the meeting, he told them to call him just plain *Coach* or *Coach D.* and leave the *Mr.* title for the classroom. "And don't worry, uh, Gina, is it? Don't worry, I will take everyone's talent into consideration. You have your summer schedules in front of you, so let's go over them. But before we do that, let's address the issue of your three captains not being present for our summer program. As most of you know, Chip, Jenny, and Annie are going to Michigan to be camp instructors for a month. I have a workout for them to do if they can squeeze it in. Oh yeah, I don't believe in letting the players vote for captain or captains. Sometimes it turns into a popularity vote, and we don't need that. I don't believe I'll get much argument by choosing these three as your captains. They've earned it. Most of the girls smiled and shook their heads in agreement. Gina rolled her eyes at Addie but didn't say anything.

When the meeting was over, the three captains walked away, discussing how much fun it was going to be playing for Coach D. especially since Coach Harbison would be his assistant. And he had already told them to be prepared to play a fast-paced running game. Gina walked away, griping to Addie that it was stupid to have an offense in mind before he got to see all the varsity players play. Addie was in total agreement.

"So is Gina going to be as much trouble in basketball as she already has been in softball?" asked Jenny.

"No doubt about it," said Chip. "She better be careful. I think Coach D. is like Coach Brown. Those two don't put up with a lot of nonsense. Hopefully, she won't be very good, which will make her just a minor annoyance."

Bulldog Tough

Coach Brown addressed his team in the bleachers before their big game against Fort Worth Carlisle. Before the team meeting, he had talked to his three pitchers, and they all agreed with his strategy of going strictly with Annie. She was their best shot at getting to the next level. Tammie was all smiles, and they appeared to be genuine. She was surprised when the coach said she would start in right field. He wanted the best bats in the lineup, and she was the best hitter of the remaining outfielders. She had only played a few innings this season in the outfield, but Coach Brown didn't think she would get many chances to touch the ball with Annie pitching. It was somewhat risky, but the tall former starting pitcher was hitting a little over .300, and he needed as much firepower as he could get in a game like this. He figured it would be a low-scoring affair with possibly only one run separating the two teams. This was typical for two teams that sported quality pitchers. At the end of the meeting and before the Lady Eagles went out to their respective practice stations, their coach invited them out to his place for a post-season party a couple of days after the season was over.

"Will there be barbecued chicken?" asked Annie.

"Absolutely," answered her coach. "But you get to decide on what else you are going to have. All my wife asks is that we let her know ahead of time."

"Does she know how to prepare Viking food?" asked Chip. Her coach gave her a thoughtful look not knowing how to answer that one.

"Ignore her, Coach," said Jenny. "She has an obsession with Viking food even though there's no such thing."

"All right," said Coach B. "Let's get out there and get after it. Hopefully, this won't be our last practice this season."

The bus ride to Fort Worth on Saturday was a nervous one. The girls knew what they were up against. The Carlisle pitcher, like Annie, was one of the best in the state. This was undoubtedly the biggest game of their young lives. Already, Chip was not having a good day.

"What's the matter with you?" asked Luke as he picked her up in the punkin. "You're not your usual perky self."

"I'm okay," was all she said as she slumped down on the seat next to him.

"You're not sick are you? That would be an unbelievable coincidence. You know because Jenny got sick just before the big basketball game with Dunbar."

"I'm not sick," moaned Chip. "It's a girl thing, okay. I've got cramps."

Luke didn't know how to respond to this statement, so he didn't say anything. In all his sports research and writing, this was something he never even thought about.

"Here," said Chip, rubbing her hand on her lower stomach area then reaching over and rubbing his stomach. "You take some of them so they don't hurt so bad."

"If that was possible I'd do it," said Luke. "Don't you take pills for your predicament?"

"They don't always work. Scientists haven't come up with something that *decrampifies* women. When they do, they will make millions. Would you really take my cramps for me?"

"Yup, I would. You're the all-star shortstop. I'm just the guy who writes about the stuff you and your teammates do. If I could, I would take them for the team. Do they hurt bad?"

"Bad enough. Don't tell Annie or Jen, okay?"

Coach Brown and Coach Harbison both gave their team a fantastic pregame pep talk. Coach Harbison talked about playing with honor and representing their school and community. Pops told them the bulldog story that his commanding officer told his unit before boot camp started. One day, a little bulldog came strolling down an alley between houses. He stopped when he saw two big dogs sitting on the back porch of a fenced-in yard. He got the big dogs' attention when he started to dig a hole under their fence. They sat up and looked at each other as if the little guy was crazy. Crazy or not, he kept digging. The bulldog squeezed under the fence and immediately got the thrashing of his life. He barely made it back through the opening and limped all the way home.

Two months later and all healed up, the bulldog came sauntering down the alley again like he owned the place. He stopped at the big dogs' fence and saw that the hole had been filled in. Determined, he started to dig a new one. The big dogs sat up and waited. If they could have grinned at each other, they certainly would have. Once the little dog was through the hole, they gave him another thrashing. Again, he limped painfully down the alley.

This went on every two months for an entire year. One warm spring morning, the little guy came bopping down the alley, acting like he didn't have a care in the world. He stopped at the big-dog yard, looked the situation over, and started to dig. Once under the fence, he looked straight at the big dogs. They were still sitting on the porch, watching him. Getting no response, he walked over to their food dishes and helped himself. Then he drank out of their water dishes. He finally relieved himself on their favorite tree. After checking out their entire yard, he exited through the hole and strolled back down the alley. The big dogs lay back down and closed their eyes for a nap. There was just too much fight in that little guy. No matter what they did to him, he refused to accept defeat.

Annie stood in the pitcher's circle and looked around at her teammates. It was the bottom of the fourth, and there was no score. Two Carlisle runners had reached base—one on an error and the other one with a walk. Chip saved a definite hit in the second inning when she went to her right, backhanded a one-hopper, and had to jump in the air to get her throw off. Her throw beat the speeding runner by a step. The Reston fans and several of the Carlisle fans, gave her a huge ovation. After she made the throw, she stood with her hands on her knees as if she were going to be sick. Coach Harbison started to come out of the dugout, but Chip stood up and waved her back. When they went in for their turn at bat, Coach Harbison motioned for Chip to come to the far end of the bench. They talked quietly for a few minutes and then her coach put her arm around the little shortstop's shoulders and gave her a hug. Chip told her she was trying to be bulldog tough, and she would get through it. Coach Harbison's eyes watered when Chip went back to sit by her teammates to cheer for Maria as she stepped into the box. Players and students are supposed to learn from their coaches and teachers. It is a bonus when the tables are reversed, and the ones doing the teaching end up learning something themselves.

The Lady Eagles and the Carlisle Coyotes battled each other for all they were worth. The Reston nine had accumulated four hits three singles and Annie's double in the first inning. She died on second when Courtney struck out to end the inning. Chip started off the game with a hard-hit grounder to the Coyote shortstop's right, and she made a nice play on the ball. Normally,

Chip would have beaten the throw on a ball hit in the hole, but she didn't get there in time. When the play was over, Coach Harbison looked over at Coach Brown who was standing in the third-base coaching box and shrugged her shoulders. Hopefully that play wasn't going to be an omen on how the game was going to go.

In the top of the seventh, Annie singled sharply to start the inning. Courtney sacrificed her to second on the first pitch. When Jenny grounded out to the second baseman, Annie took third. Tammi came up with a look of determination on her face. This was an opportune chance to make up for some of the stunts she had pulled in the past, and she was all too aware of this. A hit, an error, and a passed ball—any of these would bring Annie home from third. Tammi took a ball and a strike, and on the third pitch, she made excellent contact. It was the best ball she had hit all year. Her heart leapt when she felt the bat hit the ball right on the sweet spot. The streaking sphere took off toward left, and as it rose, so did the hopes of the Reston squad. For some strange reason, the Carlisle left fielder was playing Tammi as deep as the outfielders were told to play Annie. She was only a few feet from the fence. Neither coach had caught the mistake in positioning, and as a result, she was standing in the perfect spot. A ball that was destined to hit the bottom of the fence, landed in the left fielder's glove instead. The Carlisle players and fans let out a whoop as their girls came in to bat in the bottom of the seventh.

◊

Luke sat in the front row of the bleachers behind home plate and took notes. From time to time, he spoke into his little tape recorder. No matter the outcome of the game, he was going to write a great article. As Tammi walk across the infield, several of her teammates high-fived her. Rachel came out of the dugout with her glove. She acted like she was going to hand it to her and then threw it over the right fielder's head into the outfield.

Tammi laughed. It felt good to finally be one of them. The tall twin had to wipe away a few tears when her sister gave her a thumb up behind her back as she stood at first base. Luke took in all of these events and said something quietly into his recorder. Clarice, his freshman assistant, was furiously sketching on a pad as she sat next to him. Chip thought they were sitting a little too close, but she couldn't worry about that now. She had other problems at the moment.

Annie threw her warm-up pitches to Darby. So far, Carlisle did not have a hit, and the hard throwing hurler was determined to keep it that way. The first batter tried to bunt her way on. Maria came in on a ball that jumped off the bat and into her glove after one hop. She had the runner beat by two full steps, but her throw was wide, and it pulled Jenny off the bag. At six feet tall and with long arms, Jenny was a good target at first. But the throw was so far off the mark that she had to leave the bag to catch it. A lot of coaches would have been upset at the throw, but the Reston bosses both shouted encouragement to their players. Jenny had made a good decision. If she would have tried to stay on the bag and had the ball gotten past her, the runner would have ended up on second. In a game like this, with two first-rate pitchers throwing, one mistake could cost you the game. Maria looked over at Jenny and pointed to herself, signifying that the throw was her fault.

"C'mon, Annie," hollered Maria. "She's my runner, and I don't want to see her over here at third. Bail me out."

Annie nodded toward her third baseman and threw a rise ball to the next hitter. Most everyone there figured her to try to bunt the runner along, and that's just what she did. The pitch was popped-up right in front of the pitcher. Annie was on it like a cat, and after picking it up, it looked like the play at first was the only one she had. She gunned the runner down. The next batter also showed bunt, so Maria came in fast from third. The batter pulled the bat back and took a called strike. Chip was watching the runner at second out of the corner of her eye, and when the runner attempted to steal third, the shortstop got there several counts ahead of her. The throw from Darby was a little high, but Chip brought it down and made a nice tag. The runner slid right into her glove. Even the visitors were shocked when the base umpire called the runner safe.

"Hey, ump," said Chip. "She slid right into my glove, and my glove was between her foot and the bag."

"Don't argue, short, or you'll be out of here," said the umpire in a defiant tone.

Coach Brown asked for time and headed for the plate umpire. "Is there anyway we can ask for your help on that one? You saw the reaction of the opposing team when your partner said, "Safe" didn't you? Even they were surprised at the call."

"Only if my partner says he didn't see it clearly enough and wants my help with the call," explained the plate umpire.

Coach Brown walked to the base umpire and asked him to ask for help from the plate umpire. The base ump crossed his arms across his chest and refused. He said he saw it plain enough—the runner beat the throw. Then he told the Reston coach to go back to the dugout. The plate umpire was listening, and he thought that was a rather strange comment because Coach Brown was already headed back toward the dugout. After the game, he went up to the Reston coach and told him he liked the way he handled himself and his team. He also said if he were asked, he would have said the runner was out at third.

With one out and a runner on third, the Reston infield moved in. If the batter tried a squeeze bunt, they wanted to be ready. It would be easier to get one through the infield with everyone playing closer, but that was a risk they had to take. Annie stood in the circle with the ball, running scenarios through her mind. When she was comfortable that her infielders were in place, she toed the pitching rubber. The batter showed bunt, then she pulled the bat back and tried to hit it.

Annie had thrown another rise ball, which was one of the hardest pitches to bunt. If you didn't judge the rising ball right, you would get underneath it and pop it up. That's exactly what the batter did.

The ball went up about eight feet in the air a few feet down the first baseline in foul territory. Darby was on it immediately. She whipped her mask off and made a diving catch. This was a scenario that Annie hadn't counted on, but she sprinted in to cover the plate just in case. Sure enough, the Carlisle coach sent his runner. Darby caught the pop up in a total layout position. As she slowly came to her knees, she heard everyone yelling, "Home, home." She put her mitt on the ground for leverage, and with a flick of her wrist, threw the ball back over her shoulder to Annie. The throw got there ahead of the runner, but it was too high. Annie caught it and swept her glove back, tagging the sliding runner on the thigh. The plate umpire was in perfect position to make the call. When he spread his hands face down, he took the air right out of the Reston players and fans. Annie knew the call was good, and she shook her head in resolution at the umpire.

"Tough break," he said. She thought about his comment later. *Was he referring to the call at third or to the fact that she had just thrown a no-hitter and lost?* She had no way of knowing.

The girls moped around for most of Sunday until it was time to meet at Daggert's farm. The whole group was there. Jenny suggested they each bring something from home to eat, and they made a picnic out of it.

"I can't believe we lost," lamented Chip. "I thought we were better than they were. Annie threw a no-hitter at them, and they still beat us. There's no justice in that. If I knew the address of the guy in charge, I'd write a complaint letter to him."

"How do you know it's a guy?" asked Lu.

"It has to be a guy," answered Chip munching on a piece of celery. "That's how things got messed up in the first place."

"Why do you keep blaming the guys for everything?" asked Luke. "I think the women of the world have done their share of messing things up too."

"Puh-lease," said Chip. "Look at the facts. There has never been a woman president or vice president. There has never been a female Supreme Court chief justice. And the base umpire that blew the call at third was a guy. If just one of us gets in, things will change for the better."

"How about this," argued Luke. "The United States is supposedly falling behind foreign countries in education, right? Well, the majority of teachers in the United States are females. Explain that."

"Do you really think the teachers are to blame for our country's poor showing on those goofy standardized tests?" asked Chip. "I don't."

"Whose fault is it then?" asked Lu.

"It's the kids, smart girl. You know that most of our classmates don't study at all. And I bet each of us can name at least ten students that stay up until 2 a.m., playing video games or messin' around on their computers or phones. They don't take school seriously, and I partly blame their parents for that."

"If that's the real problem, why don't we attack it and fix it?" asked Scott finally feeling comfortable enough to get in on discussions like this. In the past, he had only talked with his dad on subjects that required level two or three thinking. It was fun and educational to hear what his peers were thinking, especially peers that had put some rational thought into the subjects being discussed.

"I've got this one," responded Luke. "Most politicians don't want to lose votes they already have, and they want to gain new ones. That seems to be their agenda from the time they first get elected. Do you think they'd lose votes if they blamed all or even part of the country's poor test scores on the parents' or their kids' attitude toward education? It seems that the new American way is to blame someone other than the person or the people responsible."

"I agree with you on that one," added Rod. "They even come up with new words or phrases that make the ridiculous sound almost logical."

"Give us an example," said Luke.

Rod thought on it for a minute then came up with, "How about being *overserved* at a bar? If a guy drinks too much, which is obviously his own fault unless he has some sort of mental condition, defense lawyers will try to blame the bartender. He didn't drink too much, he was overserved. And believe it or not, juries will sometimes side with the idiot that went out and got hammered."

"That's crazy," said Annie. "Back to the teacher thing, Luke. There's tens of thousands of teachers in this country, and they vote too. Won't the politicians lose their votes?"

"Sure, but there aren't nearly as many teachers as there are parents," explained Luke. "They're just playing the odds, blaming the smaller group so they lose the least amount of votes. And because of this, the problem won't even begin to get solved. You all know that the first step to solving a problem is identifying what the problem is in the first place. So far, the men and women in power refuse to admit what the problem is, and it's all in the interest of getting elected or reelected. It's all pretty sad if you think about it."

"You make some good points," said Scott, reaching for another cookie.

"There's a six-cookie limit, Scott," said Jenny. "And I think that's about it for you."

"I've only had three," said Scott in his defense. He felt accepted by the group since they were now making fun of him on a regular basis. "Besides, this serious discussion requires a lot of energy.

I'm actually learning something here. I never thought of the politician's view on things."

"I wouldn't worry about that," said Chip sarcastically. "There are books full of stuff you don't know." Chip thought her last comment was quite clever, so she fist bumped the other girls. "Another thing about men," said Chip. "Food is almost always at the top of their list." As soon as she finished her statement, the town squad car came into view on their left. On their right, Mr. Daggert's tractor came chugging at them. "Ha, I rest my case. The cop and the farmer both smelled these goodies from miles away."

"Let's talk about the Michigan trip," said Jenny as she winked at Annie. "We leave in a few days. Should we pack stuff for cold weather? I mean, there's a reason the state is shaped like a mitten."

"Michigan is pretty close to North Pole," said Chip. "They should have stores that carry parkas and gloves and stuff if we need them."

"And she wants women to run the world," said Luke. "I don't think you will get frostbite, trust me."

Officer Rubio pulled up followed shortly by Mr. Daggert. They both complimented the girls on their softball season. Officer Rubio said there was going to be a big celebration at the school for them in a couple of days. This is the first that the girls had heard about it. He went on to say he was surprised that there wasn't a big convoy coming back into town after the game the way they did at the end of the basketball season. He said it was probably because softball wasn't as popular as basketball was with the locals. Chip said when they win the state championship next year, that would all change. They all sat and talked and ate until well after sunset. There were only three more days of school left and plenty of adventures ahead of them.

When Annie got home that evening, she called her friend Dr. Snyder back in Jones Ferry and told him all about the game. Then she called her sister at college and talked to her for half an hour. When she hung up, she decided to call Tank and Ralph to give them an update and catch up with them. She didn't get to bed until midnight. It was no big deal because there would be no practice tomorrow. She already missed it.

Chip sat up with her parents and rehashed all the *fantabulous* moments, as she put it, that she had in softball and basketball this year. She went on and on about what great friends she had and thanked them for being such awesome parents. Then she went to her room and called her boyfriend. They talked well into the night about what the team was going to be like next year.

Luke didn't mention it to anyone, but he was already halfway through his final softball article. He wasn't sure what gave him the biggest sense of pride—Chip's great performance under duress, or his article that focused on the narcissistic attitudes of some teens. Before he fell asleep, he decided that it was okay to be proud of both accomplishments. Since school would be out, he was going to send it to the local papers. A few of them had published his work in the past.

Jenny sat at her kitchen table with her two sisters and her parents. They talked about her upcoming trip and what she would need. Tammi said she had found a job for the summer. She was going to be a lifeguard at the public pool. Jenny finally went to bed with a smile on her face. Her sister had quit acting like she was a big star and was actually fun to talk to again. That was worth more to her than a state championship trophy any day.

Lu was tired when she got home form the celebration at Daggert's farm. She was feeling better every day and couldn't wait to get back to running. Scott and Rod said they would run with her while the others were away, but only if the temp was under ninety. You'd have to be crazy to run in the middle of the day in Texas during the summer. Annie figured that out the first time she tried it.

Rod went to bed, thinking about his summer schedule. He was doing an internship at a physical-therapy facility in Fort Worth. His dad would be home soon, which meant they would be doing a lot of family activities together. He would miss Annie, but one month was no big deal. Heck, on more than one occasion, his mom went without seeing his dad for almost a year at a time.

Scott was excited about his summer prospects. He landed a job at a sporting goods store in Fort Worth, and his cast would be off soon. He had also decided to ask Jenny out on a serious date when she got back from camp. Normally, he wouldn't have been so cautious when asking a girl out, but he sensed that Jenny would have said no earlier, so he was willing to be patient. One thing that did worry him was his sister. His dad would ask her to go to Rangers games with them, but he doubted she would take him up on it. She definitely had a problem. With their dad working long hours, it was like an open invitation for her to get into all sorts of mischief. He had come to her rescue before and, no doubt, would have to do it again.

The Major

The following Friday, the three softball players and Lu were gathered in Annie's kitchen, making deserts for the big post-season get together at Coach Brown's house. Chip called their coach and asked if Lu could come too, and he said that would be fine.

"Now I won't be the shortest one there," said Chip, hanging up the phone.

"That's it," said an exasperated Lu. "You and me back-to-back against the wall."

"Yes," said Chip, taking off her oven mittens. "Now the truth will come out. Measure us, Jen. You're tall enough to get a good angle. Watch her, Annie, so she doesn't stand on her toes."

The two short girls stood still so the tops of their heads could be compared. Annie grabbed a ruler out of the drawer and laid it across their heads.

"I don't know," said Jenny. "It looks pretty level. I think you're both the same height."

"Her hair is puffier than mine," said Chip. "Part it so the ruler lays flat on her head and doesn't sit up on all that hair."

"Let's cut a strip across the top on both of them," said Annie, pulling a pair of scissors out of the same drawer. "It's the only way to get an accurate measurement. It'll be cool like a reverse Mohawk."

"I'm game if she is," said Chip.

"All right," said Jenny, knocking the ruler off their heads and pointing to Lu. "Were going to have a serious talk. Annie, grab that little one. I've got this one."

Annie took Lu by the shoulders and sat her down in a chair. Jenny did the same with Chip.

"Look, you two," said Jenny, staring at them. "You are both the same height, so stop worrying about who is taller. There's nothing wrong with being short. Randy Newman, the famous singer, even wrote and sang a song about short people. It was a big hit."

"Really?" said both of them at the same time.

"Yup, so let's drop it, okay?"

"Fine with me," said Lu as she went to the oven to check on their chocolate chip bars.

"Me too, I guess," said a dejected Chip.

"Did he really sing a song about short people?" asked Annie later when she and Jenny were alone in the living room.

"Yes," answered Jenny. "I've never heard it. I just saw it on a list of popular songs from the late seventies. It was all I could come up with to get those two to stop arguing about who is taller."

"Well, that song better be in favor of short people because if it's not, you will go straight to the top of her list," said Annie. "Luke will be grateful for that. That position is usually reserved for him."

The four girls drove to Coach Brown's place early in the afternoon so they could help with the preparation. Everyone was told to bring their gloves and bats as they were going to play a little game before the big feast. Rod and Luke volunteered to help with the cleanup, so they were coming out later. As always, Luke saw this as an opportunity to get a couple of quotes from the coaches for his last softball article of the school year. The girls couldn't believe the ball diamond that was in back of the house. It appeared to be regulation size with a backstop and real bases. When the rest of the team showed up, Gendra, the coach's wife, told the four kitchen helpers to go outside. Ellie, Coach Brown's niece, was waiting to show Annie how much she had progressed with her pitching. Reston's star pitcher was impressed with the younger girl's speed and control. The onlookers gave Ellie an ovation after she threw her last pitch.

When the rest of the team got there, Coach Brown called them all in and told them how proud he was of them. Then he told the team about the big celebration in the school gym that was planned to recognize their achievements. He told them that he probably didn't have to mention it, but they should dress fairly nice.

"Dress and act like you are deserving of all the nice words people are going to say about you. No jeans with holes in them and no tiny little shorts. That being said, I'm going to break you up into two teams, and we're going to play a little slow-pitch game before we eat."

Ellie, her dad Nate, and both coaches played too. The players were told to play a different position than the one they usually played. The smack talk was flying back and forth. The second time Chip came up, she hit a hard grounder to the right of short. Annie backhanded the ball, planted her right foot, and threw a bullet to first. The regular shortstop was flying down the base path, but the throw beat her by a step and a half.

"No way," yelled Chip as she was called out. "Get her out of there, Coach. If she takes a bad hop to the nose, you will never forgive yourself."

"Whats the matter, Fullerton?" hollered Rachel from third base. "Afraid she'll take your spot next year?"

"You know it," responded Chip. This drew laughs and jeers from most of them.

Tammi surprised everyone when she added, "I know what that feels like." She got a lot of apprehensive looks from her teammates and coaches. "Don't worry, everybody," she said with a huge smile on her face. "I learned a lot these past few weeks and will work hard to earn a spot next year somewhere."

Man, these hick girls are corny, thought Gina. *'I'll work hard to earn a spot.' Give me a break. I think I'm gagging here. It's like I moved to Mayberry or something. I wonder if that cop, Rubio, only gets to carry one bullet for his gun, like the goofy deputy did in the TV show.* The new girl continued to raise eyebrows with her strange play. She slid hard into second when no one else was sliding. Some of her comments seemed to be ill-timed like she was trying way too hard. Her softball T-shirt from her former school also drew some attention. The old saying, It's Not Bragging If You Can Back It Up, didn't quite fit in with the Reston way of doing things. Most of the players just shook their heads and were grateful that the start of the next season was several months away. As her twin brother had already warned them, his sister was going to be a real handful.

When Coach Harbison came up, the outfielders dropped their gloves and came in to stand behind the infielders.

"We've seen your act before, Coach," said Sandy Johnson. "If you get it past us, we'll buy you a steak dinner." The rest of the outfielders agreed and started to razz her. The assistant responded by hitting a fly over their heads to medium left field. She was on third by the time Sandy retrieved the ball and got it back into the infield.

"That's going to be one sweet steak," said Coach H. "I want a rib-eye with all the fixins."

Annie came up in the next half of the inning with the bases loaded.

"Tell you what," shouted Coach H. from deep left field. "If this hack can get one over my head, you don't have to buy me that steak." Then she took about ten steps farther back. Everybody started hollering at once. Some were in support, and some were against. Annie watched the first pitch go by. She stepped into the second one and nailed it right on the nose. Coach H. turned and started to run as soon as she saw the ball heading in her direction. When she got to the ball, Annie was already moonwalking backward from third to home. Ellie was catching and several of the fielders shouted for her to stop Annie. The middle schooler met Annie halfway to home and put her hands on her lower back, trying to hold her there. The muscular right fielder turned pitcher, picked up the coach's niece, and threw the smaller girl over her shoulder and kept on going. The ball had just made it back to the infield when they crossed the plate. The crowd went wild, but that was brought to an abrupt halt when Gendra stepped out on the porch and rang the dinner bell.

Three guys were walking up when Annie hit her home run over her coach's head. One was Luke, another was Rod, and the third looked like a shorter, older version of Rod minus all the muscle.

"Wow," said the older Foster. "Who hit that one?"

"That's my girl, Dad," said Rod. "Pretty impressive, huh?"

Annie shook the major's hand and gave him a hug when Rod introduced them to each other. Coach Brown was right behind her. He also shook the major's hand and hugged him. Annie figured it out right away. With Leroy Brown being a Medal of Honor recipient, it made sense that a Special Forces major, whose hometown was close by, would know him quite well.

The talk around the picnic tables was mostly about next year's chances to go even farther in the playoffs. Coach Brown stood up and toasted the outgoing seniors—Kris Ritter, Darby Quinn, Maria Baltierra, Katie Renfro, and Carmen Lopez. They received a standing ovation for their contributions to Reston softball. The two coaches then handed out the individual awards. Chip and Annie received plaques for being the co-Most Valuable Players. Jenny and Courtney both received the Most Improved Player award. Kris Ritter was given the Coaches' Award for her attitude and sportsmanship. The people around the tables knew that Chip and Annie would receive more accolades from the local papers and local coaches within the next few weeks. Jenny's .385 average and great defensive play would also draw a lot of attention. All in all, it was a great season that the Reston Lady Eagles could be proud of. Tammi and Darby joined their teammates in enthusiastically congratulating the award winners. Jenny was beaming and it had nothing to do with her award.

Luke stirred up some interest at his table when he started talking baseball history. The discussion turned a little more intense when the guys, and some of the girls, started comparing great Major League centerfielders from the past. Names like Mickey Mantle, Willie Mays, Joe Dimaggio, and Ken Griffey Jr. were thrown around. Luke surprised them all when he mentioned a real old timer, Tris Speaker. Luke explained that Speaker was not only a great hitter, but he was also considered the greatest centerfielder of his day. He played so shallow in the outfield that he would often make plays at second base. Of course when the ball got a little livelier, he had to move back several steps. Rod cautioned his dad, who thought he knew a little bit about baseball, not to go up against Luke. He was a veritable walking baseball encyclopedia.

The celebration was considered to be a big success, especially when Gendra brought out her made-from-scratch apple pies. There were a lot of comments on how Pops stayed so thin with a wife that was such a superstar cook. Major Foster figured that the retired gunnery sergeant probably ran five or six miles several days a week just like he did. In the coming months, he would be up at four thirty at least once a week to drive up to the gunny's place so they could run together. At the end of the meal, Ellie and Annie urged Coach Brown to bring out his medal. They were surprised when he made no objection. Most of the girls didn't realize it at the time, but this would be the only time they would ever see in person the highest award that the US military gives. The medal was passed around in its display case. Gina asked Carissa, who was sitting across from her, to use her phone to take a picture of her wearing the medal as soon as she could figure out how to open the case. Major Foster stood up and briskly walked around the table. He held out his hand for the case, and Gina gave it to him. Luke whispered to Chip that it was against the law for anyone but the recipient to wear the medal. Gina just shrugged her shoulders.

After several thank yous and even some tears, the visitors headed for their cars. When Gina got in the backseat of Carissa's car, she asked the two girls she was riding with. "How good was Smith in basketball this year? I mean, compared to softball."

"Where did that come from?" asked Carissa.

"Well, I'm a pretty fair basketball player myself, and I think I can beat her out of a starting spot next season. I'm taller than her, and we play the same position."

"Oh, she's not really all that good," said Sandy Johnson from the front passenger seat. "Wouldn't you say so, Carissa?"

"Definitely overrated," responded the driver with a grin that Gina couldn't see. "Yeah, Gina, you should be able to worm your way into the starting lineup with no problem whatsoever. Especially if you play basketball as tough and aggressive as you play softball."

"That's what I like to hear," said Gina with a hint of smugness. "I tell you what, some eyes will be opened once b-ball starts. Somebody is going to get the shock of their life."

Major Curt Foster was glad to be back in Texas. He hadn't told his wife and son yet, but his traveling days might be over. He was up for a transfer to the recruiting division, and if that came through, he would be working in Fort Worth or Dallas until he was eligible to retire. He figured he had done enough traveling and fighting for his country. It was time to live the good life with his little family. There were plenty of younger guys ready to take his spot.

The first item on the list that his wife gave him was to fix the back steps. Rod was supposed to take care of this little chore a few months ago, but he never got around to it. Curt drove up to Denton around 7:00 a.m., thinking the lumber store would be open. As a career military man, he felt guilty sleeping past 6:00 a.m. The sign on the door said the store opened at 8:00 a.m., so he pulled into the store's empty parking lot and sat for a few minutes, deciding on his next course of action. Never one to sit around wasting time, he reached back into the backseat and grabbed his running shoes. A five-mile run at about eight minutes a mile should get him back to the store just before eight. After stretching, he took off at a brisk pace through the streets of Denton.

A mile later, the major was still in the business district. He ran by a bread truck parked on the street. It was the kind with a big flat windshield. In the glass, he saw the reflection of a taller man running behind him. Two blocks later, another reflection showed that the other runner was catching up to him. He made a left at the next corner and could now hear the trailing runner's footsteps. He was now in what looked like a shipping/receiving area. There weren't any storefronts here, just loading docks and side doors. The guy behind him had turned too. Curt decided to stop and put his hands on his knees, feigning that he was having a hard time catching his breath. It was probably nothing, but his military training told him to always be on the alert. Hopefully, the guy behind him would just cruise on by. As he waited, he looked between the buildings and saw two men standing beside a van that was backed into the alley. By the looks of them, they were up to no good. Just before the runner behind him caught up, he saw one of the guys by the van throw a shoulder into a door and break it in. He went in quickly, followed by his partner.

The runner stopped next to him and looked in the same direction that the major was looking.

"What was that noise?" asked the taller Hispanic man. "It sounded like something fell."

Curt looked the taller man up and down with the experienced eye of a trained observer. He was Hispanic and appeared to be in his early twenties. He also appeared to be in great shape because it took him only a couple of breaths to return to normal breathing. The younger man had a dark complexion with medium-length hair and a neatly trimmed goatee. Curt also noticed that his fellow runner's manner didn't seem threatening. His UNT T-shirt indicated that he was more than likely a college student.

"Two guys just broke a door in and went into that building," explained Curt pointing down the alley. "I don't have my phone. Do you have one?"

"No, I don't like to run with it in my pocket," said the younger man. "I know the guy that owns the place, so I'm going around the building to get behind them when they come out. Maybe they've got a phone we can borrow. Stay here if you want, otherwise, go back up the street and try to borrow a cell phone."

The major thought it was somewhat ironic that a guy twenty years younger than him was giving orders. Before Curt could answer, the guy in the college shirt ran around the corner of an adjacent building. He appreciated the kid's sense of humor. *Maybe we can borrow their phone.* That was a good one.

This is crazy, thought Curt. *Two dudes are apparently ripping off a place, and this guy wants to play superhero. The smart thing to do is to memorize their plate number then get back out where I can borrow a cell phone and call it in. But I can't leave this guy all by himself. These clowns might have weapons. Welcome to the civilian world, Foster.*

The major knew a few things about taking guys down. He crouched down low and moved toward the front of the vehicle, using it for cover. It was obvious that these guys were planning on leaving in a hurry. He was only a few feet from the front of the vehicle when the two robbers came busting out of the same door that they originally entered. They were almost to the front doors of the van when someone hollered at them from behind. Both of them stopped, turned toward the voice, and pulled out handguns. The man that hollered quickly ducked behind the building. Curt was stuck in no-man's land, so he dove off to the side and out of the way. The van started up and roared out of the alley. *Got to get to a phone*, he thought.

As the van went by, Curt heard the unmistakable sound of a firearm going off. What were they doing, shooting at the guy in the back? The one that hollered at them? A sharp stinging sensation in his side answered that question for him. No, the fool on the passenger side had taken a shot at him. He looked down and saw his Army T-shirt start to turn red. His fellow runner ran up to Curt and took in the situation. He ran out into the street and flagged down a car that was coming their way. When he got back to Curt, he had propped himself up against the building. The younger man took off his shirt and lifted Curt's to see the damage. Then he gently pressed his shirt over the wound.

"It's a small hole," said the man. Then he leaned Curt forward to look at his back. "It went clean through. You were lucky. It was probably a .22 caliber. Big time crooks, huh? All they could afford was a .22. I stopped a car in the street and asked the driver to call an ambulance. The hospital is only a few blocks away, so they should be here soon."

"Thanks, man," said the major. "What did you plan on doing when those two came out of the building?"

"I was going to take one of them down, and I figured you would take the other. You are army, right?"

"Yeah, Special Forces. That was a pretty gutsy plan. You're not a cop, are you?"

"Not yet," said the man, standing up as he heard a siren in the distance. "But I'm thinking about taking some law enforcement courses in college. My name is Victor, by the way, Victor Reyes."

Rod and his mother stood at the major's hospital bedside. "I can't believe it, Dad," said Rod. "You spent all that time in Iraq and Afghanistan and never got shot. You're back here for a few days, and you're already drawing gunfire."

"Pretty ironic," said Curt, smiling. "I can't figure out why they shot at me. I wasn't a threat to them. I was just trying to get out of the way. That guy, Victor, was lucky he wasn't shot too."

"Did somebody mention my name?" asked Victor as he walked in to the room. He shook Rod's hand and gave him a quick hug. He also hugged Grace Foster. "Dude, your dad's in great shape for an old guy. Not fast enough to dodge bullets though. How are you, sir?"

"I'll be all right," said Curt. "Like you said, it's a small hole. I hear they caught those guys already."

"Yeah, we both had their license plate right. The cops caught up with them about a half hour after they bungled their little burglary attempt. They were after flat screen TVs. They got spooked when they heard a noise inside the storage room. It turned out it was the owner's cat. They startled it, and it jumped up and knocked over some stuff on a shelf. Those two went running for the door, thinking someone was shooting at them. So you're the big guy's dad, huh?"

"Yup. He caught up with me in height in the sixth grade. Then he kept right on growing. Hey, thanks, Victor, for sticking around and for getting that lady to make the ambulance call. I appreciate it."

"No problem, sir. I think the two of us could have taken those guys easy. There are way too many people out there who are willing to turn their heads when they see people doing rotten things. I think it's time the average citizen took a stand against lawbreakers. A lot of young people are in to the no-snitching thing, and that's the way the bad guys want it. You know, don't tell on us, it's not cool. Kids can't figure out that it's just the lawbreakers asking for a free pass to do anything they want. Somebody needs to wake up."

"I like this guy, son," said the major, looking at Rod. "You ever think about the military, Victor?"

"Enough talk," said Mrs. Foster. "You can tell war stories later. You two, out of here so he can rest. And thank you, Victor. I worried about him enough when he was deployed overseas. But I guess there's danger everywhere. It's a pretty crazy world."

"You're welcome, Mrs. Foster. And you're right. It is a pretty crazy world."

"Speaking of crazy," said Rod, looking through the door at Chip and her parents coming their way. "It's about to get crazier."

Chip's dad walked down the hallway and looked into his only daughter's room. He couldn't believe what he was looking at so he went in for a closer look. Her bed had clothes piled neatly on it. It was obvious that she was getting ready to pack for her trip up north. He chuckled and shook his head. The clothes that Chip had chosen were all for cold weather—hooded sweatshirts, long pants, hats, and gloves. He called for his wife to come and take a look. They were both standing there, laughing when Chip walked in.

"Melinda," said her mom. "What's with all the cold-weather clothes?"

"It's going to be cold there, Mom. It's not Texas, you know. I'm just wanna be prepared. We're going to a state that looks like a mitten. That should tell you something."

"I don't know, Karen," added Chip's dad. "Those igloos do get pretty cold even in the summer. Do they still eat whale blubber up there? I heard they used to add some kind of flavoring to it and call it ice cream."

"Stop that, John," said Karen. "Let's get on the Internet and check out the weather for southern Michigan in June."

They went over to Chip's computer and brought up the weather for Kalamazoo in June.

"That's not bad," said Chip. "Upper seventies for the average high. I can live with that."

"The nights can be chilly though," said Karen. "You'll need one hoodie but not all that other stuff. You're only taking one bag, right?"

"Yeah," answered Chip. "That big duffle bag over there against the wall. I found it in the garage. If it's too heavy, I'll get Annie to carry it. She's the one with all the muscles."

"You girls stick together at all times even on the train," added her dad. "There's safety in numbers."

"We will. Ya'll don't have to worry about us. It's going to be perfectly safe. What could go wrong on a simple train trip?"

"Still," added her mom, "I wish Rod or Luke were going with you."

"They did say that they might drive up for a long weekend," said Chip. "That would be fun. Cheryl said there are a bunch of lakes in the area and other cool places to visit. I wonder if Annie can swim. Maybe I'll take my swimsuit, just in case. Dad, do you think thong bikinis are legal in Michigan?"

"Why not just go naked?" asked her dad. "You did know that Michigan is the most popular destination for nudists?"

"You better be kidding," said Karen. "This little one is barely out of diapers. We don't need to put any ideas in her head. However, I do remember her coming out of the tub and doing the bare dance for us. She was pretty cute."

Mr. Fullerton chuckled and headed for his favorite reading chair. Over his shoulder, he remarked, "I think I'll go look for those pictures we took of the famous bare dance. Maybe Rod and

Luke would like to see them. Hey, maybe the school yearbook would be interested too."

"He's kidding, right, Mom?"

"About the dance or the pictures?"

"Destroy those pictures, and I'll take out the garbage for a month."

"That's already your job."

"Then I'll do it without complaining, and I'll keep my room spotless for a month too."

"Deal," said her mom with an outstretched hand. Chip shook it. *I got the best of that deal,* thought Karen. *I just made a deal using nonexistent pictures as leverage. And she thinks she's such a wheeler-dealer.*

That was easy, thought Chip as she watched her mom leave the room. *How can I complain about taking out the garbage if I'm not even going to be here? I think my room will stay pretty clean because I'll be like five thousand miles away. Parents, they're just too easy.*

Leroy Brown sat on his back porch and watched an assortment of nieces and nephews playing on the grass. The sun was setting to his left, but the temperature had only dropped a few degrees from the day's high of ninety-two. The kids didn't seem to care. They were used to the hot Texas climate. The retired gunnery sergeant reminisced about his days in the military. The last six months before he retired were especially tough. He needed to have a plan for the rest of his days as a civilian. There wasn't a lot of opportunity out there for a weapons expert. With only a month to go, he sat down and made a list of what was important to him. He was on his third list when it occurred to him that the number one item on all three was the only thing that really mattered—family. A modest job with insurance benefits for his wife and him was all that was necessary to supplement his military pension.

The job as head custodian at the Reston High School came only a month after he was discharged. His aptitude for fixing things and his status as a veteran were the deciding factors. There wasn't much floor-sweeping involved. He had a small staff to take care of the menial chores. He was more like an assistant to the head of maintenance, making sure the equipment ran smooth and fixing the smaller stuff. It didn't take long to realize that working around young people was something he also enjoyed. Most of them talked to him and several would even joke around with him once they got to know him. The school had its share of jerks and weirdoes, but they usually gave him a wide berth. The new custodian had a reputation of being a no-nonsense guy, and he looked like a guy that you didn't want to mess with. Pops proved this when he came in to the school one night last fall around midnight.

The evening janitor or *sweeper* as he was commonly referred to, had to leave early due to an illness. Pops had to drive back to school to see what needed to be done and to do the security check, which involved walking around the school, testing doors and looking for anything out of the ordinary. As always, he moved quietly. When he came to the computer lab, he saw beams of light dancing off the walls and ceiling. After watching for two minutes, he confirmed that there were two people in the room, and they weren't there to get in a little late studying. Pops moved back down the hallway and phoned the police on his cell phone. While he waited, he grabbed an industrial broom that was leaning up against the lockers and twisted the handle off. Moving back to the doorway, he listened to what was happening. It sounded like two people were loading computers on a cart. The two thieves were whispering back and forth and their comments indicated that they were probably teenagers.

A few seconds later, the cart started to roll through the doorway. Pops waited until both men were in the hallway before he hollered at them. He was hoping they would run down the hall and out the door right into the police. That way, no school property would have left the building and the culprits would be caught. The first guy threw a wrench into his plan when he turned and came after the old guy that had just yelled at them. The thief was about six feet two and was built like a linebacker. With catlike agility, Pops dropped down low and hit the lead guy across the shins with the broom handle. He followed that with a sharp rap to the side of the head. The big guy was dazed a little, but then his adrenalin kicked in. Before he could act, his partner got into the action. The janitor made short work of him with a side-thrust kick to the stomach. The attacker flew back against the lockers with the wind knocked out of him. He sunk to the floor, holding his stomach.

Pops squared off again against the thief. "C'mon, big un, I'm just an old man with a stick. You want some more of it?" The man charged again. Pops went low again, striking the charging man on the ankle. He yelped and turned on the older man. He was limping now, but still determined to get the stick away from the guy that appeared to know how to use it. Pops faked low, and when the attacker put his foot up to defend the swipe, he rapped him across the jaw. He followed that up with several compact blows to different parts of the big guy's body. The trespasser finally sunk to his knees, saying, "No more, old man."

The janitor was leaning on the broom handle, looking at the two would-be thieves when he saw a powerful spotlight outside the door at the end of the hall. He told the two guys on the floor to stay put while he walked down the hall and pushed on the door's crash bar. Officer Jenkins, the Reston cop on duty, walked next to the head custodian back to the two guys on the floor.

"You didn't kill them, did you?" asked the officer.

Pops grinned. "No, they're all right. Don't even need an ambulance. That big one went down hard though. I don't recognize them, do you?"

The officer said he had never seen the teens before. He checked them out for injuries, read them their rights, then he cuffed them. After calling the county sheriff's crime scene investigators and taking Pops' statement, they sat down to wait. Pops asked the officer if he wanted a soda. He got up and went into the teachers' lounge and brought back four of them.

"You brought one for the bad guys?" asked the cop as Pops handed him one.

"Yeah, they took a beating and are probably going to jail for a while," said Pops. "I reckon this will be the highlight of their evening. Can you move the cuffs to the front so they can drink these?"

"You boys aren't going to try anything, are you?" asked the officer holding up some keys. "I assume that's your truck sitting outside, and I'm holding the keys."

"No," said the smaller of the two. "I'm not going to run from a scene where we were only trying to get some answers for final exams. Jeez, Detective, what are you some kind of Bruce Lee or something? My stomach is still hurting."

Officer Jenkins and Pops both laughed at the guy's question. "I'm not a cop," said Pops. "I'm the janitor. And your final exam explanation is pretty lame. You better come up with a different story."

Later, Pops slipped under the covers, trying not to wake up Gendra. She gave him a sleepy look and asked, "How did it go at school?"

"Nothing I couldn't handle," said her husband. *It looks like the old guy's still got it*, thought Pops as he drifted off to sleep.

Train Trip

The four camp assistants were gathered at the Dallas Amtrak station. There were enough people there to see them off to fill an entire car. Parents and friends were giving hugs along with last minute advice. Cheryl, Annie, and Jenny all had cold-weather hats and gloves on, mocking Chip. She thought it was marginally funny.

"Don't mess with her," warned Luke in Cheryl's ear. "She's extremely tenacious if she thinks she's been wronged. Once she's on your scent, she's worse than a bloodhound."

"Okay, Cheryl," said Chip. "If you're going to hang with us for a while, you're going to get an education on real music."

"What are you talking about?" asked Cheryl.

"Girls," said Chip, looking at Annie and Jenny. "Give me some train lyrics quick."

Annie went first. "Hellbound train / I'm on its tracks—Savoy Brown."

Jenny followed with, "Train kept a rollin' all night long—Aerosmith."

Cheryl was racking her brain for a train song.

"Train, train, take me on out of this town," sang Chip. "I believe that's Blackfoot."

They all looked at Cheryl. She had to come up with something, but rock lyrics weren't her forte. She was more of a country fan.

Then her face lit up in a big grin. "Chuga–chuga-chuga / I think I can / I think I can—*The Little Engine That Could.*" The crowd laughed and gave Cheryl an ovation.

"I can see that you've got a lot to learn about music, girl," said Chip. "You're lucky that you are traveling with three rock dogs. We'll have you whipped into shape by the time we get to mitten country. Let's get on board before the good seats are taken."

Cheryl's parents were standing next to the Fullertons. "Is she always like that?" asked Cheryl's dad.

"Like what?" they both answered in unison.

For more reasons than the obvious, something told the Williamses that this was going to be a memorable trip for their daughter. The crowd stood and waved at the girls through the train windows. Just before it pulled out, a large black man with an old-style fedora hat on stood up and got on board. He had been sitting on a bench, watching the festivities. He pulled four small pictures out of his inner jacket pocket and looked at them one more time. Each picture had a handwritten name written under it.

Chip, Annie, Jenny and Cheryl.

They were four high school girls traveling with no adult supervision. Didn't they know that it was a dangerous world out there?

Ω

"This is awesome," said Chip, looking out the window at a field with cattle grazing. "Hey, if we could open the window, we could holler at the cows."

"In the early days of railroads, the passengers were given rifles so they could shoot at the buffalo," said Jenny.

"Why would they want to do that?" asked Chip in a concerned voice.

"I guess they figured that since the Indians relied so much on the buffalo, if they could get rid of the buffalo, the Indians would disappear too."

"That's terrible," exclaimed Chip.

"And after they shot them, they just left them there for the coyotes," added Cheryl. "I bet there were packs of coyotes hanging around the tracks, waiting for the train to come by and blow the dinner whistle."

"That's not funny," said Chip as she looked out the window. "I feel sorry for the buffalo and the Indians."

"Well," said Jenny. "If you study history, you'll find out that mankind has come up with some pretty creative ways to be mean to each other."

"It looks like your boyfriend's love of history has rubbed off on someone," said Annie, nodding toward Jenny.

"Ya'll are lucky to have such nice boyfriends," said Cheryl. "The pickings are pretty slim at Lakewood. By the way, good old Morrie and his little group are in serious trouble. A few of them are having charges brought up against them. Are you like me, Jen, still looking for that perfect guy?"

"Well, there is this new guy in town, but—"

"She doesn't know it yet, but he's her boyfriend," interrupted Chip. "Some people are just too stubborn to realize it." When Jenny gave her a frown, Chip leaned back in her seat and gave the tall girl a knowing look. "Let's talk basketball," said Chip. "We've been shooting around for about a week now. Will we get to play, or are we just coaching?"

"I think we'll get to play some," answered Cheryl. "There will be some other girls there that are our age. We're not the only assistant coaches. I'm sure we will have a chance to play them. It'll be nice to see some different styles of play."

"Whatever your uncle wants us to do is fine with me," said Annie. "As long as we stress sportsmanship too. Eighth and ninth-graders will imitate whatever the older players do, so I think we need to set a good example."

"Right, Mom," said Chip. "So, Jen, no foul language and no tobacco chewing for you."

"Speaking of foul language," said Jenny. "I heard what you said to those two little boys that were wrestling outside of school on the last day."

"What, I didn't swear at them," said Chip.

"No, but you did say, 'Hey, niceness counts, you little dirtbags.' You told them to be nice, but then you called them a name. That's kind of an oxymoron, isn't it? You know, contradicting yourself in the same sentence."

"Did you see those little dudes?" asked Chip. "Those little monkeys were dirt from head to toe. What was I supposed to call them, distinguished gentlemen?"

Cheryl was taking in the conversation with interest. She hadn't been around Chip for any length of time, so this was an education for her.

"I have to go to the restroom," said Jenny. "Who wants to go along?"

They had promised their parents that they wouldn't go anywhere on the train by themselves even to the restroom. Chip got up and followed the taller girl toward the back of the car. When they passed the black man in the fedora, Chip nodded at him and said hello. He looked up from his book and smiled at her. When they were about ten feet past him, he turned slightly and watched them. Jenny went in to the restroom while Chip sat outside the door. *Smart*, he thought. *Travel in pairs. There's safety in numbers.*

After a few stops, the train took on more people, and the car they were riding in got crowded. Chip, as usual, busied herself by trying to figure out everyone's story. She pegged the man in the suit as an executive. The lady with the concerned look on her face was going to see her boyfriend, hoping that her husband bought her story about visiting her sick aunt. The real tall guy was a basketball scout for the University of Texas. And the short pudgy guy with the red face was a circus clown heading home for a well-deserved break. When she was asked who the black guy in the hat was, Chip said she hadn't figured that one out yet.

The trip was going smooth. The four friends busied themselves reading magazines, listening to music, and texting family and friends. Jenny decided to liven things up a little. She gently elbowed Cheryl in the ribs and then leaned to look at Chip across the aisle.

"Chipper, did you know that sometimes the engineer will let a passenger drive the train?" asked Jenny. "I think all you have to do is ask a train employee, and if you're the first to do it, and don't look like a crazy person, they will ask the engineer for you."

"Are you serious?" asked Chip starting to get excited. "Wait a minute. You're setting me up. You still think you're special because you got to drive Daggert's tractor first."

"Hey, all they can say is no," added Jenny. "There's no harm in asking, right, Annie?"

"I don't know," said Annie, closing her phone. "If they let her drive the train, what's next, the space shuttle? Maybe she should quit before she does some real damage."

"That does it," said Chip, getting up and heading down the aisle. "I'm going to the cafe car to talk to a railroad worker."

"We're supposed to stick together, remember?" said Cheryl.

"I'm only going to the next car," retorted Chip. "If I'm not back in five minutes, send out a train search party."

Chip went through the passageway and into the cafe car. Coincidentally, at the same time, the large black man in the fedora decided that he needed a little snack. He rose and followed the short girl into the dining car. Chip was standing at the snack counter, waiting to be waited on, when the tall man walked up and stood next to her. She looked up at him and smiled.

"That is one cool hat, mister," she said. "What do you call it?"

"It's a fedora, uh—"

"Chip from Texas," said the girl, extending her hand. The big man's hand totally encompassed hers.

"Herman from Chicago," he said.

"Is that the kind of hat that Chicago gangsters wear?" asked Chip, still waiting for the guy behind the counter to come her way.

"A long time ago," said Herman. "I like it because you don't see them all that often any more."

"What do you do?" asked Chip in her usual straightforward manner. He was the one guy that she hadn't figured out back in the other car.

"I'm self-employed," answered Herman as the attendant came over and asked Chip what she wanted.

She ordered four sodas, and when the guy brought them back, she motioned for him to lean over the counter. "I heard that sometimes the captain, er engineer, will let one of the passengers drive the train if they are the first to ask. Has anyone asked yet?"

"Not that I know of," said the man, looking at Herman for an explanation. The big guy just smiled at him and raised his eyebrows. "I'll check and see if someone has already asked. If not, you might be the lucky one. How's that?"

"That's fine," said Chip, taking the drinks. "I'm in the next car with some other girls."

When Chip walked away, the attendant looked at Herman and said, "I don't think I've ever had anyone ask that before. She can't be serious."

"I think she was," said Herman discreetly handing the young man a twenty-dollar bill. "Why don't you ask for her. All they can do is say no, right?" The stranger from Chicago then bought an orange juice and a sandwich and returned to his seat.

An hour later, the four travelers were busy drawing out-of-bounds plays when the conductor came up to them and addressed Chip. "I'm looking for a temporary assistant engineer that wants to run the train," he said.

"You just found her, sir," said Chip, standing up. "I'm ready. Can my friends come too?"

"The engine area is pretty small, so you can only bring one more," said the man. "Follow me please."

Jenny looked at the other two with pleading eyes. Annie and Cheryl said for her to go ahead. She and Chip could tell them all about it when they got back. Chip was telling the conductor how she had driven big machinery before and didn't think the train would be all that hard to drive. She looked back at Jenny and grinned. Jenny would now be taken off her list for conniving her way into Mr. Daggert's tractor before she could drive it. Chip was a little disappointed that this was just a passenger train, and there weren't more cars on it, but she was willing to take what she could get.

Back in their seats, Annie explained to Cheryl that Jenny was quite an instigator when it came to Chip, and it would probably go on for the entire trip. It was usually easy to fool the little one, but sometimes she surprised everyone. If she did get to drive the train, this would be one of those times. The passengers watched the conductor and two teenage girls go up the aisle. Most of them assumed the girls did something wrong—teens, always getting into trouble.

The man in the fedora started to get up when he saw Chip and Jenny rise but decided that there wasn't anything he could do when two of the girls got up and followed the train conductor toward the front of the train. He sat back down. He looked over his shoulder at a guy in a white shirt and tie. He was also watching the two girls as they got up and left the car. The guy in the tie looked back down at his magazine when he saw Herman looking his way. Herman made a mental note to keep an eye on him. Sometimes appearances were deceiving.

Jenny couldn't believe that the engineer actually let Chip sit in his seat for a few minutes and blow the whistle. There were so many things that the person running the train had to do. The conductor told them on the way to the engine that they had a brakeman with them today, so he would be able to describe what was going on. He also told them that it was a rules violation for them to be on the engine, but sometimes engineers let one of their children or a VIP ride up there with them for a short period of time. Since there were two engines pulling the train on this trip, they had to wait for a station stop so they could leave the coach area and get on to the engine. If there were only one engine, it would be possible to go from the coach area to the engine. When there were two, the engines would be placed back-to-back, so when you opened the door of the first coach car, you would be looking at the front end of the second engine, and there would be no way to get on to it while the train was moving. They were coming into a station, so the girls had only a short wait. There were only three seats in the crowded engine room, so Jenny had to stand.

The brakeman explained that Amtrak actually owned very little of the tracks that they traveled over. They rented the tracks from other railroads. If they were held up for any reason by other railroad business, they didn't have to pay the full rent price. Since Amtrak was carrying people, it was very important that they follow their schedule as closely as they could. He went on to say that his job was being eliminated. Amtrak rarely had to throw switches anymore, and the few that they did have to throw, could be done by the engineer.

Cheryl and Annie were napping with their earbuds on while Jenny and Chip were up at the front of the train. Cheryl opened her eyes and looked over at her fellow camp coach. She had to use the restroom, but didn't want to wake up Annie to go with her. She figured that there was no harm in slipping off to the back of the car by herself. She would only be gone a couple of minutes. Cheryl got up quietly and walked to the back of the car. The big guy with the strange hat appeared to be sleeping too. When Cheryl came out of the restroom, there was a man blocking her way. She put her back against the wall so it would be easier for them to pass each other. The man looked harmless enough. He had a white shirt and tie on, and he smiled at her. When they were face-to-face, the smile disappeared. He grabbed her by the arm and put a hand across her mouth. He turned the surprised teen so his body blocked her from the rest of the passengers.

"Let's make this short and sweet, darling," whispered the man. "You need to give me all your cash and your credit cards. If you do, I'll let you live. The train is about to stop. You go back into the bathroom for five minutes, and I'll be gone. Do you understand?"

Before Cheryl could answer, a large muscular arm snaked its way under the thief's chin from behind and put the man in a chokehold. The thief's hands immediately went to the arm at his throat. Cheryl was stuck in the hallway and couldn't get by.

"You rob young girls," said the man softly into the other guy's ear. "Man, the only thing lower would be stealing from little old ladies and babies. I'm going to let you breathe for a minute. While you're doing that, get your wallet out. Nod your head if you understand."

The thief decided to comply. The guy that was choking him knew what he was doing, and he appeared to be extremely strong. He was in no position to negotiate.

Cheryl was still in shock, so she just stood there, watching. The tall black man that was choking the man in front of her smiled and winked at her. She didn't know what to make of this. He added to her disbelief by saying, "Everything will be all right, Cheryl." How did he know her name?

The thief slowly withdrew his wallet and held it up. Herman told Cheryl to take the wallet and remove the man's driver's license. He then told her to hold it up to his face to see if the man's picture on the license matched the man's face. She said it did and then gave him back his wallet when instructed to do so. Herman then told the thief to jam his hands into his pockets and turn around. They could feel that the train had stopped and some of the passengers were getting up to leave. No one was paying attention to what was going on back in the restroom area. Herman now had the guy's arms pinned to his sides.

"You need to get off now, and don't look back. Understand?"

The guy in the tie shook his head in the affirmative. Herman picked him up like he was a little doll and turned around so the guy had an open aisle in front of him. The man walked briskly toward the exit and left the train. Herman turned back to Cheryl who was standing there, shaking. He motioned for her to give him the thief's driver's license, and then he offered her his arm.

"Name's Herman," said her rescuer. "I'm here to protect you. Are you all right?"

Cheryl took a deep breath and said she was okay. She took his arm, and they walked back to her seat. When they sat down, Annie opened her eyes. She looked over her shoulder and was surprised see Cheryl sitting behind her with a large black guy. He had his right arm around her shoulders, and she looked like she had been crying. Annie pulled her earbuds out and gave them a questioning look. The man looked at her and smiled.

"Annie Smith, I presume," he said extending a clenched left fist toward her. "I'm Herman, your bodyguard."

Annie bumped his fist and nodded toward Cheryl. "What happened?" she asked.

"We had a little run-in with a lowlife back there," said Herman, nodding in the direction of the restrooms. "Don't worry, he left the train."

Before Annie could ask any more questions, Chip and Jenny came back and sat down across the aisle from them.

"Hey, Herman," said Chip as she sat down. All three of her traveling companions looked at her in astonishment. She shrugged her shoulders and sat back with her hands behind her head. "What have ya'll been doing while I was running this train? By the way, *running* is the correct terminology. You don't *drive* a train. Anyone with a little train experience knows that. Cheryl, you don't look so good. What's the matter?"

"The guy in the white shirt and tie tried to rob her," said Herman. "She'll be all right. She's in shock right now."

A more composed Cheryl looked at Herman. "Thank you so much. That guy was real scary. He said if I gave him my money and credit cards, he would let me live. You saved my life. I do have a credit card that my dad gave me for emergencies. If you hadn't come along, I would have given it to him. What did you mean when you said you were our bodyguard?"

"I was hired to watch over you," said Herman, handing her his business card. He also took his wallet out and showed them his investigator's credentials.

"Did my dad hire you?" asked Cheryl.

"That's confidential," said Herman. "I will tell you that the party that hired me is not related to any of you. That's all I'll say on that."

"Why did you let the thief go?" asked Annie. "Shouldn't you have called the police or train security?"

"I know some people," answered Herman showing them the thief's driver's license. "I'll make a few phone calls. The cops will pick him up soon. You girls need to relax. I'm going to sit behind you. No one goes to the restroom alone, okay? Just because we got rid of one snake doesn't mean that there isn't another one in the area."

"Right," said Chip, putting her open hand out in the aisle. "What could go wrong now that we have our own personal snake killer?" She motioned for the rest of them to join in. Herman's hand completely covered theirs. "Quietly," whispered Chip. "Herman rocks on three. One, two, three."

The train rolled north and east through the night. Herman made some phone calls to some people he knew in the area. In his business, it helped to have people. He also called the man that hired him and filled him in. The girls didn't know his name, but the three from Reston had seen him before. He had attended a few of their early season games. They knew him as the mysterious man with the dark tan and sunglasses. He had a vested interest in one of them.

The four of them huddled together, and Cheryl told them the details of what happened back by the restrooms. She said Herman was awesome. He acted like he really knew what he was doing. Whoever hired him, booked the right guy.

Chip had her eyes closed, picturing her circles. They were now very similar in size. Discovering balance wasn't all that difficult, once she had put her mind to it. She remembered what her psychology teacher had said to the class once, "Just thinking about something doesn't make it happen. You have to act on your thoughts." She decided to send a text to Luke asking him to look into a private detective from Chicago named Herman. When Luke checked his text messages in the morning, he got right on it. Even though they were separated by hundreds of miles, technology enabled them to carry on their sleuthing. He drew a blank on this one, however.

Annie sent her mom a text, telling her things were going just fine. There was no use in alarming anyone about what happened. They had all agreed on that. They could tell their parents all about it when they got home. Surprisingly, Annie received a text message from her mom a few minutes later. She was going to have dinner with the doctor that she had mentioned earlier. Martha Smith said Annie already knew his kids from school. They were twins named Scott and Gina.

Cheryl sent a message to her parents also saying everything was fine. She didn't like keeping the incident from them but didn't see any other way to handle it. She would straighten everything out when she got home. As far as the girls she was traveling with, well Annie was supposed to be the action magnate, but she had not figured into any of the excitement yet. She had decided that she really liked being around this group. A plan began to form in her mind that Chip would have been proud of.

Jenny had a hard time getting to sleep. She was thinking about Scott. What if he had a girlfriend when they got back? She now knew that she really liked him and that he was the genuine person he appeared to be. He still seemed a little too good to be true, but that was just his nature. He gave her a small bouquet of flowers just before she got on the train. The others didn't see them as she immediately stuffed them into her duffle bag.

Herman lightly slept behind his charges, snoring softly. He had earned his fee. Just before he fell asleep, he was humming a little tune to himself. If Annie didn't know any better, she thought it sounded a little like the theme song from her late father's band. With all this excitement going on, she must be hearing things.

Other Works by T.L. Hoch:

In the works---book three: Establishing Presence